THE ARTICHOKE QUEEN

OWEN DUFFY

Livingston Press
The University of West Alabama

ISBN 13: 978-1-60489-158-4, trade paper
ISBN 13: 978-1-60489-159-1, hardcover
ISBN: 1-60489-158-0, trade paper
ISBN: 1-60489-159-9, hardcover
Library of Congress Control Number 2015941913
Printed on acid-free paper
by Publishers Graphics
Printed in the United States of America

Hardcover binding by: Heckman Bindery
Typesetting and page layout: Amanda Nolin, Joe Taylor
Proofreading: Teresa Boykin, Joe Taylor, Amanda Nolin, Tricia Taylor,
Joseph Seale, Mary Slimp
Cover design: Amanda Nolin

Cover photo: unknown photographer, copyright Prototyp Museum,
courtesy of Prototyp Museum
back cover photo: 1954 poster, courtesy Robert Walsh

This is a work of fiction:
any resemblance
to persons living or dead is coincidental.

Livingston Press is part of The University of West Alabama,
and thereby has non-profit status.
Donations are tax-deductible:
brothers and sisters, we need 'em.

first edition
6 5 4 3 3 2 1

THE ARTICHOKE QUEEN

for my mother

I

<u>*One*</u>

*P*RUDENCE *B*AYLOR *snuck back in the house at sunrise and dragged her suitcase down the steps. Her eyes burned and her shoulder ached from falling asleep in the car. She was grateful for the discomfort.* It kept her looking ahead and not at the time-smoothed banister, the worn red carpet that ran the length of the stairs. Nor the old house itself, which in preceding weeks she wasn't sure she'd be able to leave when the time came. Out the window a Willamette Lumber truck blasted along the road and suddenly it felt like any other morning and not her house at all, full of all the comforts a person should want, but she no longer did.

She stopped short when she saw her father was up early and already in the kitchen, sitting at the table, listening to the radio. The lights were off and a block of grey daylight reflected off the floor. He was dressed in his chinos and a checkered flannel, his hair smeared over his forehead. His hands were folded and his head bent as if in prayer, but she knew he was just fighting another hangover. As she came and stood in the doorway, she folded her farewell note deep into her palm.

He plucked his cigarette from the ashtray and looked up at her with bloodshot eyes, the pupils like two bottomless wells. "You know I don't like you taking your mother's car like that." He sucked on the wet end of the cigarette, ignoring the suitcase by her feet. "Where do you go all night anyway?"

Prudence touched the cord to her hearing aid, its earpiece

plugged in her right ear. "Just for a drive," she replied, raising the volume knob on the box that was clipped to her skirt. She looked out the kitchen window, where the '50 Dodge sat in the driveway. A vision of the previous night came to her: its clattering engine, its tires skidding along the wet cinder logging roads. The headlamps trembling as they swept through the forest, as she sped deeper into the mountains than she ever had before.

She'd been driving those unmarked roads for years, a private way of clearing her mind. Last night she'd been gathering the courage to leave home, lost somewhere along the Luckiamute River, when the road ran out. She screamed and hit the brakes. The car shuddered to a stop just feet from the tree line, the engine ticking, tire smoke tumbling over the car. Prudence collapsed there on the seat, her cheeks wet with tears. She awakened under those dripping alders, out where the woods were dark and full of noises that made her heart shake like a rattle.

"Just for a drive," her father said, stubbing out the cigarette. "Well, it's an odd thing to do. What if you broke down?" He shook his head, as if at the futility of posing the question to her. "I don't know anyone who goes out driving God knows where in the middle of the night. Go get drunk in town like everyone else. *That* I wouldn't mind."

"I'm sure you wouldn't." She glared at him when she spoke, as even now he was trying to whittle her down to nothing. She straightened herself, squaring her shoulders. "I'm leaving today, like I told you," she said. Her voice sounded more confident than it ever had in her twenty years. "There's nothing keeping me here any more. You've seen to that fairly well."

Her father looked as if she'd just shaken him awake. He leaned forward and set his elbows on the table. "So you're going to leave your old man behind and head for greener pastures? Well, let me be the one to tell you that there's nothing out there. Not a God damned thing."

He scraped back his chair, stood and walked to the sink. His shoulder brushed a calendar that hung from a cabinet, and Prudence watched the calendar swing back and forth on its nail. On the top page was a cartoon of a boy and a girl scrubbing a dog in a laundry basin while a horrified mother looked on, her hands smacked to her cheeks. It was an Ivory Soap Flakes advertisement her mother had mailed away for. And there it sat now, still turned to December, 1953.

Prudence remembered the promise she'd made to herself in the preceding months. She stepped forward and steadied the calendar, watching her father's back, the slow rise and fall of his shoulders. "I'm leaving today," she said. "Nothing you can say will change that." She took a deep breath. "And I'm going to take Mother's car."

Her father dumped the remnants of his coffee in the sink. Prudence watched it drip down the porcelain, then as he rinsed it away with a trembling hand. He flipped off the faucet and turned. He looked at her a long time, his tongue working inside his mouth, as if tasting his disappointment. No, she knew that look too well. This was different. He was savoring the cruel and awful things he knew about the world that she'd soon understand. Some truth that would excuse the way he'd been lost in his own private miseries nearly her whole life.

The only sound in the room then was the radio, and he walked over and snapped it off. "You can go," he said, snatching his mackinaw from the back of his chair, "but you're not taking that car." He threaded his arms in his coat sleeves and went to fetch his keys, as if giving her time to change her mind.

Prudence looked down at her mother's suitcase, which she'd

found hidden in the back of his bedroom closet the day before. Although it was pasteboard and very old, it still looked brand new.

Her father scooped on his hat and jerked the door open. "Well, if you're really leaving, let's get going. I have a lot of work to get done today."

HE DROVE her to the McMinnville bus depot in silence. Rain dotted the windshield of his red work truck, *Baylor Radio and TV Repair* scripted on the door in gold letters. On the way they passed the First Presbyterian Church, the one he'd stopped going to months before. The ivy covered Twin Falls High School where she'd graduated two years earlier, the rubber boot factory with the busted out windows. People walked along the downtown sidewalks carrying lunch pails, their heads bowed in the constant drizzle; lives that to Prudence always seemed without hope or desperation. Lives consumed with the daily struggles of just getting by.

Her father parked across from the bus depot while she went in to buy a one-way ticket to Los Angeles. It all went just as she'd rehearsed so many times: her hand not faltering as she tendered the money to the clerk, who eyed her uncertainly, as if wondering why a young woman was traveling alone. As she stepped back outside, her father followed her inside the Busy Bee Café while she waited for the bus, and sat down across from her. While her coffee went cold, Prudence watched the clock on the wall.

She knew that he was waiting for a sign of weakness that he could utilize to get her to stay. He stared at her while he leaned back in his chair, fingers laced across his chest. The other patrons, some of whom she'd known her whole life, looked at her and quickly away. She'd been getting that a lot lately. The pity that comes in quiet ways: a pinched smile, the extra room on the sidewalk, the way no

Owen Duffy

one ever asked how she'd been, because they all knew.

After a few minutes, her father dropped his hand on the table. "I just don't know why you want to leave. Everything you have is here."

"You know why," she said, matching his volume.

He shook a cigarette from his pack of Old Golds, ignoring the stares from the other diners. She looked at him. The deep wrinkles around his green eyes, the faded red hair and square jaw, his still muscular build. "Fine, go back to school next fall." He tamped the cigarette on the table and then tucked it in the corner of his mouth. "I suppose your mother would've liked that."

Prudence pushed her coffee away, the spoon clanging against the saucer. At the teachers college, she'd been the captain of the women's swim team and had even petitioned to ski on the Willamette University men's team, which always struck him as a bit *funny*. And then he'd made her quit the crummy teachers college before her winter exams to come home to help out around the house. She had planned on attending there for two years, then transfer to a co-ed college, somewhere far away. She resented him for pulling her out of school at the end of the semester, and she resented him now for telling her she could just go back, as if that would solve everything.

"I'd have to start the year over," she replied, folding her arms. "And besides, everyone would feel sorry for me."

Prudence knew it didn't make much difference to him why she left, only that she was leaving him alone. They both knew he needed someone to look after him. That he'd never cooked a meal in his life and fell asleep every night with a cigarette in his hand. And although she knew he loved her in his own hard style, there was a trace of burden in it. As if she was, with her hearing aid and her lack of interest in anything *normal*, the source of his disappointments. But

Prudence knew there wasn't enough love that she felt any remorse in leaving him now.

As if sensing this, tabulating all the jabs he'd made at her expense — at least in the times when he bothered to acknowledge her at all — her father glanced down and shook his head. For a moment it was as if he was about to explain why he'd been intolerable the past few months. That he'd vow to quit drinking yet again.

Prudence cut him off. "You can sit here with me, Daddy, but I don't want you to apologize. And I don't want to hear your promises, your talk about God, or Mother, or anything at all. I don't want to hear it any more or I'll just scream."

He looked down a moment and touched the hem of his faded mackinaw. "That's not what I was going to say."

When he looked up, she made sure her hard gaze hadn't faltered. He sighed and buttoned his coat, staring at the suitcase while he did.

"That was hers," he said. He spoke without sentiment, without understanding why it looked like it had been purchased just the day before. It was pasteboard, covered in a sticker to make it look like leather. He kicked it with the worn toe of his boot. "Damn if it still looks brand new."

He tried to give her some money as they parted, but Prudence waved it away; she had thirty dollars tucked in her suitcase that she'd saved from waiting tables at the Twin Falls Diner. The money wouldn't go far, but it was enough for the bus ticket, a handful of hash house meals, and a bit of spending money once she got to Los Angeles.

"I was going to say," he said, clearing his throat, "if things don't pan out, you always have a place here."

After he walked her out of the café, Prudence stood on the corner and watched him a while. She was gripped with a sudden feeling of lonesomeness. For a moment she wanted to run after him and bury her face in the scratchy wool of his coat. But she knew that if she did, she'd never leave. If she didn't go and at least see what was out there, she would be breaking that promise she'd made to herself.

She crossed the street to the depot before she could change her mind. While she waited for the bus, she watched her father stop to talk to a neighbor on the street like it was an ordinary morning. If her father felt as lousy as she did, it didn't show. In fact, she sensed that her father resented being held up, as he was about to go into The Foxhole for his customary first drink of the day. The back of her father's head was dusty grey and his shoulders had become stooped with age. It made her wonder how little she knew him, to only notice this change now. That perhaps she was equally responsible for the rift that had grown between them.

She wondered what he was talking about with the neighbor. Her hearing was awful: less than a quarter remained in her left ear and only fifty percent in her right. As she often had to do, she read lips. She made out the shapes of the neighbor's words and guessed at the nature of her father's. She saw that they weren't talking about her, and it didn't surprise her that she hadn't even come up in the conversation. Her father opened the door to the bar and said to the neighbor, *Don't do anything I wouldn't do.* She watched him remove his hat and slip inside the dark bar. That was the one good thing about her father: she'd always been able to guess what he was going to say next.

RAIN SPECKLED her window as the bus drove west to the coast, the grey Pacific and the dark clouds hanging above it. Her fear at being alone and the oppressiveness of the last four months slowly began to lift. Life now savored a fresh perspective, and the feeling intensified as the silver bus continued southward along the coastal bi-way, across Coos Bay and Gold Beach. It was the farthest she'd ever been from home alone. And then as they entered the deep forests of northern California late that afternoon, under the soft canopies of the giant redwoods, the bus windows alight with the setting sun, the events of that past winter began to replay in her mind.

Her mother had suffered a long illness that her doctors were never able to diagnose. Dizzy spells, headaches, a general melancholy. She'd lost interest in the things she enjoyed, shut herself in her father's dark study, surrounded by his electronics manuals and spare radio parts, not rousing for days. Her doctor assured them it was a phase some people went through, that it would pass in time.

A year passed. Nothing changed. Then one day Prudence read an article in *LIFE* magazine about clinical depression. It described her mother's strange moods perfectly. But the words *clinical* and *depression* sounded terminal, like some asylum where they tied patients down with leather straps and let them wither away, their skin going ashy and their minds going as soft as the food they were fed.

Prudence threw the magazine away before anyone else could read it, and told herself to forget about it. She watched as her mother grew more detached from friends and family. During the Thanksgiving vacation, Prudence noticed her mother was healthy again, happy that Prudence was home from school for the holiday. And yet in private, when she didn't know she was watching, Prudence recognized that same tremendous sadness in her mother as she wiped the windows with vinegar, set a freshly washed dish in the strainer.

Prudence realized then that her mother's problems were not within her mind. She had always seemed out of place in Twin Falls. She had beautiful chestnut hair that seemed to catch fire in the sun. A warm singing voice that had a lonesome sound, like it had a big wet tear dripping from it. At family gatherings, when her family invariably goaded her mother to sing at the piano, her aunts would always remind Prudence that her mother used to perform in night clubs, that radio and recording contracts had been offered to her. They always spoke in hushed tones, so her mother wouldn't overhear. And not in the way women often spoke of those who'd suffered the usual sacrifices of marriage and motherhood. They spoke softly because something of great value had been lost, like a bodily limb, or even a child.

A few days after Prudence left to finish her semester at the teachers college, a secretary came and fetched her from class and led her to the dean's office. Prudence stood from her desk and followed, assuming it was another reprimand for having been caught past curfew with a boy that past weekend. She went into the office and sat across the desk from the dean and his secretary, her feet together and palms on her lap, as they explained that her mother had died the day before of unknown causes.

Prudence sat there, unmoving. Her mind went white hot and her stomach felt as if it had been pitched down a hillside. She stared back at them. It couldn't be true — she'd seen her mother only days before. And yet somehow she had expected it. And then it suddenly seemed a perfectly reasonable thing, lacking any sort of mystery. She knew immediately that her mother had simply willed herself to die, after enduring a long and intolerable sadness.

She didn't cry there, not in front of the secretary or the dean, with the smell of the damp and out the windows the mossy trees, heavy with rain. She looked around at the dusty office and imagined her mother scrubbing it down, and knew that despite what anyone said, her mother had died while occupied with a task of no importance.

In the following days, she learned that her father had come home to find her mother on the kitchen floor, a bucket of soapy water beside her, the sponge still in her hand. It hadn't been a grotesque thing, she'd overheard him quietly telling their neighbor. Her father said she had looked peaceful, like a girl lying out in the sun while on a picnic, watching the clouds pass overhead. Her eyes wide open and her long hair spread out, a faint smile on her lips.

Prudence imagined the scene and pondered that instant where a person is here one moment and gone the next, with no apparent cause or reason. She was haunted by the image of that smile, as if her mother wanted to show her father the peaceful way in which she'd been willing to leave his world.

Sometimes these things just happen, the doctors had said, when explaining why a healthy, forty-three year old woman could just die without warning. In their clinical way, it seemed like an admission to the fact that the rules of medicine were unexplainable, or worse, unpalatable: that a heart can just stop beating at any moment.

At the wake, Prudence stayed beside her mother's younger sister, Doris. She was the one level-headed person there. Her Aunt Doris helped her endure the distant relatives, who hadn't seen her in years, as they told her how much she resembled her mother. Her neighbors' clammy sentiments, the whispered consolations that *This will pass*, that her mother *is in a better place*. Prudence wished she could find comfort in God, but she could only think of the literature class she'd taken, in which her professor identified the heart as a metaphor for the soul, his fingers held out, opening and closing in the air as if to simulate its simple rhythms. Horse puckey. To Prudence, the heart was just an organ, the last thing to have given up on her mother.

Her mother hadn't always been a sad, moody woman. She remembered moments of sheer joy from her childhood. But as Prudence grew she understood that their house and town were too small. Everyone in Twin Falls seemed to know it too. Prudence had seen women being petty towards her mother. The way men were often overly polite to her. Her mother never reveled publicly in her beauty or her talents, but in private she cared for them like they were borrowed, valuable possessions.

As a child, Prudence used to stand and brush her mother's hair before bed, holding it in one hand as she ran the faux pearl handled brush over it. She'd never felt envy like that before in her life up until then, as her mother sat in front of the mirror, humming the refrain of an old jazz tune, Prudence counting the many different shades of brown in her mother's hair.

Her own hair had a light auburn hue, and although her own eyes were an impossible shade of green like her father's, and her skin tanned well in the summer, she wished she shared her mother's darker hair and skin coloring, if only to be more like her, to feel more like she was a sister, drawn from the same blood.

As the funeral neared, Prudence understood that her mother's talent had been a calling, one she had ignored. And that talent of such power should not have been disobeyed. Prudence promised to herself, on the morning of her mother's funeral, that she would live the life her mother should have. Never let someone like her father control her. A man who had always despised her hearing aid, which he treated like a deformity. The way he hated how she went walking alone by the river, or driving out in the deep woods at night. As if these were the signs of dementia or some other ailment, and not just the general restlessness she always felt when she was alone with him.

During her mother's funeral services, as their priest stood in their church graveyard, Prudence looked over at her father. He lifted his head and their eyes met. The same green eyes as her own, their hair the same faded brick color. He locked eyes with her, as if her face conveyed everything to him that she'd been thinking. As the casket was lowered, she released her aunt's arm and pushed free of the other mourners, hurried across the cemetery, feeling their eyes on her back. Prudence ran home and into the empty house and gazed at the polished tiles in the vestibule, the wood floors buffed to a high shine. The house was quiet. She stood in the kitchen and gazed out into the sloppy yard at the swaths of uncut grass, the rotting fence. She hadn't cried since her mother passed. But she was ready to cry now, and she did so, sitting on the kitchen floor where her mother had died, her hands clapped to her face.

Her father stormed up the front steps hours later, went straight into his study and slammed the door, as if unaware that Prudence was even home. She heard the clanking of liquor bottles, the angry voices on the big Zenith Transatlantic shortwave radio he had in the study: the politicians deploring the Communists, the traitors, the villains of the world. Sitting up there alone in her room, she wished she had a microphone so she could broadcast how she felt. That as much as she loved her father, she was now wedded to his every sour mood and effort to keep her with him in that old house.

As THE bus continued south, Prudence thought of him going to work that morning. Lifting his hat and wiping his boots as a housewife directed him towards a television. Walking slump-shouldered with his tools across the carpet, chomping on a wad of Chiclets to hide the whiskey. Spreading out his blanket on the floor in front of the television, setting his toolbox beside it. His faint reflection in the blank screen. Opening the cabinet to find a vacuum tube or a fuse blown, and after setting it right again, tipping his cap as he left to go on to the next job. Coming home that night to the empty house, turning on the lights

Owen Duffy

to find the kitchen, the den, and the bedrooms empty.

Prudence knew it would take years for her to forgive him, or even understand him. How he'd done everything to put a stop to her success. The way he'd made pointed jokes about her going off to college to play games, even when those games had garnered her state swimming trophies; the newspaper articles of how she'd been the first woman to compete in the state finals in college downhill skiing.

At times it still felt like she was standing at the starting gate on a snowy mountain top. Gripping the wooden poles with her gloved hands, staking them beside her freshly waxed skis. Staring down the steep mountain, the shadows of the trees splayed across the slopes. The creak of the snow beneath her, the tightness of the leather bindings. The clang of the bell and the launch. Pushing herself upwards on the poles and plopping down again, already at speed and hurtling towards the first flag. The icy wind against her cheeks, the nearly hydraulic movement of her knees as she tucked into each turn, brushing the flags with her shoulder. Carving her way down the mountain, spinning through the finish line, looking up with her breath steaming from her, the sun in her eyes and on her smiling face.

Her father had taken her from that. Said he needed help, couldn't take care of the house alone. When she did return from school, telling the displeased headmaster that it was her solemn duty, she found the house a mess. Clothes strewn about, dishes overflowing from the sink, her father staggering about with a cigarette clamped between his teeth and a whiskey bottle in his hand.

Her only solace came at night when the house was clean and she was alone in her bed. There in the house still cold from her mother's death. She would dream of a place far away. A snowy mountain top. A dark logging road. An open lake. A place where she could feel the breeze or the water in her hair, where she could again find that athletic sense of order and control.

Come see me and stay a while, her Aunt Doris wrote from Los Angeles shortly after Prudence returned from school. She was a pretty but frivolous woman who had had some success in film acting, and had never married. *Tell your father you're coming for a long weekend. I have an empty room where you can stay rent free. And I've shown your picture to a friend of mine who is a big film maker. He wants you to do a test screening for him in a month.* Prudence crushed the letter to her chest, there in her bedroom, the moonlight shining on the pages. She promised herself that she would go. She loved her aunt; she was everything she wanted to be. Better yet, she promised herself that she owed it to herself. She would simply tell her father that she loved him, but that he had to quit drinking, or she would leave. If he did, she would stay. Otherwise she would go.

As THE bus exited the deep woods, her reflection in the window took on the setting sun's muted rays. Her fingers brushed her hearing aid's thick cord, running under her coat to its bulky battery box. It was a Champion tube model, fragile and needing constant maintenance. She'd relied on the heavy, ungainly contraption for years. It was the size of both her balled fists pressed together. She'd rarely been without it, afraid she might miss a word. But now she unclipped the unit and stuffed it in her purse. She saw her mother's sewing scissors in there too, wrapped in tissue; a gift from a long time ago, thrown in there as a memento. She stroked the metal blades as she looked out the window, sensing that soft hiss coming from her bad ear. She pushed her finger into it and felt her pulse with her fingertip, brash and violent. It was the same sound she'd been making her whole life, but it was no longer just the sound of her heartbeat. It was the sound of time passing.

<u>*Two*</u>

Prudence emerged from the restroom in a San Francisco bus station in a red chambray shirt, cuffed blue jeans, a pair of worn penny loafers. Gone was the long hair, the skirt, the stockings. She tucked her mother's sewing scissors back in her purse as she crossed the terminal and stood beneath a large Western Union clock that hung above a row of candy machines. The lights flickered overhead. She set down her suitcase, took a deep breath and tucked a loop of shortened hair behind her bare ear. Old men loitered on the benches, leering at her as they smeared their cigarette butts on the floor. Announcements blared from a loudspeaker as passengers shuffled across the terminal and out into the dark street.

Prudence eyed a photo booth that stood nearby, thinking she might commemorate this moment. She fixed herself in the mirror of a cigarette machine, deciding she liked the new look this hair gave her; a bit like Audrey Hepburn in *Roman Holiday*. She drew back the booth's curtain, fished some loose change from her jeans. The inner mechanism whirred as she dropped the coins in the slot, and they found home. She then slid onto the bench and gave her best Hepburn impression. The camera flashed four times and she sat waiting in the dark booth until the pictures were dispensed. Satisfied, she slipped them in their waxed paper envelope and tucked them in her pocket.

"That yours?" A man in uniform pointed at her suitcase as she stepped from the booth. As her eyes adjusted to the light, she dialed up the volume on her hearing aid. His hair was cottony white and his ears stuck out beneath his brimmed cap. He knitted his brow and slowly shook his head. "You all need to keep a close eye on your things so someone don't steal them. I don't like walking around here looking out for all you college kids all the time."

Prudence touched the suitcase with the toe of her loafer. She had avoided talking to anyone all day, afraid they might want something from her. So she draped her short, brown mouton coat over her shoulders and busied herself fastening it.

"You know where you going?" the man asked. His eyebrows arched when he noticed her hearing aid. Prudence saw *Greyhound* on the patch that was sewn above his heart and she held out her ticket stub for him to see.

"Los Angeles." He shook his head. "Ma'am, that bus just left. They called it a bunch of times."

Prudence looked at him, feeling as if she'd just been punched in the gut. The driver had told the passengers there was a strict half-hour holdover in San Francisco to drop off and pick up passengers. She'd gotten off with her suitcase so no one stole it, then became lost in the restroom mirror, her hearing aid on the counter, as she cut her hair.

Prudence put her face in her hands. "Then I guess I'll need some place to stay," she said, lifting her head. "A hotel or something."

The man looked at her, as if there was something even more helpless about her than the other runaways he saw every day. "Come this way," he said, snatching up her suitcase. "Hold onto your ticket and come back in the morning. First bus to Los Angeles is at eight." He continued that way, muttering under his breath, rushing towards the door.

She hurried behind him out onto the curb, pressed a quarter in his palm as she climbed into the first cab in line. She then grabbed her mother's suitcase from him and clutched it on her lap.

"You don't talk much," the attendant said as he shut the door behind her and leaned on the cab. "Say, I never seen one of those up close before." He pointed at the hearing aid.

"One of what?" she asked, shooting him a hard glare.

He grasped onto the open window, his fingernails thick and yellow, hands formed nearly into a claw the way workingmen's hands often are. "You're a Cracker Jack, ain't you?" He chuckled. "Well, if you aren't careful someone's gonna eat you up, Cracker Jack." He gave the address to the driver and smacked the cab's roof.

The driver shot off from the curb and turned down some dark back streets. Prudence replayed the man's words in her head and cursed herself for missing the bus. She looked out the window at the run down neighborhoods, the stained buildings and rotting cars. Filthy looking people, sitting on crumbling steps, watching her pass by.

Her hands trembled and she wanted to ask the driver where he was taking her. As they drove, she took the photo strip from her pocket, studied them in the slats of light that fell in rhythm through the window. The photos were slick and shadowy, but she looked nothing like Audrey Hepburn. She looked like everything she'd been trying to keep from the camera: a lost, crazy and exhausted girl. In the picture, her eyes were big and bright, her hair cut in such a wild way that it made her look modern and fresh. Although her face had taken on the lovely almond shape of her mother's, there was a tension to it, a hardness. And, with her full lips pinched together, her brow creased, the photographs made her seem as if she were looking at a new, braver version of herself.

Prudence turned to the window. The city continued to pass by, tinted green under the sodium street lamps. Los Angeles was already fading, her aunt and the film test, like a mirage at dusk. She continued staring out the window, cursing herself, until the taxi stopped a few minutes later in front of a brick building. The driver stepped out, walked up to a building and rang a bell. A bent, grey-haired woman came out and waved to Prudence, cinching her bath robe closed. Prudence paid the driver, grabbed her suitcase and climbed the steps.

At the door, the woman informed Prudence that she ran the boarding house. Her face was dry and puffy, a cigarette stuck between her lips. As she talked, ashes fell from her cigarette, her eyes aimed at Prudence's hearing aid. After the woman turned, Prudence followed her down the sallow hallway to a desk, nodding as she explained the rules, signed her in, took the nightly fee and a deposit for the sheets and towels.

The landlady then led her upstairs, slowly climbing the wide steps, clutching the railing with both hands. Women's haggard faces peeked out from doorways as Prudence walked by, and when the landlady opened the door to one of the rooms, Prudence paused in the doorway. The room was stuffy and small and smelled as if someone had just been sleeping there. Prudence said she wanted a different room, but the woman looked her up and down with half-closed eyes, then walked past her and out the door.

Prudence tried to bolt the door shut but found there was no lock. She put a chair up against the doorknob, tested it, and then tried to crack a window but it was nailed shut. She opened the closet and checked the nightstand drawer. Both empty. She then sat on the squeaky bed with the overhead light still on, looking up at the stains on the ceiling. After a minute, she opened her suitcase and purse and dumped her things out beside her: clothes that still smelled of home, here in a city where she wasn't even supposed to be.

The scent reminded her of leaving her father at the bus depot. In a way, she wished she was still there. She looked around the squalid room again, then slipped her hand into a sweater's pocket and removed what remained of her money. She counted nineteen dollars and then forty-seven cents. She set the money on the nightstand along with her bus ticket stub. Then she removed her hearing aid, took the wax paper envelope from her pocket, slipped out the photos and held them up to the bare light. For a moment she envisioned herself a film starlet, and again recalled her Aunt Doris's letter from two weeks earlier: *He wants you to do a test screening for him in a month.*

Prudence hoped that she would turn out as pretty as her mother. She had her pretty face and wide smile, and when she wasn't skiing or swimming her body became less muscular, more like her mother's slender but curvy figure. And maybe this director had seen that she was about to develop into a beautiful woman. *Beauty is on the inside*, her mother always said. Her mother's eyes were large and bright, the lids pulled down at the sides ever so slightly, just as her own did in the photos. *The world is a wonderful place*, her mother had also said, and after Prudence turned off the light, she curled up with all her possessions in her arms, and lamented that her mother hadn't seen much of it.

Prudence lay awake for an hour, afraid if she slept too deeply she would miss the bus. But she soon felt her mind go, and she awoke at dawn when the sun cracked over the nearby building. She shielded her face, wincing at the stained walls a moment before she remembered where she was. She knew she'd slept deeply from the way her body felt all loose and warm. Looking at her wristwatch, she saw she only had two hours to get back to the bus station.

There was an acrid scent in the room that smelled faintly burnt, like sulfur: no doubt the dusty radiator that stood by the window. Without her hearing aid, the street and building and the rest of the world were quiet. As she jumped from bed and began to fling her belongings back into her suitcase, a pang of guilt shot through her, that she should be in Los Angles by now, not here in some flophouse.

If her father had just let her take her mother's Dodge, she'd be cruising along the California coast right now, the windows down and the briny sea spray dotting the windshield. But she knew that he'd wanted to make her trip as hard as possible so she'd have to go home to him. But she wasn't going back. She knew that, even if she had to starve, there was a life out there waiting to be led. A future unlike what the teachers college promised. A life teaching restless children about history and arithmetic. Each day a drop spilling out of her until there was nothing left.

As she looked out the window, she recalled the dream she'd been having just before she awakened. In it, she was parked in her mother's Dodge on the logging road the night before, too exhausted to drive any further. In the distance she heard the sound of snapping tree trunks as something moved through the forest, shaking the damp ground, rattling bedrock. She'd sat perfectly still as a creature stopped outside the car and hovered, invisible through the black haze. Closed her eyes while it leaned over and sniffed her through the open window, its sodden breath against her cheek.

Prudence shivered as she stood by the ticking radiator, looking down at the street and warming her hands. She could see a child sitting on the curb, kicking his shoe heel against the street, and an old woman pushing a trash filled cart. Prudence rubbed away the gooseflesh, the dream clinging like morning dew, reluctant to leave the leaf.

When she turned she noticed something odd: a few burnt matches lay on the carpet. And as she bent and picked one of them up, she noticed the chair that she had leaned against the door was overturned. She went rigid. Someone had been in her room. It wasn't

Owen Duffy

just a dream: something had been hovering over her as she slept.

Prudence felt that same shot to the gut that she had the night before. She crept towards the closet and opened it slowly, her fist cocked in case someone jumped out. It was empty. Her eyes then shot towards the nightstand. She sucked in a fast breath when she saw that the shelf was bare and her money and the bus ticket were gone. And then, as she fell to her knees and rifled through her suitcase, she saw that the thief had also stolen her purse with her hearing aid inside it.

She swore and tore open her bedroom door and looked down the dim hallway. Her pulse banged against her temples and now she felt like her guts had been sucked out of her. The thief was long gone, and her cheeks grew hot, knowing that she'd been such an easy mark: the deaf girl who'd run away from home.

"You bitches!" she yelled, her shout sounding faint and hollow to her own ears. "Why doesn't the thief who stole my things come out here!" She stopped there in the hall, her hands clenched at her side. Nothing moved. She yelled again. Still nothing.

As she walked along the hallway she continued to shout, knowing that she was making a pathetic display of herself. But as she came to the stairway, she saw, discarded by the filthy baseboards, her mother's sewing scissors and her tooled leather purse. She ran to them and knelt on the floor, but saw that the purse was empty except for the photo strip from the night before and her tiny, dog-eared copy of the Holy Bible.

She looked at the nickel-plated scissors, which were the length of her outstretched hand. She'd brought them as a keepsake of her mother's, a good luck charm. She gathered the scissors, book and purse, went back to her room and began throwing her things in her suitcase.

When she came from her room, she saw that her yelling had

awakened most of her floor. Swaths of light came from each room, disheveled heads peering out to see what had happened. As she walked the hallway and descended the stairs with her suitcase, she looked at the women she passed for any sign of guilt; they all just frowned and shut their doors.

A different crusty old lady was sitting there behind the desk this morning, adjusting the tuning dial on an old radio. Prudence couldn't hear what came from its speaker. As she stood there, she noticed that there was a sign pinned to the wall behind the woman that read:

Management Is _NOT_ Responsable
For Lost Or Stolen Posessions!!!!

Perfect, she thought, walking up to the desk. *Of course.*

"Hold my room for me," Prudence spat at the woman. "Room 3H. I'll be back before dark to pay."

Prudence turned from the desk, her suitcase banging against her leg as she pushed open the door and hustled out onto the street. She walked several blocks eastward before she stopped and leaned up against a store window and pressed her face into her coat sleeve, thinking she was about to cry for lousing her trip up in only a day.

But the tears wouldn't come. After a minute she blew her nose and straightened up, before anyone came and tried to help her. But people were walking by as if she wasn't standing there, wiping her face with a handkerchief. She looked up to see where in hell she was. Oak Street, the sign said. Despite all the traffic, the world was very quiet around her, and she was trying to keep her hand from shaking as she returned the handkerchief to her purse. She stood there on the corner while people continued to brush past, all of them heading to work. From where she stood, she could make out the Golden Gate Bridge to the north. Above her, a ridge of clouds passed along the skyline and for a moment, the sun burst through the fog and the wet street glowed.

She turned around and looked in the window that she'd been leaning against. The window showcase was filled with hundreds of pairs of shoes of all different types, more than she'd ever seen in her life. A forest of plaster legs modeled high heels and loafers. She noticed a contraption under the store's awning and she walked up to it and looked into its well worn eyepiece. **Insert Feet Below**, it said in the viewfinder, and when she put her feet under the device, she saw an X-ray image of her feet bones. She wiggled her toes in her old loafers and felt a smile come to her lips.

The wind stung her face as she continued eastward towards downtown. A drifter staggered around the corner of a building with his hand held out to her. He was bearded and toothless and filthy. Just then a trolley came over the rise in the street. Prudence had never seen a trolley before, and it was just like she imagined. She rushed to it, unsure where it was going. She grasped the brass handle, pulled herself onboard and huddled in with the other passengers, avoiding the driver's eyes. He looked at her a moment and then called the next stop. As the trolley emptied and refilled, each rider depositing their fare in the metal box, Prudence felt in her purse, as if there might be an errant coin in there. Nothing. She hunkered down behind the new passengers as the trolley lurched and continued north. She looped her arm around an outside pole and watched the city pass by.

As the trolley crested a hill she saw that she was close to the bay and had come a great distance. While the trolley was still moving, she leapt from it, onto the busy street, dodging oncoming traffic, ending up on a boulevard lined with blossoming trees.

She knew she'd have to beg a dime and call her Aunt Doris or her father, ask them to wire her some money for a bus ticket home. But she didn't want to bother her aunt, reveal to her how unworldly she was. And how smug her father would look as she stepped from the bus back in Oregon, leaning against his truck. Driving back home the same way she'd come only days before, the same people walking to work in the rain.

Prudence walked along Lombard Street and noticed a sign taped to the window of a corner cafeteria: **WAITRESS WANTED**. She'd never been in an automat before, and as she stepped inside, she gazed at the wall of little glass doors, each compartment containing a serving of food. She walked along the rows of windows, peering in at perfect slices of cheesecake, each with the same size sliver of strawberry on top. The hot plates of roast beef and gravy, steaming the glass. Her stomach gurgled and her mouth watered at the sight of them.

Patrons swirled about, businessmen in grey fedoras and flannel suits, women in wool skirts and jackets. They watched her in the mirror behind the counter, while she stared at a man at the soda fountain in his white uniform and cap expertly jerking out egg creams and chocolate malts.

The soda jerk looked at her after a minute. She merely intended to ask to use the phone, but found herself instead inquiring about a job, as a waitress or even a dishwasher. Her speech was often loud and distorted without her hearing aid, and the man looked her up and down, as if trying to figure out what was wrong with her. When he spoke, she read from his lips that they'd already found help. Prudence moved closer and explained that she had worked as a waitress back home, but he had already turned his back on her. *Asshole*, she muttered, turning and heading onto the busy street.

She spent the rest of the morning dragging her suitcase into other cafés. She just needed enough for a bus ticket to Los Angeles, a dozen meals, and several nights in that cheap boarding house. But even if there was a sign in the window, the owners all looked at her like she was a defective and told her they didn't need help. Later, she stepped into a florist and stood watching the service bell shaking silently over the door. She thought that such a quiet and gentle place might embrace her. The florist looked up from behind the counter, his words a messy jumble underneath the moustache covering his lips. Blushing, she backed out onto the street and rounded a corner. She leaned against the building and pulled her still damp handkerchief from her purse. She stood with her back against a window and pressed the shaking handkerchief to her nose.

She looked up at the street signs a minute later. Kearny and Broadway. Miles from where she'd started her day over in Haight. Her feet were aching to the bone. She looked down at her loafers. She was dressed like she was still on the campus quad. And her crazy haircut, she thought, turning to her reflection in the window and ruffling her short cropped hair. Her mouton coat. No wonder everyone had turned her away.

A milky fog had settled over the neighborhood, and she knew she'd soon be making the long trek back to the boarding house in the rain. She didn't know where else she could go, and she knew that they couldn't turn her away after what had happened. They would have to take her in so she didn't have to sleep in a doorway, where anyone who wanted could overpower her and violate her, or worse. She would make sure of it.

As she put the handkerchief away, she noticed the marquis that hung above her: *The Scotch House*. Large black sign with white neon letters. She stood, transfixed in their hot white glow. It looked like the type of nightclub her mother might've sang in years before. As Prudence stood there, the front doors flung open and two laughing men came out, arm in arm. She eyed them curiously and then grabbed the door before it shut. She walked into a dark corridor, feeling the thump of drums in her chest. She parted curtains and entered the main room and saw a small jazz combo on the bandstand, their shirt sleeves rolled up as they played to a room that was, despite the early hour, packed.

Smoke curled from the low ceiling; a long curved bar stood on the far side of the room, the wall lined with liquor bottles. People no older than herself rimmed the bar and sat at the small tables at the base of the low bandstand. She could faintly hear the stark, plaintive music. Not brassy and bawdy, but relaxed and fresh sounding. A few people turned and looked at Prudence as she neared the bar. She knew she looked out of place, but she walked as if she'd been there before. Something about this place intrigued her; something about it felt right.

"I've come to apply for a job," Prudence said to the bartender, a woman who looked only a few years older than her. The bartender didn't look up. She was wearing a white Rayon blouse, unbuttoned halfway down, a patent leather waist belt, black skirt and stockings. Prudence had never known of a female bartender, and she watched as she shook a drink, poured it neatly into a cocktail glass. The bartender finally looked up and smirked at Prudence, wiping her hands with a dishtowel.

The bartender turned and pushed through the swinging door behind her. Prudence stood there among the drinkers, stealing glances at the trumpet player on the bandstand, his loose curls spilling over his closed eyes and his cheeks puffed out like a cherub.

The kitchen door opened a minute later, throwing a blanket of light into the dark room. A woman appeared in the doorway, gazing out, as if she'd been tasked with something far beneath her. The light hit the woman's face and Prudence felt a jolt rip down her spine, as she always did when confronted with a woman far more beautiful than herself. After a moment scanning the bar, the woman noticed Prudence and came forward, the tail of her alabaster chiffon dress wafting behind her.

As the woman neared, Prudence saw how worldly and self-possessed she appeared, and she tried to arch her own back, quiet her fidgeting hands. She couldn't hear a damn thing anyone was saying in the club, and again felt the coming disappointment of being turned away from another job. Prudence held her breath as the woman came and stopped right in front of her, hands on her slim waist, chin slightly lifted. She was tall and slender and looked to be in her late twenties.

The bartender pointed Prudence out to the woman, as if implicating her of a crime. Prudence returned the woman's frigid gaze as she came and stood in front of her. Standing close, Prudence caught the scent of perfume that positively screamed of Paris. The woman had a coiffed hairstyle that looked both timely and expensive. And although Prudence knew nothing of fashion, she knew this woman hadn't just cut herself out of a fashion magazine. That she'd cultivated her own style and had done a fine job of it.

"It looks like it's Howdy Doody Time," the bartender said, nodding at Prudence's suede skirt and gingham blouse. The woman in the white dress shushed the bartender, while staring Prudence up and down like she was a piece of furniture. The woman had bright, sparkling eyes, and sharp features. A large diamond ring dangled by a silver thread from her neck. Her hair was bright blonde, her skin clear and fair. Most striking of all, she looked — unlike the bartender — intelligent.

"New in town, are we?" the woman asked in a tired voice, eying Prudence's outfit with an amused expression. Prudence read her lips clearly. The bartender laughed as she soaked cocktail glasses in the wash basin. The other woman turned and shot the bartender another displeased look.

"I'm Violet," the woman said, "the floor manager. Call me Vi. And that's Jeffie. She's quite *cruel*." Vi sat on a high bar stool. She crossed her long legs and narrowed her eyes at Prudence before she continued. "So you think you can just walk into the best nightclub in the city and ask for a job?"

Prudence watched Vi's mouth but didn't speak, afraid her muddled speech and uneven volume would betray her.

"You look like a nice girl," Vi said, squinting. "Why would you want to work here? Don't you know jazz musicians are hopped up degenerates?" She fished a blue packet of French Gauloises from behind the bar, lit one and blew a stream of smoke at the ceiling. "You could get a job in a nice department store downtown, by the look of you."

"I've waitressed before, back in Oregon," Prudence said as clearly as she could manage, setting her tooled leather purse on the black, polished bar. She looked up at the bandstand and saw that the band was mercifully taking a break.

Vi rolled her eyes as she puffed her cigarette. Prudence was already growing tired of the upperclassman routine. She'd dealt with it on the swim and ski teams back at college, and she wasn't going to be humiliated here by two glorified soda-jerks.

Vi pulled on the cigarette and gave Prudence a curious half-smile. "How old are you anyway?"

"Twenty-one," Prudence lied, tacking on a year.

"Married?" Vi asked. "Pregnant?"

Prudence shook her head, her heart beating a little faster.

"Good," Vi said. "That's very good."

Prudence noticed a cocktail waitress across the room, yet another pretty girl in a stylish outfit. There seemed to be no men operating the entire bar. She glanced down again at her gingham blouse, then back up at Vi. Her expression suggested she understood how Prudence felt right now. As if Prudence had just told a joke that Vi had heard a hundred times.

"What are you running away from?" Vi asked, leaning against the bar.

Prudence thought she'd misheard. "What?" she asked.

"We're all runaways here," Vi said. "So what's your story?"

Prudence paused, looking into Vi's eyes, afraid she might tell this stranger her whole story, of her mother and father, and even about her stolen hearing aid and money. And she knew if she tried, if Vi heard her mumbled voice, she wouldn't get the job. Her cheek began to tremble, her lip twitched. It felt as if whatever had been holding her up those past few months, that invisible bubble that holds people afloat, had finally popped.

Vi's mouth had suddenly gone slack, her eyes trained on Prudence's nose. Prudence stared back a moment before she felt something warm on her upper lip and running down her chin. She touched her face, and when she withdrew her hand, her fingers were shiny and red. The taste of blood was already trickling down the back of her throat, bitter and metallic. Prudence felt her heart quicken and her eyes widen. She shoved her hand in her coat pocket, withdrew her handkerchief and pressed it to her nose.

When she looked up again, Vi pursed her lips and shook her head very slowly, the way people in church did when someone was testifying. She motioned for Jeffie to bring her a clean hand towel. Prudence kept the hanky held to her nose, her heart still racing and wanting to leave her silly suitcase and this whole crummy adventure behind her and head out the door. Jeffie came with a towel, and Vi leaned forward, reached out her hand and squeezed Prudence's wrist, pulling the bloody hanky from her nose.

"Tilt your head back," Vi said, pressing the towel into Prudence's hand, and then holding them both to her face. "I'm from a small town in Montana," Vi said, her hand still on her arm. "My family disowned me when I was sixteen over something I did." Vi snapped her fingers again, "just like *that*." She looked even more closely at Prudence. "But when I got away from them and that place, it was like I was," she shook her head, as if trying to find the right word, "*emancipated*."

Prudence stared at her with her head tilted back, nodding, knowing that this was just a pep talk to see her back out into the chilly city. That she'd have to go back home and that this was the period on the end of her story. As if to confirm this notion, Vi patted her quickly on the arm and sat back in her stool and looked across the room. With the towel still pressed to her nose, Prudence looped her fingers through the handle to her suitcase and lifted it from the floor.

"I'm sorry, honey," Vi said. "I'm just full up with girls right now. If you come back in a couple of weeks, maybe I'll have an opening."

Prudence nodded and looked at the floor, but didn't move.

"Oh Jesus, you're not going to start crying on me, are you? Shit. Jeffie," Vi snapped her fingers, "bring me another towel. This one's leaking again."

Jeffie came with the towel and handed it to her. Prudence blotted her eyes and thanked them both, and then began shuffling away.

"Jesus," Vi called out. "Look, there's a girl who showed up

tonight with an eye that looked like a plum. A gift from her big galoot of a husband. I sent her home for a few days. If you want to come in tomorrow night, you can cover for her. It's a one night thing though. Don't go thinking I'm in the business of taking in strays here. I'll tip you out at the end of the night and send you on your way."

Vi leaned forward. "On a good night here," she said, "a girl can do real well." She cracked a crooked smile, lowered her gaze to meet Prudence's. "So, tomorrow night. Five o'clock sharp. Wear something dark and short."

Prudence grinned, her cheeks stretched wider than they'd been in months.

"*Very* short," Vi added. "None of this Oregon tomboy shit." Vi waved a manicured finger at Prudence's outfit. "Even if there are women with them, men buy the drinks and leave the tips."

Prudence nodded quickly, pinching her nose even tighter.

"You know, you'd be pretty if you took the time," Vi said, slipping off the stool and stubbing out her smoldering cigarette in the ashtray. Vi winked and then stared at her for a while, but Prudence didn't feel the slightest unease. Only a sensation of lightness, as if something heavy she'd been carrying had been unburdened.

"It looks like you've had a rough run of things," Vi added. "And you look hungry. I'd have them send out a sandwich for you, but right now, hungry is good." She winked. "See you tomorrow. And keep pressure on that nose."

Prudence grabbed her suitcase and slipped back outside, where already it was growing dark and the rain was falling in puddles that now dotted the street. She stopped and leaned against the side of the building to break the wind, and found herself absently reaching to turn up the dial on her hearing aid. Her other hand instinctively reached to adjust the earpiece, but then with a start, she remembered that the unit was gone.

PRUDENCE HAD lost most of her hearing at a place her relatives used to meet up every summer in Bend, Oregon. Where an old woman lived alone in a farmhouse, newspapers nailed to the walls for insulation. She was an aunt of someone, a grandmother; none of her cousins really knew. They just called her the woman in the paper house. Her mother would nudge Prudence into the kitchen where the woman sat year after year, gazing into the woods. The woman would turn in her chair to greet her, spread her toothless mouth, hold out her branch-like arms.

Prudence always felt an unspoken kinship with this woman. And sometimes after dinner, when the old woman went back to her chair, Prudence would go with her to see what the woman was looking at, but there was nothing out there except the woods.

The last time her family went to visit her, Prudence was thirteen. After the usual greetings, her boy cousins had chased her out of the house and into the hay fields. She watched the girls standing on the porch, glaring at her. The sunlight that time of year was the color of wheat; and Prudence remembered the way it exploded in vibrant prisms through the trees. The way it caught the dandelion seeds that floated in the breeze, holding them aloft as if to invite the memory to return to that moment.

The boys had chased her down to the stream and she stopped short when she came to its edge. There was a textile mill up the stream, and the stream often changed colors with whatever they were dyeing on a given day. She'd nearly forgotten the time it had turned indigo blue and her father had said that's because they were making denim. But that day they all stood watching the bubbles float over the stained rocks, as the water suddenly became bright red. When she saw the boys were afraid, Prudence knelt and laved handfuls of water at them, laughing as she did.

She stopped splashing when she saw she'd gotten the red dye on their dress clothes. They stood frozen, mouths agape, as if tabulating the punishments they'd get from their parents for ruining their church clothes. And then they came and grabbed her and held her wrists and ankles. She remembered the surprising pain of their nails raking her skin as they dragged her roughly over the ground. Prudence kicked at them but they kept pulling, the girls coming to yank at the straps of her brassiere to help them along.

Often, Prudence would think of this place, feel time turning backwards until she arrived just at this moment. It was just a cruel, childish game gone wrong, and she could've fought her way free. But in a child's world, justice is served decisively. Without calling for parents, without squealing. Sometimes you just had to sit there and take it.

Someone had laid out a large picnic blanket at the top of the hill. They all stopped dragging her and told her to climb on the blanket and to make like a stone. She crawled across the blanket and obediently pulled her legs up under her, watching as they each took a corner of the blanket and began tossing her up and down. She shrieked a few times as they did, to show them that they were getting their retribution.

Higher, higher, higher, they'd yelled to one another. She shrieked louder as she flew high enough to see into the kitchen window of the farmhouse, where the old woman sat pointing at Prudence, her mouth silent but working frantically as if she was trying to warn her parents what was happening outside.

And then Prudence heard her cousins counting aloud in unison. Something in her clenched, awaiting what was coming. She yelled for them to stop but she watched their contorted faces as she flailed even higher in the air.

Then Prudence looked down and saw the blanket was crumpled on the ground. She looked at them and saw that she was higher than they'd wanted to throw her. Their faces went slack as she fell twenty feet, head first onto the hard dirt.

She was lying on the ground when she came to, coughing and blinking at her cousins' pale faces staring down at her. Her mother ran from the house and knelt there beside her in the grass. There was a loud ringing in her ears, and everyone was talking and yelling and she couldn't hear them. As her mother rocked her, Prudence felt a warm trickle of blood ooze down her cheek.

At home, she fell behind in school, unable to hear what her teachers said. She couldn't hear much of anything, not while playing games with her old girl friends, not when the school bell rang at the end of the day. And even after school, when she went and stood by the Luckiamute River, it rushed by in silence. But she didn't want to tell her parents, afraid they'd send her off to a school for the deaf.

And then, after nights of Prudence not coming when she was called to dinner, her mother took her to the doctor to be fitted with a specially made hearing aid. A large, clunky device that was big even for a grown man. The friendly, pretty girl was now ruined. She saw it in her teachers' faces. She saw it in her father's face too. She felt it too, in the way her old friends began to tease her, and how her best friend simply ignored her.

The boys gladly let her play baseball with them. But they tripped her the first time she ran to home plate, and she landed face first in the dirt with her hearing aid tumbling away from her. The boys began tossing it back and forth between them while she just sat there, coughing. Prudence felt as if she had swallowed a hot coal. Soon her grip tightened on the bat, her eyesight sharpened, her muscles discovered some untapped strength. Her bat connected with every pitch thrown at her, and it sailed over their dumb heads, and she'd smile as they all went stumbling after it as she handily rounded the bases.

Within a month she'd hit more homeruns than Mickey Townsend, the schoolyard hero. He sat there crying one afternoon in front of everyone who'd come to watch her play. Blubbering that *it ain't fair, it ain't fair, she's a girl.* Prudence stood there with the whole schoolyard gawking at her. All she saw when she looked back at them were the faces of her cousins as they let her fall from that blanket and into the eternal quiet. And in that moment, listening to Mickey wail, she turned off her hearing aid and just stood there watching him. Crying over a game where nothing was really at stake. It made her feel very alone, as she realized that no one in that schoolyard was like her, because they didn't know what it was like to have truly lost something.

THE SAME landlady from the night before was sitting at the front desk when Prudence walked through the flophouse door that night. As she walked the long hall, under its dim yellow lights, she knew this was the only place where she could talk her way into a room. And she had walked thirty blocks in the cold deciding just what she was going to say.

The landlady looked up at Prudence as if she was surprised to see her. Prudence explained that she was broke, but that she had a job and would pay her by the end of the week. She didn't bother telling the landlady that she had been robbed; it was clear from the woman's expression that she was already aware of the theft.

"Promises don't pay the rent," the landlady replied, taking a slow drag on a cigarette, her eyelids half-closed. Her long, speckled fingers reached for the volume dial on the old radio beside her. "We aren't a charity."

"Then I will just walk myself over to the police station and explain my situation." Prudence dropped the suitcase at her feet. "That the boarding house and the landlady who is supposed to be watching me, put me out after one of her tenants robbed me."

The landlady stubbed out the cigarette and squinted at Prudence. She knew that if the woman called her bluff, and she went to the police, they would just call her father and buy her a bus ticket home.

"And why would they believe that you even stayed here?" the landlady said.

Prudence looked down at the guest book, splayed out in front of the woman. It was still open to the same page as the night before when she signed in. Without pause, Prudence reached out and tore the page from the book and held it out. "Because that's my name and signature right here," she said, pointing. "Signed in at 11:05 last night."

Prudence folded the page and stuffed it down her shirt. She had a mind to tell the woman what she thought of her, but she was tired of hearing her own garbled voice.

The old woman just sat there, arms crossed, her face flat as a puddle. "I'll give you three days to pay or you're out on your own," the woman said. "You can keep your old room. No one's took it yet."

Prudence flashed a false smile, climbed upstairs and pushed open her door. She saw the burnt matches had been swept off the floor, the chair had been righted and the bed made. And then she saw something else and she stopped short and stared at it. Her hearing aid was sitting in the middle of the bed. She rushed to it and picked it up, flipped it on to see if it still worked. It didn't. She swore and pried open the battery case and reseated the three miniature glass tubes, as well as the battery. She closed it back up, held her breath and prayed as she flipped the volume dial.

She held the receiver in her hand, the earpiece by its twisted, flesh-colored cord. She moved the cord closer to the beige body of the unit until she heard the earpiece squeal and cry as it began to feedback. It was a delightful sound. As she fitted the earpiece and turned the volume, a car honked down the street and she heard it clearly.

She smiled, but it quickly dimmed. She knew that the hearing aid hadn't been returned in an act of remorse. That no pawn shop would take it, and the thief must've realized this shortly after lifting it. And as much as it being stolen gave her an understanding of the type of people that lived out there in the city, she knew that not even a hard up store keeper would buy it. No, she thought, looking down at it, even the lowest of people aren't that low. The thief had probably dumped it in a trashcan in the building and the janitor had brought it back up.

It was a large, unsightly thing with an electric sensitivity that required constant adjustment. It looked like a prosthetic — a flesh colored earpiece nearly as large as her ear. The earpiece itself was hard Bakelite that pinched and chafed the inside of her ear. And the long thick cord that ran under her clothing to the heavy battery box, which had to be clipped to a belt. It had always made wearing a nice dress an impossibility for her.

She knew its limitations too: the way it amplified voices and background noises, obscuring the ones she intended to hear. And as she stood by the window, picking up nearby noises and distant ones with the same volume, she wondered how she'd be able to cope with working in a noisy night club. If Vi would retract the job offer when she showed up wearing the hearing aid the next day.

She lay down on the bed with the unit in her hand. There were new noises here. Ones without memories of her mother or father or her town. No sound of rain tapping on the window, her mother singing over the piano, her father yelling at her for taking the car out alone. No, here it was just sounds that she would've never heard had she not left. But then she turned the dial and found that familiar sweet spot, a fundamental tone that fell beyond a person's natural hearing. It was a private joy to hear that old tone. She had come to believe, from years of living in the quiet, that things lived in the layers of sound, and that she'd spent her life moving between those layers.

And as she lay there on the bed, she heard a strange frequency, one she'd heard before. She looked out the flophouse window at the dark city. She shivered. There again was that monstrous rumbling sound from her dream. A sound of rattling earth, wood, and stone. The shapeless, sodden creature moving with primordial purpose. It was too clear an image, too true a sound to be just a dream. She closed her eyes and saw it bursting from the black sea, crawling over the sand and crashing through the woods. What it was, what it wanted, she didn't know. But as she lay there she took the scissors from her purse and clutched them to her chest, imagining moonlight on its scales, feeling the trembling as it moved along the earth, rolling slowly towards her.

Three

PRUDENCE SNUCK a few trolley rides from The Haight towards The Scotch House the next night in a grey wool skirt and a pair of mended stockings. Pale coral blouse and her mouton coat. She stepped off the back of the trolley and passed the other women on Broadway, dressed in expensive looking dresses and fine coats. Her own clothes had come from Black's General Store in Twin Falls. A dusty old place that also sold hunting rifles, tin toys and comic books. As she walked along the busy street towards the night club, she tried to appear like she belonged there, although she was shaking apart inside at what awaited her: the possibility that she would spill drink trays, misunderstand orders, smack some man silly if he pinched her ass.

A line stood beneath the marquis, young men and women in their long coats, puffing cigarettes and stamping their shoes against the pavement to keep warm. They watched as she approached, their eyes trained on her hearing aid. She slipped down an alley towards the sign marking the service entrance and went into the kitchen. Painted across its back wall in bright red letters was: *DO NOT THROW FOOD IN SINKS – PLEASE USE TRASH*. Steam hissed from boiling pots, and a woman stood at a table prepping oysters. Prudence watched the flash of knife as the meat was extracted and neatly flopped back in its shell. The cook frowned at her outfit, but she did her best to ignore her and pushed open the door leading onto the main floor.

She was affronted by a loud wall of noise. She dialed back her hearing aid and scanned the crowd. Guys wearing black turtle necks and horn rimmed glasses, girls with long straight hair parted in the middle. No make-up except dark eye shadow. They were all packed against the bar, watching the band playing onstage. It was standing room only save for the area closest to the stage, where there stood a dozen small tables and several round booths, filled with people shouting drink orders at the waitresses. Prudence felt the sweet anxiety of the coming rush, just like at home, waitressing on Sunday mornings at the Twin Falls Diner.

Prudence found Vi behind the bar, looking striking in a dark red taffeta dress, gazing up at the bandstand. Suddenly Jeffie appeared and grabbed Prudence by her arm.

"Vi told me to keep an eye on you tonight," Jeffie shouted, releasing her grip. "I sure hope you know your Vodka Gimlet from a Whiskey Sour." She wrung her hands in her apron. "And don't let anyone buy you a drink. Vi doesn't let us drink on the job, not even on the sly."

"I don't drink," Prudence said.

"Idaho, is that where you said you're from?" Jeffie smirked. "Well, I didn't either until I came here. I picked up the habit pretty quick."

Jeffie grabbed her arm again, turning Prudence around. "What the hell is that?" Jeffie asked, pointing at the earpiece to her hearing aid. "Jesus, are you deaf or something?"

"No," Prudence said, covering the earpiece with her hand, her eyes flashing around the room. "I can hear every damn thing in here. So don't worry about it."

"Well, Vi's not going to allow it," Jeffie said, handing her a drink tray, a ticket book and pencil stub. "So if I don't see you again tonight, it's been nice knowing ya."

Prudence watched Jeffie walk away and then headed out on the floor, looking back over her shoulder for Vi. Throughout her shift, running back and forth between tables and the bar, Prudence watched the band. The musicians looked affected, acting too nonchalant to put any feeling into the music. The band itself was stripped down to a piano, saxophone, trumpet, double-bass and drums. Ties askew, buttons unbuttoned, eyes quivering behind their instruments. Cool Jazz, they called it. There was a purity to the sound of the horns, a deep tug of the strings on the bass. The cascading wash of the drum sticks on the cymbals.

Despite its simplicity, the music had a pulse that drove the drink orders. During the slow numbers, a hush fell over the room. For the fast numbers, men leaned back in their chairs and tossed bills at Prudence. Within an hour, she was slipping between the packed tables, balancing the drink tray on her finger tips: Pink Ladies, Old Fashioneds, Manhattans, Three Dots and a Dash, and a drink that Charlene, the head bartender, called the Evening Gun.

Halfway through the evening, Vi came and blocked Prudence's path as she was heading from the bar with a full drink tray.

"That's going to be a problem," Vi said, nodding towards the earpiece.

"What, this? I barely remember I'm wearing it," Prudence replied. She stopped and looked at Vi. "I really can hear just fine. I know it's nothing to look at, but I have to wear it. I wasn't wearing it last night because someone stole it from me."

"Jesus kid, you're breaking my heart." Vi said, with a trace of a Western drawl that she hadn't noticed before. "Well, it's just for tonight, anyway. So okie dokie, Oregon. Get on back out there."

Prudence nodded to Vi, then turned to face the crowd. She sucked in a breath. Balanced the drink tray in both hands and as she walked slowly through the room. Everywhere she turned, some drunken lout was swinging his arms or trying to back into her, screw her whole night up. She weaved between them on her tiptoes, her drink tray rising higher in the air, just like she had working back at the diner.

Soon she was standing at a round booth filled with five well-dressed men. As she prepared to place their drinks on the table, someone ran into her backside, knocking her forward. In an instant, she was face down on the table, afraid to look up and see the drinks spilled all over the men's suits. *I should just walk out of here right now*, she thought, still looking down. *Never come back.*

She heard the slow clapping of hands, and when she slowly lifted her head, she was face to face with a young blue-eyed man of about thirty. Well-tanned, jet black hair, grey suit and a black tie. It took another second to notice that the drink tray was still in her hand and not one of the drinks had spilled. She didn't move for a moment, but kept gazing up at the man. He wasn't applauding along with the others, just looking at her in a curious, amused way.

"Well done," another man at the table cheered. Prudence set the tray down and turned to confront the jerk who'd knocked her over. He was standing there, thick trunked and towering over her, wearing an outdated zoot suit. His face was covered with acne scars and he had a woman with him who looked to be no older than sixteen.

"You need to keep this aisle clear," he declared, in a slow, hoarse voice. "For the patrons."

"Well pardon me," Prudence said, "but you were the one who almost spilled these drinks on the *patrons*."

"I said 'Excuse me' when I was walking by." He looked at her hearing aid. "Maybe you didn't hear me, Sweetheart."

"I didn't hear you either," the blue-eyed man said in a calm tone. "Did any of you?" He looked at his table-mates, who all shook their heads. "So please, tell her you're sorry. We haven't seen her in here before, so she must be new."

Prudence blushed, but continued to glare at the man in the zoot suit. "Well, go on then," she said.

"What's that?" he stammered.

"Maybe it's you who can't hear so well." She put her hands on her hips. "I said, why don't you say 'excuse me' to me and these gentlemen?"

The men at the table whooped and cheered while the lout just stood there with his hat in his hands, running the brim through his fingers.

"Excuse me!" the man shouted. He plopped his hat on his head, turned and stormed away with his girl in tow.

Prudence watched him leave, then looked back at the table. "Anything else?" she asked, as she placed each of their drinks in front of them.

"Yes." The blue-eyed man asked. "Your name?"

"Prudence," she replied, blushing again.

The man repeated her name and everyone looked at him, but he didn't seem to notice. He just sat there with his eyes wide open and his mouth settled into a loose grin.

She spun on her heel and headed towards the bar, hoping she would get another chance to wait on him. She'd never felt so white hot inside about a man she just met. He appeared so dignified. Sober. And although it seemed impossible, it seemed he felt the same way too. But she didn't have time for them. Everywhere she turned there was some guy ogling her, staring at her fanny, and there were drinks to be served.

When she came back to the table a while later to settle their bill, the men were gone. She let out a withheld breath as she collected their empty glasses. Where the blue-eyed man had sat lay a crisp ten dollar bill, folded lengthwise. She'd never held a bill that big in her life, and as she studied it, she saw that it had something written on it in ink:

Good save, Prudence. Keep the change.
~ Charles

"So," Vi said at the end of the night, counting out Prudence's drink tickets on the bar. "Not bad. Looks like you served more drinks than anyone here."

"Did I?" Prudence said. "I was just keeping up."

"You have hustle," Vi said, leaning against the bar and scanning the nearly empty room. "Not these other girls. I like to think they'll go onto something better. At best, they'll end up with some stooge who knocks them up and beats them around." Vi picked up a cigarette from the ashtray and took a drag. "Speaking of which, that girl you're covering for. She quit today. Came in and cleared out her things."

Prudence felt her stomach lift. She glanced around the room, Charlene wiping down the bar with a rag, Jeffie turning chairs over onto the tables. When she glanced back at Vi, she was writing in her ledger, talking over her shoulder.

"Be here tomorrow at the same time and we'll try you out again." Vi spun around and pointed her pen at Prudence. "But don't go thinking you've got a job. If I hear one word from the customers about that thing on your ear, I'll send you on your way."

THE NEXT night went even better, and although Vi didn't offer her a job, she kept asking her to come back. By the end of her first week working at The Scotch House, Prudence had earned enough money to move to a nicer boarding house in The Haight. Once she was settled in, she bought some decent dress clothes at The Emporium, the department store down on Market Street. And as a week of work passed, and then another, with barely a day off to see the rest of the city, she had saved enough cash to think about heading down to Los Angeles. She'd written her Aunt Doris to tell her where she was, but didn't tell her about the theft or leave a return address, as she didn't want her aunt sending money for the bus ticket.

Prudence often marveled at her luck at finding such a great job, and so quickly. For once, her days felt natural, easy, as if her intuition that first day at the club had been realized. And it made her feel important to get a taste of this trendy West Coast Jazz scene. Occasionally, a big act would come to the club and bring in droves of reporters, music critics, and an even wealthier clientele.

On those nights, the owner of The Scotch House walked the floor, shaking hands with the guests. He was a light-skinned black man named Hurley. Always dapper in his pinstripe suits, Hurley liked women and they liked him; he was always off in some part of the club, in a booth necking with a blonde, or in the stockroom necking with a brunette. Sometimes Prudence caught him eying her and knew he would inevitably hit on her, and she wondered if she would be able to deflect his advances without losing her job.

There were always musicians walking in and out of the club too, dragging their instrument cases, chatting up the waitresses. As talented as they were, Prudence found them to be feckless and unreliable. She wasn't attracted to grown men who couldn't show up sober to their job on time, famous or not. She liked men who earned what they owned. To her, most of the musicians looked like spoiled prep school boys when they got up onstage, in their oxford shirts, club ties and wool suits.

"See that man over there?" Vi said one evening in mid-April, pointing at a handsome man standing at the end of the bar in an expensive looking double-breasted suit. He was drinking with a bunch of other well-dressed men. Something in Prudence's chest lurched when she recognized him.

"That's Charles Pieretti," Vi said. "He owns some hi-tone business over on Fillmore. Shoot, he's no Montgomery Clift," she added, "but there's something about that man that makes me fucking swoon."

Prudence felt a pang of jealousy, and then laughed at herself for being so naïve. The man stood out. Even in a room of famous musicians, artists and rich local businessmen, she could tell that he was somebody. Vi and every other girl there had a better shot at a man like that than she did. But as she watched him, she was surprised that the feeling she had at his table a couple of weeks earlier hadn't dulled.

"A man like that is almost enough to change my mind about things." Vi turned and looked at Prudence. "But if I ever fell for another man, I don't know what I'd do."

Prudence examined Vi closely, wondering what she meant. "I'm not looking for a man right now either," she replied, baiting Vi to tell her more. She turned her back on Charles for now, set her drink tray on the bar and watched Charlene finish mixing her drink orders.

Vi leaned against the bar and moved closer to Prudence. "You know how I told you that my parents disowned me?" Vi leaned in even closer, so close she could feel her breath against her ear. "It's because I had an affair with my Arithmetic teacher." Vi paused. "Her name was Miss Dewee."

Prudence looked at Vi and nodded quickly, as if to show Vi that this revelation didn't bother her, that she'd suspected it all along. But

Owen Duffy

in truth, she'd never met someone who admitted to liking the same sex. Sure, there were men back in Twin Falls who were rumored to be homosexual, but they were just the bachelors who still lived with their mothers and went with them to the movies on the weekends.

Vi was different than them, of course. But it made Prudence wonder if Vi thought *she* was homosexual. That Vi was only keeping her around the club to make a pass at her.

Prudence returned Vi's searching stare for a moment, their eyes locked together, as if each was waiting for the other to flinch. A crashing noise came from the opposite end of the bar as a tray of drinks hit the floor. Vi spun around and went to see it cleaned up, but she looked over her shoulder at Prudence as she walked away. Prudence was left standing there in the bustling crowd, a tray of sweating drinks in her hand, a heavy question now hanging in the air between them. One she was afraid to answer.

As she delivered the drinks to a table of noisy beatniks, who were swallowing Bennies and tossing them up at the bandstand, laughing as the musicians gobbled them up between songs, she spilled a beer right down the front of her skirt. She swore and apologized, but the man just sat there in his black sweater, horned rimmed glasses and unwashed hair and said, "*Drag* ..."

She rushed alongside the opposite end of the bar, searching for a clean rag. She hurried down a long dim corridor, where the restrooms and stockrooms were located. She grabbed a rag and fanned herself with it. Then she stepped out the open back door service entrance into the alley to cool off, catch her breath. Some of the musicians were standing there, smoking a stick of reefer and leaning against the walls. They all thought reefer made them more intelligent, made them play better. But having overheard their conversations, both musical and verbal, Prudence knew it was all an illusion.

"Oh here come Miss Strawberry," said the tall, lanky bassist, who often sat in with traveling bands that didn't have their own. She could see that he was high on the Bennies, the jitteriness to his movements. He smiled at her with his big, frog-like face as she tried to turn back into the building. "Oh my, and she is all ready for me." He laughed, pointing at the wet spot on her skirt.

"Oh my, Miss Sweet Red," the drummer said, grinning at it too. He was also tall, but stockier, and with a lot of gold rings on his fingers so the audience could see his hands as he did his corny tricks with his drumsticks.

They all laughed and blocked her path as she tried to pass. She stopped and glared at the drummer, then at the others. He was the only black person among them and she hated the way the others were always talking like they were black too. It had gotten to their heads so much it was as if they actually believed they were black.

"Hey asshole," she said, glaring at the drummer. "I don't go around calling you names because of how you look." She flashed her eyes around the group. "My mother was *Irish*. Got it?"

"Hey now," the bassist said. "That's Dexter Jones. You can't talk to him like that. If Hurley heard you, you'd be out on your ass."

"Screw you," she said, staring the drummer up and down as if he was nothing. "And screw Dexter Jones."

The drummer stepped back, his mouth falling open. The others all went quiet and looked at the bassist, who suddenly popped off the wall he'd been leaning against.

"Hold on now." He passed off the stick of reefer and came and stood in front of her. "*What* did you say?" He suddenly seemed larger, a dark intensity in his eyes that she hadn't noticed before. He grabbed her arm and put his face in hers. "Now, no one's taught you your place here yet. So I'm gonna make this real easy. You come with me into that stockroom and do what I say, you won't be out of a job come tomorrow."

Prudence gasped, looking up at him as if he'd just knocked something from her hands. Something fine and pristine that she'd been carrying around her whole life. She looked at the others, but they had the same dark look to their faces. As if they were happy to stand there and admire the shattered pieces on the floor.

"I'm sorry," she said, wriggling her arm in his hand. "I'm sorry."

"Huh," the bassist muttered back, his lips curling over his yellow teeth. "You hear that, Dex?" He kept his eyes locked on her. "Miss Sweet as a Strawberry is sorry."

Dexter pulled on the stick of reefer, staring at her. She felt her shoulders rising and falling, her arm burning where the bassist was holding it. Dexter exhaled a cloud of smoke and squinted at her.

"What the hell is going on out here?" A familiar twangy voice called into the alley. Prudence and the band members turned and saw Vi standing in the doorway beneath the lamplight, her hair aglow, her skin pallid and white. "Leave her be. And all of you get back to work." She clapped her hands together. "Go on now!"

When the bassist reluctantly loosened his grip, Prudence twisted around and hurried down the corridor with Vi beside her, her pulse rattling in her ears, her breath coming short and fast. As she came to the bar, she stopped and braced herself against it, her chest tight and her eyes stinging. She began gathering the empty drink glasses and beer bottles that sat there. As she did, she lowered her head and pinched the bridge of her nose with her fingers to stop the tears.

"Thank you," Prudence said.

Vi leaned in close. "Don't think there's always going to be someone to save your candy ass. Be smart. You have to fend for yourself. If one of those motherfuckers says 'boo' to you again, say 'boo' right back. Scream if you have to. Kick him where it counts."

Prudence nodded and stood there with her head in her hands until Vi left. When she looked up a minute later, she saw the bassist and the rest of the band standing at the mouth of the corridor, waiting for the emcee to re-introduce them to the stage. She held in her breath, hearing their suggestive comments, their continued threats. When she turned back around she nearly dropped all the empty glasses when she saw Charles walking along the bar towards her, dressed in a dark suit, his hands stuffed in his pockets.

As he neared, he smiled. "I was hoping I'd run into you," he said. He looked at her a moment before his smile faded. She could tell her hair had fallen out of place and she was covered in a fine sweat, her cheeks feeling hot and rosy. As she set the empty glasses down and brushed back a few strands of hair, she could still hear the band muttering behind her.

Charles glanced over her shoulder and seemed to understand what was happening. When he looked back at her she recognized the unmistakable look of pity, but underneath it, something else. Something in his gaze that reminded her of the times she'd asked her father about his time in The Great War. The way his eyes fogged over and his face went flat. How she could tell in his expression that he'd killed men and seen men killed.

"It's okay," she said, avoiding his eyes. As she finished sorting the dirty glasses, Charlene yelled and pushed a fresh tray of drinks her way. Prudence pulled it towards her and let it sit there. She looked down at the floor and then back up at Charles.

"Well, back to work." She shrugged, wiping her eyes with the back of her hand.

"See you around?" he asked, as she brought the tray to her shoulder.

"Sure." She nodded, as if to thank him for not intervening or even trying to lift her spirits. She stood there a moment longer, looking up at him, before she returned to the floor, her arm burning and her hair still a mess. Looking back over her shoulder as the night began to pass, she saw him standing at the bar with his friends. She cursed at herself for what had happened in the hallway. She was an old hand at sorting out bullies, as the hearing aid always aroused their cruelty. And that was the problem with people: no matter where they came from, they were always ready to remind you of your weaknesses.

When she had a break she scanned the room, and saw that Charles and all the men with him had vanished. She sighed and tossed her drink tray on the bar, lit a cigarette and stood there smoking, hoping he might re-appear. She swore when she looked down and saw the wet spot was still there on her skirt, and then began to laugh as she blotted at it with a clean cloth. By then Charlene had already loaded up her tray with fresh drinks, and she crushed her smoke and went back out on the floor, continuing to scan the crowd for Charles, but he was gone.

She was still thinking about him as she walked home from work, as she fell asleep, as she awakened each subsequent morning. The thought of him inexplicably filled her with a hot pressure, one that built over the coming days to a near scream. She soon bought some shorter dresses for work that minimized her athletic build, applied a lipstick that made her lips look plump and full. She told herself that she would talk to him if he came back in, devising ways to lighten the mood after what had happened. And each night for the next week she stood there at the bar, waiting for him to appear and give this urgent feeling some release, but he never did.

WITH THE Scotch House closed on Monday nights, Hurley

threw late night dinner parties for the staff and their friends at his home over in Tiburon. Although she'd been invited several times by Hurley himself, Prudence had never gone to one, as she had heard stories about how wild the parties were. Lots of reefer and other illegal drugs, whisperings of illicit sex acts and late night orgies. Prudence knew she sure as hell wouldn't fit in with that crowd. But then Vi insisted she go, assuring her that the parties weren't *that* good. And that she'd keep an eye on her, just this once, to make sure she didn't get in trouble.

Vi pulled up outside the new boarding house on Monday night and picked Prudence up in a navy blue 1949 Dodge, which was uncannily similar to her mother's car. She stood on the curb and looked at Vi, her window rolled down and her arm hanging out. Her sharp chin line and neat profile, her blonde hair held back with a thin black headband. It was the first time Prudence had seen her out of the club, and was unnerved to see it did little to diminish the cool confidence she exuded.

"You talked me into this," Vi said sarcastically, sliding over on the bench seat when Prudence appeared on the curb. "So you can drive."

Prudence slipped behind the wheel and shut the door, flashing a glance at Vi. It had been nearly a month since she'd driven a car. There was a strange familiarity to the large wheel, the fluted gauges staring back at her like eyes. The engine rumbling when she tapped the pedal, the pleasant vibrations reaching her hands.

"Jesus. You *live* here?" Vi asked, looking up at the institutional looking boarding house she'd been living in the past two weeks. Prudence blushed as she dropped the car into gear and pulled out onto the street.

"They don't have bedbugs and they serve a good mystery meat

Owen Duffy

on Sundays," Prudence said as she accelerated.

"You should really spend some of that money you're making," Vi said. "You could move in with one of the other girls at the club. No need to live in squalor."

The engine noise obliterated most of what Vi was saying. Prudence had forgotten how good it felt to press the gas pedal to the floor, and she couldn't bring herself to let it up. As she tore towards the corner she downshifted, double clutching the pedals and swinging the car around a busy street corner. Vi cussed and grabbed the dashboard as Prudence kicked out the tail end of the car, the rear tires singing as they skidded past a row of parked cars. A few boys that were standing on the corner jumped and cheered as they roared past.

Vi sat up when Prudence straightened the wheel, looking over at her as if in disbelief. "What the hell has gotten into you?" she screamed. "Slow down!"

Prudence grinned at Vi cringing in her seat. But then Vi smiled and let out a playful wail as they shot down the street at fifty miles an hour, the engine's gurgle ending the conversation. The truth was, Prudence knew that her time in San Francisco was up, that this party was a last hurrah. Los Angeles still loomed like an oasis in her imagination, and she figured she would have over twenty dollars saved by the end of the week, if Vi kept her on that long.

As she yanked the wheel and soared through another turn, she realized, just like that first time she'd walked in the club, that this still felt *right*. More than that, it had all been a lot of fun. Strike that, she thought, shooting down the street with Vi gripping her arm. It had all been an absolute scream.

They crossed over the Golden Gate and pulled off the highway towards Hurley's place. The roads quickly turned ashen and wet, reminding Prudence of the Oregon logging roads back home that she used to race along. The long nightly drives she'd taken in the past months to clear her head. And how nearly every Friday and Saturday night in high school she had piled into an old souped up car with her friends. A '32 Ford Roadster, a '47 Chevy Coupe, a '39 Lincoln Zephyr; it didn't matter, as long as it was loud and fast. They'd cruise around town with all the other kids, drinking Rainier beer, the radio blaring Doris Day and Frankie Laine. They'd stop at the Five Spot for hamburgers and fries before they'd drop off the other girls and tear deep into the woods.

The boys had taught her how to drive those roads, and eventually she'd memorized the curves just like they had, until she could take them faster than any of them. There was something about being behind the wheel that gave the world a sense of order. As if something could be deciphered from the trail her tires left on those soft logging trails. That by pushing the car to its limits, kicking its rear end out over a ledge with a bunch of boys in the back yelling out to God for her to slow down, the world lost its sense of mystery.

And she remembered too, at the end of those long nights, how those boys would invariably crawl drunk from the car after she'd smacked them off of her. Boys that were all too ready, overeager and pressed hard against her. Boys who would soon enough have children of their own and be wedded to the same town they too had been trying to escape.

There was only one boy, Davy Monahan, who she hadn't smacked away. Who truly didn't mind her hearing aid or her blue jeans, nor she his wispy haired frailness and painful sensitivity. She'd driven out with him one night in their senior year, after everyone else had gone home. Down a road that dead-ended at an abandoned lumber mill, a waterfall spilling beside it. It was near dawn when they arrived and shut off the engine, the sound of rushing water through the open window. The rising sun obscured by a blanket of heavy branches. Her heart pounding, her mouth dry. Their cold sweat, their beating hearts, out there where they were hidden, where what happened in that car would be a secret. She kissed him hard, pulling at his trousers and he at her underpants, both of them breathing fast, gasping and pleading as they coupled, the tight rocking rhythm, and then as he pulled away and moaned, then afterwards they lay there, shivering, the cool forest breathing over their naked bodies.

PRUDENCE BLINKED, watching the headlights pass over the trees as they rounded another bend.

"We're lost," Vi said, looking out her window as she lit a cigarette.

Prudence began to sing "Let's Get Lost," mimicking Chet Baker's flat-toned, effeminate voice, which they'd heard that entire weekend at the club. As she belted out the refrain, her foot jabbed the accelerator and the car surged forward. She grazed trashcans at the end of driveways, seeing how close she could get without knocking them over. Cat's eyes stared back from the tall grass, indolent, phosphorescent. When Prudence finished the song and looked over, Vi was braced against the door jamb.

"Oh loosen up," Prudence laughed. "You're too damn stiff!"

"You're going to hit something!" Vi yelled, laughing now and loosening her grip on the door.

"If you tell me to slow down again," Prudence said. "I'll just speed up, so skip it."

Vi whooped again as Prudence flew around a blind corner, spinning the wheel in her hands, the car's engine racing as they tore through a residential neighborhood.

"There it is!" Vi shouted a minute later, as they shot over the crest of a hill. She pointed at a brightly lit house sitting atop it. A row of cars lined both sides of the street. Prudence slammed the brakes and they surged to a stop. She parked behind the last car and they jumped out, laughing as they walked up Hurley's driveway.

"Did you learn to drive in Oregon like that?" Vi asked. "Not bad." She was wearing black capris that showed off her hips and a tight black blouse, a thin red leather belt around her trim waist. Her hair was coiffed and her make-up neatly applied, her lips accentuated by reddish orange lipstick.

"Some boys taught me some things back in high school," Prudence said.

"I'll bet they did." Vi reached out and touched Prudence's hair, which had grown out enough that she now had a proper Audrey Hepburn hairdo. "And I bet they were crazy about you."

Prudence blushed, feeling both uneasy and flattered to have Vi's attention focused on her. Music and laughter poured from Hurley's place. Vi looped her arm through hers as they climbed the stairway to the front door, snapping her fingers and swaying lightly to the music, her hips thrusting into hers. As they banged together, Prudence felt a burst of warmth shooting through her, and she looked at Vi and smiled.

Inside Hurley's house, Prudence noticed that there wasn't any dinner at all. The dining table was littered with half-empty liquor bottles and spilled bowls of peanuts and potato chips. Everyone from the club was there, the entire staff and dozens of Hurley's friends, all beatnik types who looked to be there only for the free liquor. Some were reading poetry aloud, some were dancing to race records, and some were necking with the waitresses along the wall.

"See," Vi said, handing Prudence a glass full of scotch and soda.

"It's not at all like what you heard."

Within the hour, the house was empty and everyone had shed their clothes and were standing naked by the pool in Hurley's back yard. Hurley himself was the first one in, doing a fancy dive off the diving board. Prudence and Vi just stood there, shaking their heads as a dozen nude bodies leapt into the pool. When they surfaced, they called for Prudence and Vi to join them.

Prudence had never been naked in front other people like that, and her heart began to throb at the thought of it. But then Vi lifted her shirt over her head and began to undo her brassiere. Everyone in the pool began to whistle and cheer. She smiled at them and ceremoniously flung her clothing on a nearby chair and then slipped down her pants, pumping her hips from side to side. Prudence blinked, but didn't look away. Soon Vi was standing there, the light reflecting off the water on her skin, her small breasts, the pure blonde hair between her legs. She laughed and dove in the pool with a small splash, surfaced, and looked up at Prudence.

"Come on in," she said, and the others joined. Prudence smiled, bit her lip and looked down at them. She'd been initiated into groups before, and this was no different. And besides, she thought, I won't see these people after the end of the week anyway. She slowly unclipped her hearing aid and lifted her shirt over her head. Someone whistled as she covered herself with her blouse and began to undo her brassiere, then her skirt.

Within moments she was completely nude, the cool wind against her skin, the world gone quiet. Looking down at her bare, full breasts, her flat stomach and strong legs, her painted toenails gripping the edge of the pool.

"Holy Christ," Hurley said, gawking at her, and everyone in the pool laughed in agreement.

Prudence turned backwards, her toes on the lip of the pool, raised her arms straight into the air and flung herself up, tumbling and flipping once in the air so she landed feet first in the pool. She closed her eyes as the warm water slipped over her, places where it felt foreign, but pleasant. When she came back up, everyone was clapping. Vi moved over towards her and clung to the wall beside her.

"That was pretty brave. I never would've thought you had that in you." Vi brushed back her hair with her hand, wiped the water from her eyes. "You're beautiful, you know that?"

"Do you think so?" Prudence asked, feeling Vi's leg brushing against hers, soft and slippery.

Vi closed her eyes and nodded, water glimmering on her lips. When she opened her eyes again, a drunk, naked girl was staggering out of the pool with two men following close behind.

"Hold that thought." Vi swam to the ladder and pulled herself up, grabbed a towel and covered the girl up, shooing the men away. When Prudence turned, Hurley was swimming towards her. She swam to the ladder and climbed it quickly, but Hurley grabbed her ankle on the last wrung.

"Just wanted to enjoy the view a moment," he said in a warm, soothing voice, looking up at her bare ass. Prudence turned and put her hands on her hips, and gave him a playful frown.

"Well, enjoy it," she said. "But you know what I'd really like right now?"

"What's that, Sweetheart?"

"A sandwich."

He laughed and released her ankle and told her to go help herself. She covered herself with a towel, plugged in her hearing aid and went to find something to eat in the icebox.

As she was stuffing Swiss cheese and lettuce between two pieces of stale bread, Hurley came into the kitchen. She gasped when she saw him standing there, completely naked and dripping wet. They were the only two people in the house and the rest of the party suddenly seemed far away.

"Well, well, well." His eyes were heavily lidded, his fist pressed into his kidney, his dangle like a rolled up pair of socks. His entire body leaning tipsily and suggestively towards her. Prudence stared at him, her heart beginning to pound.

Just then Vi passed by the kitchen, only half-clothed, holding the drunk girl upright with the towel wrapped around her. Prudence called out to her and Vi immediately set the girl down in a chair and ran into the kitchen. She stopped short and gasped when she saw Hurley standing there naked.

"This one's mine, Hurley," Vi said, coming and standing directly in front of Prudence. Vi slipped her hands around her waist and pulled her close. Prudence stumbled and threaded her arms through Vi's. She stared into Vi's eyes a moment, her heartbeat soft and muted, the rest of the room becoming hazy. She leaned forward and pressed her lips against Vi's. Felt the slickness of them as they met, finding it no different than kissing a man, only softer, better. Then Prudence pulled Vi's body even closer, her tongue touching her own now, a trickle of warmth washing through her.

Vi pulled back a second later, releasing her grip on Prudence. They stood there, blinking at one another.

"What a waste," Hurley said. He shook his head at the both of them. "What a waste of two beautiful women."

Prudence didn't move until Vi led her out of the kitchen, leaving Hurley standing there alone in a pool of water. Prudence let out a laugh, partly because of the look she must've had on her face, and partly out of relief. Vi reached to cover her mouth, but Prudence grabbed her hand, and after they gathered up their clothes they were both rushing out into the cool damp night together.

They threw themselves into the car and sat on the cool seat with their clothes in their hands, their breath steaming the windows. They laughed and then dropped their clothes and moved closer on the seat, kissing again. Prudence closed her eyes, chanting in her mind that this is wrong, this is wrong, even as she took Vi's hand and guided it to her breast. Prudence stopped and leveled her eyes at Vi. She was breathing hard and Vi was staring back at her.

"I've never done this before," Prudence blurted, the sound of her own voice surprising her.

Vi nodded and kissed her again, slowly this time, her hands thumbing her breast. Prudence closed her eyes and felt the sweet anxiety, the rush of alcohol through her blood, heady and cool. The rush of something else, fire hot and urgent. She pressed Vi's hand down between her legs, her own hands reaching out for her there too, the fine hair and then deeper, the warmth and the scent of her, wild and unexpected, until they were both moaning and rocking with their lips pressed to each other's ears, hushed and moving together until they were both gratified, collapsed against each other.

AFTER DAYS of Vi's pestering, Prudence checked out of her new boarding house the following Sunday morning. She grabbed her suitcase and turned in her key, took the long ride over to North Beach. It was a bright, sunny morning and people were hurrying along the sidewalks, coatless, hatless. Vi's apartment was only blocks from the bay and she walked from the trolley stop, the sun warming her face. She followed the directions Vi had given her and came to a yellow door on a corner apartment building on Grant Street.

Prudence removed a letter she'd written that morning and slipped it under Vi's door. She rang the bell, then she ran down the street and stopped in an alleyway, watching as the door opened a minute later. Vi's face peered out a moment before she noticed the letter at her feet. She tore it open, there in the doorway with the light spilling on her. Prudence felt her eyes fill with tears when she saw Vi's shoulder slump. Vi looked up and down the street once, then closed the door slowly behind her.

The wind blew at her back and she squinted and pulled her coat tight around her. Vi had offered her a job that past week, invited her to move into a spare bedroom for a while. Prudence initially hesitated at Vi's offer, until Vi put it in terms in which she couldn't find fault. Particularly that they would both be helping each other out: she would be helping pay the rent, and Prudence would be in a safer neighborhood, within walking distance to work. And besides, Vi said, they got along *quite* well.

Prudence turned and headed back towards the trolley, to ride it over to the bus depot. Los Angeles was waiting, and if she put it off any longer her frivolous Aunt Doris might forget her offer, and the director would too. Perhaps it was cowardly to have told Vi in a letter that she was leaving, that she wouldn't be coming to stay. To not get a chance to thank her face to face, offering only the promise that she would write.

She got on a bus headed towards the depot. As it wound through the city and stopped at Fulton and 30th Street, she knew she might come to regret this. That Los Angeles and what awaited her there would be nothing like she had imagined. When she stepped off to again change buses, she saw hundreds of people jamming the sidewalks, heading south into Golden Gate Park.

"Where is everyone going?" Prudence asked a man passing by,

a boy in tow.

"To the races," the boy said, dragging his father along. "They're just starting."

Prudence looked down at her suitcase and then up at the long tunnel of people hustling past. *Races?* She followed them into the park until she came over a hill. She heard the scream of a dozen engines as a row of brightly colored cars rounded a bend lined with hay bales. She stood there with her mouth hanging open. She watched them head north along the closed off park roads, speeding away in a cloud of blue smoke, and when it cleared she saw there were thousands of people lining the long, winding course, and more of them brushing against her as they went to find a spot close to it.

She found herself wandering along the track, between the spectators, removing her hat and unbuttoning her coat. Each time the cars came, small and wimpy looking, but sleeker than any car she'd ever seen, she dialed back her hearing aid. Soon she was standing by the starting line, having pushed her way to the front of the crowd, watching each race car pass over it and a man in a white suit jumping and waving a checkered flag. A woman in a two-piece bathing suit handing the winner his trophy, a banner draped over her shoulder which read *Miss Dangerous Curves*.

Prudence stood there as a new group of cars entered the racetrack and lined up for the next race. The course was seemingly made from the narrow public roads in Golden Gate Park, that wound between the lakes, trees and grassy hills. She watched as the flagman waved the green flag and the cars shot off, the drivers wearing helmets and goggles, leather gloves gripping their steering wheels. She looked at her wristwatch and counted how fast they rounded the course, most of them in just over six minutes.

She stood there through each successive race, nearly a half dozen in total. Her knees aching, her stomach growling. Some of the final race heats featured cars that could be bought at the local dealership. Big Chevys and Chryslers, Dodges, DeSotos, some of them driven by kids who looked like they'd just gotten their licenses. After these races, she turned and hurried back up the hill, grabbed a bus back to Grant Street.

"Well, well, well," Vi said, when she answered the door, her hand on her hip. She was wearing only a red kimono, holding a half empty highball glass. "I thought you were riding off into the sunset. Or did you come back for your girl?"

UPSTAIRS, VI showed her around the two-bedroom apartment. Brightly lit by the large east-facing windows, the bamboo blinds half open. An Oriental carpet filled the main room where there was a wingback chair and a porthole television, which was tuned to a re-broadcasting of the Jack Benny Show. To the side, behind the worn leather sofa, stood a small artist's studio, replete with easel and a table full of paints and brushes.

She then showed Prudence the bedroom: it was cozy and clean with a single window facing Lombard Street. A Murphy bed and large dresser, and a desk tucked beneath the window frame. Vi took Prudence's suitcase and set it on a rack in the closet.

"And that's it." Vi dusted off her hands. "Welcome to Chateau de Prudence and Vi."

Prudence nodded, looking down at her own hands. "Thank you, Vi. I mean it. And I'm sorry for the letter. I didn't sleep last night and I wasn't thinking clearly. Didn't know what I wanted to do."

"Forget it, kid," she said in a mock W.C. Fields voice, slipping her arm around Prudence's shoulder. "Ya hungry?"

Vi sat her at the small Formica table in the kitchenette while she made lunch: bacon, lettuce and tomato sandwiches. Prudence learned that Vi's full name was Violet Louise Greene. She was indeed from Montana. Missoula, to be exact. Prudence then told Vi all about her mother and her father, her reason for leaving home for Los Angeles. Her Aunt Doris, the movie director. Missing her bus and getting robbed her first night in town.

They ate slowly and read *The Chronicle*, then spent the morning organizing and decorating Prudence's room. They drank Bloody Mary's that afternoon and at dusk they walked down to a café on Beach Street that Vi liked and they sat looking through its large windows at the shipping vessels moving in and out of the bay.

Prudence felt a complete calm, just sitting there in silence as they ate dinner, then walked the long way home along the waterfront, the salty air damp against her skin. And the cool sheets of her bed in her room as she lay down that night, the wind blowing through the open window, smelling of the Italian bakery across the way.

Prudence stared at each car's headlights as they whipped around the corner, listened to their engines and soon she began to guess the car's make. She knew a Dodge when she heard one, like a sewing machine in need of oiling. A Ford, with their rattling exhausts. A Hudson, loud and raspy. She decided she was going to save up to buy a Hudson Hornet, enter one of those races.

But first, she flipped on the lamp and wrote her Aunt Doris a letter, thanking her and explaining that she was safe and happy in San Francisco. After a while she got up for a drink of water. As she passed Vi's bedroom, she noticed the door was open and Vi was sitting in bed reading a worn copy of Jack Kerouac's *The Town and the City*.

"Can I come in?" Prudence asked, sticking her head in the door.

"Sure." Vi set the book on the nightstand. "Can't sleep again?"

"My mind won't quit." Prudence sat on the bed beside Vi, leaned back against the wall and shut her eyes. The sound of cars still rattling by. Rain ticking against the window. Soon she heard the light flip out and felt Vi's fingers, soft in her hair, like her mother used to do, long ago.

Prudence opened her eyes a minute later when she felt a single tear slip down her cheek. The room was lit only by the streetlights outside, and for a moment the tears gathered and refracted the light, so the room looked as if it had inexplicably filled with sunlight. Vi stayed there beside her, unmoving, out of focus, as the tears pooled and dripped on her chin. Soon she felt Vi grip her hand and squeeze it, as if she'd been standing at the end of some long, dark tunnel with an outstretched hand. Waiting for someone to join her, here in this room that suddenly looked like a field carpeted with colorful flowers, its only window like a painting standing on one of her easels, of a gray and rainy city.

Four

PRUDENCE READ an article that May in *The San Francisco-Examiner* about the all-female staff at The Scotch House. She was standing in the center of the accompanying photo, her hair grown out and styled modernly at Vi's suggestion. A cream cashmere short-sleeve sweater, five buttons snapped across her clavicle. Pleated wool lamp shade skirt. The article noted how the women completely ran the club, from bookings to advertising, liquor orders and accounting. How they had attracted the top jazz performers, booked sell-out shows for months on end. And that the club had been named in *Down Beat* magazine as one of the top five jazz clubs in the country.

Vi hung the clipping on the kitchen wall of their apartment so they'd see it every time they walked by. It became a trophy of what she and Prudence had achieved in a few short months. And although Prudence had grown comfortable in those stylish clothes, wearing her hair longer again, she lamented that she didn't possess Vi's intense beauty. And then there was that damn hearing aid. You couldn't miss it. But then, as Vi had noted, Prudence stood out from all the other girls in the photo: she looked bright eyed, smart, and full of promise.

Often, during long nights at the club, she and Vi would stop on the floor to talk and then suddenly start laughing. A hard, deep laughter that masked their exhaustion. They'd walk back to the apartment in the early morning hours, their eyes burning and their feet aching, deeply in need of continuing those conversations, restoring a bit of the humanity they lost every night serving a bunch of drunks.

What happened that night at Hurley's party never happened

again. Once or twice they had petted and necked, but never with the same intensity. Prudence felt as if she had let Vi down somehow. It all seemed so unnatural, wrong, and it filled her with the worst kind of shame. For wanting it, but not in the same way Vi did, who never pestered her about it. It was as if a private part of her had been opened for that one night, and then quickly covered back up, before anyone — even her own self — could see.

Each morning, they'd sit at the breakfast table, passing the newspaper sections between one another. Vi always joked how Prudence reached for the sports section first, flipping to the back pages for coverage of the local amateur car races. She loved the pictures of the sports cars, the winners sweaty and happy as they gripped their trophies. That day in Golden Gate Park, the cars whipping by, still haunted her. Lately she found herself cruising the local used car lots, chatting up the salesmen, talking about engines and tires, even though they knew she didn't have the money to buy anything.

The article that hung on their wall marked some changes at the club. With the popularity of Cool Jazz at its peak, Hurley had taken a private financial investor that spring and opened the top level to the club, relying on his girls to furnish it in a modern, tasteful style. They adorned the tall windows with heavy drapes, placed small tables on the tiled floor. They saw that the bar was lit by blue neon lights that ran the length of it. That a bigger bandstand with a state of the art public address system was installed. The front section of the club would be reserved for dancing. The large, deep leather booths lining the walls would be held for special guests.

Vi had hired a dozen more girls to work upstairs for the opening night of the second floor. Clifford Brown would be performing upstairs, and a house band would be playing downstairs. They had anticipated opening night for months; they'd overseen the carpenters and the new staff, and made sure everything went together smoothly. As the night of the grand opening arrived, Vi was scrambling to make sure nothing was amiss, not a bottle of bitters or a jar of cocktail onions. By five o'clock of opening night there was a line of ticket holders formed around the block.

Prudence stood clicking the metal counter as they opened the front doors, to keep track of the number of people. She hoped Charles would be in the line, although she hadn't seen him in weeks. Long enough for the glow of their momentary encounters to have dimmed, but not enough to have burned out. As she stood there, she reminded herself that if he liked her at all, he'd show up tonight.

Patrons brushed by her quickly. As she took the cash and tore the tickets, she scanned the line for Charles or the group of men he usually came in with. But, as the room reached its capacity of a thousand guests, there was no sign of Charles. She scolded herself for setting herself up for this. Dozens of viable men had hit on her since she started working here. And she'd let them slip by because of a connection she felt with a man she'd only bumped into a couple of times.

She sighed, standing alone at the ticket booth, sorting through a metal box full of ticket stubs and cash. She rubbed her eyes and sat heavily on a stool. In just over an hour, she had stamped the hard metal clicker so many times that her thumb had blistered. She counted out the money, then tossed it and the clicker in the cashbox and headed for the stairs.

As she looked around the packed club, she smiled. She had wanted to see the top level of the club opened, to make sure it all went as planned. And although she still hadn't become popular with the other girls, she had worked hard, and gained their respect. As she carried the cashbox down to Hurley's office, she stopped in the dark stairwell, listening to the noise coming from above and below her. That heavy, uneasy feeling she'd had back in Oregon had returned. That she still hadn't yet made good on that promise she'd made to herself.

After she'd set the cash box on Hurley's desk, who sat smoking cigars with his clients, she slowly climbed back upstairs and saw Vi at the bar, helping the bar staff fill drink orders. There were bags under Vi's eyes, her hair was out of place, and she looked thin. Hurley hadn't even looked up when Prudence handed over the cashbox — hadn't even looked at her since that night Vi kissed her in his kitchen. She could've walked right out the front door with the money. Vi ran the club and oversaw the staff, but it was Hurley and his investors who pocketed the cash. And they doled it out to Vi so meagerly that she couldn't afford new canvasses on which to paint, nor the time or energy to do so.

As Prudence stood watching Vi, their eyes met. Vi's face expressed everything she'd been thinking. She stopped working, reached down in the bar's well and came up with a bottle of whiskey and two shot glasses, and waved Prudence over to the bar.

"Let's have a little of the sacrament," Vi said, pouring out a shot for them both. "And remember why man invented liquor to begin with. For nights like this."

They tapped glasses and Vi tossed hers back. Prudence had never drank straight liquor before, and she looked down at her glass tentatively, then tilted her head back and poured it down her mouth. She felt the cool burn of it in her throat, the swirling hot sensation as it settled down in her stomach.

The liquor burning in her, she grabbed her drink tray and headed out on the floor. Onstage, the musicians played in that soft West

Coast style. The trend had pervaded even the most die-hard east coast musicians. Prudence longed to hear the hard bop of Clifford Brown's earlier records. In a way, his softer songs had influenced this stark, elegant style. And yet how he must've yearned now for the snap of a snare, the boom of the kick drum, the dizzying stick against the ride cymbal.

That first day she'd walked into The Scotch House, she'd heard untrained California boys who'd sunned on the beach all day, went sailing and skin diving, then came onstage with sand in their hair and played raw music that reflected that lifestyle. Truly *cool*. And as Prudence heard the boisterous applause, it made her wish she had something of her own to offer the world.

She went to wait on the customers in one of the red leather booths lining the wall. All the booths had been reserved weeks in advance for special guests, who were always brought in through a private rear entrance. As she neared, she saw a man in an olive drab Army uniform at the head of the table, his smile so large it was as if he had a few extra teeth. She'd seen him downstairs before and rumors had spread about who he was. Jeffie swore that he was looking for Communists, but Vi quickly set them all straight: he was Hurley's private investor, Colonel Brown.

He looked distinctly out of place in a jazz club, with those gold bars on his shoulders. He was smooth-bald, broad-shouldered, with an impassive face and deep set eyes. He was a strange contrast to the beatniks who lined the bar in their moth eaten sweaters, banging their Anchor beer bottles on the bar along to the music.

The Colonel was flanked by two men in tailored suits who looked equally out of place. They portrayed an image of success, if not menace. Prudence wasn't the only one noticing them. Some of the bohemian types at the bar glared at this group, sullying their idea

Owen Duffy

of what a jazz club should be. And that they had taken a booth that seated eight and fit only three people in it, was a gesture of offhand confidence that impressed Prudence. That here among those working so hard to look like rebels, was a group of real rebels.

"Anything else?" she asked, scanning the table, after taking their drink orders.

"Campari and soda for me," a man said, as he slid into the booth beside the three other men. He took off his sunglasses, brushed back his black hair and looked at her.

Her throat tightened, and his smile slipped away as he recognized her, tucking his sunglasses into his inner suit pocket.

Prudence tried to play it cool, but she knew from her burning cheeks that it was clear to the entire table the effect Charles's sudden appearance had had on her. As she tried to write his order down on their drink ticket, she broke the tip off her pencil.

"*Damn it*," she muttered, tucking the pencil in her pocket. "I'm sorry," she said, looking up, "those drinks will be out in a minute." *That man makes me swoon too*, she thought, twirling around and rushing over to the bar.

"You okay?" Vi asked, popping the top off a bottle of beer. "You're all flushed."

Prudence touched her sweaty forehead and pushed back a few strands of hair. She fanned herself with the drink ticket, breathing through pursed lips. She looked back over at the booth. Charles had an arm draped back over the seat, his head tilted back, rocking gently to the music.

"I hate to splash cold water on you, Pru," Vi said, raising her eyebrows. "But he's married. And he must be about my age, if not older."

Prudence's heart felt like it had been flung into an icy river.

"Are you sure?" she asked, scanning Vi's expression for any hint of jealousy. "I mean, that he's married?"

"Go see for yourself," Vi said, as she finished making the drinks, and placed them on her tray.

Charles smiled when Prudence returned to their table. As she set down their drinks she focused on his voice, soft and lilting, with a trace of an Italian accent. He was telling the others about the local car races, and she lingered a moment after she'd served the drinks, sneaking a look at him. When he spoke her eyes were drawn to his lips, his teeth, his dimpled chin. There was something alluring about him that a camera could never capture: his demure and detached expression, as if he knew something no one else did.

When he lifted his left hand from beneath the table, she saw the wedding band. She hadn't noticed it before. She turned from the table, scolding herself again for hoping, for dreaming, as long as she had.

Prudence had one of the new girls wait on Charles the rest of the night, unable to bear standing that close to him and knowing she could never have him in the way she wanted. But then as she was rounding a corner later in the evening, she bumped into him. She apologized and tried to pass, but he touched her arm and she glanced up at him.

"Excuse me," Charles said, looking directly at her. He didn't move aside and again she felt her face get hot. He was taller and slimmer than she remembered, his shoulders square and set back, his skin a light olive color.

"Do you want another Campari?" she asked.

"No, thank you," he said. "I just wanted to say hello. I saw you in the paper a while back."

"Oh that." She put her hand to her face. "That *picture*."

"It was fantastic." He looked off at the bandstand. "You really stand out."

Prudence felt her smile slip away and she looked at him more closely, to see if he was teasing her.

"And I was thinking," he said. "About that night. Those musicians."

She shook her head. "I'm sorry you had to see that."

"I'm glad I did." He shook his head, leaning towards her. "You have what the Italian call *vigoria*. Strength."

She listened closely, hearing more of his accent, the way he phrased his sentences. As she looked at him, his smile didn't fade. Prudence crossed her arms and examined him. She called her drink order to Charlene, then began sorting through her drink tickets.

"Maybe it's this that makes me different," she said, pointing to the hearing aid.

But when Charles looked at it, it was as if he'd never noticed it before.

"Or maybe this is a pick up line?" She tossed the drink orders on the bar. "Is that it?" She could barely keep the weariness, the ache from her voice. She had foolishly put so much of herself into this man, and it had all been in her crazy head. And he was just like every other guy, always looking for something else on the sly.

"I'm married," he said, staring at her, unblinking. He then fished inside his suit and pulled out a business card. He put the card on her tray when she didn't take it. "Come and see me sometime."

Prudence took his card from the tray. When she looked up, he hadn't moved, and he was still staring at her. And again it was like that exchange they'd shared the first time they met. The room went quiet, her heart beat more softly, and yet — now that she knew he was married — she felt like she was a bubble slowly floating towards a spike.

"Why is it that women always think men only have one thing on their minds?" he asked, lighting a cigarette. He squinted at her through the smoke.

"Because they do," she said, shaking her head.

"And women don't?"

"Well, perhaps they do too." She shrugged. "But it's different."

"How is it different?"

She squinted at him. "Because it just *is*." She turned his card over. *Charles Pieretti, Pieretti Motor Company.*

"Please," he said, before turning. "Come and see me. We will continue this conversation then."

PRUDENCE WALKED back to the apartment that night, after locking up the club with Charlene. *Married,* she muttered. She'd known a lot of men in the club who didn't act it. Women too. And what a strange convention, she thought, listening to her own footfalls along the empty sidewalk. In the windows above, golden lights glowed behind drawn blinds. The neighborhood was asleep, or soon would be. She thought about the girls back at the teachers college, conventional in their desires and aspirations, and then the beatniks who came to the club, how they all railed against that conventionalism. One way or the other, it was controlling them. As she crossed the street and neared the bright yellow apartment door, she knew that it was controlling her too.

And yet she felt peaceful lately, in knowing where she'd be at a certain time each day, knowing which door she'd walk in and out of each night at the club. The way her hand fell to each glass as she lifted and neatly delivered each drink. The way the key slipped into the lock at the apartment, how the rooms smelled of Vi's oil paints and thinner. But lately it had become an automated rhythm, as natural as her own beating heart, and she knew that there was some flaw in her that made her want to break any staid, rhythmic chain in her life.

Prudence pushed open the apartment door and heard familiar laughter coming from upstairs. She climbed the stairs slowly and crept into the den. She saw Vi and Jeffie sitting Indian style on the floor, listening to the hi-fi. They were laughing and nearly spilling their wine on Vi's prized Oriental rug. They didn't notice as she set her things down and came and stood beside them. Candles flickered on the table and the apartment smelled like Vi had cooked something good.

"Oh hi, Pru," Vi said when she finally turned. She knelt forward and lowered the volume on the hi-fi. "Jeffie and I are listening to this comedian, Redd Skelton. He's a scream." She held up the album jacket for her to see. "Get some wine. Come sit with us."

Prudence looked over at Jeffie. There was something rat-like about her, something awful. She was a tag along, a fair-weathered friend, a mooch. Prudence had never seen her outside the club, and as tired as she was now, she wasn't prepared to be cordial.

"Hey Prude," Jeffie snickered, grabbing the album jacket from Vi. She missed it and fell face first on the floor and began laughing. Her hair had recently been dyed raven-black and it made her look pale and sickly as she lay there.

Prudence didn't say anything. Something about the situation hinted at more than just a friendly get together. It looked more like a date that she'd interrupted. She didn't know if Jeffie was a lesbian, but then she'd never seen her with a man, nor heard her talk about one. Prudence dropped her keys on the table and went into her room, shut the door and sat on her bed. She took off her shoes and stockings and unbuttoned her blouse, took a fresh towel from the closet. When she turned, Vi was standing in the doorway.

"You okay?" Vi asked, stumbling a bit, her lipstick smudged.

Prudence rubbed her eyes and then dropped her hands. "It's late and I'm tired. I'm gonna wash up and get some sleep."

"I'll tell her to go then." Vi shut the door behind her and leaned on it. "We got a little tight at the club tonight and we left early." Vi came and sat on the bed next to her. "Are you feeling okay? You seem down lately."

Prudence looked at Vi. "It's nothing."

"Tell me about nothing?" Vi asked, smiling. "What's nothing *like*, Miss Prudence Baylor?"

Prudence shook her head, blew out a thin stream of air. "Well, if you really want to know, I've just been thinking about things. What I'm doing here, where this is all going." She removed her earrings. "Do you ever feel like everyone knows something you don't? Some secret about life or something?"

Vi nodded and leaned closer on the bed.

"And maybe this sounds ungrateful, but I feel like I'm just getting by," Prudence added. "Like nothing's really changed since I got here. Maybe I should've gone to Los Angeles after all."

"Oh please," Vi said, laughing. "When I first met you, you were a girl on the lam with a bad haircut and not a penny to your name. And if you'd gone to Los Angeles that director would just have had his hands up your pants. And then where would you be?"

"Back home, girls my age are married," Prudence said, looking at her. "They're having children. They know who they are, what they want. And I can't figure it out."

"Shit, they don't know what they want either," Vi said, staring up at the ceiling. "They just never bothered to ask. They did what they did because that's what you're supposed to do. Right?"

Prudence pulled her legs up under her, resting her chin on her knees. "I guess."

"When you're my age," Vi said, turning to her, "a family starts sounding pretty good. I've been running around a lot longer than you, remember." Vi sat back on the bed and leaned against the wall. "And you want to know what this great secret is? If you ask me, it's that meaning comes with a pound of flesh. So that's why people sit in front of the television, practically sticking their dinner in their ears. Because that's a lot easier. That's something they can *have*."

"God, you're an old maid," Prudence said, jabbing her softly with her elbow.

"But it's true," Vi said, laughing. "After a while you just start taking the world for what it has to offer."

"I don't know." Prudence shook her head and set her earrings on the nightstand. "I'm always putting down those musicians at the club. Because I'm jealous. I remember being great at something too, back when I was swimming or skiing back in school."

"You were pretty good, huh?"

"The best," Prudence said. "Well, maybe I could've been, but I didn't get to find out. And it's dumb, but back then it was like things made sense. All that mattered was how fast you went down some crummy old hill."

"Then you have to do that again."

"It's dumb," Prudence said, looking at the floor. "And I don't miss the cold."

"So what? Everything's dumb if you think about it. And having a talent is a burden, trust me. You either ignore it or go out and see where it takes you."

A loud knock rumbled the bedroom door and Jeffie's harsh voice sounded through it: "What are you two doing in there? You aren't necking are you?"

Prudence slumped back against the wall and groaned.

"I'll be out in a minute," Vi yelled. She shook her head. "That damn girl. She has no tact."

They heard Jeffie go and change over the record and turn up the volume on the hi-fi. Prudence drew her legs up at her side, tight against her skirt. "Does she know about you? I mean, about your affair and all?"

"Most of the girls at the club do." Vi sighed. "Jeffie's just like me. And you know, for a minute I thought I had a live one on the hook with you." She leaned back in the seat. "Not all of us set limits on who we fall in love with. And if anyone has a problem with that, screw them."

Prudence toyed with a jagged fingernail. "Do they think that you and I ...""

"No," Vi said, glancing at her, letting out a haughty laugh. "You aren't like me. And they all know it too. Even Hurley knows that was all a game we were playing just that night."

Prudence shook her head. "Why does everyone think they know me? Is it because of this damn thing?" She pointed at the hearing aid. "I'm sick of it."

"This isn't about that." Vi's brow furrowed. "You're just not like me, Prudence. It's not something you decide, or can play pretend about, so let's not act like it is."

"I just meant," Prudence said, glaring back at Vi, "that there's things you and everyone don't know about me yet."

"That door swings both ways, sister. But it doesn't mean our problems are the same." Vi stood and walked to the door, where she turned. "And I'm not trying to tell you who you are. But I can damn well tell you what you're *not*."

On her day off later that week, Prudence rode the trolley towards Polk Street, wearing a strapless pair of heels and her favorite new dress: a black short-sleeved number that came just above her knees. The pavement sparkled in the June sun, and an easterly wind brought with it the Pacific's brisk scent. As the city passed by, she worked Vi's words back and forth in her mind, like a finger wiggling a loose tooth. At last she had met someone who knew her even better than she did herself. And yet she knew that, like the tooth, if she tested it too much, the relationship would yield.

As she stepped off the trolley she pulled her hand from her pocket. Her mother always said that you could count your true friends in life on just one hand. Prudence stuck out one finger. She stood there, staring at it and nodding her head. *Try not to screw this up*, she muttered, before stuffing her fist in her coat pocket and crossing the street.

She came to a stop in front of Pieretti Motor Company, a whitewashed building standing amid several warehouses, just blocks from the bay. Dirt lined the broken pavement and morning shadows cast deep into the alleys. The sidewalk was cracked and gated by a rusty iron fence. Prudence walked underneath the humming electric sign hanging in the archway and across the lot. It was filled with brand new European cars that she'd only read about on the sports pages: Ferraris, Maseratis, Alfa Romeos. They were all painted the color of freshly shed blood, their chrome bumpers gleaming like sunlight. A four-bay garage stood adjacent to the main showroom, and as she approached she heard power tools and mechanics shouting in foreign tongues.

One of the mechanics watched as she stood gazing at the cars. A small, wiry man with a crow's wing of hair slicked back on his skull. He came out of the garage like a troll blocking her passage, said his name was Rudy Wulff, that he ran the garage.

When she told him why she was there, his eyes narrowed and his tongue slithered around inside his open mouth, as if dislodging something he'd eaten. He then shut his mouth quickly, turned and led her through a concrete floored showroom where a black convertible Ferrari sat, wire wheels and saddle leather interior. The showroom smelled of grease and tire rubber. But she wanted to run a finger along the car's tanned hides and sculpted fenders. A matched luggage set was stacked behind the front seats, lashed down by thick leather straps and deeply chromed buckles. She envisioned the type of person who'd buy such a car, the places they'd go, the clothes they'd pack inside those suitcases.

"Don't touch it," Rudy said, as if reading her mind. "That's a Ferrari 212 Barchetta. There's only two of them in the world." He rushed her past the reception area, and as he did she saw Charles sitting at a large desk inside an enclosed glass office. She brushed her sweaty palms against her dress and sucked in a quick breath.

"Well, what took you so long?" Charles said when he saw her through his office windows. He stood as she came to the doorway, dressed in a blue suit, the coat tapered neatly to his trim waist. He crushed a freshly lit cigarette in an ashtray and thanked Rudy, who nearly bowed before he walked away.

"I'm glad you came," Charles said to her, in that soft, lovely accent of his. "Please, have a seat."

As she sat in the chipped wooden chair, gripping its armrests, she noticed the stacks of papers on his desk and on boxes on the floor. Racing trophies and framed photographs lined the rear office wall. Charles was smiling in all of them, his racing suit tarnished, his face smeared with grease. Two other photos stood on his desk, of Charles with Colonel Brown, and a larger picture of a beautiful, raven haired woman. Beside them sat a shiny, leather bound copy of the Bible. Prudence stared at it a moment: her father always said you should never trust a man with a Bible on his desk.

"Well," Charles said, sitting and leaning back in his chair. "How are things at the club? Are they treating you any better over there?"

"I suppose so," she said, fidgeting with the cord to her hearing aid. "Mostly I just try and stay out of everyone's way."

Charles nodded and put his elbows on his worn desk, looking at her in the same way he had at the club. She released the cord and again wiped her palms on her dress. He sat there a moment, still staring at her. Here in the light, she studied him better. His face was square, his eyebrows broad and wing like, the bridge of his nose beginning between them. His hair was coal black, parted and combed back neatly.

"Look, I'll get right to it," he said, leaning back again. "I've been thinking about you. My secretary quit a few weeks ago and I haven't been able to find anyone good. And you came to mind that night at the club." He laughed softly, fiddling with the mess on his desk. "I need someone to help out with these. But someone tough too, to sit out front and guard me from the tire kickers."

Prudence had covered her mouth with her fist as he spoke, to hide her smile.

"But I need a pretty woman too, who can use it to her advantage," he added, glancing at the floor. "I have a lot of clients who are slow to pay their bills, so I need someone sharp out there. It's doctors and lawyers mostly. Rich kids too. And then when I'm out at the races, I'll need someone here to watch over the office."

Prudence sat there, her fist still pressed to her lips, trying not to show him how flattered she was. He offered her a cigarette from his pack of Murattis, which she declined. He took one himself, lit it, then described the job: answering phones, keeping up with payroll, being a liaison between the shop, the dealership and their accountant.

"My last secretary was starting a family." He glanced at the floor again. "Are you seeing anyone?" He cleared his throat. "That is, you don't intend to get married anytime soon?"

Prudence crossed her arms, blinked, and shook her head.

He pulled on his cigarette and appraised her through the smoke. "So then, are you interested?"

Prudence looked at him, feeling the heavy, persistent beat of her heart in her temples. "In what?" she asked, playfully.

"The job," he said, narrowing his eyes.

"Well," she said, looking around his office, "I'd have to think about it."

"Working at the club," he said, crushing the cigarette. "Well, it must be fine. You women run the show, and it's impressive. But here you won't be mistreated or have to deal with drunks. Or some musician who passed out in the john with a needle in his arm."

Prudence smiled: he knew life at the club all too well. "It's not that," she said. "I'd have to give notice. I'm very close with the manager. She wouldn't like me leaving just like that."

"People change jobs all the time. That's how you move up." He stood, went to the window and looked out over his lot. He was neither tall nor short, but with a good build. He limped slightly as he walked, something she hadn't noticed in the nightclub. "Relationships are very important, but you can't let them hold you back."

Prudence met his stare when he turned, then looked out into the lobby. The sun appeared from behind a cloud and the windows glowed. The black Ferrari drew her eye again, and she thought

Owen Duffy

of those races at Golden Gate Park in the back of the papers. The pictures of that week's top drivers. God, what she'd give to get behind the wheel of one of those cars.

"Do you like cars?" he asked.

"Of course," Prudence crossed her legs, deciding that she needed to play this ice cold. "Wouldn't I have to, to work here?"

"No," he said, shaking his head. "I like cars too, but what I really love is racing. As you can see." He pointed at the trophies and photographs behind him. Then he patted his knee. "I had an accident a few years ago in Europe that ended my career. But then I met Colonel Brown, who you've seen at the club. He helped me out when I needed him, got me back on my feet."

A silent moment passed and she looked up at him. She appreciated his genuine manner and the way he spoke honestly, as if time was too valuable to be wasted. And yet she glanced at the Bible on his battered desk, the display of old trophies and photos, and wondered what all of that was meant to convey, why he'd told her these things without really knowing her.

"Did you ask me down here because you think I need help?" she suddenly asked, unable to stop a quiver from slipping into her voice. "If it was just a secretary's job you could've just said so at the club and I would've said no."

He looked at her and leaned back against his desk. "You'll be helping me grow this business. Not many people here in America know what a Ferrari is. Anyone who finds their way down here has seen them at these races." He cleared his throat. "I wouldn't have asked you down here if I didn't think you'd be perfect for the job. I know this place might not look too great, but everything in it is state of the art."

"Thank you," she said, rising from her seat. "But I do pretty well at the club. And I know my way around there fairly well."

"I'm sure you do." His phone rang and he looked at his slim, gold Hamilton wristwatch. "Well, whatever you make there in a good week," he said without looking up, "I'll add twenty-five percent."

He then stood and held out his hand. "I'm glad you came, Prudence." He shook her hand and held it a long time, ignoring the ringing phone. "Take some time to think about it."

As he finally picked it up, she stood and walked back through the showroom. Past the glittering Ferrari and out into the street, where she broke into a wide smile. *Twenty-five percent.* She could feel him watching her until she was out of sight. Somehow she just knew he was; that uneasy feeling in each quick step along the sidewalk. As she rounded the corner she took a cigarette from a pack of Pall Malls from her purse. Smoking was still a recent, secret habit for her. Although cigarettes still tasted bitter, she smoked this one down quickly and felt the headiness of the nicotine wash through her. She sat a while on the curb to steady herself. She watched traffic pass, the rich smell of exhaust, the cool of the concrete beneath her.

On her way home she passed by Delaney's department store and stared at the white manikins in the window against a black cloth backdrop, their painted eyes looking out. She wandered inside, through the scent of perfume and racks of bright clothing, the saleswomen cheerful as they helped her pick out some dresses and then showed her to the dressing rooms.

Maybe she wouldn't find what made her happy working for Charles, she thought, but she sure wasn't going to find it working for Hurley. As she slipped on the first dress, a coral colored crinoline fabric, stiff and formless, she stood there in the dark enclosed space. Listening to the other women changing in the room beside her, the sound of rustling fabric and silk slips, the soft grunts and groans.

She stood there looking at herself in the mirror, touching her face, deciding that she liked it, finally. Her focus shifted down to her legs, as some of the dresses were a bit short, which was the style here in the city. She'd never shown off this much of her legs before, not even in college. But without the bruises and cuts they'd always had back then, they didn't look so bad. A bit muscular, but well shaped. She turned from side to side, eying them uncertainly, but decided that they would make due.

It was late-afternoon by the time she returned to the apartment. She'd spent over an hour in that dressing room, for a while consumed only with the task of looking good. She set her shopping bags down on the coffee table and pulled off her shoes and rubbed her feet. She picked up the mail and sorted through it. In the pile was another letter addressed to Vi from a John Knowles. At least the tenth such letter she'd seen since she'd moved in. As she studied the envelope, she felt herself dozing off, replaying her meeting with Charles. She could still feel his hand in hers as she shook it. *I've been thinking about you*, she thought, closing her eyes. As she drifted off, she knew she had the entire day to make her decision, and that all she needed to do now was rest.

Five

ON HER first day working at Pieretti Motor Company, Charles walked her around the building and introduced her to the staff, before sitting her down and outlining her daily tasks. There was an old phone switchboard to operate, with six separate lines connecting to different parts of the building. There were file cabinets in need of re-organizing, stacks of mail to sort daily, lunches to fetch from nearby restaurants. She loved walking down Van Ness Avenue into its dark Italian restaurants, being greeted by their wait-staff, who always threw up their arms and hugged her. They served food she never tasted. Her favorite was a sandwich that they made just for the mechanics: olive, prosciutto and provolone on sourdough bread.

Besides a small staff of salesmen, of which there was only one on the small lot at a given time, there was a garage of six mechanics who serviced European cars from the area. It was a specialty shop, and when the customers came by to have their cars fixed, the staff knew them by name and would invite them to have a cup of coffee and chat. There was even a big RCA Orthophonic player in the showroom, and when they were all working late Charles would stack on Mario Lanza records and turn it up full tilt.

The work was a welcome change from serving drinks in a jazz club. She was off her feet, and it was easy talking to people without having to contend with the noise. And although in school she'd never possessed the patience for sustained reading or rote tasks, this was different. She was handling paperwork dealing with the importation and sales of foreign cars. Charles even gave her an English-Italian dictionary so she could make sense of the many forms she had to translate and re-type onto carbon paper. As she did, she would daydream about visiting the cities where the cars came from: Milan, Modena, and Maranello.

She and Charles were the only people who worked in the offices, and he gave her complete freedom to do whatever she wanted, from tracking down an errant lien holder, to warming up a prospective client before a sale. And when they passed each other in the showroom, or stood talking in his office, she still felt that unspoken current passing beneath them, like water, swirling and rising at their knees.

Her third day working at the dealership, a long Cadillac pulled into the lot while the only salesman was out on a test drive with another customer. Prudence watched a handsome young man step out of the car, joined by two women wearing short dresses, despite the cool weather. They all stumbled around the lot looking at the cars. Prudence recognized him immediately as the actor who played a villainous cowboy in a Western she'd just seen. He came inside and ceremoniously took off his sunglasses, as if waiting to be recognized. His hair was sandy blonde and his eyes bloodshot. The stem of a pipe stuck out of the pocket of his sport shirt.

"Hello, Gorgeous," he said. "Who do I talk to about taking a drive?" He knocked on the lip of her desk and winked. He reeked of liquor. Vodka gimlets, she guessed, by the look of him. The two girls behind him positively bubbled.

"You talk to me," Charles said, appearing in his office doorway just behind her.

"*Fantastic-o*," the actor said, mocking Charles's Italian accent, then turned and motioned for the girls to follow him outside.

"Watch this." Charles looked over at Prudence. "I bet you ten dollars he's going to ask if I will take a trade for his Caddy." He shook his head. "I fucking hate Cadillacs."

Prudence followed after him, walking briskly to keep the girls from banging their handbags against the cars. The lot itself had a long portico roof over it, with four large skylights. There were about two dozen cars on the lot, packed close together. She stood by Charles as the actor assessed each of the cars, each too small or racy for his tastes, his unlit pipe clamped in the corner of his mouth.

"What kind of engine does this one have?" he asked, leaning over a large convertible Alfa Romeo. "Is it a V-8? Does it have power brakes?"

Charles answered politely, but she could tell he didn't like the actor's haircut, his huarache shoes, or his taste in cars. Charles had always called this particular car an Italian Eldorado, because of its size and weight, and because it was built to cater to bloated American tastes. When Charles told the actor the price, the actor removed the pipe from his mouth and shook his head.

"What will you give me in trade for that?" the actor asked, pointing at his long taupe Cadillac. It was a '53 model, but its left front fender was already dented.

Charles winked at Prudence, shoved his hands in his suit pockets, and slowly shook his head. The girls looked at the actor, who dropped his pipe in his shirt pocket. By then it was clear to all of them that the actor was just showing off to the girls. And that Charles wasn't going to suffer his charade any longer.

"I see how it is." The actor put his sunglasses back on. "The joke's on me, huh? C'mon." He waved the girls into his Cadillac, started it and lumbered off down the street.

Charles lit a cigarette and shook out the match. "You think I embarrassed him?"

Prudence crossed her arms, watching the car recede into the

distance. She didn't say anything, just watched the car until it disappeared.

"Well, I don't like to turn away business," he said, walking with her back towards the building, "but these cars are hard to get and I don't sell them to just anyone. And besides, he couldn't have afforded it anyway."

He grabbed the door and held it open for her, his hand absently falling to her arm to guide her in. She stopped and looked at him, an unexpected jolt running up her shoulder and then deep down along her spine. A faint blush came to his cheeks as he removed his hand and then followed her inside. She hurried to her desk and distracted herself by shuffling through some paperwork. She watched over her shoulder as he slipped into his office, where he remained the rest of the afternoon, his door closed, the showroom filled with a charged, uneasy quiet.

BACK AT the apartment, she rarely saw much of Vi, as their hours were so different. Prudence had bought Vi a new easel and canvasses with her first paycheck, to show her the appreciation she felt for all she had done. Of course Vi had been hurt that she was leaving work, and warned her about men like Charles, having overheard things about him at the club. That he ran with a fast crowd, that he would take advantage of her, make her work for that extra twenty-five percent. But then Vi admitted that she was simply jealous that someone was stealing her away, that she'd have no one to talk with at the club. Soon they were back to their usual routine, talking and laughing until the early hours.

One afternoon in July, back at the shop, Charles's wife Maria called and Prudence connected her to his office. A minute later he came out and told Prudence that his horses had broken out of the stables at his ranch down near Palo Alto. He looked at his wristwatch and began pacing. Charles cursed, went back into his office, gathered a few things, then came out and grabbed Prudence from her desk. He unhooked a set of keys from the rack on the wall, then rushed them both outside towards the convertible Ferrari, which now sat on the lot. Deep ebony paint and white leather interior, chrome wire wheels, white sidewall tires. A barchetta, he often called it. *Little boat,* in Italian.

Rudy Wulff came running out from the garage to object to his taking the car, then gave Prudence a dirty look as she climbed in beside Charles. Charles ignored him and started the car and put on his sunglasses as it settled into a steady rumble. He clicked the car into gear, turned north on Fillmore, and then they shot east along the Embarcadero, over rough, broken stretches of pavement, towards the Bayshore Highway. He blasted past other cars, weaving between them so fast that she braced against the door frame to steady herself.

His driving stole her breath. Powerful and wild, as if he had grabbed the car by the scruff of the neck and was dragging it along. As he drove, he handed her his pack of Murattis and she bent beneath the dash to light them as the air rushed overhead. He smoked them casually as he continued to dodge traffic, blasting the horn, the tachometer edging off scale.

As they headed farther south on the highway and traffic cleared, she saw the speedometer indicating a hundred and twenty miles an hour. She leaned back in the hard leather seat, the cold wind tearing through her hair, the entire car humming beneath her. She closed her eyes as a tickle suddenly fluttered through her belly. Like sea waves licking against her insides, hot and cold, hot and cold. Soon she had to bite her lip and cross her legs tightly, to keep them from completely washing over her.

The engine screamed as he balanced the steering wheel with his fingertips, flicking the gearshift back and forth as they slowed and turned from the highway onto two-lane county roads. She was as moved by the scenery as she was with his driving. It had been so long since she'd been out of the city. Here the hillsides were burnt gold, splotched with green bushes, livestock grazing along the fence lines. She shivered as he passed other cars at a hundred miles an hour. The car's power felt urgent, insistent, and its exhaust wailed as they rocketed down into a valley.

The valley was bound by mountains and small hills that undulated into soft peaks. Thickets grew on the tops of them, and small dusty driveways led to handsome houses. Soon Charles turned off the road into one of these driveways. Tall poplar trees grew on each side of it, and as they passed over the edge of a hill, she saw the reaches of his property in a shallow valley, a glittering creek running through it.

Charles swore when he saw the horses grazing on the distant hillside. He sped up the gravel driveway and skidded to a stop. He opened the door and stepped out, stretching his bad leg as he looked up at the house. A large stucco building with a red tile roof and groves of elm trees on each end, casting shadows on the circular drive and the fountain that sat in the middle of it.

His wife Maria stepped out the front door at the sound of the car. Long and slender, a doll-like face, dark eyes, a knee length green dress. Her skin was olive-toned and her black hair was neatly bundled, falling to the small of her back. Prudence watched as Maria came and stood in the center of the driveway, shading her face with her hand, her gold bracelets sliding down her slender wrist. Prudence took her in, the lithe and delicate neck, the sharp brow, her gaze like the point of a knife blade. For a moment she looked like an Egyptian princess rising from her chambers to see what the trouble was.

Prudence sat there, feeling as if she had been shaken awake. She blinked and looked at Maria again, her foolish dream evaporating, replaced by a simple truth: Maria was perfect, everything a man could want. And yet, most of all, she looked expensive.

As Prudence sank down in the car seat, Maria spoke to Charles, her English surprisingly good, her voice soft but clipped. She pointed at the horses, which stood on the burnished hillside, chewing the dry, gold grass. She wondered why Maria hadn't gone and fetched them herself. But then she studied her polished leather heels, the earrings and necklace, and she felt her own head begin to nod slowly.

The salesmen at the shop often spent the slow hours gossiping beside her desk. She'd overheard their stories about Maria, how they didn't understand why Charles was married to a bitch of a woman like her. Prudence always sat there, nodding her head, just as she did now. She looked at the house and the land, Maria standing on it proudly, as if she'd made it all herself from earth and stone. Prudence finally understood the reason for the salesmen's contempt: it took a certain kind of man to possess a woman as beautiful as Maria. Charles was that kind of man, and they were not.

Prudence stayed in the car, protected from the sun by the house's shadows. She looked off at the rolling hills and the late afternoon light creeping across them, wondering if Maria even knew who she was. Maria's gaze had passed over her several times, but she had yet to acknowledge her. It felt as if she was just one of Charles's servants, come to help him with a task that was beneath her.

Suddenly, a large doe-eyed child of six or seven stumbled from the house and clung to Charles's waist. He was dressed in a collared shirt and pressed pants, holding a small rag doll by its head. The boy's eyes were dull and half-closed, and didn't seem to focus on anything. Charles groaned as he picked the boy up and kissed him.

Owen Duffy

The boy's head just lolled to the side, working the doll's arm in his mouth.

Maria spun around and spoke in Italian to a squat, grey haired woman in a heavy black skirt, stockings and sweater, who had appeared in the open doorway. Charles set the child on the ground and he began to jump up and down. Maria yelled at him and pointed towards the doorway, where the woman remained, her eyes trained on the floor, holding out a wrinkled hand. When the boy didn't respond, Maria smacked his backside and a slowly building wail issued from his mouth.

Maria glanced over at Prudence, then quickly away. The proud look she'd had before was gone, replaced by a beaten, shamed expression. Maria led the still wailing boy towards the doorway, her voice softening. The old woman still stood there holding out her hand, as if she was afraid to pass over the threshold. When Maria had the child in the house, she knelt and kissed his cheek and brushed back his hair. The old woman, eyes still trained on the floor, shut the large wooden door closed behind them.

Charles stood there a moment, staring at the front door. He then turned and began walking down the lane towards the barn, his limp more pronounced than it had ever been before. Prudence opened the car door, stepped out and watched him loping down the hill with his hair all out of place. She followed after him, keeping her distance, then came to a stop as he paused to light a cigarette.

"Do you know anything about horses?" he asked, without turning to face her. He pulled on the cigarette and brushed back his hair.

She shook her head, but he kept looking straight ahead, as if he already knew the answer to his question.

"Well, just don't stand behind them, whatever you do," he said. "They are skittish right now, being out of the barn." He continued walking and she followed, until he stopped again, just a few dozen paces from the barn door.

"I want you to stand right here. And don't go anywhere." He turned and looked at her. "I will go up and send the horses down this way. All you have to do is block them from going anywhere else but into the barn. Just hold up your arms and they'll know what to do. Then shut the gate after each one goes in."

She nodded, her pulse quickening at the thought of a horse running straight at her.

"That's the thing about horses. They want to be in the barn." He looked at her again, then shook his head. "They just don't know it."

Prudence stood there as he went and climbed the nearest hill, without even removing his suit coat. It was a gradual slope, but his leather soled shoes didn't slip as he worked his way towards the grazing horses. As she watched, her hand shading her eyes from the sun, she considered how effortlessly he did everything: the way he switched between languages, drove a car. How quickly he had returned a sense of purpose to the day, as easily as his wife had shut the door on him.

He walked through an open gate in the fence and then even farther up the hill. Beyond the wooden fence, the three unbridled horses stood grazing on the slope of the hill. Large and muscular, their dark coats shining in the sunlight. They looked up as Charles approached from behind, just as he had told her not to do. They shook their tails and continued pulling up swaths of grass. Prudence watched as Charles began walking slower, his hands held up and his mouth moving, trying to soothe them.

He was only feet from one horse's rump when another of the horses spooked. The others followed, moving farther up the hill, where they continued grazing. Charles stopped and crouched, as if anticipating what was coming next. Suddenly the black horse began trotting in small circles. As if on his cue, it split off from the others and took a few steps down the slope and began prancing. Charles came abreast of it, lifting his hands to steady it. The horse paused, then took a few steps down the slope even closer to him. But as Charles advanced again, the black horse trotted down the hill towards her.

Prudence felt its footfalls in the earth, hardy and heavy. She kicked off her shoes and held up her arms as the horse approached. It lowered its head and began to gallop, flinging clods of dirt out behind it. As it neared she made out the sheen of its coat, its mane ruffling in the breeze, the sound of its footfalls growing louder. For a moment time seemed to slow as the horse grew larger and larger. Each pump of its legs sending ripples through the muscles in its chest. Its head bobbing lower, its strides increasing as it neared.

She felt her body tense, her arms still lifted high, unmoving, just like Charles said. She feared the horse didn't see her and wouldn't stop before it ran her down. But when the horse was no more than twenty feet away it swiftly cut left and trotted into the barn. She stood there a moment, stunned, then she ran and slammed the gate closed behind it.

Charles whistled from the top of the hill and raised his fist in the air and shook it victoriously. But when she looked over again, she saw the other two horses had spooked and were coming down the hill towards her, galloping in a nervous, jittery way. Prudence opened the gate again and the black horse came back and nudged it open further, throwing her off balance. She fell on the hard dirt and when she looked up, Charles was limping down the hill, waving his hands and shouting, although she couldn't make out the words.

Prudence sat on the dry grass, watching through the gate, the two horses rounding the side of the barn, bouncing off one another, like race horses fighting for the lead. They looked as if they were about to cut right and circle back onto the hill, and so she pulled herself up and waved her arms. But when the horses saw her they cut left instead of turning, and began heading straight at where she stood.

She watched them both coming, goading each other, galloping even faster. She gripped the gate with one hand and stuck the fingers of her other hand into her mouth and let out a sharp, high whistle. A whistle that shocked even her in its volume and pitch, tripling that which Charles had issued moments before. The horses planted their feet and came to an abrupt stop there in front of the barn gate, as the sound of her whistle echoed off the distant hills.

Charles rounded the side of the barn then, hobbling a bit, and came up beside the horses and yelled at them. They lifted their feet, whinnied, then went inside the barn with their heads down. Prudence ran and shut the gate behind them, surprised how willing they were in the end, after putting on such a show.

When she turned, she found her arms were covered in a cold sweat, the adrenaline still pumping hard through her. She leaned on the gate, catching her breath a moment before dusting herself off and straightening her hair. After she had collected her shoes, she saw Charles was just standing there in the shade of the barn, his face glistening, his eyes focused on her.

"What?" she asked, looking back at him.

He came forward and pulled out a white silk handkerchief. "You're bleeding."

Prudence didn't feel anything, and couldn't imagine where she'd been injured.

"No," she said, as he came forward with the handkerchief. "I don't want to ruin that for a little blood."

But he came and took her arm and gently pressed the handkerchief to her forehead. She winced, feeling how tender it was along her hairline. He pulled the handkerchief back and showed her the blood, the size of a small leaf.

"I can do that," she said, averting his eyes, her hand touching his as she tried to take the handkerchief from him. As she did, she felt a warmth spread through her, as if she wasn't standing in the shade, but still basking in the warm sunlight. She held his hand, looking at him.

He looked back at her a moment, then turned and went into the barn. Prudence sat in the shade with the handkerchief pressed to her forehead, listening as Charles finished settling the horses and putting them in their stables. She felt a burning sensation in her lower body, a blunt outward pressure inside. She had felt it in the car. She had felt it the first night she met him. She'd been feeling it for so long that she wanted to stand, swing open the gate and find out if he felt it too, there on the dirt floor of the barn.

She breathed deeply, slowly, willing the thought away. And yet she knew that there was something here that was also four-footed. Something that, having met Maria, made no sense. And yet which felt more natural and true than anything she'd felt before.

"Come," Charles said, walking out of the barn a few minutes later, wiping his face with his hand. "Let's go and have a drink. The day is lost." He didn't look at her, as if equally unsettled by what had happened a moment before. His hair was out of place, one of his shoes untied, as he walked just ahead of her along the dirt road leading down to a tool shed. There, he undid the latch, went inside and came out with two bottles.

"You pick," he said, holding up both the labels up for her to see. A bottle of scotch and a Canadian whiskey. The dark fluid gathered the warm sunlight as he lifted the bottles, swirling what remained in them. She picked the whiskey and he set the scotch back on the shelf, and grabbed two dusty looking tumblers.

"Maria doesn't like me having a drink in the house," he said, closing the shed door. "So I have to come down here with the livestock."

Together they walked back towards the barn and sat in some old cane chairs. The chairs creaked as they leaned back in them, the air smelling sweetly of hay, sawdust, and the cool earthen scent of the barn.

He poured them each a snort of whiskey in the fading sunlight that shone through the open barn doors. Prudence took a sip of hers, and as she did, she looked through the bottom of the glass and up to the house, across a field, and into a window. She lowered the glass when she saw Maria standing in the window looking down at her. Not more than fifty yards away. Prudence felt herself shrivel a moment before the bedroom curtains snapped closed.

Prudence swirled the whiskey in her mouth before swallowing it. She replayed the drive there, the scene up at the house, the horses. Soon her drink was gone and he had poured them each another, and was telling her about his racing career, working for the Scuderia Ferrari racing team in the early days. And then about his accident, how he'd met Maria in Italy, in the town where he recuperated after the crash. As he told her this, something in Prudence lifted, realizing that he'd chosen Maria in his weakest moment.

She was quiet a minute after he finished his stories, the wind rustling through the trees, and it seemed that it was a large world, and she was a very small thing. She would be gone in fifty years and may not have experienced half of what he had. She would be a tick in the time-line of the universe. And yet she knew that a person's life just happened, irrespective of what they wanted.

"Was it hard to give up racing?" Prudence asked suddenly. It was a question she'd been meaning to ask him for a while, as he'd never addressed it.

"Hardest thing I ever had to do," he said. "I was good. It's what I was meant to do. But after the accident, I just didn't have it any more. The nerve." He looked at her, his voice lowering. "I just wish I had a couple more years of racing. It was like jumping into a raging river every day. And this," he said, looking out over his property, "is like sitting beside a very still pond."

She watched the fading sunshine, the air quickly cooling as dusk neared. She looked up at the house again, the drawn bedroom curtains, the little black Ferrari sitting there by the fountain. She wondered why Charles had hired her, why he'd brought her with him today when he could've brought one of his mechanics.

"Do you ever race in those races I see in the paper?" she asked, after a long silence. "Over in Golden Gate Park and down in Palm Springs? It seems like you could take one of your cars there and clean up."

He poured himself another drink, quickly tossed it back, then poured himself another. "No," he said, looking at her. "I go to them to talk with the other drivers before a race, try and sell them a car. But sometimes I stick around in the grandstand with the other fans. Being down with the drivers and cars only reminds me how much I miss it."

He looked away from her and began humming a tune she recognized, "A Hundred Years from Today." She knew the song's lyrics all too well: it was one of her mother's favorites. She recalled her mother singing the song, which dealt with all our earthly concerns: love, wealth and happiness. And how we should pursue the simple things in life, because in a hundred years, no one would know how freely we loved or how much money we had.

Hearing the song reminded Prudence of that past October, when she'd made a surprise visit home after her mother had won a mail-in songwriting contest. She'd ridden the bus and stopped at Black's General Store and bought the only flowers they had, a bouquet of artificial roses. She'd seen her mother working on the song all spring, and hoped it might be the one thing that could lift her from her doldrums. Each morning she would sit at the piano in the den, etching little dots on paper she'd carefully lined with musical staffs. The sun spilling in through the windows, the curtains blowing. Her long chestnut hair in a bun, her eyes clear and focused. Leaning close to the piano, plunking a note and humming over it, shaking her head and pulling a pencil from between her red lips and rubbing away a note, scribbling a new one in its place.

Sitting in her chair at night while Prudence and her father listened to the radio, staring at the ceiling and mouthing words, finding some coming through the speaker that twisted and twined in a pleasant way. Prudence had only heard the song in this fashion, pieced together, never knowing what would be kept or what would be rubbed away. A minor chorded, dissonant bridge. A bouncing, tumbling verse or a stout, joyous chorus.

And she remembered late that summer, her mother holding the envelope and letter, inviting her up to Portland to accept her prize and to perform the song. While her father stood there, shaking his head, her mother threw her arms around Prudence and pulled her to her breast and cried. It felt as if, at last, her mother had flung open the windows in her own self, and the sun and wind were pouring in.

Prudence walked up outside the house the day of the ceremony, to ride with them up to Portland. As she neared the house she saw two men lifting the piano down their front steps. An upright Baldwin that had stood in their home longer than she'd been alive. And as she bound up the steps and into the den, there was her mother on the floor on her hands and knees, scrubbing the dusty rectangle where the piano had been. Prudence stood clutching the rubber flowers as her mother looked up at her. Her hair a dull, twisted rope. Her face hollow, her eyes like two blown out candles.

Just then her father pulled up in his work truck, got out and opened the back doors. The same two movers went and lifted a heavy box from the back of his truck and carried it up the front steps. Her mother stood and stepped back, pressing against a chair to make room for the giant box, *ADMIRAL* marked on its side. One of the movers pulled out a knife and with three swift cuts, the front of the box fell away to reveal a large console television, with a record player to its side, a radio and hi-fi. All of it encased in a cabinet that rivaled the largest wooden furniture in the house.

Her father peeled off his coat while the workers removed the rest of the cardboard. He tipped them and sent them on their way, shut the door and turned to the unit. He plugged it in and knelt before it, flipping a knob on the television. It began to glow, filling the dim room. The hi-fi's faceplate lit up, a warm orange light, and soon the sound of a commercial boomed through the speakers: The Arthur Murray Party. *Brought to you by 5-Day Deodorant Pads,* the announcer said. *Use 5-Day Deodorant Pads. They're 5 times more effective!*

Prudence looked as her mother turned, toting her dusty rag, and walked down the hall and into the kitchen, as her father adjusted the dials on the television, the screen filling with spinning dancers, the shriek of violins, his face breaking into a broad, wide smile.

CHARLES was still humming the song a half hour later, as they walked up the driveway towards the car, holding the nearly empty bottle at his side. She figured that he'd had six drinks, and as he walked ahead she stopped and looked at the high wispy clouds. It somehow didn't seem unreasonable that she'd be here, on a ranch in California, when only a year before she was studying to be a teacher.

When she looked up, Charles was well ahead of her on the driveway. He was limping but had settled into a kind of stroll under the effects of the alcohol. She watched his tall figure and the fading sun in his tousled black hair. When he reached the Ferrari he leaned unsteadily against it and waited for her, twirling the car keys around his finger.

"I should drive back," Prudence said, and she came and stood in front of him. "I'm too young to die."

Charles set the whiskey bottle in the gravel. "I don't think that's a good idea. I can walk the tightrope very well, thank you."

"No," she said, shaking her head. "As your employee, I insist I get you back safely."

"You know how to drive a car that doesn't have a slushbox?"

Prudence flashed him a playful glance. She had only been half-kidding until he said that. She grabbed the keys from him. "Just get in the car, please."

"I'll humor you," he said, opening the door and falling in the passenger seat, "just until I feel a bit steadier."

The sun sat low on the horizon, a brilliant mixture of orange and red. Prudence felt gooseflesh rising on her arms as she slipped the key in the ignition, eying the chrome rimmed gauges. She started the car and let it idle while she removed her heels and set them in her lap. Charles instructed her about the stick shift pattern, but she ignored him and clicked it into first gear, let out the clutch and pulled up the driveway.

She paused when she reached the road and adjusted the rear-view mirror. The bucket seat gripped her, the soft leather against her bare thighs as she depressed the clutch and revved the engine. The large wood wheel, with the prancing horse emblem in the hub, felt pre-worn in her hands. The gauges displayed long, elegant needles. The tachometer rose in notches as she tapped the accelerator. The exhaust gurgled and lowered to a hollow rumble.

Prudence turned back the way they came, down the long sloping road. She pressed the accelerator, felt the engine surge, the cool evening wind in her face and hair. The car felt so light and nimble, its steering tight and responsive. She was eager to unspool the engine's power. But she drove conservatively for the first few miles until Charles was done talking about the virtues of this particular car: engine displacement, chassis construction and its suspension.

"There are only two cars like this model," he yelled over the noise, resting his arm on the door jamb. "Henry Ford has one, and I have the other."

The car felt as if it could do anything. It had looked so chic in the shabby showroom, like an expensive piece of jewelry. The small glass windscreen, gleaming leather interior. And now it responded to her every input, and as she finally depressed the accelerator to the firewall, she sank back deep into her seat.

"Whoa!" she yelled out, releasing the throttle and letting the car coast.

"It's something, isn't it?" Charles took a cigarette out of his pack. He waved his hand, his droopy eyelids opening a bit more. "Go ahead, let it out."

Her mother's Dodge was so sluggish, it had always felt like she'd stepped in a basket of overripe tomatoes when she pressed the accelerator. But the Ferrari felt stiff and tight, gushing power and control. The engine screamed up to redline as she let her foot sink deeper and deeper as she hunched behind the wheel.

Her thoughts began to wander, and she went someplace in her mind she hadn't been in a long time. She used to lie in her bed as a child and will herself to fall asleep against the frightening thoughts closing in on her. And like then, she made her world seem simple. For a moment, it was just a car, a road and herself. She was terrified of the speed, but ever since she was that little girl, she had always confronted her fears. As overcoming them gave her an exhilarating sensation, as if she was holding a strange jewel that sparkled with its own kind of light.

As the car rocketed faster, her heart began to pump steadily. After a few minutes she began to feel a lightness, as if she was floating. As she slipped into that graceful state, she found herself driving over ninety miles an hour down every slope and bend. The sun had set and a dusty moon glow had fallen on the countryside. The air stung her eyes and she crouched even lower behind the windscreen, pushing even harder.

She looked over and saw Charles gripping the dashboard. He yelled for her to slow down, glancing at the speedometer as she approached a tight turn. Prudence had casually done the same as he rounded certain turns on the way to his ranch, and now she shot towards this bend at an even higher speed than he had. She wasn't being reckless: by now she knew what she and the car could handle. She took up both lanes of the empty road as she cut through the corner neatly, braking smoothly in and accelerating out.

Those Oregon logging roads came back to her, the rattle of that old car beneath her. The boys she'd often driven out there with had been much the same as Charles: frightened, but impressed by her driving. And when she glanced at Charles again he was looking back at her in a different way. Her hair had grown long since she'd come to California, and she felt the wind unfurl it to its full length over the seat. It fluttered over her ears and her wide-open eyes.

"What are you looking at?" she yelled over at him.

His expression softened, and he smiled and shook his head.

A half hour later Prudence was still keeping up her pace. The moon hung full above the glittering roadway and she turned off the headlamps and drove by moonlight. It broke over the hills and the road itself looked like some ghostly mirage, but she could still make out the white stripe down its center. Suddenly Charles pointed at a pair of headlights cresting a hill. Prudence didn't lift her foot and passed the oncoming car at sixty miles an hour. She watched its taillights flicker in her rear-view mirror, the car shuddering to a halt at the side of the road.

"Holy Christ!" Charles turned around in his seat. "I bet he needs to change his underwear," he yelled, then laughed.

She ripped along the highway as they headed north, weaving through traffic until they came to the city. When they reached the shop, she pulled up to the front gate, cold and windblown. Charles climbed from the car and took his keys from his pocket. It had only been forty-five minutes since they left his ranch and he was still stumbling a bit as he fumbled with the lock. The old electroliers lighting the street cast their green glow on the car's hood as he waved her in through the gate. She pulled in and backed the Ferrari between the other cars and when she got out and gathered her things, a light blinked on in the office and she saw Charles was already inside, his shadow moving along a wall.

Prudence felt that same internal pressure, moving lower and lower, like a weight was dangling beneath her. A crude sort of ballast. She stopped at the showroom doorway. She knew she could turn around right here, walk right home, but she walked across the showroom in her bare feet and hung the Ferrari's keys back on the wall.

He'd uncorked a bottle of Strega and was sipping it from a paper cup when she arrived in his office doorway. He sat on his desk, removed his jacket and tossed it in his chair. Prudence stood with her shoes in her hand, dangling by their straps. He loosened his tie and she saw, despite the cool night air, his forehead glistening with perspiration. She poured a cup of water from the water cooler and turned to him. His office smelled of leather, wax polish and fresh tire rubber. The clock ticked smoothly and a car whistled by in the street; the office softly inviting after all that wind and engine noise in her ears.

"Where did you learn to drive like that?" he asked.

"Back home." Prudence smiled. "Cars were about the only way to pass the time."

"That is the same way it was in Italy. But I never saw a girl do that." His eyes narrowed, as if focusing on some detail in her that he hadn't noticed before. He stood and looked at the photographs in his office a moment before he picked one off the wall, of him as a young man with an older woman. His eyes seemed to soften, his mind retreating to the past. "My mother used to say that she'd love me even if I became a thief," he said. "She loved me whether I won or lost, when I was poor and when I had money."

Charles set the picture down, rubbing the frame with his fingers. "But Maria. She's not like that." He glanced at her and shook his head, laughing, as if shocked by his confession. "This business Prudence, I'm afraid it has turned me into a windbag."

Prudence took his cup of Strega from the desk and fell into the chair across from him. She looked at him. There was something about the drive home that had forged a connection. As if her driving was a sort of confession, prompting him to make his own.

"What happened to your mother?" she asked, taking a sip of his drink.

Charles sighed, rubbing his cheek. "She died not long after my brother Luca did. He was killed in Sicily during the war. I was too young to go myself. We were her only children. My father, well, no one knows where he is." He sat on the edge of the desk, letting out another longer breath, as if he was ready to confess things he'd never told anyone. "And after the war, the plant I was working in began making engine castings. One day I turn around and it is Enzo Ferrari. He says he wants me to work on his race crew." Charles managed a smile. "And then, very soon, I'm behind the wheel, racing against the greats."

"Maria, well, she was my nurse. In the hospital after the crash. The papers were all saying my career was over." He crossed his arms and looked down at his shoes. "I was in pretty bad shape, but she fixed me up. She was married to a farmer there. He beat her with anything he could find."

"I was still just learning to walk again when I got out of the hospital, so I stayed in town. Maria came and looked after me every night. And then one day she came to me, telling me she was going to have a child. That it was mine.

"We wanted out of Italy. No one wanted much to do with me, and the politics after the war were terrible. We got her a divorce in Livorno, and lived there until Charlie was born. Then we came to America so I could race. Maria, well, she wanted something else. I guess she believed what the papers wrote about me back home. And after a while, I suppose I did too."

Prudence watched him, nearly wincing every time she heard

Maria's name. But she nodded, leaning closer.

"So here I was, married, a child, no job. I improved my English, lost my accent." He added, laughing, "Well, most of it. And with the money I made selling off my race cars, bought some Ferraris through my connections back home. I sold those here, made more money, and bought more." He held out his hands, palms turned upwards. "And here I am."

He picked up the bottle of Strega and took a swig straight from it. "And now, everyday, I see Charlie. Starting to look more and more like Maria's old husband." He shook his head and looked at her, steadying his gaze. "I should've gotten out of the hospital and gone right back to racing."

Prudence stood slowly from the chair. She picked up the cup of water that she poured for him earlier. "My mother died too, not very long ago," she said, holding out the trembling cup.

"She did?" he asked, staring at her.

Prudence nodded. "So please. Please don't tell me that no one's going to love me like that again. Because I don't think I could stand it."

As she held out the cup he took her hand and studied it. That same warm sensation ran the length of her arm, but it went even deeper into her flesh, down to the bone. Her lips parted to speak, but Charles set the water on the desk and pulled her towards him. She felt loose and light as he did, her body cupping neatly into his. It was so simple a gesture that it felt as if they'd done this a thousand times. He closed his eyes and she pressed against him, his breath warm against her cheek.

"I need to go," she said, without turning loose of him.

"Yes," he said, pulling her closer.

She felt her body sinking even deeper into his and she closed her eyes, her head tilting back. She felt complete darkness then, like she was moving through an unlit room, searching to find the light. As his lips touched hers, impossibly soft and warm, his hand fell to her waist and she felt a bright flash pass through her body, so strong that her eyes opened and she pulled back. She stood there, blinking at him, breathing hard.

He was staring back at her with the same astonished expression. "I'm sorry," he said, shaking his head. "I never meant for this to happen."

"It's okay," she said, still wide-eyed and staring at him. "You're a little tight, that's all."

"That's not what I mean," he said, looking at her.

"I should go," Prudence said, biting her lip. "Will you be all right?"

"I keep a damn cot in the utility closet." He laughed, still looking at her. "I feel more at home sleeping here than I do in my own bed." He reached into his pocket for his car keys. "I'll drive you home."

"No, I'll be fine." She looked at him a long while, then stepped forward and kissed his cheek. "Goodnight," she whispered, and then turned and walked out of the office, out of the building, into the cold street. A hard drizzle bit at her face and her bare legs. She walked as quickly as she could into the bluster, and yet it felt as if she was strolling along some warm Roman promenade. That everything from now on would feel as easy as that kiss. She knew it was a fleeting emotion, sure to pass, but she stopped at a street lamp, gazing up at the spitting rain in the halo of light it cast down upon her. She smiled and closed her eyes, for a moment feeling as natural and pure as a budding tree, being soaked by a warm spring rain.

Six

W<small>HEN</small> P<small>RUDENCE</small> arrived at work the following morning, Rudy Wulff came storming in from the garage, waving a metal object. The showroom glowed with sunlight, the shapes of the windows printed on the farthest walls. As Rudy brushed past her desk, he looked smaller and more tightly bound than usual. Although his hands were greasy, his coveralls were clean except for the cigarette burns littering the front placket. His hands shook as he muttered under his breath, the cords of his neck straining as he went into Charles's office and dropped the metal part on his desk. Rudy stood there and picked the cigarette from between his lips, letting the ash crumble to the floor.

"Why did you let her drive the car? Now see what she's done?" Rudy shook his head and pointed at the part. "This is ruined. I won't be able to find another one like it."

Rudy turned towards Prudence as she came and stood in the center of Charles's office, the sunlight burning against her cheek. She shot a look at Charles and then the broken part; a bent lever of some sort, a bolt sheared from its threads. Charles looked as if Rudy had just flung a dead rat on his desk.

"You have no business driving a car like that," Rudy said to her, his thin-lipped mouth looked as if it had been cut out by a punch press. "This kind of damage only happens with inexperienced drivers. Charles never would've done this."

Charles rubbed his temples and then his eyes. She remembered all he'd drank the night before. But when he opened his eyes he appeared bemused, as if Rudy were a petulant child and he was used

Owen Duffy

to this sort of behavior. He waved his hand in the air. "The best drivers don't respect their cars, you know that. That's why Enzo Ferrari never made it as a driver. He respected the cars too much."

"She is *not* Enzo Ferrari. And this is carelessness." Rudy waved the part in his face. "This sort of thing will ruin your business. I'll be on the phone all day trying to find another and then who knows how much it will cost."

"Let it alone, Rudy. It's just a car. We will get another part, or we will make one." Charles shook his head at Rudy, a man who may have understood his business more than he, particularly when it came to the delicate nature of automobiles.

"How long will it take before we can have the car back out for sale?" Charles asked, leaning back in his chair.

"A long time." Rudy lifted the greasy part off the desk. "It might be a month!" He glared at Prudence, then rushed out of the office to the garage and slammed the door. The noises in the garage ceased as Rudy yelled at someone, and then after a moment the tools continued their chattering.

"He's intense, but he's a great mechanic." Charles wiped the grease off his desk with his handkerchief. "The best. And he's right. I shouldn't have taken that car. It was a mistake." He glanced at her, standing there with her legs crossed at her ankles.

Mistake. Prudence puckered, brushed a strand of hair out of her eyes. He averted her eyes, folding the greasy handkerchief, before he sighed and threw it in the trash.

"He doesn't like me much, does he?" she asked, after a long silence. A meek tone had crept into her voice and she cursed herself for appearing fragile in front of him. For seeming disappointed that the bond they shared the night before was gone.

Charles came from behind his desk and walked past her. For a moment she thought he'd said all there was to say about the previous evening, and something fell inside her until it hit bottom. She wanted to turn and tell him that she wasn't promiscuous. That before she came to San Francisco, she'd known boys, but they'd been just that: boys. She wasn't an ass-aching Puritan or anything, but neither was she one to get carried away like she had last night, and certainly not with a married man.

"Let's talk," he said, as he closed his office door. She watched him gaze out at the lot of sparkling cars, his hands clasped behind his back.

"I've been thinking about last night," he said.

"Oh," Prudence said, sucking in a breath.

"I was thinking," he said, turning, "and this may sound ridiculous, but you asked about it." He looked at her and shook his head.

"What?"

"Forget it. It was just an idea I had."

"What?" she blurted. "Spit it out."

He sat on the edge of his desk and looked up at her. "Okay, well. Those races you asked about. They're open to the public, you know. All you need is a car to race with." He fidgeted with the brass lighter on his desk. "I mean as an advertisement. For me. You never see women out there. You could do a race. Or two. In one of my cars."

Prudence stared at him, her mind swirling and her stomach feeling washy, as if the room had been tilted on its side. She put her hand on the wall to steady herself. This was the moment she'd been secretly dreaming about since those races at Golden Gate Park. She thought it would take a year before she could even broach the subject with him. But now, after last night, the timing of it just felt … *wrong*.

"So?" he asked, squinting at her.

"Sorry, I thought you were going to say something else," she said, shaking her head.

He cleared his throat. "Well?"

She recalled the drive the previous evening, the enticing trance she entered. She decided to keep playing it cool. "I guess I've thought about it before, but I don't know." She looked at him sitting there on his desk, just as he had last night, his arms wrapped around her.

"Of course I'd supply the car and pay you, and let you keep your winnings." Charles crossed his arms. "These are all amateur events and I could get you a license with a quick phone call. It would be great publicity for the shop if we got you out there to cruise a couple laps."

Prudence stood there, again hiding a smile behind her closed fist.

"I wouldn't have asked if I didn't think you were up to it. Last night was just kidding around. You're better than most of the drivers out there." He lit a cigarette. "So how about it? There's a race this weekend in Monterey. I'll make Rudy paint your name on the car door to pay you back for that little scene in here."

"God, is that what he was so upset about?" Prudence asked, leaning forward. "Does he know you're asking me to do this? You should be asking him to drive for you."

"This isn't about who is the best driver. It's about publicity," he said, grinning. "There was a French woman I knew back in Europe who raced a Delahaye. She wasn't much good but she got so much press that she became a well-known actress. Just think about that for a second."

Prudence sat down in a chair, taking a deep breath. She looked at the cars in the showroom and then out on the lot.

She turned back to Charles. "I'll do it under one condition. You have to let me race. I don't want to go out there and parade around in the back of the pack. I just can't do that."

"No, I don't know about that now." He shook his head. "Those boys are really rough out there. You could get hurt. Even killed. I'd want you to just do a couple of laps in a Ferrari with the business name painted on it."

"Look, if you think I'm any good, then you'll let me race. Really race." She tapped out one of his cigarettes and lit it. "*That* would be good for business."

He sighed. "I don't think so, Prudence. I have to think about the car too. You've never seen twenty men breaking their necks to see who can get off the starting line first."

"Oh yes I have," she said, standing up and looking at him, her face feeling hot. She squashed the cigarette in the ashtray, thinking of all the swimming blocks she'd stood on, waiting for the whistle. "So if you let me race, I'll do it. If not, thank you very much, but I'd just as soon get back to work."

She spun on her heel and left him sitting there in the office. *Mistake*, she thought, letting out a laugh. If that kiss was a mistake to him, she'd be sure not to make it again. She went and sat at her desk and slapped papers into a pile. As she did, she felt Charles's eyes on her back as he picked up the phone, and a broad smile formed on her lips.

CHARLES PULLED up to her apartment early that following Saturday morning in a two-tone Chevy station wagon, towing a flatbed trailer with a small red coupe lashed to it. Prudence and Vi ran to their apartment window at the sound of his horn. The sun beaming in, they gazed down at him standing beside the double-parked wagon, wearing a pair of gabardine slacks, white sport shirt and Panama hat. The street was busy with weekend foot and car traffic but he seemed indifferent to the people who slowed to gaze at the race car.

As Prudence opened the window, a rush of fresh air blowing in, it all felt like a dream. He smiled and waved his hand at her. "Come down here." He climbed on the trailer with his good leg and leaned against the race car's fender. Traffic on their corner had all but stopped, and a crowd had formed around him. She stared at Charles leaning there, his hands on his hips, unlike anyone she'd ever known, seemingly able to pursue and achieve anything he wanted.

"Good Lord, Pru," Vi said, in an exasperated tone. "What the hell have you gotten yourself into now?"

"I don't know." Prudence stared back at her. "Pinch me."

Vi pinched her arm and laughed. She then left the open window and headed quickly for the door, knocking the chain loose, the sound of her feet fast on the steps.

"C'mon!" he yelled, smiling back up at Prudence. "Come have a look."

Prudence slipped on some blue jeans and grabbed her purse. Downstairs, Vi was assessing the race car with a dour expression, dressed only in her kimono, despite the small crowd. The dark red car was dented and chipped. Covered in grease stains and old advertisements for Ken Rad radio tubes, Vitalis hair tonic, Chesterfield cigarettes. Stenciled across the doors and hood, over fresh white paint, was *Pieretti Motor Company*. It wasn't exactly the Ferrari he'd been talking about. But as promised, her name was also freshly painted on the upper driver's door, along with a four-leaf clover beside it.

"It is a '49 Maserati A6 Coupe. It has seen some action, but it is a great car. And that clover was my racing sign," he said, pointing at it. "It's an old Italian racing symbol, and I want you to use it." Charles opened the driver's door to give them a clear view of the inside, which looked like the cockpit of a burned up fighter plane. All that remained of the interior was the ratty driver's seat, the wooden steering wheel, three pedals and a row of faded instrument gauges. "Rudy's been through it from top to bottom. In good hands, it will cut past anything at the track today."

"What a piece of shit," Vi said, unable to keep a look of disgust from her face. "You'll die in that thing."

"God no," Charles said, putting on his black sunglasses. "Easy to handle. Nothing to be intimidated by at all." His face grew serious as he looked at Vi, as if he was bidding for a mother's approval. "These races are a bunch of rich college kids and doctors with fancy cars. Worst that could happen is she gets banged around a little bit."

Prudence assessed the car again, swallowing hard, then looked at Charles.

"If you want a race car, this is it," he said. He then went and reached inside the wagon and pulled out a shiny red and white checkered racing helmet, brown leather straps dangling from it.

"There's a thirty dollar cash prize for First Place in the men's races," he said, handing her the helmet. "And when you win, you can keep it all."

Prudence glanced over at Vi, who was slowly shaking her head. Prudence felt the adrenaline pumping through her, intermingled with the warm rush she still felt whenever Charles was around.

"You're crazy," Vi said, as Prudence took the helmet.

"I'll call you after the race," she said, running and jumping in the wagon after Charles. As he started its engine, she leaned her head out the window. "Wish me luck!"

"Good luck!" Vi shouted, finally cracking a smile, holding her kimono closed.

The crowd parted as Charles pulled the wagon and trailer down the street, and headed out of the city. He talked all the way down to

Monterey, his wrist dangled over the wheel, sunglasses on the bridge of his nose, cigarette smoke curling towards the open window. *God*, she thought, looking at him. *He makes everything seem so easy.*

They entered the Salinas Valley, its black pastures and the mountains shrouded in mist. She watched migrant workers walking along the bi-way as Charles told her the lessons he'd learned in car racing, how they could also be applied to life: how to get an early lead, how to overtake a slower driver, how to put pressure on a lead driver so he makes a mistake. By the time they reached the track, Prudence felt that he'd told her offhand stories about himself that he otherwise wouldn't have shared.

A pleasant anxiety was building as they wound along a dirt road and parked at the edge of the airfield, where the race was to be held. Although it was only eleven in the morning, several dozen cars were readying for the amateur heats. She caught the acrid smell of fuel and heard the unbelievable roar of the engines. Hundreds of spectators milled about, and off in the distance she heard the bark of tires as the cars wound along the far end of the track, the air heavy with exhaust and burning motor oil. A sensation came back to her, tinged with nostalgia: the will to master a sport, to understand and overcome its challenges. Her stomach tightened, and when she saw the other drivers, intense and distant in their own way, she felt her competitive urges return.

She eyed the other race cars, the trailers, the booths set up with toolboxes and ice chests full of soda pop. It was just like the race she saw in the park, she thought, as Charles led her over to the paddock. He walked past the drivers, some nodding in his direction as if they recognized him. Then they looked at her, as if wondering why she was dressed in a race suit.

Even though she was wondering the same thing, she glared

back at the other drivers, feeling her blood grow hot again. But then she forgot about them as she looked beyond them at the racetrack, patched asphalt in the sand; a winding short course with sharp turns, the retired military airstrip as the straightaway. As she watched, a Hudson Hornet screeched past the hay bales that outlined the course, its engine so loud that she reached down and dialed back her hearing aid.

As Charles stood watching the racing, she went to check herself in for the races at a row of tables that sat along the fence. A long line of other racers stood there, and Prudence joined them and watched them sign their names. Then each of them were handed forms from the men manning the table, who were all wearing red sport coats with SCCA patches over their breasts. As Prudence neared the table, the officials looked up at her and began whispering to one another.

When her turn came up a minute later, she told her name to one of the officials, who wore a white baseball cap. They all stared at her a moment, and then the man rifled through their metal file box and came up with her race card. The man looked at it a moment as if there was a mistake. He leaned over and conferred with the official sitting beside him.

"Miss," the man in the white hat said, turning to her and removing his glasses. "I'm afraid there's been a mistake." He shook his head. "They won't allow you to race. I'm sorry, Honey." The man put his glasses back on and called the next person in line.

"And why not?" Prudence set her helmet and driving gloves on the table. She looked over her shoulder at the line of racers forming behind her.

The official looked up. "Because there's a weight requirement." He looked her up and down. "You have to be at least a hundred and forty-five pounds to race. It's just the rules, so no one has an unfair advantage."

She looked back at the other drivers, taller than her by half a foot and outweighing her by fifty pounds. Last she stepped on a scale, she was a hundred and twenty-five pounds. Not exactly skinny for her height. But she knew damn well that most women didn't meet their requirements.

"Well that's a pile of horse puckey," she said, her hands on her hips, any reservations she'd had about racing suddenly gone. "And you know it."

As the official sat there glaring back at her, Charles came up through the line of drivers and stood beside her.

"What's the problem here?" he asked, glancing at the man in the white hat.

"And who are you, sir?" the official said. "This is a private matter. Now please step aside."

"Please," Prudence said to Charles, "let me handle this."

But Charles stepped even closer to the table. "I'm Charles Pieretti."

The three men went silent and looked at one another, as if this was all some sort of joke. They then looked at Charles, standing there in his grease-stained sport shirt. She watched their expressions change as they recognized what she had the first night she saw him in the club. That Charles was *somebody*.

"Carlo Pieretti?" another of the officials asked. He was an older man with white hair who sat near the end of the table.

"That's right," Charles said, nodding towards the man.

It was the first time Prudence had ever heard that name. It made her wonder at his past, all that she didn't know about him. She watched as the man in the white hat laughed nervously, looking back at the other officials, who were still staring at Charles.

"Well, I'm sorry, but there are rules that everyone must follow. There are minimum weight requirements for the cars, and for the drivers." He held up a form and pointed to it. "Your driver here must be at least a hundred and forty-five pounds." The man looked her up and down again. "And I don't think she meets that requirement."

"I saw Helle Nice race in Italy when I was a boy," Charles said, pursing his lips. "She was a driver if there ever was one. And she couldn't have been more than a hundred pounds. So you're telling me that if she were here, you wouldn't let her race?"

"Please sir, we have a lot of drivers to sign in." He looked at his wristwatch.

"If you don't hand over that card," Charles said, leaning on the table. "I'll see that you're selling hot dogs in the grandstands at the next race."

"Now just wait a minute," the man in the white hat said, standing. He put his hands on his hips and looked at Charles. "Last I read of Carlo Pieretti, he was on his death bed. Shattered both of his legs in a wreck." The man put on his glasses and inspected Charles a moment. "And you really mean to tell me, that's you?"

Charles didn't take his eyes off of the man. Prudence watched as Charles pulled an empty chair from nearby, set it in front of the table. And while the line of racers continued to back up, Charles put his foot up on the chair and began to roll up his pant leg. He then undid his sock garter, and pushed his sock down. Prudence noticed the netting of pinkish white slashes that crossed over his shin and calf. The deep, smooth pink scars. The place where his kneecap was supposed to be looked oddly empty, and seeing it, she understood the reason for his limp and the pain he lived with every day.

He held up his pant leg a moment longer, looking around to see that the men were satisfied, then refastened the sock to the garter, and rolled down his pants.

"It wasn't both legs," Charles said. "Just the one. Don't believe everything you read."

"I'm sorry, sir," the man in the white hat said, sitting down. He talked with the other men at the table. "The best we can do is give her a waiver for this one race. You'll have to have her weighed here, and then add weight to your car to make up the difference."

WHEN THEY arrived back at the trailer, both of them silent after what had happened at the table, Charles unbolted a chain from beneath the Maserati. He stood and rolled it backwards onto the pavement. As he reached inside to set the handbrake, Prudence looked at the car's hood. *"Miss Hot Rod"* was painted across it. She hadn't noticed it earlier, and the blush that had formed on her cheeks as the officials weighed her at the table deepened.

"It's awful, I know, but people will eat it up." He laughed, as if he'd forgotten about it. "I think you will understand, after today. Racing is about much more than just driving."

He then took a large metal toolbox from the Chevy and set it on the floor beside the driver's seat in the Maserati, grunting as he slid it into place. He rubbed his knee, then turned and grabbed a jack and tire iron and set them beside the toolbox.

"It's about bullshit management," he said as he climbed in the Maserati, started it, and instructed her to sit on the hood. She looked at him a moment, then set her feet on the bumper, positioning her rear end above the headlight. She knew what he was doing, and figured she owed him this much. As he drove her down to the paddocks, racers parted from their path, looking at the sleek coupe and her in her sparkling white race suit, the cord of her hearing aid disappearing into it, her hair held back in a ponytail. Some of the younger boys stared and off in the distance she heard whistling and cat-calling.

Prudence knew then that she had to beat all of them. If she was going to make a spectacle of herself, then she needed to be able to back it up with a win. She turned and looked at Charles behind the wheel, grinning in a way he never had before. He stared back at her a long time, nodding his head slowly. As they arrived at the paddocks and he prepped the car for the race, it seemed like he was reliving an old version of himself. That in a way, he was racing again through her.

After a race official inspected the car, she was ushered to the pre-race proceedings and a briefing on the rules. Some of the other drivers shook their heads and whispered at each other when she arrived. She looked away from them, listening as each driver was assigned a starting position at random, realizing that she was about to enter her first real race. She stood there, her hands clammy, wondering if she could really do it.

"Hey good luck out there, Sweet Tits," one of the other drivers called out to her as she was leaving the tent. She heard the echoing laughter of the other drivers and she flipped them her middle finger over her shoulder.

Charles walked her over to line up for the start of the race, talking rapidly the whole way, as if to give her a crash course in this type of racing. He told her there was no qualifying for the amateur heats, that each racer had been assigned a position at random. As he talked, Prudence remembered the bustle and excitement before her college swimming events. Hundreds of people all consumed with their own tasks. Tasks that overshadowed the fear and the nervousness of the coming race.

Soon she was behind the wheel of the Maserati, staring through the split windshield. She strapped on her helmet, working it down over her hearing aid. Then she gripped the wheel and worked the pedals, turned the key and started the engine. *This is it*, she thought, tapping the accelerator and watching the tachometer needle surge. *This is what you wanted.*

"Okay," he said, his voice shaking a bit. "Remember that you can pull out of the race at any time. Just pull outside the hay bales and shut off the car."

"I'm going to be fine. And I'm going to finish the race," she yelled, waving him away. "And then you're going to buy me dinner."

He winked at her. "I wouldn't have let you talk me into racing if I didn't think you were up to it. Just pass as many as you can at the start. Then block them from passing on the straights, and beat them through the turns. Got it?" He smacked the roof. "Good."

Charles climbed over a metal railing and watched her enter the racetrack for a few warm up laps. She trusted him implicitly, his confidence becoming her own. She cruised around the track, memorizing each turn, finding their apexes. Nervousness fell way to a calm focus as the flagman ended the practice and she was lined up in her starting position. She looked out at the five pairs of cars ahead of her and one beside her. She adjusted her rear-view mirror and glanced back at the empty track. The car trembled and she looked ahead at the flagman. The sky was clear blue, the racetrack a bleached blacktop rimmed by dust.

She was fast on the throttle as the green flag dropped, cutting to the left along the outside of the track, around the cars that were caught behind a car that had stalled at the start. A few other drivers had broken out of formation too and she revved up to redline between each gear shift, passing them handily. When she came to the first turn she was still on the outside of the formation; she gave a two-count after the other cars began braking for the turn. As the hay bales neared, she jabbed her brake pedal. The car slowed precisely and she cut inside the slower cars, five spots ahead of her starting position.

The sun shined directly in her face and the car's cabin was hot and loud, as if the engine was in there with her, a steaming, blistering thing. Its tone was insistent and sharp, blatting and popping as she swung the steering wheel and downshifted, her leading tire dipping into the turn. The car lurched, the rear end squealing, tires smoking, the weight of her body thrust against the door as she spun the wheel and slammed the shift lever down. The cabin was filled with the rank scent of raw fuel, wisps of burning blue oil seeping out of the dashboard.

Time became elusive, blurry. She blinked and a few laps were gone. She could anticipate every action she needed to make, and made each movement with precision. Here in a race car she didn't need to hear well, here she had no shortcomings. Now it was just her, the car, and the race. For a moment it felt as if everything could be fine, that nothing could ever harm her as long as she stayed in this race.

Every time she passed Charles, he stood there waving his arm forward, an indication that she was closing in on the lead. The car was tight in her grip, feeling strong as she pushed through the slower cars and neared the two lead cars. A small Porsche and an MG. They were running clean laps, but she closed the gap at each turn, finding a smoother line. On the airstrip straightaway she had the car all out in fourth gear, the engine redlining, the speedometer twitching.

A tunnel of vague colors and shapes. Prudence felt it solidify to a fine point of light as she passed the second place car on the final turn. The Porsche was just ahead of it, but as she chased its bumper it pulled away smoothly. But then as she accelerated, she missed a shift. She ground the shift lever into its gate and hit the throttle again.

The MG passed her and she chased after it, but the Porsche and MG crossed the finish line several car lengths ahead of her.

The flagman waved the checkered flag and she felt the exhilaration of a close victory, but the burn of a third finish. She wanted to keep pushing for the win, but she cruised a victory lap behind the winners, as a fresh set of cars was already pulling onto the course to begin practicing for their heat.

The race had been nearly thirty minutes, but it had felt like seconds. Prudence drove past the paddock up to the parking lot, stepped from the Maserati and looked for Charles. The other drivers were congratulating each other and although a few looked her way, they didn't acknowledge her. She smoothed her hair and cradled her helmet under her arm. There was a compact tucked in the pockets of her racing suit, but a quick look in her side view mirror revealed it a lost cause. Her face was covered in a dirt film, a sharp line of white above where her helmet had been. She spat in her handkerchief and rubbed at her face, brushed off her dusty race suit. Prudence cinched its belt tight to her waistline and cut through the crowd. She found Charles talking to a young reporter with a tag in his hat band that read *San Francisco Bee*. He held a notepad and had a camera hanging from his neck. He looked no older than she was, his suit a size too big.

"This is my first assignment," the reporter said, his voice shaky. "So please bear with me."

Charles came and threw his arm around her as the reporter fumbled with the settings on his camera. The thrill of the race was still in her blood and she wanted to explain the exaltation to him, the heady afterward. But before she could speak, Charles was dragging her and the reporter up to the race car by the arm.

"Trust me," he said, as he posed her on the car's hood and wiped the rest of her face clean with his handkerchief. The reporter began snapping photos and she smiled. Her hair had come loose from its ribbon and was fluttering in the wind.

"You better look out, boys," Charles said, turning towards a group of other drivers that had assembled. "Here comes Miss Hot Rod."

She felt her smile soften. The young reporter took one more photo and she slid off the car, unzipped her race suit and headed towards the station wagon.

"Why'd you have to say something stupid like that?" she said to Charles when he joined her a few minutes later. She pictured that woman in the two-piece bathing suit at the race in the park. *Miss Dangerous Curves.*

"I know what I'm doing," he said. "I know how those female drivers in Europe became successful. You need to be something out of this world to them. Unobtainable." He walked to the back of the wagon. "Just wait until those photos run in the paper," Charles said as he grabbed the tow chains and swung the tailgate shut. "Then you'll see what I mean."

"I thought this was just one or two races," she said, standing by the car, hands on her hips.

"No." He stopped and looked at her, shaking his head slowly. "I really think we've got something here. Something *big.*"

Prudence awakened early the next morning, and while Vi was still asleep, walked from their apartment to the corner store to pick up the *Bee.* She spilled some pennies on the counter, tucked the newspaper under her arm, then walked home, her feet quick on the steps, and spread the paper on the kitchen table. She promised herself she didn't care; wouldn't be crushed if there was no mention of her at all.

Pages fluttered as she searched for an article on the races. And then she spotted the photo on the third page of the Sports section, with a headline *Miss Hot Rod Beats Men Racers!* It was just as Charles had predicted. She gasped and read the article while holding her breath, which mentioned how she'd passed nine cars to finish third. They'd also ran a large photo of her sitting on the car, the wind unfurling her long hair.

Vi came from her bedroom and stood in the doorway, blinking at the sunlight filtering through the kitchen window. Prudence hadn't even seen her the night before to tell her about the race. Vi yawned and threaded the belt of her kimono into a knot.

"My, my," she said, yawning while glancing at the scattered papers. "What are you getting into out here?" She picked up the paper and held it up to the light. She blinked and looked at it more closely. "My God, is that you? I don't believe it!"

"I know," Prudence said. "I can hardly believe it myself. It doesn't seem real."

"Wow, and you look great," Vi said, setting the article face up on the table and reading it slowly. "This is really something, Prudence," she said, as she continued to read. "You came in *third!*?"

Prudence sat back and laughed. "I wish you could've been there to see their faces when I stepped out of the car. *No* one liked me very much, let me tell you."

Charles had taken her to a celebratory dinner afterwards as promised. It was just a roadside hot dog stand and soda fountain, but she'd stood there dumping catsup on her hot dog, recounting every bit of the race to him. Charles just sat nodding and smiling as if he knew exactly how good she felt. As she talked, her hand absently touched his. He looked up at her and she pulled it away, and they ate the rest of their meal in silence.

"You should really be proud, Prudence," Vi said. "This is something else."

"Though I can't say I really like this Miss Hot Rod business."

Vi waved her hand at Prudence. "If they have to call you Miss Candy Ass, then so what? You could've gone out there and bombed, but you didn't. And you wouldn't be in the paper if you had. And besides, it's catchy."

"I guess." Prudence sighed, pushing away the paper. After the initial elation, it all began to feel a little strange. She looked out the window. "I feel like since I've gotten here, good things are just happening and I don't know why. I feel lucky. And that luck has to run out sometime, doesn't it?"

"Don't forget, bad things have happened in your life too. So this isn't just a fluke." Vi smiled. "And good thing you met Charles. Men have a way of making things happen for us. It's just the way it is."

Prudence looked up slowly, not sure if this was a jab or a confession. Either way, the tone in the room had suddenly changed. As if Vi knew about the bittersweet success Prudence was feeling. Vi had hinted a few times that she'd been in a relationship with a man. All those letters, and the diamond ring on the necklace seemed like important clues, but Vi had never shared the details. Prudence had never pushed it, sensing it would be revealed in time, and now the following silence seemed to pose the question.

A long, uncomfortable silence passed. Vi pursed her lips and stared out the window a moment. She shook her head and laughed. "Well, here goes. I guess I haven't told you much about the men in my life, have I? Well, I suppose this is a good a time as any." She closed her eyes, as if she'd pre-formed her words carefully and wanted to make sure she got them right.

"I was married once to John Knowles. He's a well-known painter.

I was a struggling artist until I met him, and then things started happening. He introduced me to some big people and suddenly I had shows lined up. My paintings started to sell." She laughed softly. "I felt like one day I was staring up at this big mountain, and then John picked me up in a helicopter and dropped me off at the top."

Vi went into the kitchen and rummaged through the cupboards. "To make a long story short, we got married. John desperately wanted to have children, and so did I. And so in a farmhouse up near Seattle we tried and tried to have a baby but it never happened. I felt like it would've changed things for us, made us a normal couple." Vi pried the lid off a Hills Brothers coffee tin. "But maybe nature has a way of telling you things. Or isn't that just what people say when things don't go their way?"

She turned and leaned against the counter. "And then I just wanted to get away from it all. I felt like I wasn't much of a wife. I felt like I wasn't being truthful to him. There was a woman down here that I was seeing. She'd moved away after John and I were married. It had broken her heart, but I hadn't stopped caring about her." She shook her head. "There's no way you can shut off the way you think and feel. And I told John I loved him, but I explained to him who I was, and that I was leaving. And then I came down here, but by then she was married herself and pregnant. I was just a mess. Couldn't paint, couldn't focus. I went to Paris for a month and blew what money I had. And then I came back and got the job at the club and haven't stopped working since." Vi set the coffee tin on the counter and looked at Prudence closely. "And there's something else I should tell you."

Prudence leaned forward, listening intently.

"John and I never officially got a divorce. We didn't want to."

Prudence stared at Vi. A coldness filled her, as if she and Vi had returned to being strangers. The confession stung, knowing Vi had been lying to her all along.

Vi stood there with the straps of her kimono coming undone, half-clothed underneath it. Outside there was a whole city, and Prudence lamented that she was here in this room, feeling foolish and betrayed. Suddenly the image of the cool, collected woman Prudence had first met in The Scotch House was gone.

"I know how you feel," Vi said. "I'm telling you this, because I've been thinking more and more about John. He loves me and writes me all the time. He knows that I left him because I thought I'd let him down somehow."

Prudence shook her head. She had seen the dozens of letters from a John Knowles, but never asked about them. She had so many questions for Vi, but before she could start to ask them, Vi took a step closer.

"I'm saying this because you're headed to the top of the mountain now, and don't think that there isn't a fee for that ride. I can only guess what's going on between you and Charles. He's a married man with a child. Have you thought about that?"

"There is nothing going on between us. And I'm not ready for a lecture from you right now," Prudence said. "I think it should be the other way around. And I can't believe you've waited this long to tell me this. I've told you everything about me."

"Maybe I'm ashamed. Maybe I was afraid if I told you that you'd act like this. I just want you to learn from my mistakes."

"You don't have to warn me of anything, I know what I'm doing." She walked across the room and began gathering up the newspaper. "And I thought you were excited for me, but then you ruin it and tell me that it's all just going to end badly like it did for you, and I think that's just *crummy*."

Vi put her hand on the newspaper. "Look, just think before things start getting too wild. Don't get in over your head. I'm happy for you. I really am. But this is serious. You could get killed, for God's sake."

The phone began to ring in the den but they both kept staring at each other. After several rings, Prudence slowly went and picked it up. It was Charles.

"It's my day off from the shop, why am I talking to you?" Prudence said, smiling. She brushed back her hair and saw that Vi was listening.

"You saw the paper?" he asked.

"Yep," Prudence said. She heard his Zippo cigarette lighter click open on the other end, then snap shut.

"Well, if people start calling for you, tell them they have to talk to me."

"Why?"

A silence passed in the receiver; traffic in the background. He wasn't at home, not at the office either.

"Because, I'm your manager now. I had my lawyer draw up a contract."

Prudence crouched, her hand covering the mouthpiece. "What do you mean?"

"I mean that we are sitting on a gold mine. I've been getting phone calls all morning about you. I made some phone calls and got you entered in some upcoming races, bigger ones. We'll get you your own car, we'll go on the road. I will incur all these little costs for twenty percent of your future earnings," he added. "But one thing's for certain. Things are going to change for you."

Prudence closed her eyes and rubbed her temple. Yesterday's race was still so close: the crash of sunlight through the windshield, the hammering engine.

"So what do you think?" he asked.

Prudence glanced over at Vi, who was still looking at her.

"Make it fifteen percent and you have a deal," she said, setting the phone in its cradle without waiting for his reply.

Mistake, she remembered him saying, the word still hanging out there like an omen. She turned and found herself looking at a watercolor Vi had started months ago. A modern styling of pastel-colored shapes, each the size of a corn kernel, forming into a pattern that created depth and relief. The colors reminded her of air blowing through trees just before a thunderstorm. The subject was unmistakably a woman's unclothed figure, her face cast away from the viewer.

"Why is he calling you this early on a Sunday?" Vi asked, breaking Prudence's trance as she came and placed a cup of coffee in her hands.

Prudence shook her head, afraid if she answered honestly, the conversation would continue and never amount to anything. Instead she took the coffee and looked at the painting, wishing Vi would finish it. She then stood and put a 78 on the Scott Hi-Fi, "Berceuse de Jocelyn," letting the music fill the room. She gazed at the bookcase, rough wooden planks supported by bricks. The battered easels with used canvases on them, scarred wooden brushes sitting in a jar of thinner. Prudence sipped her coffee, realizing that Charles had come to the same conclusion that Vi had months ago: for better or worse, things were going to change for all of them.

Seven

A MONTH later, on Labor Day Weekend, Prudence was standing on the rooftop of the Horace Stevens Ford Company in Sacramento. She was wearing a light blue organdy dress, a white sash draped from her shoulder to her waist that read *Miss Hot Rod*. Banners had been strung across street lamps, proclaiming this as the dealership's grand opening. She waved at passing pickup trucks, the drivers staring up at her as they turned into the lot. She smiled down at the crowd that stood amid the rows of sparkling new cars, all for the twenty-five dollars this appearance promised. It was more than she would make in a week as a receptionist, and more than two weeks' pay at The Scotch House.

Lately, she'd become a bit of a celebrity in the local papers. The woman who raced cars against the men and regularly beat them. The requests for personal appearances had been pouring in from grocery stores, town parades, high school football games. She hadn't turned any of them down. There was money to be made and she needed to be making it. But most of all, she just loved the racing, and she was proud of the statement it made. Even if they had to call her Miss Hot Rod.

Charles was milling through the crowd, eating free hot dogs and talking shop with the salesmen. Men bought raffle tickets for a new Ford Country Squire wagon. Children stood under the awning, tittering as they tried to a get a peek up her dress. She glared at them, her heels stuck in the tarred rooftop, her hearing aid box clipped to a cloth loop she'd sewn to the back of her dress. Behind her a high school band played brassy, triumphant Sousa marches. Beyond the car lot stood miles of open farmland, flat and dry, irrigated by shallow lanes of muddy water.

Late that afternoon, after she'd watched a dozen new cars drive off the lot, Prudence sat inside the shop drinking an RC-Cola. Her dress was sticking to her and her sweaty hair was sprawled over her shoulders. Her arms and face were sunburned and her skin there felt tight, and she gazed at her reflection in the large showroom windows, sipping the soda through a straw. Outside, a big-boned mother and her children stood staring at her as if she were a manikin in a department store window.

"Can I help you?" Prudence asked through the window to the mother, who was dressed in dirty jean overalls and a faded flannel shirt. The children stared back, their mouths rimmed with melted ice cream. The small boy reached forward with a grimy finger and touched the glass, leaving a white ice cream smudge.

As if sensing that she was indeed real, the boy retreated and knocked back against his mother's leg, slurping his ice cream. The mother hoisted the girl farther up in her arm, balancing the large child on her hip. The woman was no older than Prudence, and she eyed her up and down, took a bite of hot dog and chewed slowly.

"You married to that man?" the mother asked, nodding her head towards Charles. "The one you come here with?"

Prudence blinked back at the woman while the band broke into another marching tune. She put the straw back in her mouth and sipped her soda, looking beyond the woman, through her, into the hard dry earth from where she'd come. Other women had looked at her the same way over the past month when she did similar jobs at other dealerships and town fairs, and she was surprised how little their pettiness affected her.

"I'd bet you'd lick the floor if you had to," the mother said, moving close to the window as her husband came and stood behind her.

Prudence stood up and glared at the woman. The husband, a big burly man in bib overalls, slipped his arm around his wife's broad shoulders.

"Looks like you been licking something even dirtier," Prudence said, staring at the husband. Charles walked into the showroom just then, tucking an envelope in his inner jacket pocket. He brushed back his hair as he came and stood beside her, dark rings under his eyes. She wished he hadn't appeared at that moment, as she hated women who only picked fights when men were around.

"Let's get the hell out of this hayseed town," Prudence said, staring at the woman. She clanked her unfinished soda bottle on the windowsill and quickly gathered her things. When she looked up a minute later, the mother and her children were already gone, the kid's finger smudge still on the window. Outside, the sun was beginning to set, and there was a long drive ahead of them, and suddenly the whole day felt heavy inside her like a thing that couldn't be left behind.

They climbed in the Chevy wagon, the Maserati strapped on the trailer behind them. They would be driving all that evening to a raceway in the town of Cotati, where she would be racing in an amateur event the next day. She looked out the window as they pulled onto the road, back at the thinning crowd at the dealership, wishing she could've had that woman alone for a minute. Feel the flat of her palm connecting with her cheek.

"When am I going to see some of this money?" Prudence asked, turning to Charles after they'd passed the outskirts of town. "That's the purpose of all this playing pretty, to make some money, right?"

"I told you, Steve, I'm taking care of things," he said, leaning back in the seat.

"Steve?" she asked, smiling at him. "Who the hell is Steve?"

"You are," he said, looking over at her. "Steve gets uptight a lot lately. So *Steve*, let me take care of it. I have the money all accounted for and I'm going to open a bank account for you." He rested his arm over the seat, his voice sounding impatient. "Or if you want, you can keep track of it."

"I didn't mean that I don't trust you. I'm just ready to see how much I've made." She patted his arm. "You don't have to get all bent out of shape. Geez."

"*Geez*," he replied. "Then that settles it. And I know you don't like it, but this is the best way to get you exposure. A few more of these, and you'll be able to ask for some real money. Racing's going to get expensive and the competition's going to get tougher."

She touched the cord to her hearing aid and looked at him again. He slowly slipped his arm around her shoulder and shifted in his seat. She glanced back at him as he did, craning her neck away. But then she felt her body go loose, light, as if she'd just admitted some long withheld truth, here in the car. A truth that unburdened her from putting up this fight that she knew, deep down, neither of them wanted to win.

He winced and adjusted himself in the seat so his leg didn't hurt. She moved closer, cupping her shoulder into his arm, her hearing aid cord catching on his suit. She grabbed the cord and pulled. The hearing aid's earpiece popped from her ear and she unclipped the battery box and shut them away in the glove box.

As she looked forward again, out the windshield in silence, he kept his arm there, even as she leaned her head against his shoulder and fell asleep. A sleep so deep it felt like she'd let go of the edge and was falling, deep into some bottomless chasm.

IN THEIR room in a motor court in Cotati that evening, Charles took out a pint of scotch and sat on the bed, leaving the curtains open so he could keep an eye on the Maserati. Across the road stood a filling station and a diner, polished aluminum facade, a large painted sign promising twenty-five cent blue plate specials. The filling station and the diner were packed with drivers headed to the race the next day. In the sky above, the contrails of a plane faded into a burnt orange skyline. The diner's neon lights shined into their room, where they hadn't yet turned on the lamp, and the filling station's white globes spun high in the darkening sky, reading *Esso, Esso, Esso.*

There were other racers at their hotel too, leaning against their Jaguars and MGs in the string of parking spaces, drinking beer and staring at the Maserati.

"Quit worrying," Prudence said, fresh from the shower, wrapping her wet hair in a towel. "No one's going to touch it."

He laughed, looking at her as she drew the strings of her robe closed. She laughed with him, as he was likely thinking the same thing that she was. It was the first time they'd had to stay someplace overnight, and they'd gotten the last room in the only motel in town, and there was only one big bed to share. That night in his shop a month earlier felt like a long time ago now. As she came and sat beside him on the bed, she felt that same warm, natural feeling she had that night. But now it was like something either of them could touch, the battered dresser or the chipped mirror hanging above it.

She looked out the window, the cars glowing under a string of streetlights. The moon appeared high and luminescent over the far away hills, and Charles looked equally at ease sitting beside her, as if he'd also been put there to please and mystify her. And yet she remembered Vi's warning and closed her bathrobe even tighter. She reached over on the nightstand and turned on the little green Arvin radio that sat there. Country and western music spilled from its speaker, a Davis Sisters song, "I've Forgotten More."

"I've been thinking," he said, after a long silence. "I'm hoping you can get a top three finish in the race tomorrow. I think people would take you more seriously, help them get past the Miss Hot Rod name."

She leaned back and sighed, twisting the towel tighter in her hair. He was right. The papers would stop covering her unless she did well in this race. Her novelty was wearing off, and she needed to capitalize on what remained of it.

"They won't give you too many chances to prove yourself. And now is the time to show them what I see. A top driver," he said, looking back out the window. "There's plenty of people out there who want to see you fail, and I want to prove them wrong."

"I'll do fine," Prudence said, but her voice sounded flat to her own ears. In her last few events she knew she'd been inconsistent. She'd work her way to the top of the field, only to overshoot a final turn because she'd overcooked the brakes. "I feel like everything's going to come together tomorrow."

Prudence propped her feet up on the vinyl turquoise chair and looked at the faux wood paneled walls. Her eyes were aching and she didn't want to talk about tomorrow any more, as it would keep her up all night, worrying. She just wanted to sit here, off her feet and in the cool, dark room with him.

Charles took another sip from the bottle of scotch and set it on the nightstand. "I'm nervous. I feel like I'm the one racing tomorrow."

"So why don't you? You could enter one of the other heats with the car."

"My leg's too screwed up," he said, shaking his head. "And things change after a wreck like I had. After you see all your friends die in crashes. You lose the nerve." He turned back to the window. "And besides, I'm too old now."

Prudence knew that these little SCCA events were beneath a driver of his level, but she thought it would be good for him, easy win or not. She watched as he rubbed his hands together, looking down at the orange carpet.

"You aren't too old," she said. "And you said you wished you went back to it."

"I suppose I did say that." He laughed. "It was a mistake to tell you all those things. Now you have something to hold against me."

She took another snort from the bottle and set it back down. She whispered that everything would be all right. That she would win tomorrow and everything would be fine. She still heard the hollowness to her words, and she knew he did too. They sat there together on the bed, the wagon and the trailer outside the window, the Maserati's fenders gleaming in the fading twilight.

"I'll make up the floor," he said after a while, taking a pillow and a spare blanket from the closet.

While he unfolded the blanket and set it on the floor beneath the window, she took her underwear and nightgown from her suitcase and walked past him to the bathroom. When she opened the door she looked at the toilet, inches from the shower, the rusty radiator wedged behind the door.

"Don't look," she said, glancing at him. He froze by the window, the light from the street lamps and the gas station spilling in. Her heartbeat quickened as she shook off the damp robe, the air cool against her bare skin. She threaded her arms through the nightgown and let it fall, loose and cottony, over her. He'd already finished making his bed, so she tossed her underwear and brassiere back in her suitcase and slipped into bed.

She pulled the covers close to her chin as Charles unbuttoned his sport shirt, threw it over the back of the chair. He stood there in front of the window, looking out. Square shouldered in his sleeveless undershirt, thin hipped in his tailored trousers. He brushed his hair back and untied his shoes. As he undid his belt and lowered his trousers over his boxer shorts, she began to look away, but she didn't. She stared at the netting of scars that covered his leg, the smooth, pale flesh against the rest of his dark skin.

"You take the bed," she said, kicking off the sheets. "I'll sleep on the floor."

"No, no," he said, sitting on the edge of the bed to remove his socks. "I need my driver fresh in the morning."

The radio played, the verse of another song came and went.

"Charles," she said, sitting up, placing her elbows on her knees. "Thank you for all you're doing for me. I know you've given up a lot to do all this."

"And I don't regret it for a second." He flashed a smile and kept looking at the window.

Prudence swallowed, feeling her words rising up in her, the unavoidable purge: "Do you regret that night, in your office?"

He snapped his head around at her. "No."

She looked at her hands, twisted into a ball. "Then why did you say it was a mistake?"

"I never said that." He leaned towards her. "I said taking that Ferrari was a mistake."

She stared at him, his eyes clear and open. "It's hard to tell sometimes, exactly what you mean."

"Well, maybe I don't always know what I mean when it comes to this." He peeled off a sock. "It's harder for me than it is for you."

"Because of Maria?" She sat back in the bed. "Does she know

where you are right now?"

"She thinks I'm in Los Angeles on business. If she knew I was here she'd have my head on a stake." He gazed back out the window. "Maria and I don't exactly get along, if you get my meaning. We haven't in a long time."

"Well, I've never really gotten along with anyone," she said. "Well, not *anyone*. But it's never felt right, you know."

"Well, in my experience, sometimes things feel wrong because they are wrong. But you ignore them because you think you have to." He turned again, leaning closer this time, his words hushed but urgent. "How does this feel now, right here? Does it feel wrong?"

Prudence blushed and shook her head.

"Then there's our answer." He pursed his lips and nodded.

As he did, Prudence reached down and shut off her hearing aid, removed it from her ear and set the unit on the nightstand. She swallowed again, harder now, staring at him, her heart clenched like a fist. When she leaned forward he put his hands on her shoulders, as if to stop her. He looked at her a moment before he drew her to him, pressing his lips to hers. His skin was soft and smooth, and as she rubbed her hands over his arms and the fine hairs on his chest, her heart fell into a slow, deep rhythm.

As he put his arms around her, her hands dropped beside her body, hovering, reaching in the space around them. His tongue pressed against hers, and it seemed like the room had flooded and they were swimming in warm water, being washed together into a deep, clear pool.

She pressed back against him. He lifted her nightgown over her head, the pads of his fingers dragging lightly against her skin. As he let the nightgown drop to the floor, she lay back on the bed, bare and clean, her wet hair twisted in a rope between her breasts. His eyes didn't leave hers as he reached for the curtains, and when it was dark they moved inward with the current in a rush. His fingers tracing her body, her hair, her own hands studying him. She was shaking, breathless and burning as she grasped and guided him in. She gasped, as much as for the warmth of him as for the way the world now seemed so small, and for once, so simple.

WHEN SHE awakened the next morning, Charles wasn't in the bed beside her. As she rose, dressed, and fitted her hearing aid, she threw open the curtains. The room filled with bright, water-clear sunlight. Charles was standing on the trailer with the Maserati's hood open, fiddling with the engine. She knocked on the frosted window and he stood up, waved, and stepped down from the trailer. When she opened the door, her breath coming out in puffs, she heard shouting. She looked across the road and saw that all the racers were out of their rooms, gassing up their cars, preparing to drive towards the track.

Charles came to the door, where he paused a moment before he kissed her. "Get your things," he said. "We've got to get going. We're running late."

He washed his hands and threw on his clothes as she slipped on her shoes and jacket. They rushed out the door, jumped in the wagon and followed the stream of racers, one of his hands draped over the wheel, the other behind her neck. She grinned and leaned back against him, feeling as if she'd been washed and scrubbed and left to dry in the breeze. As his arm tightened around her and he kissed the top of her head, she knew that this was the way it was meant to be, since the first time they met. And thank God, she thought, lighting a cigarette. As they parked and unloaded the Maserati, she heard the pop of its chain as it came loose, and the sound resounded through her body.

At the racetrack, they quickly prepped the car for the first heat, checking the engine fluids and tire pressures. Charles then placed the toolbox and jack in their usual spot on the passenger footwell. As she slipped on her race suit beside the car, a passing driver made a lewd comment. When she walked over to him, zipping up her suit and shaking her fist, Charles came and looped his arm around her waist pulled her back to the car, telling her that she could deal with him on the track.

During the first race, she was bullied so much that she was sure all the drivers had banded together to make sure she lost. Within the first lap, she was blatantly run off course into a sign that read *CHAMPION Spark Plugs: Dependable!* She pulled back onto the track, waiting for the offending driver to be given the black flag, but it never flew. She raced back up to the front of the pack and was set to win when another driver banged her rear fender on the final lap, knocking the toolbox open and spilling the tools at her feet. As she cursed and kicked the tools aside to press the brake pedal, she overshot the apex of the last turn. He tried to cut inside her as they neared the grandstands, hundreds of spectators rising to their feet as she downshifted and mashed the pedal to the floor. Her engine wailed up to redline, and she slammed it in third gear and beat the driver by one car length.

After she'd pulled in the paddocks, her radiator steaming, Prudence climbed from the car and peeled off her helmet, huffing over to where Charles stood. "Those assholes hit me!" she yelled. "Didn't the judges see that? If I'd done that to someone I'd be thrown out of here."

"That's how it is, Steve," Charles said, shaking his head. "They're turning a blind eye to what's happening out there. You need to get tougher and stop leaving that inside line open or someone will knock you out of the way and take it. You need to close that gap when the pressure is on."

Prudence glared at him, but she knew he was right: it wasn't ever going to be a fair race. She handed Charles her helmet and wiped the sweat from her brow. "Well, that doesn't change anything. It was dirty driving and I don't like it."

"It's only going to get tougher for you out there." He put his arm around her and led her away from the pits. "And this is just practice for the real races. So learn your lessons now. You won't forget to close that gap later on, and you'll know how to play dirty too."

Prudence stopped near the grandstands and bought a Coke from a vendor. She reached deep in the ice chest to fetch it, letting her hand linger in the ice a moment before she lifted out the bottle and pressed it to the back of her neck. When she looked up she noticed spectators had come down from the bleachers and were staring at her. Boys in Davy Crockett coonskin caps and their blue jeans rolled up at the ankles. Their fathers stood smoking in their weekender jackets, arms draped over the chain link fence, wry smiles on their faces.

"What are they all doing down here?" Prudence asked Charles.

"They came down to look at you," he said, laughing.

Prudence adjusted her hearing aid and brushed her fingers through her hair, trying to remove the impression her helmet had made on it. "I look like hell," she said as one of the spectators yelled out her name, congratulating her.

Prudence smiled as best she could, her face feeling hot, flushed. She waved at them and saw the boys were holding out pencils and race programs for her to sign. As she walked over to greet them,

Charles leaned in close.

"You hear that? They're using your real name now," he whispered. "Goodbye, Miss Hot Rod."

Eight

ONE EVENING in late October, they went to The Scotch House, where The Gerry Mulligan Quartet was playing a week-long engagement. Multi-colored lights shone across the stage, and the band's rainwater tone made her feel melancholy as Charles squeezed close beside her in the deep leather booth. The club was filled to capacity and the show sold out. Prudence caught sight of Vi across the room, rushing between tables, making sure all the guests were happy. She didn't like Vi seeing her with Charles this way. He was still married and as far as Prudence knew, had every intention of staying so.

Prudence sank lower in the booth, getting lost in the music and drinking steadily. She had learned to love Pink Ladies, a sweet, frothy cocktail made with egg whites, gin, and grenadine. It was the only drink that didn't upset her stomach, which had grown increasingly delicate. Lately, she felt a constant burning sensation in her belly that felt like she'd swallowed a jagged stone.

"You should take it easy," Charles said, putting his hand on hers after she'd had her fourth drink. "You're not used to drinking this much."

Prudence shot him a look and lifted the glass to her lips. He just shook his head.

"Suit yourself, Steve," he said. He'd brought some racing magazines with them, and he resumed thumbing through them as the band played, looking for any sign of her name in their pages. She'd grown accustomed to seeing her face in the local papers and racing rags, but lately some national magazines had taken an interest.

She'd placed in seven of her last ten races, and already Charles had her booked through to the fall of the next year with races and paid appearances.

During the intermission, regulars stopped by the table. Many of them recognized her from when she worked there as a waitress, and were curious about her racing career. Prudence leaned far back in the booth and glanced at them, dialing up the volume on her hearing aid. She always said that she wouldn't let this sudden, fortunate success of hers go to her head. But when she spoke, her voice sounded indulgent, her tongue like a snake being charmed from its basket.

"I have a race coming up next month where I drive across Mexico," she shouted to one woman. "A big one. How do you pronounce it, Charles?"

"*La Carrera Panamericana*." Charles set aside the race journals, smiling. "*LOOK* is going to have someone there just to cover Prudence."

Prudence tossed back the last of her drink. "And then we're going to Europe next summer," she said. In her haze she vaguely remembered him mentioning a race called the *Mille Miglia* in Italy, and then the *Targa Florio* in Sicily. Prudence felt dizzy at the thought of them. The biggest one was the race in Mexico, and she knew she wasn't ready for it. A nineteen hundred mile, seven day road race from the southern end of Mexico up to the Texas border.

As the girl continued to talk, Prudence stared off across the dance floor at Vi. Mexico seemed very far away and the thought of the grueling race made her stomach churn even more. Charles would be with her, but she'd be away from Vi. And although they were all in the same room tonight, it felt as if they were all separate from each other, and alone.

When Vi appeared at the table a few minutes later, hands on her hips, Prudence leaned her head back on the plush booth and looked up at her.

"You okay?" Vi said, looking down at her with a concerned expression.

Prudence nodded and reached out her hand, wanting to lace her fingers into Vi's.

"She's okay," Charles said. "Just a little overwrought."

Vi grasped her hand, squeezing it, and stared at him. "Take her home and put her to bed, Charles," she said, "now that you've gotten her good and tight." Someone called to Vi and she patted Prudence's hand, then turned and disappeared back into the crowd, the scent of her perfume lingering.

Prudence watched her go and then looked at Charles. He sighed and left the racing magazines on the table and took her by the arm, half-carrying her through the club and down the stairs. As they were walking out to the car, Prudence stopped in a puddle and declared that she wasn't going to Mexico with him.

He stopped beside her in the middle of the parking lot and looked at her. "What is this all about? You told me you wanted to go."

"I did, after you made all the plans. You seemed so *thrilled* about it." She leaned against the wagon. Rain drizzled on her face as she gazed into the black sky, the rain falling beyond the rooftops, lit by the city lights so it looked like ash. "I just keep going and going. And I can't keep up."

"So what do you want then?" he asked, the shoulders of his suit darkening.

She stared at him a moment, knowing that the answer was on her face, naked and exposed.

"I'm giving you what I can," he said, moving closer. "But I can't give you everything. Understand?"

"Don't," she said, glaring at him, "talk to me like I'm a child."

She got in the wagon and slammed the door, cigarette butts spilling from the overflowing ashtray, the seat's vinyl sticking to her. He walked around the car and got in beside her. They sat there, rain tapping against the roof, water dripping from them, their breath fogging the windshield.

"Maybe I am just a novelty. The girl who races cars," she said. "I'll just be another flash in the pan. And then what, where will you be when it ends?"

He turned in his seat, facing her. "I'm going to Mexico with you. It's a big race, I know. But if you just stay here doing these little races, you *will* just be a novelty."

"Please stop," she said. "Please stop talking to me like a manager. I'm talking to *you*." She pointed her finger at him. "Tell me, where would you be right now if you weren't my manager?"

"Do you think there is somewhere else I'd rather be? At first I thought we could make a little money, but now it's more than that, and you know it." He turned and started the car. "And if you think you are giving me everything, then you are wrong. You just wait until Mexico. Then you'll see that there is more of you to give than you know."

He pulled out of the lot and they drove quietly through the wet, foggy streets to her and Vi's apartment. She leaned her head against the cold window, the vibrations of the car, the tires, the road. Shaking the inner parts of her mind, thoughts that could never be named or held. She watched the city passing by, as it had the night she arrived here. She recognized these streets now. Had walked and touched them, left a part of herself there: the scuff of her shoe sole, ash of a cigarette, strand of hair. She wondered, as they drove with the lights of passing cars shining in on her face, if the old version of herself was to see this woman, in her wet dress and with this man, his Roman profile and his jeweled fingers dangling over the wheel of the two-tone Chevy, if she would find herself equally strange as these grey buildings had seemed on that first night, and see some dark part to her that she could no longer see now, no different than a frightening alley or a black doorway, a pair of glowing eyes peering out.

Then climbing the unlit stairway of her apartment, the sound of her breath in her ears. Charles's goodnight kiss still damp on her cheek. Perhaps he had wanted more. The usual hanky panky they'd partaken in nearly every night since Cotati, there in the wagon, in the empty shop, anywhere they wanted. The warmth of him inside her like a river through a rock canyon. She wobbled up the last steps to the apartment, cursing herself. She had betrayed something unspoken, she knew. Made fragile what had been strong. And as she fell into bed, the light still burning above her, she tried to think of what she hadn't given him, but then the room began to spin, and her thoughts washed down into a black whirlpool, and she closed her eyes and then she went down with them.

CHARLES WASN'T in his office when she arrived for work the following morning, his door locked and the lights turned off. As Prudence sat at her desk, the large Pirelli Tires clock ticking above her, the sun working its way across the showroom, she wondered if she'd scared him off, and regretted what she'd said the night before.

She washed down some aspirin with a bottle of Moxie soda pop. Her stomach was churning as usual and now her head felt as if it was stuffed with cotton. She rubbed her temples, swearing she'd never drink again. As she waited for the hangover to pass and for Charles to arrive, she busied herself by filling out paperwork for incoming inventory. She paused on one of the forms, noticing that a check had been drawn in her name for seven thousand dollars, the word 'PORSCHE' written in the memo line.

She'd picked the car for herself because it was the model that was always passing her at the track. The Porsche 550 Spyder. A brand new, sleek design that Charles hated, but Rudy loved because of its German engineering. Charles cherished his Ferraris, but racing one of them would put her in a larger engine size class, with drivers far beyond her experience. She knew that she would make a killing in her class with the Porsche down in Mexico, as its engine was big for the car's small size and light weight.

As she set the form aside, Rudy came into the showroom, as if on cue. He stopped beside her desk, cocking his head to the side, wiping his hands with a rag.

"They called from the shipping docks," he said. "The Porsche is arriving tomorrow morning." He grinned at her as he picked the grease from his nails. It was the first time he'd shown any enthusiasm in front of her, and she thought maybe it was good thing. Maybe he'd lighten up and they could get along after all. But he lingered beside her desk, staring at her legs and then up at her breasts. Something he never would have done with Charles around.

She picked up another form and glared at him. "Oh fuck off, Rudy."

He smirked and walked back towards the garage, letting the door slam behind him. *Swine*, she muttered, remembering what the salesmen told her about Rudy. That he'd been a German aircraft mechanic in the war. Prudence imagined him loading the bombs into planes, and knew that he was an industrious bastard who had played a role in killing her own countrymen. A man who had moved with fluidity into a new country and career, burying his old allegiances a bit too easily; if those allegiances were buried at all.

The thought of Rudy's past caused a cold chill to pass through her. As did the filthy looks he often gave her, as if he had the right to gawk at her as he pleased. Perhaps in Germany, men treated women as sexual material, but that was the exact kind of piggishness that set her aflame. She vowed that if he ever looked at her like that again, or made a pass at her, she'd be ready for him.

She worked on paperwork until lunch, still without any sign of Charles. One of the mechanics, a kid named Adam, came and delivered a sandwich to her desk. She set down her pen and rubbed her eyes and thanked him. He was only a few years younger than her, a fresh-faced and ambitious trainee that Charles had hired part-time. As soon as Adam turned around, Prudence sank her teeth into the sandwich, suddenly ravenous.

The phone rang a moment later, the tinkle of its bell echoing across the floor. When she picked up there was a pause, and then a woman's voice came on the line, asking for Charles. Prudence knew from the sharp, strong accent that it was Maria, and she felt her body tense.

"He's not in," she said, swallowing a bite of the sandwich.

"Well, where is he?" Maria asked.

"There's no telling. Out, I suppose."

"Well then, I need you to make a deposit at the bank," Maria said. "I had some furniture delivered and I need to send a check."

"Okay, but I can't leave until he gets here. I'm the only one out here."

Another pause. "Is this Prudence?"

"Yes."

"Well Prudence, I will need this taken care of today. Not tomorrow. Today. When he comes in, you go right to the bank, okay?" Maria cleared her throat. "And I hear you are quite a star. With your driving and your pictures in the papers."

Prudence paused, unprepared for Maria's cordial tone. "Why yes, I suppose."

"That is good. Very good for you," Maria said, a sudden warmth flooding her voice. "But Prudence, maybe you don't think I'm so smart, because I don't-a speak-a English a-so good," she mocked. "But then you do not speak my language, do you?"

"No," Prudence mustered, leaning back in her chair.

"And so you do not know who he is, or where we come from. I will tell you that he and Charlie are all I have, and we are all he has. So I will have to stop this racing of yours if I need to. I only allow this because if I tell him to stop, he will just keep going. That is the kind of man he is. So I wait, because I know he will tire of this soon. Do you understand? I want to be sure that you do. You are very young. And when you are young you don't understand these things. How people can hurt you."

Prudence held the receiver close to hear hearing aid, the sound of her own breath coming through it. Her heartbeat tapping against the hard Bakelite earpiece.

"Good," Maria said. "You are listening. So I will tell you this one last thing. I am not a stupid woman. I am very proud. So. If you ever try and take advantage of him in any way, I will come and I will find you. Because if you hurt Charles, you hurt his family. Do you understand?"

"Yes," Prudence said, biting her fingernail.

"Good. Now don't forget about the bank."

At that Prudence heard a click, then the line went dead. She held the receiver a moment before she set it down and stared at it, sucking in her breath. Maria's voice continued to play in her mind, and with it, the feeling that she'd just committed a crime. Prudence pressed her hands to her face, shaking her head. Perhaps Maria was a good wife after all. But then, something about her warm tone felt off. After a minute she stood and looked into Charles's dark office. She scanned the showroom, then slipped her key from her desk drawer, went and unlocked his office door and flipped on the light.

She looked at the ashtray, full of butts, the pictures of Charles on the wall, the trophies, the Bible on the desk. She stepped inside, her pulse quickening, and went and fitted the key into the lockbox that sat on a shelf under a stack of papers. She opened it and counted out only a few hundred dollars. He hadn't prepared any deposit forms for her as he usually did each week, and she opened the top drawer of his desk to see if he'd misplaced them. There, she found a large burgundy book with Bank of America embossed on it. She looked out into the showroom before she pulled it from the drawer and clutched it to her chest, turned off the light and closed the office door behind her.

She sat at her desk and began pouring over the statements, which were both for his personal and business accounts, written in his own careful pen. It took her only a minute to find that, as she'd often suspected, Charles was over-extended financially. There were checks paid to European accounts for thousands of dollars. And although large sales came in to the shop regularly, she saw that Maria was constantly making lavish purchases that offset his profits. She saw checks written in her name to jewelers, hi-tone clothing shops, and dozens of swanky furniture stores throughout the city.

Prudence shook her head, realizing that Maria was running Charles and his business into the ground. Maria's voice played again, proud and righteous, and the guilt Prudence felt vanished. Maria was the one taking advantage and committing the crimes. And if she had truly given Charles what he needed, then he never would have bothered with her or her racing career.

Prudence lit a cigarette, her fingers trembling as she drew from it, as she reviewed his earnings as her manager. It was the only place where he'd come out on top, and it was clear, that he needed her as much as she needed him.

She exhaled and flipped to the last pages of the book, where she came to the payroll forms. She saw Rudy's paychecks, which far exceeded what anyone else made. After she returned the bank book to Charles's desk, she looked out through the showroom windows, into the garage. Rudy was underneath a Ferrari on a lift, twisting his wiry body, his face wrinkling as he fitted his wrench to its exhaust and yanked on it.

In her dealing with him in the past, Rudy had insinuated that she was getting by on her looks, that she wasn't a real driver, or appreciative of a good mechanic. He'd pinned her as the type who only offered themselves to men who could do something for them. Prudence decided, as she looked at him slinking around the garage, that she hated everything about him. Most of all, she hated that he'd be in the car with her during the race in Mexico, to navigate and fix the car if something broke.

Rudy stopped working when he noticed her sitting there, watching him. He grinned and held her in his stare as he stood beneath the car, rubbing the grease from the wrench. Even as Charles walked in the door, smiling, twirling a set of car keys around his finger, Rudy stood there, grinning at her.

THAT EVENING at the apartment, Prudence soaked in a hot bath while reading the *San Francisco Bee*. A photo of her appeared in the sports section from a recent race at Torrey Pines. The caption above it read, *Baylor Lands Big Sponsor*. She scanned the article, which noted that *Crèma Nivea* would sponsor her in the *Carrera Panamericana* in Mexico, a deal Charles had recently negotiated. The reporter, the same young one who'd snapped her picture at her first race, seemed to have secured a role covering all the races. He speculated that this race would decide if Prudence was a real driver, or just the novelty so many predicted she would be.

Prudence tossed the paper aside. She dried her hands with a towel and lit a cigarette and lay there in the steaming bath. Her hearing aid sat on the sink, and she could only faintly hear the sound of traffic outside, hollow and distant. She tapped the ash from the cigarette into the soap dish, feeling naked without the earpiece in her ear, but knowing that this would be the last of the quiet for a long time.

After her bath, as she stood drying herself with a fresh towel, she heard a soft noise. She stood there, listening. Again came the faint sound of the door buzzer. She grabbed her hearing aid, threw on her robe and went to the front door and drew the chain. Charles was standing in the hallway, and he puffed madly at his cigarette as she let him in. He hung his hat on the rack and straightened his hair.

He paced around the room as she fitted her hearing aid, set the battery box in her robe's deep pocket. She thought he was here for another of their evening love making sessions before he went home, but as he continued to pace, she knew something else was on his mind.

"This came today, registered mail." He sat on the edge of the sofa, pulled a manila envelope from his coat pocket and handed it to her.

Prudence looked at him as she took it and removed its contents. A letter typed on a sheet of green paper, an artichoke stamped in the corner in gold leaf. She read it quickly, then looked out the windows.

It was still foggy outside and through the telephone lines the sky was the color of milk spilled on a piece of glass.

It was an invitation for her to appear at a festival in Castroville, a small farming town a hundred miles south of the city. She'd submitted her photo and application a month before and had completely forgotten about it. The gig offered over four hundred dollars, more than she'd made at all her other personal appearances combined. Prudence knew she had to accept, that the exposure would be good for her.

"You know who was the first to wear that crown?" Charles asked. "Marilyn Monroe. Before she was big." He crushed his cigarette in an ashtray on the end table. "And they picked you because people know you. People will come to see you."

He unfolded a copy of the *San Francisco Bee* that he had tucked under his arm, folded to the same article she'd been reading earlier. The photo of her posed on the hood of her Porsche, her long hair flowing from the back of her race helmet. "Put these two together," he said, holding the invitation up with the newspaper, "and we've got something good."

Prudence held the straps of her robe. The weight of the battery box in her pocket had drawn it open and she saw her bare skin was exposed from her ankle to her neck. When she looked at Charles she saw that he hadn't failed to notice.

"Appearing at a high school football game is one thing, but this, I don't know," she said, drawing the robe tightly closed again. "I'm not sure they've got the right girl. I'm not a Marilyn Monroe."

"Look, Prudence, the timing is perfect. We'll leave a day early, drive down, do the fair on Saturday, be on the road to Mexico the next day." He set the invitation and paper on the coffee table. "I have everything taken care of at the shop while we're away. This is the big time."

Prudence blinked. The soft white light shining through the windows made it hard to concentrate and she went to let down the blinds. As she did, an ice truck rumbled down the street, a man her age hanging on the back, his clothes wet and dirty. She turned and looked at Charles.

"The big time," she repeated, mimicking Marilyn Monroe's breathless voice. She laughed and covered her face with her hand, shaking her head. She couldn't picture herself as a beauty queen any better than she could imagine herself racing across the length of Mexico in a German race car.

He pulled a check from his pocket. "They sent an advance." He handed it to her. "Two hundred dollars."

She took the check and sat on the sofa beside him.

"There's nothing wrong with showing a little leg if it helps you do something you want. You're pretty, so why not take advantage of it?"

"You don't have to sell the idea to me. The offer is here, and I have to do it." She looked at him. "We need the money."

He looked away as she set the check on the table.

"I just want to be taken seriously. I don't want to be their pin-up."

"You are being taken seriously. That's why they chose you."

Suddenly that dull, insistent pain returned to her stomach. She winced and waited for it to pass as usual, but this time it didn't. She excused herself, stood and went to the bathroom, shutting the door behind her. She grabbed the sink and looked into the mirror, her face sallow and washed out, feeling cold and hot at the same time, the sting of bile in her throat.

She splashed some water on her face and sat on the edge of the

Owen Duffy

tub until the feeling passed. She came from the bathroom and heard the bay out the open windows, as if hearing it for the first time. The broad windows offered the bridges' silhouettes, the lit up wharf and the noises down the street. An old, dirty bar that played cocktail jazz into the night. Standing there, she could smell the beer and smoke, hear the laughter.

"I'll do it," she said, still gazing out the window. "That Porsche cost me a pretty penny."

"Don't worry about money," he said. "You'll make plenty if you do well. I'll pay my own way, and Rudy owes me some favors. I've got the salesmen covering things at work while we're gone."

"If I do well, you know I'd give you all of it. But I have my own debts."

She turned from the window and looked at Charles, sitting there patiently, nodding because he knew just how she felt. In her way, she really did love him. She loved him because she understood him and saw past what everyone else saw, even Maria, down to what lay beneath: a man caught in the dissatisfaction and compromises of his own life. And she knew that he had given his time and money to help her despite the fact that he was nearly broke. As she watched him stand and put on his hat, slipping his cigarettes into his coat pocket, he looked lovably pitiful.

After she kissed him and he went out the door, she promised herself she'd forget how ill she felt lately. How she had missed her monthly cycle, which was always regular. She fell asleep on the damp bedsheets with the sounds of street life below, but awakened in the middle of the night with a hard rain beating against the windows, and knew that she wouldn't be able to forget about it at all.

She was pregnant. She knew it more clearly that she'd known anything, the way a person knew when they'd broken a bone. She must be over a month along, counting off from the first time she and Charles had been together. She covered her face with her hands and began to cry. She looked up at the ceiling and knew that if she told Charles, he'd feel trapped and think that she'd tricked him. That she had done this on purpose, despite his attempts to be careful in his lovemaking methods.

Prudence knew she couldn't have the child, that it would ruin everything for both of them: her career, her image, their relationship. That she would have to have that procedure like all those irresponsible girls she'd known back in college. Abide by the woman's code that dictated it as a necessity of life. She'd always hated those girls for throwing a life away for their own good.

As she lay there, an image came to Prudence, of a large eye out her bedroom window, looking in. Yellow and glistening, worms crawling across it. That same earthen creature that had been following her, its breath now fogging the glass. The eye scanned the small, unadorned room and the twisted sheets on the bed, the woman lying atop it. Alone and shaking. Then the eye blinked and pulled away, as if satisfied that soon she would be ready, and at last he could be fed.

Two weeks later, just before she, Charles and Rudy left for their trip to Castroville and then on to Mexico, Prudence awoke feeling nauseated yet again. As she was making coffee, she ran and wretched in the bathroom. She cleaned herself up, then came and sat at the kitchen table, looking out the window to steady herself. Rain speckled the glass as she stared at the building across the way, its windows illuminated by lamplight, the sizzle of tires in the street as cars passed by.

Although it was just past eight in the morning, she heard Vi stirring in her room. Prudence sat up straight in her chair, busying herself by completing the itinerary she intended to leave for Vi. It had been nearly a week since they'd crossed paths long enough to exchange more than a few words. As Prudence watched Vi's bedroom door slowly open, she felt her blood surging because she knew she had to tell her that she was pregnant, and Vi wasn't going to take the news easily.

Vi came from her room with a cigarette dangling from her lips, her kimono sash trailing behind her. She stopped and looked at Prudence a moment, then went into the kitchen. She continued to glance at Prudence while she poured them both a cup of the dark coffee, then sat across the table from her, crossing her bare legs.

The only sounds in the room were the rain hitting the window, the percolator quietly burping steam. Prudence looked down at the two steaming cups of coffee.

"I'm headed down to Mexico in a few days," Prudence began, breaking the silence. "Yes ma'am. Big race down there. Big money. And I need it. I couldn't quit now if I wanted to."

Vi took a sip of her coffee, returned it to its saucer. "Do you want to quit?"

"No." Prudence smirked. "Hell no."

"Seems like you've been doing pretty well," Vi said. "I like that photo in last Sunday's paper. The one of you on the hood of that new silver car you have. Very sexy."

Prudence smiled, pleased that Vi had been watching in the papers for her. "Yeah, that's the picture they all use." She glanced up at Vi and then back at the peeling linoleum. "We're going to Europe after this for some more big races. I wish you would come with me."

Vi stubbed her cigarette out in the ashtray but didn't answer.

"I meant," Prudence said, leaning back in her chair, "that you could get out of here if you wanted. See some place new."

"What's wrong with here?" Vi asked. "And I've seen Paris. What else is there?"

Prudence glanced at the easels, the half-finished paintings. Brushes sitting in paint thinner, rings in the jar where some of it had evaporated.

"I meant that you might get inspired again if you had a change of scenery."

"I don't need someplace new." Vi crossed her arms. "I'm perfectly happy here."

Prudence picked up her spoon and stirred her coffee, the silence returning, as if neither of them wanted to talk about what had awakened them both.

"Not that long ago you were a girl fresh off a bus," Vi said, looking at her.

Prudence nodded slowly. "A lot has changed since then."

"It has," Vi said. "It has."

Prudence's pulse felt hard and insistent, her tongue dry, even as she sipped the coffee. She held it in her mouth a moment before letting it trickle down her throat.

Vi narrowed her eyes at her. "What do you want to tell me, Prudence?"

Prudence cleared her throat, opened her mouth, but didn't say anything. She knew it was useless to speak, as the truth was already being unburdened by her face.

"Well that didn't take long," Vi said. "Are you sure that's what it is?

"I'm sure in the all the ways you're supposed to know. All the usual signs." Prudence set her coffee cup down in its saucer and put her hand to her forehead. "He's not going to leave her, Vi. At least I don't think he will. She'd probably just turn a blind eye to all this."

"Is that all you're worried about?"

"I knew you'd be this way. Things just happened and I'm not proud of it."

Vi tamped a fresh cigarette on her thumbnail. "This isn't the first time this has happened to a girl that's worked for me. This is why girls always quit at the club." She lit the cigarette and blew smoke at the ceiling. "I just thought you were better than them."

"Well, it's not going to be a problem for long. I'm going to get it taken care of," Prudence said. "But it's going to have to wait until I get back."

"You're not going to do that," Vi said. "And you know it too."

"Well, I know one thing for certain. Things are moving even faster than I can keep up with them." Prudence looked out at the building across the way again, watching shadows moving in the lighted windows. "All I can tell you right now for sure is that I don't want to leave here. I would just give anything not to go down to Mexico."

II

Nine

Prudence studied the photograph of Marilyn Monroe that hung in the civic building, in a trophy case, where any visitor was sure to see it. She imagined farmers removing their hats as they entered the building, lost for a moment in the photo. Heading into drab offices to discuss irrigation access, acreage disputes, county spillways. Men who had arrived in battered trucks, carrying legal documents to be signed, copied, in triplicate. *Marilyn Monroe,* they probably mumbled as they climbed the stairway, wiping their dusty faces with a handkerchief. *I'll be damned.*

Marilyn appeared younger in the picture, her hair famously blonde, her skin almost platinum. She was standing in the back of a pickup truck, waving as she was paraded through Castroville. Flash bulbs threw her faint shadow on the men gazing up at her from the street, wearing Levi jackets and crumpled hats. The soft curve of her breasts, the thin waistline. Her frantic smile, as if she was waving at someone she hadn't seen in years, far off in the crowd.

Prudence stared at herself in the mirrored backing of the trophy case. She was no Marilyn Monroe, but perhaps she looked the part of the wholesome small-town girl who'd made it out. She had carefully cultivated her look for the occasion. She washed and curled her hair that morning, and it now fell full and shining on her bare shoulders. She had chosen a sleeveless green chiffon dress, which fell below her knee, and accentuated her eyes.

She freshened her orange tinted lipstick and smacked her lips in the mirror. But as she stared at herself, her smiled dimmed. At times she nearly forgot she was pregnant, that she really wasn't all that wholesome. She dropped the lipstick back in her purse, the hearing aid battery filling most of it, and snapped it closed.

Prudence turned and looked out the glass doors facing the main street, where in two hours the parade would begin. Her stomach fluttered as she looked at the banner that hung loosely across the street between two lamp poles. It read: *"Castroville Artichoke Festival 1954: The Artichoke Capital of the World!"* A group of men stood beneath it, investors and local officials, clapping as the workers pulled the banner taut.

Charles had instructed her to keep her interactions with these men short and succinct. *Don't be your usual sullen self,* he had said. *Perk up. Bullshit a little. And don't bite anyone's head off if they pinch your ass.*

He and Rudy were having breakfast in a café across the street, as the town officials didn't want anyone laying claim to her today. They wanted her to appear *available.*

The town mayor, whom she'd met earlier, opened the doors and waved the group of men inside. They removed their fedoras as they entered, looked up at the winding suspended staircase, the balcony and the elk horn chandelier. The lobby walls were wood paneled, the linoleum tiles polished to a high shine. They stopped when they saw Prudence, standing there in the lobby. The men coughed in closed fists and rattled the change in their pockets, eying her hearing aid. A phone was ringing off in the recesses of the building and no one answered.

"Gather round," the mayor said, leading the group towards the trophy case. He came and stood beside her, blocking the photo from view. He was a small, middle-aged man in a faded flannel suit. He patted down his toupee and smiled at Prudence.

"Gentlemen," the mayor said, raising his arms. "Today is an

important one for you and for Castroville. As the number one producer of a particular vegetable, this fair brings our town much deserved attention in the region and the world at large."

He continued in the same fashion, seemingly the type of man who didn't waste a chance to give a speech. A man who might've been the first to raise his glass at a dinner party and give a toast. The kind where his chin would repeatedly tuck into his neck, as if he either had indigestion, or an important message to convey.

After his speech, some of the men introduced themselves. They asked Prudence about her racing career, and when she answered, they nodded as if she was a child who'd just boasted that she could fly.

"Come see," one of the men then said, resting his hand on the small of her back and ushering her away from the crowd. He led her over to a photograph of the town's largest artichoke, hanging on the lobby wall. A grotesque, misshapen thing. Lumpy in the wrong places, the top most fronds the size of arrowheads. Prudence wondered if artichokes grew on trees or if they came from the ground. She didn't want to ask, have to smell his sour breath as he answered. She believed an artichoke was a legume. She liked that word suddenly: *legume*. The sound of it in her mind. A rooty vegetable, plump, and full of seed. The vine anchoring it to the earth. A small ensnarled thing.

She gazed at the humble wooden placard hanging beside the photo of the artichoke. Small brass plates were tacked to it, inscribed with the names of the past queens. Prudence didn't recognize any of the names besides Marilyn Monroe's. She wondered the careers they went on to, what became of them. She hoped they had gone on to great things. But whatever they had achieved, she knew that they had all, no doubt, never passed through town again.

Only a few minutes later, the men stood Prudence in the parking lot for the grand opening of a new *Giant Artichoke* supermarket. The asphalt there was fresh, soft as a sugar cookie. The mayor's wife took the crown from a hat box and pushed it into Prudence's hair. A golden tiara with metal artichokes suspended by wires. There was a speech and a ribbon to cut, and the supermarket owner handed Prudence a pair of scissors. *Don't cut it yet, Honey*, someone said, and a photographer bent on one knee to capture the moment, the ribbon in the scissor's blades.

Above, the November sun burned like a hole punched in the sky. Her feet hurt and the crown pinched at her scalp. She noticed that Charles had returned from breakfast and was sneaking through the spectators lining the parking lot. He came through them and stood beside her a moment, their shoulders touching as he secretly clasped her hand and squeezed it. Prudence smiled as he then moved unnoticed back into the crowd.

"You're really pretty," a girl said a moment later. Prudence looked down and saw her standing between three little girls, all of them wearing gingham dresses, their hair neatly ribboned. Prudence suddenly felt tears in her eyes, and didn't know why. She bent down beside the girls and resisted the strange urge to wrap her arms around them and pull them to her.

"Can we take a picture with you?" one of the girls asked in a sweet, country accent. She produced a Brownie camera and called for her mother, who came and wound it and held them all in the viewfinder. Prudence crouched between them and smiled.

"Do you really race cars?" one girl asked afterwards. "That's what the paper says but my mom doesn't believe it."

"I sure do, and I'm going to win my next race just for you three," Prudence said and the girl smiled. Prudence noticed the girl's little brown shoes, the white frilly socks. One of the shoes was unbuckled and as Prudence bent to fix it, her mother came and pulled the girl's arm and they all disappeared into the crowd.

Prudence was then returned to the civic building in a long black convertible Cadillac. She was led down into the basement into a boiler room that had been converted into a makeshift dressing room. People rushed in and out as she sat in a wooden folding chair with her legs crossed, nibbling some crackers that had been spilled out on a tray. She waited for someone to tell her what was expected of her, and realized after a half-hour passed, that no one knew.

Members of a western band strolled by in the hall wearing fringe jackets and cowboy hats, carrying fiddles, guitars, banjos. They wore red cowboy shirts and had white bandanas tied around their necks, the back of their sequined jackets reading: *Golden Flour's Crisp Crust Doughboys.*

The band leader, a tall and unhealthily thin man, came and sat beside her, removed his hat and set it on his knee. He looked no more than twenty-five, but his face was deeply lined and his hair was thin and patchy up top. His suit jacket had a musical staff and notes running along the sleeves and he reached inside it and offered her a cigarette from his pack of Camels.

He struck a match on his thumb and lit their cigarettes, leaned back in his chair and crossed his bony legs at the knee. "Boy," he said in a calm, deep drawl, "I'll be damned if anyone can tell me where I need to be."

"I was hoping someone would come along and tell me," Prudence said.

"Well, it's a mystery then." He sipped from a paper cup that he'd set by his feet, filled with a brown liquid that smelled like whiskey.

Prudence watched the people running through the halls, their anxiety becoming her own. Everything had been moving so fast all morning, and she knew that it wouldn't let up until the race down in Mexico was over. She closed her eyes and took a few deep breaths.

"You aren't scared, are you?" the singer asked, looking over at her. "Of this little country fair?"

Prudence looked at him, his nearly skeletal face and body. She wanted to confess to him that she was terrified of all that awaited her. She wanted to tell this complete stranger how she felt, but she figured that he could read it all on her face.

He chuckled and nodded at her. "They'd grind you up and sell you for dog food if there was more money in it, wouldn't they," he said. His expression turned grim and he leveled his eyes at her. "Just don't let them buy that part of you that ain't for sale."

She looked at him more closely, not sure what she was really seeing. He was young but he seemed ancient inside. He looked right back at her, sucked at the wet end of his cigarette and dusted off his red, tooled leather boots.

"Lefty Whitman," he said, holding out a long, thin hand.

As she shook it, his name was called from far down the hall. He tossed back the rest of his whiskey, dropped his cigarette in the paper cup and set it on the cookie tray.

"That's the boss man." He stood and looked down at her. "I'll see you out there, Darling. And remember what I said now."

He walked out the door and Prudence sat there in the empty room, picturing being ground up like dog food and sold in paper sacks. The image struck her as funny for some reason, and she was cackling when a woman in a blue dress came in the room, towing a fat man dressed entirely in denim. The woman stared at Prudence until she stopped laughing, then explained that they would be the ones bringing her to the stage. That the man would drive the truck she would be riding on. As Prudence sat and listened, she heard fiddles tuning up in the hall, the squeak of tuning keys as the strings were pulled to pitch.

Prudence lost the melody of the woman's voice, drawn to the sound of bows across the strings. The fiddlers warmed up by playing a reel, and she felt the knitting of the notes, and imagined the way the sun would feel as she stood on stage in front of a few thousand people, all of them looking up at her. She could already hear them out the doorway, cheering in anticipation, the sound of the public address system being tested.

A balloon popped in the hallway and Prudence jumped in her seat. She turned and looked back at the woman, then turned down her hearing aid. She couldn't speak if she wanted to, as it felt like her mouth had been swabbed in felt. She looked down at the piece of paper in her purse. A little speech she'd prepared for later, a string of meaningless niceties. The kind of speech Marilyn Monroe had likely given.

"You hear me?" the woman in the blue dress said. "Prudence?"

Prudence blinked. The woman was bent over, her eyes deep brown and below her chin a cross dangling from a silver thread. And farther, out of focus, the dark inside of her dress, pale breasts netted with blue veins. And down the hallway, the sound of a frenzied crowd and a man yelling into a microphone, the sound of exploding firecrackers in the distant alleyways.

"Prudence?" The woman touched her arm. "You ready?"

Prudence followed electrical power cords that wound through the hallway. They led out a side door, where the Western band was performing on stage. Prudence blotted her forehead with a tissue.

Blinked at the stage's rough hewn pine, the sun beating down on it, releasing a sickening resin scent. Sawdust bounced on the stage as the singer yodeled into the microphone, his long fingers fretting his guitar, *Lefty Whitman* inlayed across the fretboard. Their frilly stage clothes snapped in rhythm and the chrome microphone rocked on its stand. The speakers rattled on the chairs behind them, booming an electric sound down the main street.

When the song ended, Prudence realized that her trembling wasn't from the music or the heat or the excitement. Her nervousness was so great that she was physically quivering, as if a hand was inside her stomach, fiddling with her guts. She stood there aching for another ten minutes while a member of the Rotary Club gave a tiring speech, then as local Eagle Scouts and the Farmers Growers Association followed.

Her nose itched, her eyes burned as motes of pollen floated in the sunlight. The band played another number and then the woman in the blue dress appeared again and snatched her hand. Together they ascended the wooden steps and Prudence looked out at a thousand sunlit faces, hands shading their eyes, fans fluttering. Prudence walked to the center of the stage and planted her heels beside where the mayor stood adjusting the microphone.

The applause died and everything was quiet, save for a faint, persistent ringing through the speakers. Charles waved to her from the opposite side of the stage, Rudy standing beside him. Prudence felt as if she was detached from her own body, looking over her own shoulder at the faces gawking up at her, as the mayor repeated his speech from earlier that morning, eliciting enthusiastic applause from the crowd.

As he finished, the crowd whistled and cheered. They were so close she could feel the heat of them. Men in dusty hats, women in plaid cotton dresses. She looked down the main street at the people lining the sidewalks, waiting for the parade to begin. A fire truck idled in the shadows of a nearby building. A white convertible sat beside it, a man sitting on the rear deck lid, adjusting the banners that draped from its doors. Beyond, the buildings thinned and a haze rose off the artichoke fields.

"Such a wonderful day," the mayor continued, grasping the microphone, "to celebrate another wonderful year. And we have the people of Castroville, the Artichoke Capital of the World, to thank for it." He leaned back on his heels, enjoying another wave of applause. After a while, he raised his hands to quiet the crowd and spoke in a deeper tone. "Now, I am delighted to present this year's, nineteen-fifty-four, Artichoke Queen. You know her, she's that gal who's racing her way up in the world." He held out his hand to introduce her. "Miss Prudence Baylor!"

The mayor's wife handed Prudence an armful of yellow roses. Prudence took them and stepped towards the microphone with her speech in her hand.

"Thank you," she mustered into the microphone, looking down at the scrap of paper. As she tried to continue, a loud boom sounded from the side of the stage. The flatbed truck that was parked there to parade her down the main street had backfired. The crowd went silent as the sound reverberated through the public address system.

Prudence blushed and eyed the quiet crowd, the sun hot on her cheeks. She looked down at her speech and leaned over the microphone.

"I'm very happy to be here today," she began. "I never would have dreamed I would be standing here in front of all you nice people. I know some of you may know me from the papers, and some of you are just hoping that girl up there on stage isn't a talker.

So I'll be short."

She looked up and saw the crowd staring back at her.

"They didn't really want me racing cars at all when I first started. You know what they say about women drivers. And I suppose the men didn't want to be beaten by one."

A murmur of laughter rippled through the crowd.

"Well, I'm not used to having such a warm reception as I've gotten here today, out on the racetrack. But I think that might change soon. And I hope that I've made it a bit easier for the next girl who comes along, to do whatever it is she wants to do. So I want to thank the people of Castroville for recognizing that, and for having me out here today."

Already the mayor was at her side, pulling at her arm. The flatbed truck grunted to life again, long ribbons of red, white and blue tinsel dangling from its bed. Several men stepped off it and began ushering her from the stage.

"Thank you," she said into the microphone, blowing a kiss at the crowd. She heard an unexpected burst of applause as the men helped her onto the wood paneled flatbed.

As the band struck into another tune, the truck lurched from the stage. She fought to keep her balance while she continued to wave, giving her best impression of a beauty queen. While the crowd whistled and cheered, the truck joined the formation heading down the main street.

The parade's theme was Pioneer Years, and starting it off was a herd of cattle led by ranch hands on horses. A fourteen-mule jerk team followed, driven by a cowboy on a rickety wooden wagon. Behind them was a line of antique farming equipment, tractors with metal wheels, rolling through the clumps of manure littering the street. Then a Quota Club float covered in crepe paper artichokes.

The big truck plodded behind them all. She gazed at the policemen standing with their ties tucked into their shirts, the boys in their Davy Crockett outfits, waving little American flags. As the fireworks burst and popped in the air she waved at the women standing beside their husbands, beaming up at her.

Ten

THE NEXT morning, she watched through the window as they surged southward in the Chevy through Salinas, then Paso Robles. Faded wooden billboards pointed to nearby hot springs and mineral baths, touting their restorative powers, and promising to heal any ailment. As they drove on, Prudence felt the sweet sensation of forward motion, of moving quickly through wide open spaces. She watched the road markers as the miles fell away to the Mexican border: three hundred, two hundred, one hundred. She sat in the back seat with maps and race pamphlets fluttering in the wind. It would be like this all the way to the southern tip of Mexico, five days of driving along the Panamerican Highway, nearly two thousand miles. Over high arid mountains, sharp plateaus, and into low desert valleys.

Castroville already felt like a dream as they passed by Bakersfield. Those rows of people gazing up at her, the warm feeling of adulation they'd given her. She was sunburned from the parade and the festival that followed, where she'd walked through the crowds with women running up and shaking her hand for what she'd said during her speech. And that night, two hundred dollars cash placed in her hand, Charles telling her that she'd finally made it, that this was how it was going to be from now on.

And so, over dinner at a roadside cantina that evening, Prudence bought the beers. After they'd had a few, Charles reminded her that Rudy would be in her race car as a navigator. He assured her it was common practice to have a co-pilot during road races. She had wished it would be Charles who would be with her, but Prudence knew that she'd need Rudy in case of mechanical issues, and to guide her along the road.

The waitress came and set huge steaming plates of rice and beans and tortillas on the table. The beans were salty and good, and she scooped them up in her soft tortilla, hungry for the first time in days. She washed them down with the cold beer and when her plate was clear she sat back and smoked a cigarette down until it burnt her fingers.

As they left the cantina and pulled back on the highway, the car jerking with the weight of their new enclosed trailer behind them, Prudence felt a wave of nausea, more abrupt and threatening than ever before. She clenched her stomach as long as she could, but soon felt the bile rising in her throat, the cold sweat on her temples. She quickly stuck her head out the window and purged, her stomach muscles clenching again and again, hurling her dinner onto the road.

"You okay?" Charles said, slowing the wagon and pulling over to the shoulder.

Prudence propped herself against the door frame, her body chilly and her hands numb. "I'm fine. It's okay," she said as she wiped her mouth with a handkerchief. "I guess I'm not used to that kind of food."

His eyes flashed at her in the rear-view mirror, then he pulled back onto the highway. "If I see a place to stop we'll get you a soda pop."

"Don't worry about it. I'm fine. It was just something I ate." Prudence sank back in the seat as Charles looked at her again in the mirror. She knew that he'd seen a woman with morning sickness before. She wouldn't be able to hide her condition much longer, and when she returned to California she'd have to decide what she wanted to do.

As she sat there trembling, she reminded herself that if she finished the race in Mexico she would be the first woman to have done so. She knew she'd have to make sacrifices in her career, and yet that same forward tumbling sensation overtook her as they drove, its momentum so powerful now that it felt as if she no longer had control. As if she'd dipped her toe in a river and was taken underwater and pulled downstream. She suddenly heard the words of that singer at the festival: *Don't let them buy the part of you that ain't for sale.*

She distracted herself by studying the race maps. The race began on the southern tip of Mexico, in Tuxtla Gutierrez, and would end four days later in Juarez, along the Texas border. The race was cut into eight individual sections, with each driver departing the starting line at one minute intervals from one another. It wasn't the first driver to the finish these sections of the highway who won; it was the driver with the shortest overall time who won.

She then studied the permitted size and ply of tires, grades of gasoline. She read warnings about the poor quality of Mexican fuels, and then the designation of each class of car that could enter the race.

She had picked the Porsche because its engine put her in the smallest engine class, which would be filled with amateur drivers. She had reasoned, since anyone could enter *La Carrera Panamericana*, that most of the other drivers in this class would be those who could only afford an old Austin Healey or an outdated Jaguar; cars her modern Porsche would easily outmatch.

She noted that the larger stock classes were for the big American cars: Chryslers, Cadillacs, Lincolns and Mercurys, most of them sent down from car dealerships to drum up business. Above this group was the sport class of Alfa Romeos, Ferraris, Maseratis, and Mercedes sent by their factories, accompanied by professional race teams. The faster car classes would begin each leg of the race, long before the other slower classes were released, so there wouldn't be any race traffic.

THEY ARRIVED at the Mexican border the following morning at dawn. A row of gatehouses and Mexican officers with rifles, searching through the line of waiting vehicles. Prudence watched their twitching eyes as children wandered between the cars selling marionettes and chewing gum. She took a penny from her purse and gave it to one of the children and suddenly there were a dozen small hands being held out for her change. When it was all gone she gave them her mints and her own chewing gum, until there was nothing left to give.

She looked at the other cars, the bulging canvas water bags strapped to their rear bumpers, prepared for the journey into the hot, dry desert. The evaporative air conditioning canisters mounted in their passenger windows, big cylindrical tubes filled with water to cool the cars as they drove.

After a half-hour of the officials holding everyone up, Charles got out of the wagon, leaving the engine running.

"Where are you going?" Prudence asked.

"I'll be right back," he said. She held her breath as he shut the door and limped up to the gatehouse and knocked on the door. When the door opened, he disappeared inside. When he came out a few minutes later he was carrying their papers, the Mexican official in tow.

He got in the car, shook a cigarette from his pack and lit it. "I gave them some money," he said, and looked back over the seat at her. "This place is not like America. If you get in a fender bender, they lock you up in jail. Guilty until proven innocent." He pulled out a few large bills and handed them to her and to Rudy. "Keep these with you. American money will buy your way out of a tough spot."

Prudence looked at him, then took the money and stuffed it in her pocket. She turned again and gazed out the back window a moment. Perhaps Mexico *was* as she imagined it, the way it was depicted in the movies, as lawless and corrupt. Those border officials had held them up, no different than a grimy pack of banditos.

She stared ahead at the road. The red, barren desert was so flat it made it appear as if they were driving down into the earth. Prudence watched old women walking along the road, their eyes like olive pits, their faces like dried gourds. Their filthy robes and eagle feathers dangling from their ears. Children beside them, shirtless, black hair falling past their shoulders, their mouths rimmed with the dirt they'd been eating.

"I've heard about them. Those are the brujas," Charles said, looking straight ahead. "Clans of Mexican witches."

"Oh please," Prudence said to him, but felt a chill pass through her as they slowly passed them by. She stared at their knotted, spotted hands, and then into the women's sunken eyes. The women stared back and spread their toothless mouths at her. Prudence looked away and leaned back in the seat. Soon she saw a slow rising mound of land, and beyond it the burnt red mountains, but they were so far away they never seemed to get any closer to them.

They arrived in Tuxtla Gutierrez, the southern tip of Mexico, early on the fifth day. The banners hanging across the highway welcomed the arriving racers, a sea of them suddenly appearing in their windshield. Small airplanes passed overhead as they wound through the center of town. Sandy streets, white buildings with dark, square openings for doors and windows. Charles nudged the wagon through the crowds of deeply brown-skinned people, dressed in dirty, ragged clothing. Carrying baskets filled with fruit and grain, or pulling carts filled with caged fowl.

Prudence brushed her wind-tousled hair and slipped on a fresh outfit as Rudy sat stealing glances at her over the seat. He'd been doing that a lot lately, leering at her or trying to surprise her in the enclosed trailer when she was dressing, standing there in front of her mirror, the battery powered light bulb hanging from a string above her head. She'd known perverts her whole life, and she was convinced he was one. She shot him a hard look and he turned around.

When they reached the designated central meeting point for all the race entrants, a large parking lot filled with cars, she stepped from the wagon and saw that she was the only woman there. Her pulse quickened as she looked around. Already there were reporters gathering around the professional racers but they all turned towards Prudence when they noticed her. She stood there in her bright red blouse, gathering her hair into a pony tail. Her blue jeans were still neatly tapered and creased, her Keds stark white against the blacktop.

As Rudy backed her Porsche out of the trailer the photographers began snapping pictures. Prudence smiled at the cameras and leaned against the door and spread her hands beside her, where her name was stenciled in red letters. Looking past the reporters, she felt pristine, the only person in the parking lot not covered in dust.

"Well, that's it for now," Charles said to the photographers after a few minutes. "If you have any special requests for press information or any other material," he added as he dispensed a few promotional cards he'd had made of her, "we'll be doing an interview in Juarez when the race is over. We know that so many people are rooting for Prudence, and we thank them for their support."

Some of the photographers looked at the card Charles handed

them, then at Prudence, shook their heads and walked away, as if disappointed.

"What was that all about?" she asked.

"I have no idea. Come, let's get in the shade," Charles said. He took her by the arm and led her under a grove of trees by the edge of the lot as another group of photographers arrived.

"Silvia," one of the photographers called to her. Then another man called her the same name.

"Who?" Prudence shot them a look over her shoulder. "Who is he talking to, Charles?"

"You are Silvia de Lobos?" the reporter asked her, coming closer.

"No," Prudence turned, hands on her hips. "Who's that?"

The reporter turned and left as quickly as the others had. Charles shrugged at the only one who remained, a face Prudence had seen somewhere before. As she looked at him more closely she realized he was the young reporter from San Francisco who'd been at her first race. The one now covering all the California races. He was younger looking than she remembered, and overdressed for the climate in a heavy brown suit.

Prudence smiled at him. "Well, you've certainly come a long way."

"So have you," he said, grinning. He lifted his hat and wiped his forehead with his sleeve. "The damn heat down here."

Prudence looked up at the blaring sun, then pulled the reporter under the shade of the tree with her and Charles. "So what's all of this about a Silvia woman? Why do they think I'm her?"

"Because they see a woman and just assume it can only be her," the reporter said, looking at her, his eyes a deep brown. "She's the big deal in the race around here and she's not shy with the press, believe me. She's a showboat if there ever was one. Polka dots on her race suit and on her car too."

He put his hat back on his head. "Well, I'm glad I've found you. I want to do a story on you, and on her too." He tucked his writing pad in his pocket and slipped his pencil behind his ear.

"Well, then go find her," Prudence said, crossing her arms.

"No, no," he said, laughing. "You see, she's this British actress married to this Mexican diplomat. She's done this race every year and has never finished. But people down here love her." He narrowed his eyes at her. "She has Eva Peron painted on her car. It's disgusting, and besides that, it's not kosher. Her car is highly modified. But the officials turn their heads because it's great publicity for Mexico."

"So? What's that got to do with me?" Prudence said, as if offended her name would be mentioned in the same breath as a woman like that.

"I know you aren't like her," the reporter said. "But many look at you ... how do I say it ... as a bit of a novelty too. That is, maybe you get more press than drivers who might have more experience and better race results. So some people have put you in a sort of a duel with this Silvia woman, to see which of you beats the other. Mexico versus America and all that. A race within the race."

The sun shone now through the thin tree branches and Prudence lifted her hand to shade her eyes. She felt the sting of the reporter's words, as she had when she read the last article he wrote about her, but she knew that he was right: she was a novelty and would remain so until she could prove otherwise.

"Here," the reporter took a folded newspaper from his back pocket. He opened it to a photo of a beautiful woman leaning against a white Jaguar. A big red dot on its door and hood, and — sure enough — Eva Peron's face painted on its flanks.

"'How to Pander to the Masses'," the reporter said, handing

her the paper. "That's what the caption *should* read." He jabbed his pointed finger at the photo. "This is what you're up against. And I will tell you that she's going to finish the race this year with that Jaguar she has. Her husband has literally paved the road with gold for her."

Prudence shook her head and bit her lip. She'd been proud to be the only woman in the race, and now that hope was gone. But now she was glad she came to Mexico after all. Even if her chances were slim, she was going to push harder in this race than she ever had before, to be the first woman to finish.

The thought made her stomach lurch, as she'd read in the papers, that in the past four years that the race had been held, forty-nine drivers and spectators had been killed. Just the year before, a driver in an open topped car like hers hit a dip in the road as he approached a town, lost control and hit his head on a flower box of an adjacent house, decapitating him.

Prudence looked at the reporter and put her hands on her hips. "I'd say my chances are as good as anyone else's here," she began. "We have a great car and things should go smoothly. There's no reason that any prima donna should change that."

The reporter took out his notepad and removed the pencil from behind his ear. As Rudy fiddled with the car, she answered his questions, each response short and calculating, a way to let de Lobos and her people know that she was here to race.

"Last question for you, Prudence," the reporter said, leaning back on his heels. "Why do you want to race cars? Our readers want to know why you chose such a dangerous pastime. Most women your age are settled down and having children."

Prudence glared at him. She'd asked herself the question many times, and each time the answer changed. As if her reasons for racing eluded even her.

"I guess because deep down, I'm afraid," she said, looking up at him. "And I don't like being afraid of something. If something scares me I want to beat it. I don't like to be scared of anything."

The reporter looked up after scribbling down the words, and nodded slowly, as if she'd just said something meaningful.

"And there's something beyond that fear. It's like the sound barrier to me. I just want to break through it until I'm not afraid any more." She looked at the reporter and then at Charles. "I know that when I finish the race, whether I win or not, I can go home and nothing will be able to worry me again. I'll know that I can do anything."

"Will you print that?" Charles asked the reporter.

The reporter wrote down the last of her words and flipped his notepad closed. "I'll print it and hopefully it'll make up for every inane story I've ever had to write." He tucked away his notepad and shook both of their hands. He wished her luck and said he'd catch up with her after the first day's racing.

As she watched him go, his suit coat now slung over his shoulder, Rudy started the Porsche and revved its engine. Charles was already climbing under the car to check the under carriage. The sound of the exhaust was so loud that she turned off her hearing aid and could still feel the sound in her chest. Rudy had modified the engine back in the shop; machined and ported the head, sharpened the lobes of the camshaft, re-jetted the carburetors. Then he'd polished and waxed the entire car to reduce aerodynamic drag, and installed a headrest on the rear deck lid, to make the car even more streamlined.

A short time ago the Porsche had been a brand new, unmarked car. It was a true racer now, with the teardrop shaped headrest and its front windshield fairing producing a sort of spine, the gill-like cut-outs in the engine hatch giving it a reptilian look. Racing stripes had been painted along the fenders, two spare tires strapped to the rear hood. NIVEA CREMA was stenciled in big blue letters across the silver sheet metal, along with Dunlop Tires, Castrol Motor Oil, Tung-Sol Tubes, and several San Franciscan sponsors. Rudy had screwed the metal race plate onto the hood that morning, *MEXICO La Carrera Panamericana 1954* stamped on it in. Painted her name on the top panel of the door: *Prudence Baylor* in large red script. Below it, the number **77** inside a white circle.

She smiled when she saw that Charles had crudely painted his four-leaf clover beside her name. She stood there looking at it, hoping it would bring her luck. And yet for a second, it seemed that this had all been too easy. Soon she would be competing in one of the world's largest racing events. She had been lucky in winning the races she had, but had narrowly avoided enough crashes to make her wonder if she'd used up all the luck a person could have.

"Whoa!" Charles yelled from where he lay under the car. Rudy cut the engine, jumped out and ran to the front of it, where fresh, honey colored motor oil was spilling onto the ground.

Prudence sat on the station wagon's tailgate, watching as Rudy dragged out his tools and crawled under the Porsche to repair the leak. He'd installed an oil cooler in the front grill to keep the car running cool, with rubber hoses running back to the engine. He shouted to Charles that one of these lines had burst, causing the engine to lose its oil.

The nearby racers looked over at the commotion. Drivers with factory sponsored race cars and crews, with the panache and demeanor of flying aces, prepared to give their lives to win. One of these drivers looked over at her and shook his head. A Germanic looking man with a crew cut. He nudged one of his crew members and stuck his tongue out at her, wagging it up and down.

Prudence glowered at them and their fancy trucks and crew, adorned in matching Porsche jackets. Charles called to her from where he lay under the car. Prudence climbed from the shade of the wagon and back into the seething heat. She slid under the Porsche beside him and, with a wrench in her hand, poked her slender arm into the recesses of the car where he couldn't reach. A bolt that she couldn't see, but could feel with her oily finger tips. She drew it snug and then pulled herself from under the car and wiped her hands on a rag. She looked at the other drivers and knew that in the end, she would show them that they could be beaten by a woman, and how easily it could be done.

Eleven

THE SOUTHERN Mexican countryside looked lush and tropical to Prudence, with its thick-trunked trees and green hillsides. Tuxtla Gutierrez itself sat between two rivers, and from where they sat that evening she could see the ramshackle houses, rusted fences of corrugated metal, faded clothing hanging on lines. The rooflines cut sharp shadows across the open doorways, and nearer, the setting sun shone on the hundreds of race cars parked in the lot. Prudence stared beyond their sparkling fenders, up at the billowing clouds that hung above the churning, muddy waters.

After the sun went down, Charles cooked canned beans and potted meat over a fire. Sitting on the blanket with him after the long journey, she leaned back on her elbows and gazed through the tree branches at the stars. Around them, other race teams were cooking their dinners too. They were laughing and talking, some of them even sharing their fires with their rivals. She watched them toasting each other in the firelight and knew this would all be forgotten once the racing started.

They ate supper quietly, cleaned up and washed their hands and faces with water from their canteens. Then Charles hung his hat on the side mirror of the station wagon and took some blankets from the car. Since there was nowhere for all the racers to stay, she and Charles would be sleeping in the back of the wagon tonight, or here in the grass beneath the trees, the wind and the moon passing through the branches of the scrub oak.

As the clouds again filled the sky and dark set in around them, they heard music and laughter from the center of town, saw the strings of electric lights as they slowly began to be lit. Far off came the crack of a gunshot, and Prudence reached for Charles's hand across the blanket. They sat there holding hands a while, stoking the fire to scare off the mosquitoes and what creatures lived in the bordering woods.

"You going to be able to sleep okay tonight?" he asked. In the firelight he looked calm, contemplative, drinking a bottle of beer and smoking his Mexican cigarettes.

"Promise me that after this is all over, we'll take it easy a while," she said, leaning her shoulder against his. "I like it just how it is now."

"Take it easier than this?" He chuckled.

"I just meant let's look at any offers that come my way and consider the easier ones." She brushed away a moth and looked down at the town. "I got the chills today thinking of all the chances we're taking to be here."

"You could win thousands," he said, puffing his cigarette. "And you will prove something if you win. Isn't that worth more than money? I'm beginning to think it is."

"I don't know that I can prove anything to anybody. I'm just a race car driver. For a while I thought that meant something, but I'm not so sure it does in the grand scheme of things."

"Christ, what does anything mean in the grand scheme of things?" he asked, looking into the fire. "Sometimes you just have to do something because it's the only thing you can do. The only thing that makes sense."

"Sometimes it does feel like that. But this race," she looked around at the other race cars and their drivers, dozing beside their own fires, "it scares me."

"You are a top contender in your class," he said. "All you have to do is keep up a good pace and finish. Don't push too hard. Remember that."

Prudence stared deeper into the fire's embers. "That's not what I mean. I'm talking to you about what this all feels like. I'm allowed to think, right?"

Charles raised his eyebrows and waved his hand for her to continue.

"I'm risking my life out there. And no one talks about it. You don't talk about it. I don't talk about it." She brushed her hair behind her ear. "Because when I'm in that car, I forget too. I forget that I could die, even when I know I could at any minute."

"It's like my brother Luca said to me in the war." Charles looked at her. "When you stop being afraid, that's when you become a soldier."

The fire crackled and sparked. Prudence watched the embers rising towards the branches, the warm glow the fire cast on the underside of the tree, the way each ember faded. "I have to push it," she said, shaking her head, "if I'm going to beat that de Lobos woman and those factory drivers too. I have to go as fast as I can."

Charles looked at her without speaking. She cleared her throat and glanced over at Rudy, sitting beside her Porsche a couple dozen feet away. "After we get on the last legs of the race, I'm going alone. The highway was flat and straight up there. I'll need Rudy with me in the mountains, but I'm going alone at the end."

"You know I don't like that idea." Charles flipped his cigarette in the fire. "It's not as flat or easy as you think."

Prudence sat there, fiddling with her hearing aid, sensing that the battery was dying. She cursed, smacking it with her hand. Charles laughed as she crawled over his lap and across the blanket and began rummaging through her suitcase.

As she took a spare battery from her suitcase and installed it, she heard a loud sound, like rushing water. The sound grew louder, as if a dam had burst. She looked at Charles to see if he heard it too. Then the earth began to shake and rumble beneath them, and she felt it rattling in her spine and her elbows and her knees. She cried out as a tree branch dropped beside the blanket. The ground felt soft and hollow, and then came a deep geological thump, as if something had become unmoored deep inside the earth.

Charles grabbed her arm, steadying her. "It's just a tremor. It will pass."

"Jesus." Prudence looked at the town below, the electric lights swinging on their cords. After a few more seconds, the quaking stopped, and everything was strangely quiet. She heard shouting from far away as the parties below began taking stock of the damage. Then their boisterous noises resumed a moment later, as if these quakes were a common occurrence.

"Look," Charles said, his hand on her knee, as if the tremors had given immediacy to their conversation. "When we get back home, we are going to get things straightened out. After the race, there will be new offers coming your way. I know you have a lot of expenses now, and even if you don't win down here, you will be getting chances to make more money."

He looked over at her. "And I've been thinking. I shouldn't be the one to manage you any more. That maybe you need to hire an accountant, handle things on your own."

Prudence was relieved to hear him say it, but within her arose the latent fear that she might be on her own soon. That perhaps he would, as Maria had said, grow tired of her as his project.

"I have to protect you," he added. "From Maria. I don't know what she will do, me being with you all the time. And when we go to

Italy …" He shook his head, swatting at the flies.

Prudence bowed her head, replaying the conversation she'd had with Maria back in the shop.

"If she does something," he added, "anything I have my name on will be hers. That's the way she is. And she will have the lawyers to make sure that happens." He looked at her. "That's why I have been putting this off. Because she will take everything. And she will be able to with us off together like this. It won't look good in court."

She took his hand and pulled it to her heart, gripping it. She held it there, looking at him, glad that soon it would be like this all the time. That he would finally be free from Maria.

"She tricked me, Prudence, she really did." He shook his head. "I had to marry her."

Prudence watched the fire, their hands absently sliding down towards her belly. She suddenly released his hand. She picked up a stick and began poking the fire, tugging at her blouse.

"Soon after that, she had to have her way with everything," he added. "Whatever she wanted, she got. If I didn't have the cash, she would buy it on credit." He lay back on the blanket and crossed his arms under his head. "There was never enough money for her."

Prudence continued to poke the fire with a stick, listening to the crickets, her other hand covering her still flat belly. She turned to him, her lips parting to speak, prepared to tell him.

"I did do one thing," he said, rolling over and propping himself up on his elbow. "After my accident I bought a home on some property in Italy. I had a lawyer who said to spend what I had before I got married. So it couldn't be taken away." He glanced at her, as if waiting for her reaction. "So when we go over there for the big races, we will have our own place."

Prudence forced a smile, her hand falling from her belly to the blanket. She sat there a moment, gazing over at Rudy, working under the car with a flashlight. Then she picked up the stick and tossed it in the embers, watching as it caught fire.

He looked at the stick, then at her. "Is everything okay?"

"It's nothing. Just the race." She stared at the fire. She knew this child would ruin everything. Maybe it was his problem too, but he wouldn't see it that way right now. And as she glanced at Charles, she knew that she would ruin him the same way Maria had.

"Well, everything will seem better after a good night's sleep," he said, kissing her on the cheek and rising from the blanket. She watched him walk towards the station wagon, favoring his good leg. She scattered the embers and followed after him. He was already snoring softly as she lay down and slipped her arms around him, his bare feet hanging off the wagon's open tailgate, the parking lot slowly going quiet as she lay there with her eyes wide open.

CHARLES SHOOK her awake sometime during the night. She opened her eyes, trying to remember where she was. His face was completely dark. He was leaning over her, his head outlined by blue moonlight, his hair clinging to his sweaty face.

"You were a ball of fire," he said, gasping. "I kept calling your name but you were driving right at me and you wouldn't stop."

Prudence's heart began to beat quickly. "Stop it," she said, pushing him away. "You're dreaming. Go back to sleep."

He lay down and breathed out hard, muttering that she'd been a big ball of fire coming at him, a big ball of fire.

As he resumed snoring, she tried to close her eyes again but her heart was still banging around inside her. She'd had a dream too. That she was being tossed from the blanket as a child, her cousins looking down at her after she hit the ground. Her head was twisted so she was looking backwards up at them. And the way they were staring back at her, she realized that she was dying. And that she had dreamt the rest of her life, in that liminal moment before she died. That her life from then on was all a dream — high school, teachers college, her mother dying, coming to California. And that right now, she was still lying there in that field with a broken neck. And at any moment, it would all go dark.

Prudence shook her head to toss the image from her mind, but she knew it would be there again if she closed her eyes. As Charles twitched beside her, she lay awake most of the night to insure that her dream did not return.

AT DAWN she climbed from the wagon and stood under the scrub oak, rubbing the ache from her shoulder. Already it was hot and the sky was hazy, insects biting at her bare skin. She smacked them away and saw that the other crews were already up, carrying their tires and tools slowly, as if saving their energy for the race.

She yawned and walked towards their trailer. Rudy was crouched beside the Porsche, his face haggard from lack of sleep, his movements stealthy, as if he didn't want to awaken any of the other sleeping mechanics. She saw that he had fixed the burst oil cooler lines, the old rubber hoses discarded beside the car. He was now deflating the tires and refilling them with nitrogen from the two silver tanks he'd brought. She slipped her hands in her pockets and smiled at him.

"See," he said, looking up at her after he'd shut off the tank, the nub of a cigarette stuck to his lips. "Now you have no excuses not to win. You have the best car in your class, even better than the Porsche team."

Prudence smirked at him and started to walk away. As she did, she felt the ground begin to rattle. She gasped and held out her hands for balance. Another tremor, this one softer than the night before. For a moment it seemed as if that sound she'd always heard in her head had followed her here. That the beast she'd imagined was nearing, rolling across the earth, closing in on her. She shut her eyes until the rumbling stopped, and realized that the calm she felt the night before had been just an illusion. Now, she just wanted to get the race started, so she could get out of Mexico as soon as possible.

As Rudy and Charles ate breakfast, she nibbled an apple and some Saltines to steady her stomach. The race officially began in an hour, and although she was not slated to depart until the late morning, a film of cold sweat covered her as she thought about racing up the Pan American Highway.

Only minutes after breakfast, she and Rudy were in their race suits and tucked in her Porsche, Charles shouting instructions at her as she joined the line of cars leading down the thin roadway. He kissed her fast on the cheek and patted her helmet.

The car trembled, its small cockpit enclosing her body, which was slunk down flat in the seat so her head was just above the door. The doorjamb pressed against her left arm, Rudy wedged against her other, the race map unfolded on his lap. She tightened her helmet's strap and tossed the shifter into gear, her ass feeling like it was scraping the ground as they inched towards the starting line for the first leg of the race.

Rudy fiddled with the pockets of his race suit, filled with little hand tools, another cigarette dangling from his lips. She could hear the distant crowd over the engine's burbling as she crossed through town. She looked in her rear-view mirror and saw that Charles had joined the line far behind them, to drive up to the finish to meet them after all the racers had departed.

"Turn here." Rudy pointed between some adobe buildings. As they drove along the shady avenue, faces peering from darkened windows, they emerged atop a hill. Below them several thousand people were gathered beneath a banner that marked the starting line. She breathed as much as she could of the dusty air as she again fell in line.

From the top of the hill, she saw the Lincolns and Ferraris from the Large Sports Class being released at the starting line, each at minute long intervals. Falling on their haunches as the official waved the green flag, their rear fenders receding in a rooster tail of dust. It was just like she'd read in the rule book. The fastest cars would leave the starting line first; the classes tiered by engine size and overall speed: Large Sports, Small Sports, Large Stock, Special Stock, Stock, European Stock.

She was in the Small Sports class, the second group slated to leave. Within that group, she would be the tenth to depart. This leg of the race, from Gutierrez to Oaxaca was over three hundred miles, and would take her nearly four hours to complete.

Prudence drove down towards the bottom of the hill. Rudy's hand was trembling and he grabbed the handlebar on the dash. He lit another cigarette off the other and offered it to her. She took a few deep puffs before flipping it away. As they crawled through a tunnel of chanting mouths and shaking fists, she drew cat calls from the men, some of them reaching in the car to touch her hair before the officials pushed them back.

As she neared the starting grid, flash bulbs popped in her face. She looked up as an airplane zoomed overhead, its wings glinting in the sun before it disappeared over the crowd. Sand blew across the open cockpit and she closed her eyes and affixed her goggles. When she had them adjusted, Rudy pointed to the engine temperature gauge. The needle was nearing the red. She nodded, hoping the oil cooler would hold.

She came to the starting line, the banner strung across the highway, spectators roaring in the bleachers beneath it. Race officials stood before her in their black uniforms and hats. She looked up the highway, the dust still settling from the last car that had left. The official held the time piece and the flag, limp in his hand. It felt as if she was staring off a cliff and was about to be pushed off of it. As she waited, she felt her blood squeezing through each artery and vein. The rattle of the engine behind her, the rumbling of the crowd as the official looked up from his stopwatch and waved the green flag.

She jammed the throttle and sank back in her seat, the tires squealing beneath her. The engine spooled quickly up to redline and she nicked the shifter into second gear. The spectators in the road stepped back as she approached and Rudy yelled *Go! Go! Go!* and waved them out of the way as she shifted again and sank her foot to the floor, the road appearing as a long straight line receding into the horizon, blurred with all the hands still reaching out to touch her.

Twelve

PRUDENCE GRIPPED the white Bakelite steering wheel, her mind shattered by the wail of the Porsche's engine as the speedometer needle climbed. The sun crashed against the fluted windscreen and she sank behind it as she pushed hard, flat out towards the first turn. As she tucked the car through it in a wide, sloping arch, her shoulder pressed against the doorjamb, her head bobbing, she felt an intense focus, her movements independent of her mind. She grabbed the shift knob and pulled it into fourth gear and kicked the accelerator pedal to the floor as she and Rudy descended into a broad valley.

The tachometer neared redline and the speedometer hovered at a hundred and thirty miles per hour. The Porsche squatted down nicely at that speed, firm and stable. She knew she still had room to push the engine, that if she pinned the pedal to the firewall, the car might do a hundred and fifty. She'd never gone that fast before and she didn't chance it yet, knowing that she had to conserve the engine and the tires.

Ahead she saw the road rise and the lush trees thinning to sparse brush. Vultures sat in the road, pulling entrails from crushed armadillos, and they wouldn't move until she was upon them, the thump of their wings against her fender as she passed. Soon she passed cars sitting roadside with steaming engines, their radiators punctured. Many of the cars were dented and blood streaked from vultures and livestock that hadn't gotten out of the way in time.

Here the road surface had changed from smooth pebbles to crushed volcanic rock. The car skimmed over them, and as the sun began to rise higher, the roadside became littered with racers changing their chewed up tires. Prudence was glad that Rudy had filled hers with nitrogen, making them lighter and less prone to damage.

He suddenly signaled for her to slow down, and as she came to a blind turn, some spectators who hadn't seen her coming were still standing in the road. She stomped the brake and ground to a halt before them. They just stood there and blinked at her. She revved the engine and Rudy waved them out of the way. When they finally parted she accelerated through the town, ripping around each bend, trying to make up lost time.

By the second hour she'd passed some of the slower cars in her class, a Lancia and an Alfa Romeo, but there still was no sign of Silvia de Lobos in her white Jaguar. They had left four car positions after her, and Prudence hoped that she'd catch up with her soon. But again Rudy slowed her down for each dangerous curve and soon the Lancia had returned in her rear-view mirror.

Ahead, she saw a large maroon Ferrari lagging behind its race class, driven by an elderly man with a teenage girl beside him. There were no stickers or sponsors on the car. It looked like he'd just bought it off the showroom floor and decided to race. The slower drivers were supposed to yield, but as Prudence tried to pass the Ferrari, he cut her off, his tires flinging gravel over her and the car. He shook his fist at her, and then as the road straightened, he easily pulled away.

Prudence was alone for the first time all day, the road no longer lined with spectators. The temperature gauge sat safely at one eighty-five, and although she felt the power of the car urging her, Rudy waved at her whenever she tried to speed up, implementing Charles's plan for a careful and measured finish.

A thick cloud of oily black smoke rose ahead. As they neared the rock-lined walls of a town, she saw that the maroon Ferrari from earlier had crashed. She slowed and saw the elderly man in the driver's seat, the steering wheel bent, his face vacant and eyes open. The girl was sitting outside the mangled car, screaming. Her face and her dress covered in blood.

Rudy waved for Prudence to keep going. "You can't stop," he yelled, smacking the dashboard. "You have to go. There's nothing we can do."

She knew that the race rules stipulated it was illegal to stop for anything other than mechanical issues. That providing help to other drivers was prohibited. As she left the wrecked Ferrari behind and drove out of the town, her hands began to tremble.

Of course she knew that drivers could get killed in a race, but in the back of her mind she thought it would never really happen. But the image of the dead man and the screaming girl would never be out of her head. She would not be able to unsee them, or forget the feeling of not being able to help. And furthermore, she knew, as she shot off along the highway, that it could also happen to her.

Despite her newfound sense of caution, she passed the finish line in Oaxaca in just over four hours, and was directed to a parking lot along with all the other race cars. There, her car was inspected by race officials for damage or any mid-race modifications. The officials scanned her car and, finding nothing, she got out and unstrapped her helmet.

Journalists milled through the busy lot, and spectators stood pointing at her from behind the barricades. She thought that they'd mistaken her for Silvia de Lobos again, until a Mexican man standing nearby waved at her.

"*Mujer con el coche de plata*," the man called at her as she passed.

Prudence stopped and looked at him.

"Girl with the Silver Car," a passing journalist said. "That's what we're calling you in the papers." He took out a notebook and asked for an interview.

She removed her helmet and goggles, watching the other journalists come towards her, their cameras at the ready. Prudence combed her fingers through her hair, ruffling it with her fingers, and smiled at them.

PRUDENCE GAZED at the crowd of racers and crews surrounding her as the results for that day were posted. She fought her way forward and read from the board that she'd placed sixth in her class of thirty-eight cars, beating out nearly everyone but the factory drivers and Silvia de Lobos, who came in third on that leg of the race.

Rudy didn't even congratulate her. He simply turned after the results were posted and disappeared into the crowd. Prudence stood there drinking warm, tepid water from one of their canteens. As usual, the other drivers didn't talk to her, so she went back and sat leaning against the car alone, utilizing what little shade it provided.

She tossed pebbles into a discarded hubcap, watching mechanics make adjustments to brakes and engines, repair their damaged fenders. She caught a glimpse of Rudy talking to the Porsche team and their crews, which had likely been his reason for coming down here: to secure a better job. Prudence considered what Charles paid him and had done for him. Maybe Rudy was the best mechanic he knew, but as she suspected, he was a disloyal bastard.

She sat there, looking around the hot, dry countryside, thinking how different it looked than Oregon. All drizzly and green, moss growing on everything. She hadn't been there in almost a year. Lately, her thoughts of home had become more and more remote. As she leaned back against the car, she knew that no one from home would recognize her if they saw her sitting here. That she now had the unmistakable look of accomplishment, that same self-satisfied expression that Charles and Vi always wore.

Or her mother had, on her good days. It had been nearly a year since she last saw her, while home from school. Prudence remembered how they'd both gone to the market in the Dodge the night before Thanksgiving. How it had broken down two miles from home. Walking home together in the dark, laughing, their arms full of groceries. Not accepting rides from those who stopped and offered. Just enjoying each other's company.

That had been the last time Prudence had been alone with her mother. Her heart beating her last beats, there on that walk. And Prudence knew that she had made good on her silent promise to her mother. All her life she had believed that Prudence was bound for something great, and here was the evidence, right here: she was in another country, racing amongst the world's top competitors.

She looked down the road and pictured life happening back home, unaware of where she was, what had happened to her since she left. Her father would be coming home from work about now. Climbing from the work truck, wiping his feet before he stepped into the dark house and hung his coat on the empty rack.

As she sat there, the image of him filling her mind, Charles pulled into the lot and sprung from the wagon. He took off his sunglasses, stretched his arms and combed back his hair with his fingers. He'd made great time, curiously great. She noticed his mischievous smile as he walked towards her, and knew that he had raced that big Chevy wagon up here.

He came and threw his arms around her waist, lifted her up and kissed her. She squealed and covered her mouth. He laughed and took her hand and they walked to a nearby grease cart and sat on the benches and ate tamales that were grilled in corn husks.

She told him about that leg of the race, the sheer speed, the thrill of it. Of the journalists who'd come by to take her picture and to interview her afterwards. She didn't mention the wrecked Ferrari or the screaming girl; the sight of the dead driver's eyes had a sort of morbid privacy that she dared not betray.

He told her all about his drive, how he'd cut past so many others making their way north to catch up with their crews. She watched his eyes glow even brighter and again wondered why he wasn't the one racing, why he'd given it up.

They were standing by the trailer when Rudy appeared from the crowd an hour later, his face pale and his jumpsuit speckled with blood. She watched as he neared, dragging his feet. He stopped beside her and Charles, his pant legs bunched sloppily around his ankles, his hair hanging in his face. He told them that after the race he went to find something to eat. As he was crossing the street he witnessed two spectators, a man and a woman, get struck down by a speeding race car. He and some others ran to them and found that they were nearly dead.

"They were trying to hold hands as we loaded them in a truck heading for the hospital," Rudy said, shaking his head as he lit a cigarette. "They were in such bad shape, they couldn't even talk. All they cared about was being able to touch each other."

Prudence watched the cords in his neck bulge as he puffed deeply on the cigarette. He shook his head and put his hand over his face, exhaling the smoke through his hand. When he lifted it, the pained expression was gone, his face becoming as unreadable as it usually looked. He then turned and walked away as if nothing had happened.

She and Charles looked at one another but didn't speak as they walked back to the station wagon. Prudence imagined the two people holding hands and a chill passed through her. She knew that soon Charles would be leaving her for the night, and she wanted to linger as they walked through the crowd. But already it was late in the day. He'd now have to make the drive north ahead of them to the town of Puebla — eight hours through the mountains — partially in darkness.

"Don't leave me tonight," she said, as they came and stood beside the wagon.

"I don't like this any more than you." Charles got in and started the car, looking off at Rudy, who was talking to a member of the Porsche crew. "Remember what I said before about tonight. Don't trust anyone."

PRUDENCE SLEPT in the trailer that night with the door locked, just as Charles had instructed. She lay in front of the Porsche, her head under a clothing rack, her feet rubbing a little make up desk. As she fell asleep, all she could think about was how badly she wanted to win the race. Now that the end of the race was nearing, and she was only sixth in the race standings, she'd have to push the car to its limits. She imagined being on the cover of *Speed Age*, or even in *LIFE* magazine. She wouldn't be just some local novelty then, but the first woman to finish the Pan Am. And Silvia de Lobos wouldn't even be a footnote.

In the morning, she dressed in her race suit and went to check on her car. She stopped short when she saw Silvia de Lobos standing alone on the edge of the lot. She was tall, blonde hair, creamy skin. She was wearing a white race suit and had a silk scarf tied around her neck, a powder pink helmet tucked under her arm. Most of the other drivers were just awakening, and de Lobos was just standing there alone. For a moment Prudence felt like she had stumbled upon a rare and dangerous creature, and she stood motionless and watched.

A nearby mechanic dropped a wrench and cursed, and de Lobos looked over and saw Prudence. She took off her sunglasses and glared at her. She was startlingly beautiful, with bright red lips and cold, blue eyes. Eyes that made Prudence feel important when they were trained on her. Were they not rivals, Prudence might have even felt a bit star struck at the sight of her.

Silvia de Lobos smiled as her entourage came and joined her. A crew chief wearing an ascot, a personal photographer with a twin lens Rolleiflex camera. As they began talking, de Lobos continued to stare at Prudence. From that distance, Prudence could see her lips moving, but couldn't make out the words. And yet she knew, from the bitterness in her British accent, that it was something cruel and vindictive.

Prudence slipped on her kid leather driving gloves and headed down to the check-in station. She found Rudy there working on her Porsche. He had the hood open and he was re-jetting the carburetors for the thinner mountain atmosphere on this leg of the race.

After the officials checked over the car, she drove them down towards the starting grid, de Lobos only a few cars ahead. As they sat idling, Rudy warned her that he'd heard that spectators were removing road signs that warned of hazards. That they were building dips in the road and other booby traps to cause accidents.

Prudence nodded, inching up to the starting line. When the green flag waved she launched hard, hoping to catch up with de Lobos. But only an hour into the race they hit some metal shards and had to stop to change a flat tire. Others were parked there too, cursing the laughing spectators who had thrown the debris in the road.

Soon after they changed out the tire and got back into the race, Prudence rounded a bend and saw a white car pulling back onto the road with a fresh rear tire on it. Red polka dots on each door and Eva

Peron's name stenciled on the fenders.

Prudence sank the accelerator to the floorboard, the engine screaming as the carburetor clicked wide open, sucking in air. Within a few more turns she was just car lengths from de Lobos' Jaguar and closing fast.

"Slow down," Rudy yelled. "It makes no difference if you pass her or not."

A few old women were walking alongside the road and they ran out of the way as Prudence came abreast of de Lobos. Prudence felt her blood singing through her body as de Lobos looked over as saw her. Her eyes widened and then her Jaguar easily pulled away, taking the better line for the turn. Prudence tried to pass on the outside, but de Lobos swerved to cut her off.

As Prudence righted the wheel and pulled up behind her again, a large Lincoln from up ahead slowed and dropped behind de Lobos. It blocked the road, cruising at seventy miles per hour. The Lincoln had left earlier in the Stock Car class and should've been well up the road by now. It was covered in advertisements for a Mexico City optometrist.

"What the hell is he doing?" she yelled, slowing to avoid hitting its bumper.

Rudy laughed and then Prudence understood. The Lincoln was a pawn, placed there by de Lobos' corrupt team to insure her victory. As Prudence cruised behind the Lincoln, which cut her off each time she tried to pass, the white Jaguar disappeared beyond the next turn.

He laughed again, his teeth yellow and jagged. It was as if he was pleased to see that the world still had an order to it. That even on a desert mountain, some things didn't change in his mind: Prudence wasn't much of a driver, and she could be defeated by even a cheating actress.

Prudence stepped out of her trailer that evening, where Charles sat on a blanket, looking rumpled and weary, having spent the day driving in the heat.

"I still can't believe that bitch and her team cut me off today," she said.

Charles looked up at her and slipped his arm around her legs. "Listen, I want you to stay away from that woman from now on. Understand? You do not know what they will do to win. Next time that Lincoln might run you off a cliff."

Prudence gathered her hair over her shoulder. "So is this what you miss?" she smiled. "All of this cheating?"

He lit a cigarette and shook his head. "Remember what I said. Racing is about bullshit management."

She sat down beside him and looked off at the quiet countryside. "Tell me about Italy," she said. "Is it like this?"

He looked out at the mountains. "Parts of it," he said. "But there are no open highways like this. The Mille Miglia is raced on small roads with rock walls on each side. It is a much different race."

"I can't wait to see it all." She slipped the cigarette from between his fingers. She looked off at the horizon a moment, puffing deeply. "Charles, I want to go it alone for the rest of the race, without Rudy. The car will be lighter and I'll be able to go even faster."

"No," Charles said, staring back at her. "I don't like that idea. It's dangerous out there. The desert is not as easy to navigate as you think. You'll get vertigo driving in the dark."

Prudence exhaled and looked at him. "There's nothing you can say that will change my mind." She saw that Charles understood that she meant it, that there would be no debate. "This is my race. And I am going for the win."

Thirteen

AT THE start of the final leg of the race, winding north through the Chihuahua desert and into Juarez, the race standings board showed that only one-third of the original racers remained. Prudence watched hundreds of broken cars and their crews form a weary procession behind the racers as they assembled near the starting line. The afternoon sky was growing dim and a hot wind stirred up the desert sand, peppering her face. As she affixed her goggles and neared her Porsche, she saw that in the past days, the desert sand had pitted the headlights and stripped the paint off its nose. She ran her hand along the rough fender, kissed the four-leaf clover painted on the door, then climbed in her seat.

"You will regret not having me with you." Rudy shoved the crumpled race map in her face as the car was warming up. "You will get very tired of trying to guess what is around every turn in the dark."

Prudence took the map and watched him walk away, shaking his head. She'd already explained to Rudy and Charles why she wanted to race alone: this part of the race emphasized sheer speed, and the car would be a hundred and sixty pounds lighter without Rudy, which meant she could wring another five to ten miles per hour from the car. And besides, she'd studied the race map enough to know that this was the straightest, simplest part of the race.

She tucked the map under her thigh, put the car in gear and inched down to the starting line. As she neared it, she saw American and European television crews were filming the remaining drivers as they left the starting line. She sat idling in queue with the other cars, all of them scarred from nearly three thousand miles of open road racing. Their drivers' faces appeared haggard, but their eyes focused as they each waited for the flagman to shake the green flag and send them on their way.

A few minutes later, she sat on the checkered starting grid, watching the flagman. His eyes trained on her and hers on the silky flag, fluttering in the wind. The fading sun behind it, making it appear almost translucent as the flagman's arm extended the flag, snapping and unfurling, to its full length.

The engine grunted as she shot off into the desert, tucking low beneath the windscreen. Behind the clouds, the late afternoon sun was falling fast, and she realized it would be completely dark halfway through this leg of the race. She watched the speedometer flick past a hundred and fifty, the engine humming as she dove into a broad, wide plain. Her foot remained pinned to the floorboard for over an hour, as she weaved through slower race traffic. Before long, a trace of the moon appeared in the twilight, the cooler northern air rushing overhead, the sun's pink afterglow on the dimming horizon.

Prudence flipped on her headlights and a triangle of light spurted forth, shaking as the car rattled along. The green glow of the gauges filled the car with a soothing light. She thought of sharing a celebratory cocktail with Vi when she got home. The great press she'd receive at the finish line and all the press that would inevitably follow. The international acclaim that Charles had hinted at, should she win the race, startled her to the exciting reality that she might soon be facing.

She lifted her goggles and rubbed her eyes. She hadn't seen a tree or even a cactus for miles, just scrub brush lining the highway. She looked for the lights of distant houses, the taillights of other race cars. She assayed the map, checked her fuel gauge: already fluttering near empty. She traced her finger along the race route, then glanced up from the map at the stars above her, and for a moment she felt very small and insignificant.

She stared as far as her headlights reached, holding her pace at a hundred and fifty miles an hour. The road ahead darkened and the horizon went oil black. They blurred together for a moment, as if she was driving into space, unlit except for the bouncing triangle shape her headlights made. She momentarily drifted off the road, the tires rumbling against the hard packed sand before she righted the wheel.

She breathed deeply, telling herself that she would soon be heading home. Where she could see and talk to Vi anytime she wanted, where the secret inside her could be resolved. And then she would be free to go to Italy with Charles. Then return after the year's big races a celebrity in the racing world. There'd be more appearances, more parades, more money. And she would marry Charles then if he asked her. The thought of it made her tingle from top to bottom. There would be children then. Beautiful, happy children. And she would retire from racing, having made her mark, and her fortune.

Racing. Prudence blinked. She couldn't remember the last ten miles. She hadn't seen any other cars in an hour, nor a house, person or animal. She frantically traced where Charles's careful pen line had drawn the route on the map. She seemed to be on course, and yet something felt off. She tightened her grip on the steering wheel, her breaths quick and shallow, her foot reluctantly holding her breakneck pace.

Ten miles passed. Nothing. Another five miles. Still nothing. Then there came a faded road sign, pointing towards Juarez. She loosened her grip on the wheel and sank back in her seat, veering from one section of the highway onto a rougher section of pavement. The desert was eerily still and she wondered at the creatures that lurked out there. In the distance, she saw a faint glow of the town rising into the night sky. Gravel and rocks pinged against the underside of her car as she downshifted into third gear, the speedometer reading a hundred and ten miles an hour.

Prudence steadied the car and crouched down below the windscreen, heading for the lights. She accelerated again on the rough road, dropping it into fourth gear at redline. The speedometer needle rose again, the scrub brush lining the roadway flashing by as her engine began to scream.

Ahead, a shape flickered in her headlights. A dark object positioned in the middle of the road. She blinked, thinking that it was merely a shadow. But then it moved.

"*Motherfucker,*" she yelled, jabbing the brakes so hard that the tires squealed and the car began to fishtail. As she careened towards the dark shape, she thought it might be just another vulture, but in the fraction of a second it took her to be upon it, she saw that it wasn't an animal.

It was a child.

She felt a resounding thud inside her when she saw the wind part the child's long black hair. Then its small face was staring back at her, its eyes shining in her headlights. The child was wild and feral looking, its head no larger than a melon. It was not unlike the children they'd passed up in the mountains, following behind the ancient looking brujas.

Prudence yanked the wheel hard left, the car lifting momentarily onto its right two wheels, still speeding in a straight line. The child stood unmoving, as if mesmerized by the lights. A swift thought passed through her mind then, that this couldn't be happening, that this wasn't real. That the child was some sort of apparition and would vanish at any moment.

But it only grew larger in her headlights until she could see its fingers, its belly button, its dirty face. The brakes had slowed her to thirty miles an hour, but in an instant she felt the bump as the front outer fender struck the child. She heard its soft cry, and then saw the flash of the child as it was knocked clear of her wheels to the side of the road.

She lurched forward in her seat as she came to a stop sixty feet later, skidding sideways so her car completely blocked the road. Her hands were shaking and a cloud of dust passed over her, spewing across the beam of her one remaining headlight. She coughed, her heart hammering and the car's engine rumbling steadily behind her.

"No," she muttered, shaking her head and closing her eyes. "No."

She jumped from the car, calling out into the dark. As her voice was swallowed by the empty desert, she felt like this wasn't supposed to happen, that seeing a child out here had been the farthest thing from her mind.

But if she could help the child, she would forfeit the race and drive it into town. As she came around to the front of the car, she saw the headlight — the glass itself undamaged, but the filament and chrome bezel both broken. Then she saw a good sized dent on the side of her fender and knew the child was badly injured, if it had survived the impact at all.

"Hello!" she yelled again. Her own voice sounded foreign, unreal. A calling into the dark to something that couldn't answer. She stumbled into the brush with her hands outstretched, her car's engine still blatting behind her. As she searched, she again hoped that this had all been an illusion. She looked back at her car, its single headlight pointing off into the desert.

She cursed and continued scouring the brush. The urgency of

the race pulled at her, with only miles to go. Charles's voice flashed through her mind; that the child shouldn't have been there, that it wasn't her fault, that she should *go*. That there was nothing she could've done, no way she could've stopped in time, and there was nothing she could do for the child now. She thought of all the spectators in the road who'd been killed and injured in the past days. But this was a *child*. As her hands tore at the brush, she imagined the child coming to watch the cars pass, the intoxicating sight it must've been, and she felt something inside her fracture.

She began to cry as she stumbled over denser scrub brush, kicking at it. She recalled the hull of that Ferrari smoking on the rock wall, the elderly Mexican man, dead behind the wheel. No one had stopped for them. And as she continued her search, she realized that if anyone caught her now, she'd be disqualified from the race and implicated of something awful.

Visions of a Mexican jail came to her, lawless and corrupt officials. A trial prejudiced against the American who'd killed a Mexican child. The tainted lawyers, the media projecting her as a murderer, and a country thirsty for her blood. She imagined the entire outraged nation, seething and chanting, coming after her.

Prudence heard the whine of approaching engines. She looked south and saw headlights bearing down on her from the dark desert, as if they were descending upon her from the sky. She had been well ahead of them after all. Her pulse quickened as her hands made one last frantic sweep through the brush.

Her Porsche was still blocking the road. She ran to it and glanced over her shoulder as the cars came speeding towards her, the desert now filled with the piercing wail of their engines. She jumped into the Porsche and grabbed the wheel, the child's eyes emblazoned in her mind, so alive as she approached, unaware of what was about to happen. She put the car in gear to move it from the road, but then suddenly, she pressed the gas pedal and began to drive north along the highway.

"He shouldn't have been there," she said as she accelerated, hoping that the child had been uninjured, that it had just walked away.

The cars were upon her quickly as she raced towards Juarez with her single headlight jiggling along the highway. Teeth gritted, foot to the floor, her driving gloves tight against her knuckles. The cars fought to pass but she skidded through each turn, her car nearly sideways, spewing gravel and sand as she pulled away from them.

At the finish line, a small crowd surrounded her car, cheering her a moment before going on to the next car. She saw the Mexican police with their bandoleers and white hats and leather holsters, walking amongst the arriving race cars. She wanted to confess the accident to them now, but as they pushed back the spectators, their hands hovering near the worn butt of their pistols, their wooden batons raised, she didn't say anything. She remembered the bribed officials at the border, and knew that there'd be no protection for her here, no justice for what had happened.

Prudence turned off her car, climbed from it and saw, under the overhead lights, that the damage to the front fender was obvious, as was the broken headlight bezel. She began to sweat as the officials sorted through the line of incoming cars, and then came to hers.

"What's this?" one of the officials said, pointing his pencil at the dent.

"It was a vulture," she said, her voice trembling.

The official shook the loose headlight bezel and looked up at her. "That's a lot of damage for a bird."

He tipped back his hat, smirking, and jotted some notes down on his tablet. He then placed an **OK** sticker on her windshield and walked on to the next car. She sighed and sat heavily on the fender. She heard other drivers cheering and congratulating each other, but she sat there with her head down, pinching the bridge of her nose to stave off the tears.

When she looked up, Charles was walking towards her with a bottle of champagne. She began to cry when she saw how happy he looked, how excited he was to see how well she'd done. He wrapped his arm around her, the champagne bottle cold against her arm.

"I hit something out there. I think it was a child," she whispered. "I didn't know what to do." She pulled back and looked at him. "I want to go back. I want to go back and find him."

A photographer stepped forward from the crowd just then. He took a picture as they stood in front of her Porsche, before she could cover up the damage. Another man came and stood beside the photographer, a wire recorder on his hip, a microphone thrust out towards them both.

Charles was looking at her closely, as if he didn't believe what he was hearing. "You imagined it," he whispered back. "People see things in the dark. You're just exhausted."

She tried to protest, but he hushed her, and when she turned, the reporter had the microphone pointed at her face. Prudence stared at it. She then shoved it aside and walked past them all, through the crowd and quickly down the street, listening as Charles explained to the reporters that Prudence was tired and would give them all interviews in the morning at their hotel.

IN THE morning Charles sat holding his head, the empty champagne bottle on the nightstand beside him. As she slipped on a loose, sleeveless white cotton dress, and tied the black waist ribbon on her side, she watched him rise from the bed and gaze out the window. She looked for some sign that he'd heard what she'd said to him the night before. He stood there rubbing his temples and she knew it wasn't because of the champagne, but because he'd heard what she'd said, and a blunt reality was closing in on them: that maybe she hadn't just imagined it.

He rested his hand on the wash basin and splashed water on his face. "You have those interviews to give," he said, without turning.

"Charles," she said, stepping closer to him.

"You are already late," he said coldly. She looked at him standing on the bare stone floor, the room already hot and the sun on the dirty windows. "Just give those reporters the usual. I will be down later."

Although she knew she had finished well in the race, Prudence wished she had never come. Later in the day the officials would be announcing the race results and dispensing the trophies and prize money. They would have to stay here in Juarez for that, and then for the awards ceremony and dinner that night. But Prudence knew that she'd be worrying about the child all day, and what had really happened out there in the dark desert.

She went down to the hotel's restaurant to wait for the reporters. She ordered a coffee, and while the waiter poured it, dirt black and steaming, she searched through her purse for change. She was still carrying her old tooled leather purse, her mother's silver scissors in the bottom as a good luck charm. As she rifled through the inner pockets she found the photos of herself taken in the photo booth when she arrived in San Francisco. The photo strip was scratched and worn. Little did that girl know what was awaiting her, she thought, as she crumpled the pictures and set them on the table.

"Miss Baylor," a bellhop said, walking in from the lobby and holding out a Western Union envelope. "Telegram."

Prudence tipped him and then tore open the envelope.

18/11/54

PAPERS HERE COVERING YOU CLOSELY
STOP SO PROUD STOP EAGER FOR YOUR SAFE
RETURN STOP LOVE VI.

Prudence smiled, having forgotten that she'd left Vi with a detailed itinerary. But then the smile faded. As she drank her coffee, she looked out the window and watched the crews loading their race cars onto their trailers. Last night felt like a dream that she couldn't shake. She closed her eyes and envisioned the dark figure in the road, flickering in her headlights. A vulture's black wings unfolding to reveal a child standing between them. And then as she drew nearer, the wings spreading into a V shape, wider than her car. The giant bird lifting itself into the air, tucking its feet into its body. Leaving the boy standing in the road, his skin the color of clay, his eyes filling with light.

When she opened her eyes, two reporters were entering the restaurant. They came to her table, one waving a microphone and asking questions, winding the wire recorder that hung from his shoulder by a large leather strap. The other taking flash photos, popping the bulbs out into his hand. Prudence just sat there, her coffee cup tinkling against the saucer as she set it down, trying to hide from the camera just what she was: a scared, crazy, exhausted girl.

SHE WAS there when the race results were announced that afternoon, in a ceremony held inside a large tent. Only the drivers and the officials were permitted, and so Prudence stood with over two hundred sweating people in the stifling tent, as the official read from the list into a bullhorn. Prudence gasped when she learned that she'd placed fourth in her class of thirty-five drivers. Perhaps it wasn't high enough to win a trophy, but high enough to be listed among the official results that would be wired worldwide. And more than enough to prove that she wasn't just some novelty, that she had out-driven the top professional, factory drivers.

Charles was standing outside the tent when she walked out, rubbing his hands together. "Well?" he asked.

She paused to light a cigarette and then peered at him through the smoke. "Fourth place," she said, breaking into a wide smile.

He hugged her, lifting her off her feet and kissing her on the lips. He held her there a long time, before he set her back down and straightened her dress.

"I knew it," he said, beaming. "I simply knew it."

Prudence went to collect her race winnings, which came in Mexican bills, totaling nearly five hundred American dollars.

Outside the tent, Silvia de Lobos was posing on her white Jaguar for two dozen photographers, wearing a white two-piece bathing suit. Although de Lobos had blown her engine on the last leg of the race and didn't finish, she was smiling at the cameras with a fake gold ribbon pinned to the straps of her suit top. When de Lobos noticed Prudence standing there holding all the cash, her smile dimmed.

The other winning drivers passed by de Lobos, but the cameras didn't turn to capture them. As Prudence stood shaking her head, de Lobos looked at her and laughed, and began blowing passionate kisses at the cameras, for photos that would undoubtedly be smeared all over Mexico and England.

Charles came up from behind and put his arm around Prudence, pulled her in close to him and watched de Lobos with her.

"The world is a strange, strange place," he said and shook his head. "They should be taking pictures of you." He reached in his suit pocket and took out his flask. She handed him the money and took the flask from him, taking a long pull of the hot whiskey. She winced and looked at de Lobos, who then turned and, one hand on her trim waist, blew one final kiss in Prudence's direction.

Fourteen

PRUDENCE STOOD in a crowded Juarez nightclub that night with the racers and crews, a row of local women in bright dresses lining the wall. A smoky place with hot Mariachi music blasting from the jukebox, the dance floor swirling with bodies. She didn't pay for a single drink. As soon as she set her empty glass down there was another Pink Lady waiting, and a fellow racer toasting her from across the bar. She raised her glass to them all, before tossing back each sweet, mind numbing drink. Charles had his arm thrown over her shoulder the whole night, his head tilted back, laughing. Everyone was celebrating except Rudy, who sat in a corner nursing his whiskey, watching her.

Prudence opened her eyes just before dawn, a pair of bright headlights shooting through the open hotel window. "Oh God," she said, touching her throbbing head. She looked around the room: she was still in Juarez. She'd gotten too tight on booze to even think about the race, the boy. She looked at Charles next to her, remembered being with him the night before when they came back to the room. Falling naked on the bed, her legs wrapped around him. The intensity of their kissing, the rising pressure of his body against hers, the pleasant ache and the sweet release.

She slipped from under Charles's arm and dressed as the sun rose over a nearby clay building. "I'm going to run down and get the paper," she said, slipping on a pair of blue jeans. Her voice was more breathless and anxious than she wanted it to be. Charles murmured and rolled over.

She bought a copy of the El Paso newspaper in the lobby, the concierge cutting one out of a freshly delivered stack. A picture from the end of race was on the cover. The article on the front page stated that twelve drivers and eight spectators had been killed in the race and the Mexican public wanted future races banned.

She skimmed the article and stopped on a single line, her chest clenching, when she read that an injured boy had been found the previous morning near Juarez. The unidentified child was in a hospital in Parral, south of Juarez. Mexican Policia would begin investigating the accident by further inspecting all the race cars for undisclosed damage.

She scoured the rest of the paper, her hands beginning to shake. Prudence felt hollow inside, the image of the abandoned child standing in the road branded into her mind. She chided herself for pretending that it was her imagination. She had done the unspeakable by leaving that child there, and now she was a fugitive in a corrupt country.

She took the paper and walked slowly back upstairs, as if eluding a predator that had not yet begun to hunt her. She slipped the key in the lock and went into the room. Charles rolled over in bed, covering his head with his pillow.

"I'm driving down to Parral in the wagon," Prudence said, taking the car keys from the nightstand.

Charles pulled the pillow off his head and looked at her. She held the paper out and read to him what she'd read moments before.

"I have to make sure he's okay," she said, after she finished. "Will you come with me?"

"Are you nuts?" He sat up in the bed. "They'll throw us in jail if we show up at the hospital. Do you know what a Mexican jail is like?" He looked at her, his eyes sharply focused, as if he was noticing some flaw in her that he'd never seen before. "Once you go in, no one can get you out. Not even Dwight D. Fucking Eisenhower."

"I don't care," she said, glaring back at him. "If I don't confess before they find that damage on my car, I'll be screwed."

"Prudence," he said, moving to the edge of the bed, wearing only his shorts. "What happened was an accident. Not your fault."

"It wouldn't have happened if I hadn't been there."

He shook his head, then stood and put his arm around her. "We'll make some phone calls from home, find out how the boy is doing. We'll pay his hospital bills. But we won't show up there and invite the police to arrest us. That serves no purpose."

"No, I'm heading over to the wagon now. You've helped me long enough. If you don't want to come, that's fine. I'll go alone."

"Prudence." He stood beside the bed, a mere shadow in the room's half-light. "Doing the right thing doesn't get you anywhere. Look at Silvia de Lobos. Christ, look at me."

She shook her head quickly. "I don't believe that."

"And that's what I love about you," he said, as she put her hand on the door knob, "but this is more serious than you think. Go down to the trailer and drive it over here. I'll meet you downstairs after I pack up our things."

"No, you don't have to come," she said, grabbing her purse and pulling open the door. "You don't have to help me any more."

She left him there staring at her, walked quickly from the hotel and along the quiet street, which was littered with drivers who hadn't made it home the night before, slouched and sleeping against filthy stoops. A pack of dogs ran along the sidewalk and scurried down a dark alleyway. Above growled the neon sign of the *El Sol* theatre, ghostly now in the pale morning light, with Marilyn Monroe's, *River of No Return* in bright red letters.

El Paso and the border lay just miles away, but parked along the street were many of the American race cars, rows of Fords and Lincolns. As she walked along, a car pulled up behind her and began to follow her. She could feel a pair of eyes on her back and her pulse quickened, but she held her pace, hoping the car would pass. She heard the slow lope of the engine's cam against the valves, the thump of the pistons. When she finally turned, a Mexican patrolman was leaning out the window of the white sedan, wearing a white cap and a black uniform. He seemed to have been waiting a long time to be acknowledged.

"You shouldn't have done that," he said, pulling up beside her, slowing to match her speed.

Prudence sucked in a quick breath, glancing at him. "Done what?"

"Come out here all by yourself." His accent was strong, his skin a deep glistening brown, hair so black it was blue.

She exhaled and looked at him. "Is there a law about a woman being out here?"

"There may be," the officer said, his wrist dangled over the steering wheel. He smiled, his teeth the color of wet bone.

Prudence turned a corner, quickening her stride. She heard the sedan turn to follow. She continued on towards the trailer, which sat on the edge of a parking lot, trying not to move too fast. She knew he was still following her; she could nearly feel the engine panting. When she was out of sight she ducked off the street, ran along a red dirt berm and through a shock of scrub trees, rushing past the rows of tents, drivers still snoring inside them and their bare feet sticking out.

When she came to the trailer, she took her keys from her purse, fitted one in the door's lock and climbed inside. She stood in the dark a moment, listening, then threw back a corner of the Porsche's canvas cover. In the long square of daylight that shined through the open door, she saw the broken chrome headlight ring, the dented sheet metal. She covered her eyes with her hand, stanching the image of the child standing in the road.

She held her breath when she heard footfalls moving around the trailer. She stopped and adjusted her hearing aid, focusing the sound. She thought it might be Charles, but the footsteps were too soft, too stealthy. The world whistled as she turned up her volume, on the edge of feeding back. The footfalls stopped. Then came the scent of cheap Mexican cigarettes, and when she turned, traces of smoke curled through the doorway.

"Good morning," Rudy said in his faint German accent, appearing suddenly. He held a pint of liquor and took a swig of it, wiped his lips and set the bottle on the trailer floor. "I thought you might be here."

Prudence crawled backward and pressed against the trailer wall. Rudy furrowed his brow, climbed inside and looked at the Porsche's dented fender.

"What happened there?" He pulled at his cigarette. "It looks like you hit something."

"A vulture," Prudence blurted, not looking at him, trying to appear calm, although her heart was pumping hard. "Just a vulture."

"It must've been a big one," he said, gazing at her and back at the dent. He dropped his cigarette, ground it out on the floor. Within the confines of the trailer, he suddenly seemed very large.

Rudy knelt beside her, reached in his back pocket and pulled out the same El Paso newspaper that she'd read earlier. "I couldn't sleep last night, couldn't get something out of my head. Just a feeling I had that something wasn't right." He unrolled the paper and read it, as if for the first time. He then threw it on the floor, face up. "And then it occurred to me. This article about the boy they found." He ran his hand over the damaged fender. "A child could do damage like this. It's too high up to be a bird."

Prudence stared at Rudy, unable to think of what she could say to make herself appear innocent. The longer she waited, she knew her silence continued to implicate her, but she couldn't speak.

"I could smooth that out, you know," he said, nodding towards the damage. "Make it look like nothing happened. Because if the police find out about this, you won't be going home for a long time."

She knew if he went to the police, it would be too late for her to confess. His eyes narrowed and she glared at him, his sudden smug confidence. She felt all her muscles tense, her hands balled into fists.

"Nothing happened, Rudy," she said, standing. "I think you need to leave. Because I could have you canned just like that. And I'm sick enough of you to do it."

"Wouldn't Charles be curious why you fired me?" he asked. "And then I'd have to show him this." He smacked the newspaper against the car's damaged fender. "Maybe I'd have to show it to some other people too."

"No one wants to hear your drunken ideas," she said, backing against the trailer wall. "Not Charles, and not me, that's for sure."

"Well, maybe I should report it just the same," he said, stepping closer. "To make it official."

"Get out!" Prudence yelled, pointing at the open the trailer door. "Get out before I scream."

"If you hit that boy," he said, moving even closer, closer than he'd ever been to her. "You'll go to jail. A filthy jail. Maybe you think people from other countries are lower class. I see the way you look at me sometimes. Like I'm trash. Maybe that's how you look at that boy too." He swigged from his bottle, sneering. "Just a piece of trash."

She shoved him away from her and went for the door, but he grabbed her arm and pulled her to him. His breath was sour with booze. She tried to squirm from his grip, but he was holding her tightly, squeezing her with a strength that belied his size.

"As much as I'd like to see what's coming to you, I have another idea," he said, running his hand along her arm. Prudence winced as he gripped her wrist, grinding her flesh against the bone, and brought it towards his crotch.

"Please let me go," she said, her voice cracking. "You're drunk, Rudy."

"People will see that dent when I show it to them. And then Charles won't be able to help you." Rudy pulled her hand closer, chuckling. "And you think you've got something special there, don't you? Let me tell you that he'll never leave Maria. Never."

Prudence felt her nerve fade as quick as it came, her body suddenly going limp in his arms.

"I could pull the dent out," he said softly. "End this for you right now. Let you walk out of this country a hero, not the woman who left a half dead child by the side of the road."

Prudence felt his breath, hot on her face. His grasp damp with sweat, his eyes heavy-lidded as he looked down her blouse and smiled. When she didn't answer he shoved her aside and swung the trailer door shut, leaving only a strip of daylight surrounding it.

It was dark until he found the light switch. The battery was low and the light bulb glimmered faintly above them. Prudence watched as he unfastened his belt buckle. Soon it would be done and everything would be better, she thought, leaning back against the table at the front of the trailer. As she did, her hand pressed against her purse.

Owen Duffy

Rudy grinned at her, then leaned down and lifted his pint bottle from the floor. He tilted his head back and took a long, gurgling swig. As he did, her hand felt something rigid inside the purse.

"I'll take care of that dent after this," Rudy said. "You be good to me for as long as I want, and no one will ever know." He chuckled and put the cork back in the bottle. "I didn't even really know that you had hit that child. But now I know for sure."

She reached into the purse and the scissors fell to her hand, her fingers lacing quickly through the handles. How far those scissors had come. On the bus with her, down from Oregon, and then stolen and found again in that flop house. She'd hemmed with them in Vi's apartment, cut the threads cleanly after sewing a button on a skirt. And now as she held the scissors she imagined her mother sitting in a chair back at home, years ago on some gloomy Sunday, teaching Prudence how to sew.

"Go on," her mother says, smiling as she handed them to her. *"They were my mother's and now they're yours."*

Prudence held the scissors behind her, the blades open slightly. When Rudy advanced towards her, he was smiling and fumbling to undo his trousers. When he was standing right in front of her, his hands on her shoulders, she glanced down at his penis, a candlestick burned down to a nub.

She swung her arm from behind her back and thrust the scissors upwards. As easily as Prudence had sliced that ribbon up in Castroville, she grasped Rudy's center nostril with the scissors blades, his eyes wide and startled as she firmly snapped them closed.

Rudy shrieked and dropped the pint bottle on the floor, which shattered and sent shards of glass throughout the trailer. How easily the blades had clipped through his nose, parting the flesh as if it were paper. And how quickly came the blood. It flowed and dotted the trailer floor. Rudy gasped, swatting his hand in front of his dripping nose and cursing her.

"Damn right you won't tell anyone," she said as she stood, looking at him. "And if you do I'll come and cut off your prick."

"Police!" he began to yell, staggering around the trailer. "*Policia!*"

Prudence jumped from the table, flung open the door and ran from the trailer, the door flapping behind her as she shot past the awakening racers with the bloody scissors at her side, stumbling and falling as she hurried back along the ridge towards the hotel. As she ran, the sound of Rudy's shouting cut through the sleepy morning, shattering its calm and quiet as he continued to yell out for the police.

CHARLES WAS only just heading out of the room when Prudence returned to the hotel, sweating and out of breath. He was dressed in a suit, their luggage in his hands. She leaned against the doorway to catch her breath and looked over at him.

"We need to get out of here," she said, panting. "Rudy knows what happened. He's going to the police. He's out there yelling for them now."

The color quickly left Charles's face. He went and listened at the open window for a moment, as if he might hear Rudy out there. Then he turned and slipped out the door after her. As they walked outside, the sky was a dull white, the morning already growing hot. They hurried down the street, hand in hand, and she felt a sense of dread for the coming hours, when her iniquities would be revealed, and things would forever be changed. But now the town was still asleep and uncomfortably quiet. As they hustled towards the wagon, she no longer heard Rudy's voice, which signaled to her that he had found an officer, with his bloody nose as proof that she had evaded his capture.

Charles stopped at the corner as a hot gust blew across the street, lifting the dust, twirling it in the air. He seemed to sense that something terrible was coming. She pulled him down the same path she had taken earlier, through the grove of trees and past the now awake drivers, who were looking around to see what all the yelling had been about. Prudence and Charles rushed past them, and when they reached the wagon, Rudy was gone. Charles tossed his luggage in the wagon, checked that the trailer was securely fastened to the tow hitch. As Prudence latched the trailer door closed he climbed in the driver's seat and started the wagon.

Prudence jumped in beside him and they shot out of the parking lot and headed straight for the highway, honking at anyone who was in their way. Already traffic heading north had begun to gather at the highway entrance and in the distance she heard a siren crossing their wake, headed back to where the trailer had been parked only moments before.

It was ten long, slow miles to the American border, sorting through traffic with the trailer dragging behind them. Prudence kept looking back to see if anyone was following. Cars passed by indifferently, the sun glinting off their fenders, the drivers looking eager to return home. As they neared the border, an El Paso radio station was playing a fast Speedy West and Jimmy Bryant tune. She rolled down her window, the air smelling sweeter as they neared America.

She shivered at the thought of what had happened with Rudy in the trailer, what might have happened if she hadn't had those scissors. She closed her eyes for a minute, and all she could see was Rudy's face, could feel his alcohol-infused breath on her skin. She wished she had clipped his nose even deeper, or had immobilized him completely, sparing her and Charles this frantic race to the border.

Prudence sat back in her seat, her hands absently brushing her belly. There were other things to worry about too. She could feel the slight mound now. Soon it would be clearly visible and she would have to tell Charles, unless she had the procedure. But for now, all she could think about was Rudy's hands on her, the bruises forming on her wrist, four small dots where his fingers had sunk into her flesh.

As they drove, she confessed to Charles what had happened with Rudy when she'd gone down to the wagon. She told him, in a cold and detached voice, what Rudy had tried to do to her, and what she had done to him in return.

She looked over at Charles when she was finished. But then the image of Rudy swatting at his nose and dancing around in the trailer, instantly sobered up by the injury, struck her as funny. She leaned back in her seat, laughing, unable to stop. Soon they both were laughing uncontrollably, not knowing quite why, each of their laughs picking up when the other's had died.

After the laughter ended, it became very quiet again, except for the radio and the wind playing through the car.

"Things are going to be fine," Charles said, putting his arm around her.

"And why wouldn't they be?" she replied. "Everything has worked out so great."

"Geez, relax," he lowered his sunglasses and looked over the rims, smiling. "It's just me."

"Geez," she jeered back at him.

He pushed his sunglasses back up on his nose. "Geese."

"Goose," she said, smiling as Charles swung the wheel back and forth playfully.

Prudence's smile waned when she looked ahead and saw that traffic was stopped. As they slowed, she realized that it wasn't just traffic, but some sort of road block. Several black police cars were funneling traffic into a line. As they moved closer she saw that Mexican officers were checking through the cars heading north. Charles said that they were probably pilfering anything they could find, holding up racers for American cigarettes or booze. Or for a black Chevy wagon with a man and a woman in it.

She could see, from the batons the Policia held at their sides, that these men were serious. And as she watched them sort through each car, slowly working their way towards their wagon, it was clear that they knew what they were looking for, and for whom. When they neared the wagon she slunk down in her seat, while Charles leaned out the window.

"What's this all about?" he asked, as an officer circled the station wagon, peering inside.

"Can we see your papers?" the officer asked in fluent English, coming to a stop by her door. He was tall and lean, with half-frame glasses, appearing and sounding more Spanish than Mexican.

Charles retrieved the documents from where they were tucked in the crack in the seat, reached over and handed them to the officer. The officer looked through them quickly. He asked a few questions as he did, keeping an eye on Prudence: where they'd been in Mexico, what was in the trailer, if they were carrying anything illegal.

"Yes, if you don't mind, Miss Baylor," the officer said while she was answering one of these questions, as if bored with the charade. He placed his hand on the door through her open window. "Please step out of the car."

She was surprised how easily her name came to his lips, how natural it sounded. The pit of her stomach went ice cold. As she opened her door and stepped from the car, another officer joined them and handed him a document, and she could see from where she stood that her name was clearly marked on it. Prudence looked up at the line of cars that were beginning to back up behind them.

"It's been reported that there is some damage to your race car," the officer said to her, looking up from the document. "You were supposed to report any accidents and you didn't do this when you came to Juarez. Can you tell me why?"

Prudence felt cold and sweaty. She didn't know how to answer, as it was clear he believed she knew what this was about.

"Miss Baylor." The officer shook the papers. "I'm asking because a child was found by the side of the road just south of Juarez. He's in the hospital and there's been accusations that you were the one who hit him. That you drove off without reporting it."

Prudence stared at him, his deep brown eyes behind his glasses. His lips were large and purple, giving him a strange, perverse look.

"Wait a minute," Charles said, stepping from the car. "Prudence, don't say anything."

The officer backed up and rested his hand on his baton, staring at Charles. "Get back in the car, Mister Pieretti. I will have you both detained here until I have an answer."

"There won't be an answer," Charles said. "We just fired a disgruntled mechanic who tried to blackmail us about this very same thing."

"That's no concern of mine," the officer said. "The fact remains that in one minute, we will open up that trailer, and if there is a dent in the race car, then you both will be going to jail." He tipped his cap back on his head and glared at Charles.

Charles stared at the officer a moment, as if sizing him up. There was a fiercely protective look in Charles's eyes that she hadn't seen before. Hidden behind it was a man who was just as weary and beaten down as she was.

Charles slowly reached into his pocket and pulled out a wad of cash — her race winnings, five hundred dollars — rolled into a neat little ball. He looked at Prudence and then slapped the money in the official's palm without any explanation. A long, silent moment passed. The official looked at the wad of cash with a shocked expression, like a man who's been shot in the gut and is staring at his bloody hand in disbelief.

The officer dropped the money on the ground. "Wait right here," he said. He turned and signaled towards the other officers who were sorting through the other cars.

Charles suddenly grabbed her arm and flung open the car door and told her to get in. Prudence ran to snatch up the roll of cash that was sitting there in the sand.

"Leave it!" he yelled, waving for her to get in the car.

She saw the officers hustling towards her, holding up their batons and yelling for her to stop. Charles was already behind the wheel, gunning the engine. She took the last few steps and snatched up the cash, and with the driver's door still open and flapping, she yelled for Charles to move over in the seat. As he did, she jumped in the wagon and slammed it into gear and shot around the police officers, who banged their batons against the wagon as she passed, racing along the shoulder, past the row of waiting cars.

Prudence looked in the rear-view mirror, the officials running towards their patrol cars. Their sirens began to wail as she pushed the wagon up to seventy-five miles an hour on the hard packed shoulder, passing other cars and the trailer wagging behind them, blowing a long trail of dust.

Prudence shot past a caravan of American race crews in their cars, whom she recognized from the beginning of the race. Charles waved his hand at them, signaling them to fall back. The other drivers looked in their rear-view mirrors, saw the approaching police cars, and gave Charles a thumbs up sign. The caravan began to slow to a halt, grid-locking the highway with their cars and trailers, blocking the pursuing officers as Prudence sped ahead on the empty highway.

The Chevy's engine temperature needle rose as she pushed hard the last few miles to the border. Prudence sat forward on the seat, waiting for it to appear, Charles with his hands on the dashboard, the sirens howling behind them. In the distance, Prudence saw the signs for the border, but she was worried that the police had radioed ahead for the American border to stop them.

As they came speeding up to the border she saw two officials standing with their hands on their hips, growing larger through the windshield. Their blue uniforms and pale white skin. When Prudence looked in the rear-view mirror, she saw two black Policia cars were now close behind them. Up ahead, the border gates were open and the two American agents were waving their arms, as if they had their police radios on and knew what was happening.

Prudence could hardly believe it, and as she drove effortlessly through the open border gate, one of the officials turned and dropped the gate behind them, blocking off the Policia. Prudence looked in the rear-view mirror and saw one of the American guards raise his hand to her and wave.

As they passed through the border and on through El Paso, mixing back in with the other race crews heading north, Charles wiped his face with a handkerchief. He didn't say anything and neither did she. It was as if they were deep in their own thoughts and worrying about all that lay ahead of them.

They drove silently through the day and night, the car quiet except for the soft din of the radio, each of them lost in their thoughts. Thoughts that led her back home, to what was waiting, where the true weight of what had just happened would be there to greet her. Where she could begin to set right what had gone wrong. They drove without stopping to eat, only for gas and cigarettes. As any sort of lengthy pause would require them to speak about what had happened. Soon enough she knew they would have to talk about it, but not now, not here.

They passed through Bakersfield the next morning and sped north along the empty grapevine road. As they did, Prudence stole glances in the side view mirror for something following them. Someone or something that had witnessed what she'd done. But for now it was only the two of them on the road, dragging that silvery trailer behind them. And what a low, thunderous sound they made, rolling along that bi-way, onward across the earth.

Fifteen

CHARLES ROLLED the Porsche from the trailer when they arrived at his dealership that evening. The shop was empty and dark, and it seemed like a long time since she'd last seen it. As the car eased to a stop outside the garage, the pavement wet with fresh rain, he peeled off the cover. The car was already a relic, aged a lifetime in a single week of racing. Prudence ran her hand along the damaged fender, her fingers finding the impression, the size of her hand, larger and deeper than she remembered. As she caressed the sheet metal, Charles put his hand on her shoulder.

"I told you," she said, brushing her hair from her face. "When I got from the car after Juarez. I told you what happened."

"I thought that you imagined it," he said. "That happens on long races. But there was nothing we could do anyway." He put his arm around her and pulled her to him. "I'm sorry. But there was nothing we could do."

Prudence looped her arm around him, looking down at the battle-worn Porsche. After a minute, they turned and pushed the car inside the garage. As she set the parking brake, Charles went and unlatched the trailer from the wagon, the safety chains tinkling as he loosened them. He then swung the trailer doors shut and latched them closed.

"I'll give you a ride home," he said when he returned, wiping his hands on his handkerchief. "Let me get some of my things from the office."

"No," she said, eager to clear her mind on the walk to the apartment. "I'll be fine by myself."

He tucked the handkerchief in his pocket and inspected his

hands. "What happened wasn't your fault, Prudence." His face was as open and bright as she remembered seeing it the first time. "All those spectators wouldn't have been hurt if they weren't standing out in the road. We'll get a paper in the morning and see how the child is doing. We'll make some phone calls. Pay all the hospital bills."

Prudence shook her head. "That boy wouldn't have been hurt if I hadn't been there." She looked off in the distance, feeling as if she'd spoken a simple truth. Rain dripped from the garage overhang, and farther, over the buildings a fog had rolled in, blushing with the setting sun behind it.

"You sure you don't want a ride home?"

"No," she said, searching in her purse, her hand clasping a half-dollar. "I'll be fine."

"It's always like this after a big race." Charles shook his head and sighed. "You wonder if things could've been different. But you can't change any of it. You want to, but you can't."

Prudence flipped the coin over in her hand, minted long ago, existing while she and the world went on around it. She stared at it a moment. "My bus ticket to California cost eight dollars," she said. "I was going to Los Angeles, but missed the changeover. I never told you that, did I?" She smiled and turned the coin again. "I got robbed my first night here in town. In some lousy flop house. Nearly twenty dollars, my bus ticket, my wallet with all my identification. But maybe my wallet and my money took a bus ride, maybe someone else's little dream came true of getting far from home."

Charles was just looking at her. She wasn't sure what she was saying, but she was getting at something, and he seemed to know what it was, and that it wasn't anything that could be said, but that sometimes you had to try.

"But I'm glad," she continued. "Because if I could do this much damage with eight dollars, what would I have done with the rest of my money in Los Angeles?" She closed her hand around the coin. "And I've been thinking. What if I could go back and buy myself? And then I wonder how much I would pay, to avoid what had happened."

She looked at Charles, his rumpled sport coat and wrinkled shirt. He ordinarily wouldn't tolerate this kind of thinking, as when it came to matters of speculation he was blindly optimistic.

"But you wouldn't have sold yourself then," he said, "and you won't sell yourself now. That much I know about you." He came and put his arm around her again. "Great things come with sacrifice. And sometimes you aren't prepared for what happens. But there's always something good waiting out there, something that proves that all the hard times were worthwhile."

She nodded, knowing that in a way he was talking about himself, confessing the good changes she'd made to his life. He looked at her then, the type of sympathetic expression that years ago might've incited her to confess a secret. But her secret was still entangled in her body, like a root tapping deep into the wellsprings of her mother and beyond, in some way connected to the child in Mexico and that vein of highway, and then here between their bodies, sharing their flesh and their blood.

They stood looking at each other, both of their eyes half-closed, and then she kissed his cheek and said goodbye. She crossed the lot and began walking up the block. Before she turned the corner, she glanced back through the iron fence and saw Charles talking on the phone in his office, with Maria she guessed by the way he intimately cradled the receiver, the ember of his cigarette glowing as he lifted it to take a draw.

Around her, as she moved forward through the evening mist,

Owen Duffy

everything appeared as if she was seeing it anew; the buildings and streets washed clean in the rain, the resplendence of the salty fog that swept over her as she tucked her head and began to walk to see the one person who could frame this all into perspective, with whom there would be no secrets or silences.

Prudence gazed up from the corner at a shadow moving behind the curtains, feeling a thrill as she crossed the street and slipped the key in the apartment door. Cars passed with their wipers smacking back and forth, the sluice of their tires, waves washing to the curb and streaming in tannin rivulets down the hill. She stared at the door's cracked finish, and even before she could turn the key, she heard the pad of bare feet on the steps, the unlatching of locks and chains, and then as the door was pulled open, the flash of a kimono and the scent of stale cigarette smoke.

But it was Jeffie standing in the doorway. Cradling a bag of trash. She stared back at Prudence, who felt her smile recede as if a drawstring had just pulled her face taut. Jeffie's hair was cut severely short, trimmed on the side and top, like a man's. Her lean figure now looked hard and sinewy, her face bloodless and puffy. Prudence envisioned the dopers she'd seen pulled from The Scotch House john, the needles still in their arms, and realized that Jeffie had been turned on to whatever they were using.

"Where's Vi?" Prudence asked.

"She left," Jeffie said, blocking the doorway.

"What?"

"She's gone," she said, lifting her chin. "I took over her room." Jeffie looked strange wearing Vi's old kimono. "She went back with her husband. John or whatever."

Prudence heard noises upstairs, another woman's voice. She pushed open the door and brushed past Jeffie, who shouted at her as she bound up the steps.

Prudence stopped at the top of the stairs, in the entry to the apartment. The room was empty of its furniture, the paintings and easels gone. Now there was only a card table, a record spinning on a portable player. On the floor sat a tattered Oriental rug, and a very young couple sat on it, their faces pale and their doped eyes bobbling as they tilted back their heads to take her in.

"Where's Vi?" Prudence said, her voice sounding panicked. She was breathless and felt queasy, her hand finding the wall to brace herself.

"What the hell is wrong with you?" Jeffie asked as she came up the stairs and into the room. "You're a kooky bitch, always have been."

Prudence glanced around from where she stood, her back against the wall and her hands falling to her stomach.

"Here, relax," the girl on the rug said. She reached out, holding a burning stick of tea. Prudence smelled the pungent marijuana smoke, then looked around at all of them, feeling as if she had stumbled into the wrong apartment. She then turned and walked past Jeffie and across the den to her bedroom.

She opened her door, went inside and stood in the dark and caught her breath, telling herself to slow down, to take it easy. She sat heavily on the bed, listening to Jeffie cackling out in the den. Prudence flipped off her hearing aid and leaned against the wall, her arms wrapped tightly around her belly. For the first time she felt protective of what was inside her. This thing she was carrying inside her was *life*. And now she wanted to see Vi so she could share this sudden revelation, and foolishly expected her to be waiting there, even after the way she'd dispensed with her for Charles.

Prudence felt the burning pangs of jealousy that Vi had run off.

And left her with Jeffie as a roommate to boot. Just two weeks before they'd sat at the kitchen table in this apartment and decided that they would find the best solution to her situation when she returned. It wasn't like Vi to break a promise. But Prudence also knew that she'd let Vi down too, enough that Vi might have had no qualms about leaving her.

Out her window, slow evening traffic moved by her in the street. As she watched a passing taxi splash through the rain, she felt the sensation of something gripping her body. A tightness, an intense pressure, as if something was holding her there a moment before it started to swallow her whole.

She had to get out of this apartment, disappear for a while. She may have escaped what had happened in Mexico for a moment, but the danger wasn't behind her. There were likely charges against her. She feared they would try and persecute her, an underground network that might already be working to find her. And perhaps they already had.

Prudence turned on the light and set her purse on the bed. When she looked down she noticed an envelope on the bed, tucked under her pillow. She picked it up, saw her name was written on it, and quickly tore it open.

Nov. 23rd, 1954

Prudence,

I have so much to say and don't know how to begin. By now you already know that I've gone. I know what you felt like last time we met, to be heading somewhere and leaving something behind. Not knowing if what you're doing is the right thing, but having faith that things will work out.

John called after you left that day. He wanted me to come for the holidays, and I think I might just stay up there a while. I have no real family Prudence. I have no one. I think you know what that feels like.

I haven't even packed. The first thing I wanted to do was write you. You were here only the other day and you'll be back in a couple of weeks. I could've waited, I should have. But I know that you wouldn't have waited for me. And I would never have expected that of you.

I turned my room over to Jeffie and packed up all my art supplies. I sold off most of the furniture. Quit work. Hurley wasn't pleased, but after three years of servitude, I didn't owe him a thing. I'm going up to Raintree, Washington, that's where John has a place. It's an old farmhouse, and I've been wanting to sit on that porch swing and get back into my work, and think about some new ideas I've been having.

I still believe that a wise person knows when to quit at something. But I haven't given up on myself. I know now that I quit on myself too soon, and for the wrong reasons. You were right about that. I am going to make it on my own this time. I've made that clear to John, my intentions that is, all of them. That I want to be my own artist, and that I don't want his connections. I want to get to the top of the mountain by myself. That's the whole point right, the journey?

I do respect and admire him greatly. Maybe that's what love will be to me. He is a strong, gentle man who cares for me a great deal. And he wants to see me have what every person deserves — someone to love them in return.

When you were here at the apartment the other day, you said you knew what you were going to do about your baby. You don't need me to tell you what to do. I know you, and I know you'll do the right thing, because you aren't afraid of what that means to others.

And if you come to that decision, I have a proposition. Come up here. Stay until you have the baby. Don't go overseas with Charles — you need rest. I've talked to John, and there are good doctors here and he wants you here too. He knows I don't have many friends and he's not the jealous type. Stay as long as you like, is exactly how he put it. After all, it's just a big, empty house.

And after you have the baby, do as you please. If you have to go off, we'll take care of it — that sounds crazy of me to say — I know a baby should be with its mother, and that you'll want that too. I just mean to say that it can work out. It doesn't have to seem like such a hard thing. We're modern people, right?

I'll write again when I get there. Just know that this hasn't been easy, but I know I'm doing the right thing. That I've realized there's more to life than the one I've been living, and there are things I want more than to be free — because to be free means being alone and not having the things I want — a home, a family, and a chance to do something that <u>means</u> something..

And I'm leaving you like this, because I know you will come see us. Charles will have his things to take

care of and so will you. So I hope to see you soon.
Think about it.

Love always,
Vi

PRUDENCE WATCHED the mechanics come out from the garage when she arrived at the dealership the next morning. They shouted to her from beneath the garage overhang, their caps raked to the side, their coverall sleeves rolled up. When they broke into applause she bowed, her cheeks warming. As they whistled and cheered, the crushing sadness of what had happened in Mexico began to lift. She also realized, as their applause continued, that they were celebrating more than just her finish at the Pan Am, but also what they had heard from Charles about Rudy. As they came and shook her hand, she saw that they respected her for dispensing with him, and the way in which she had.

They invited her back into garage, where she saw they were prepping her Porsche for street use. The headlight ring and sheet metal were mostly repaired, but the paint on the hood was otherwise still race ravaged. She felt the respect she'd always wanted from them, and knew, as she looked at the new license plate and pressed her finger into the fresh tires, that this was their way of showing it. Of allaying the pain caused by the accident, pain they knew to be common to car racing. As she stood back and looked at the Spyder, she knew that she had become, in their eyes, indoctrinated into the sport.

When she looked into the showroom she saw Charles waving to her from his office window, the phone cradled to his ear, his feet propped on his desk. She thanked the mechanics and went inside, heard Charles's lilting Italian wafting into the showroom, the bitter scent of his cigarettes. A group of workers were laying marble tiles on the showroom floor, the air filled with dust and the occasional whine of a saw. Another group stood painting the walls. She knew she didn't have to be here to work today, but she was eager for its distractions, and the safety she felt here.

She dropped her things beside her desk and sat in her chair. It felt strange to be there after those two weeks. She noticed a box beside her desk, filled with bottles of Strega liquor, cartons of Muratti cigarettes, rolls of prosciutto: whenever Charles's Italian connections sent him a car, they always filled the trunk with goods he couldn't get stateside.

She moved the carton aside and immediately began working on some paperwork. She found its rhythms soothing: the scratch of her pen and the wisp of each paper as she sorted and stacked them neatly in the file. As she worked, she watched the sun gleaming off the cars in the lot, heard the mechanics' laughter out in the garage, and was thankful that it hadn't been a gloomy return.

Charles stepped out of his doorway a moment later and called her in his office. He apologized for not coming out to greet her with the others, told her that he was making some business arrangements. His expression softened as she slipped into a chair across from him.

"I should have had someone better with you during the race, not Rudy. Someone you trusted." He looked down and shook his head. "It was a big mistake on my part, and I fully intend to listen to you on everything from here on out."

Prudence nodded slowly, knowing that he had good reason to be sorry. "But that doesn't change things now, does it?" she asked, crossing her arms.

"No," he said, "it doesn't. I have been sorting things out

over the weekend." He put his hands in his pockets. "I wanted to anonymously pay all the boy's hospital expenses, to see that he gets proper care. I know some people down that way and they made some inquiries. Apparently the boy is in fine condition. A concussion and a few broken bones. But there's a problem. Hundreds of people are coming forward and claiming to be the boy's parents."

"How could that be?" Prudence asked, but then she knew the answer. She shook her head. "So what do we do then?"

"You can give the money to the San Marco de Paul Hospital, where the boy is," he said, handing her a piece of paper with the address. "Apparently that boy was living in the streets." He stood and went to the window. "The parents of that child should be liable. What you did was the right thing. If you'd told the officials about the accident, you'd be in some jail right now, and I'd have no way to get you out."

He turned back to her. "The important thing is to get you back out there. Not for the press, not for exposure, but to keep you moving forward. The papers aren't talking about the boy in Mexico, they're talking about how well you did. Have you read them?"

"I haven't had the time." Prudence shook her head. "I need a break from all of this."

"There's no time for a break," he said. "We need to capitalize on your finish in the Pan Am. I want you to do another local race to get more sponsors and investors. Then we will get ready to go to Europe. I've already made the arrangements. We will leave the week after this upcoming race."

"I need a break, Charles." Prudence pressed her fingers to her temple. "I need to think about things. I have a lot on my mind. And I'm not leaving the country with that boy in a hospital."

"To think about what, huh?" he asked, leaning closer to her.

"About how awful it is that a boy was standing there? To wish that it was different? Because if it wasn't you, it would've been the next guy to hit him."

"Yes!" she yelled, rising from the chair. "Maybe I wish you hadn't pushed me into something that I wasn't ready for, when I didn't even know the risks." She pointed her finger at him, her voice rising. "And now you're trying to put me back out there. *You* gave up racing, and then I come along and suddenly you're pushing me to do all the things you should be doing."

The tools and talking ceased in the garage, and she knew the mechanics were looking in and watching them.

"Look," Charles said, sitting on the edge of his desk. He breathed deeply. "The truth is that you are better than I ever was. I didn't just quit because I was scared, or because I'd lost my edge. I quit because I was afraid that I'd gone as far as I could. I would have gotten back in that car in a second if I thought I'd have a chance at something great. I would have risked it all. And right now, you're where I was then, and you're scared. But let me tell you this: you were risking your life out there too. Remember that. And you're going to see a lot more people get hurt and even die. You have the talent, and you owe it to yourself to keep going."

He stood from the desk again, blotting sweat from his forehead. "But I won't push you any more. I don't want you to go out there because I think you have what it takes. I want you to do it on your own from now on. You can say you quit right now, or you can say it in six months, and I will be fine with that. But you don't need time to think about it. You know what you want to do. There are bigger races out there and if you want to win them, you can. But you can't stop, you can't take a break. Not now."

Prudence took Charles's cigarettes from his desk, tapped one from the pack and lit it with one of his Zippo lighters. She ran her fingers over the brushed chrome metal, tarnished with years of use, the silk-screened commemoration of some long ago racing event, now faded and chipped to illegibility.

"I don't need a break," she said, feeling tears forming in the corners of her eyes. "And I don't want to quit. I don't need to feel good about anything that's happened in order to go on."

He handed her his handkerchief and she pressed it into the corners of her eyes.

"There's a race this Saturday in Palm Springs," he continued, his voice resolute. "It has a large cash purse and everyone will be expecting you to appear. There will be a lot of press too, so I think we should go in strong." He paused. "Colonel Brown is interested in investing in you, and as a gesture, he put up some money to buy you another car." He held his hand up to her before she could protest. "This one is mine; you don't have to pay for any of it. It's a step up in engine size, and if you want to get into the Gran Prix circuit, then you'll have to drive the bigger cars, and you'll have to do it well."

Prudence closed her eyes, imagining racing a larger car, the challenges it would bring. She blotted her eyes with the handkerchief. When she opened then again, Charles was smiling. He took an envelope from his letterbox and held it out to her.

"This might raise your spirits."

She took the open envelope from him and looked inside, running her eyes over its contents. It was a check for her *Nivea Crema* sponsorship, for three thousand dollars.

"It comes with a contract," Charles added, pulling another document out of the stack. "They want you to be the face of their products, and to sign on for a full year. And if the Colonel puts up some money too, you will be set. And if he likes what he sees, he'll put you on a nice salary too."

Prudence stared at the check, amazed at the amount written on it. She'd never earned that kind of money before.

"Now I want you to come out to my ranch this weekend," Charles said. "Maria is gone and has moved in with some relatives in Sausalito, who are no doubt harming my good name at this very moment." He looked at her. "I'll have the new car there at the house. It's a Ferrari. I want you to try it out before the next race."

Prudence was barely listening to him. She was fanning herself with the check, feeling how flimsy it felt between her fingers. Her race winnings had already been spent to cover her expenses, and this check would pay off a portion of the seven thousand she still owed on her Porsche. And then there were the boy's hospital expenses to consider.

"I'll do the race in Palm Springs," she said, standing and folding the check in half. "But I'm not so sure about promises of more money. It seems like every time I make a dollar, I've already spent three."

"Well you just became the first woman to finish the Carrera Panamericana," he said, smiling in the boyish way he had. "Magazines and newspapers have been calling all morning for interviews. You aren't going to ever have to pay for a car again, let alone a drink." He came closer and put his arm around her waist, leading her out into the showroom, heady with fresh paint, across a section of marble tiled floor. "And wait until you get behind the wheel of this Ferrari. All those worries of yours are going to slip away."

Sixteen

PRUDENCE DROVE the same road to the ranch that she and Charles had nearly five months earlier, that day they'd raced south to corral his horses. As she sped along, she recalled their decisive return trip to the city that evening; Charles clinging to the dashboard as she killed the headlights and drove by moonlight. And although the memory felt bittersweet now, there came again, as she dropped into a flat valley and pressed the accelerator to the floor, the same exhilaration she felt that night, from the intense speed and motion. A heightened sensation that she knew she could no longer live without. That unmistakable levity she felt when she was racing, as if everything was going to be okay as long as she just kept driving.

She smiled at the thought of driving the Ferrari that Charles had picked out for her, and to have him to herself for the afternoon. She planned on spending the night there with him, and then leaving together for Palm Springs in the morning. She knew the countryside was the perfect place try out the Ferrari, and that she'd be able to stretch the car's legs with impunity. Charles had doubly assured her that Maria was long gone from the ranch, had run off when he signed the divorce papers.

Arrivederci, Prudence thought, downshifting as she neared the ranch. Charles had finally freed himself. Even if it came at great cost and their future was uncertain, she knew that he was better off. That perhaps everything would come together for them after all. That their biggest fears hadn't turned out to be that bad, and that if they could go through what they had and make it out okay, then they could go through anything.

Owen Duffy

As she approached the driveway to the ranch, a black foreign coupe appeared in her rear-view mirror, the driver's face obscured by the sunlight glinting off it. Prudence waved for the car to pass, but it stayed close to her bumper. When she came to the long gravel driveway she made the turn quickly. She watched as the coupe slowed and turned down the lane behind her, obscured in the effluvium of dust that her Porsche kicked up.

In her rear-view mirror Prudence saw a face shrouded in the dust, hands gripped tightly on the wheel. She pulled in the circular driveway, cut her engine, and watched the black coupe come to a halt behind her. Both front doors snapped open and Maria and a short, older woman stepped out.

Prudence felt her body tense, as if she was being squeezed. She glanced down along the row of oaks that grew along the lane leading to the stables. Charles was moving swiftly in their shadows towards her, his gait unsteady, his hand supporting his right thigh as he walked up the sloping hill. He cupped his hands around his mouth, yelling through them as he hurried, but his voice was swallowed in the rustling trees. Prudence jumped from her car and flipped its door shut, her pulse quickening. Maria stood poised in front of the Porsche, her feet and shoulders squared, her hands behind her, as if she was clutching a weapon.

She had never seen Maria this close before, and was shocked by her fierce beauty; the trim, lithe figure, the diamond shaped face and raven black hair. Her dark eyes intensified these features and hinted at a cruel cunning. Prudence felt her own face go ashen, feeling foolishly unprepared for this, when she'd somehow known its inevitability.

Charles was still climbing the driveway as the same squat older woman, in a heavy black skirt, stockings and sweater, came and stood at Maria's side. With their eyes now pinned on her, Prudence felt herself shrink into the person that they undoubtedly saw when they looked at her — the woman who had vandalized their lives.

Then she heard another of the car's doors open. When she turned she saw Maria's boy standing beside the car with his fingers in his mouth. Prudence gasped. Even though he wasn't Charles's child, and was the pawn that Maria had used to trick him into marrying her, Prudence realized that she had disrupted the child's life too.

"You bitch." Maria spat at her. "You've ruined our family. And for what? He will be broke now. He will lose all of this." She gestured to the house and the surrounding land, her other arm still pinned behind her back. "You think you've hurt us? No, you've hurt *him*."

Maria stepped forward and paused, looking Prudence straight in the eye. Maria's lips quivered a moment before she moved her arm from behind her back. In a swift motion, she dealt Prudence a hard slap across her cheek.

The pain was instantaneous, a white hot sting shooting down to the tips of her toes, like a sharp, electric jolt. Prudence rocked on her heels a moment, too shocked to cry out. She cupped her burning cheek. The slap disarmed her, and had knocked her hearing aid from her ear. When she looked up, Maria was glaring at her.

"You're nothing but a whore," Maria spat. "A deaf, ugly woman. And because you are so pathetic, you had to steal my husband. You will never be anything more than a prostitute."

Prudence couldn't hear much of what Maria said. Her hand had clenched into a ball, and before she knew it her fist had swung through the air and connected with Maria's cheek. There was the satisfying smack of their flesh connecting. Not an effete smack, but a hard knuckled punch that buckled Maria's knees and sent her to the ground.

"Prudence, Goddamn it. Stop!" Charles yelled when he appeared just then, and wrestled with her a moment before he could pin her arm down to her side. He wrestled with her some more, Prudence's eyes still fixed on Maria's supine figure.

"What the hell are you doing here, Maria?" he asked, wheezing. He released Prudence and hunched over to catch his breath, hands planted on his knees.

"You were the one who tried to ruin him," Prudence said as she re-attached her hearing aid. "So go find some other man to bleed dry."

Maria stared back at her and then barked in Italian for the older woman to take the child inside. "I've come to get some things of theirs," Maria said to Charles, standing and brushing herself off. "And then I'll leave you to your whore."

Charles was still hunched over, the hair on the back of his neck slick with sweat. He slowly straightened and glared at Maria, his eyes wide and unblinking.

"Don't you call her that. *You* of all people," he said, giving Maria a scouring look. "You are the one who whored yourself a long time ago. Suckered me in and screwed some poor bastard over. At first it was just a dress, then a new car, then a house with everything a person could want." His voice was becoming more placid as he continued, more matter of fact. "And then you withheld all the things a wife is supposed to give. You're worse than a whore. You're a thief and a scold." He wiped a bit of spittle from his lips. "Get the last of your things that I bought you and get the hell out of here."

He turned decisively, his expression still calm. Maria stood there, her lips formed into a large and confused shape. Charles went to the child, standing in the house's doorway. As he knelt and reached out to him, the boy recoiled and ran and clung to Maria's legs. She stood there and looked at Charles, her mouth flattening into a grin.

"Take a good look at him and your house," she said. "Because it's the last time you'll ever see them."

Clutching the child to her, she walked into the house and slammed the front door, leaving Charles open palmed, kneeling in the dirt.

FIFTEEN MINUTES later, Prudence watched from a distance as the black coupe roared out of the driveway. She turned back to the Ferrari in the barn doorway, her body casting a shadow over its long hood. She and Charles were, for the moment, ignoring what had happened and trying to feign interest in the car.

The Ferrari had bright wire wheels, muscular fender arches, a dozen trumpet intakes rising from the hood scoop. It looked menacing to her, violent. It was a factory team race car, the color of freshly shed blood, with a radiator inlet like a shark's mouth, the headlights set close above it like eyes. Charles said the car had raced at the previous Mille Miglia, and had fared well. As she walked around the car she noticed how race worn the paint was.

Like her Porsche, the Ferrari had an open cockpit with no roof. It had the same sharply raked windshield and also came to her thigh in its height. It had only one seat, but the car was substantially wider and longer, with a twelve-cylinder engine, which was nearly three times the size of her Porsche's.

"This is the 1953 375 Plus. It raced in the Pan Am too and I got it at a good price. I'll have my mechanics go over it and then you'll have one of the fastest cars at the Mille Miglia this year."

As she stood looking at the car, Prudence's hand absently touched her cheek, and felt a bruise forming. She gazed up at the house, expecting to see a drawn curtain and Maria's silhouette behind it, but the house was closed and dark

"So what do you think?" Charles asked. "It's something, isn't it?

She looked at him and then down at the car, the moment soured by what had happened. The blow to her cheek had snapped her from any fantasy she had about being some international race starlet. She felt silly for having gone along with the idea as long as she had, when she knew that she'd never be able to go to Europe if she was to have the child. She leaned against the broad, open doorway and looked at the sun setting over the golden hills.

"You said Maria wasn't going to be here," she said, rubbing the toe of her shoe over the barn's dirt floor.

He brushed back his hair and leaned on the Ferrari's hood. She could tell it was still close in his thoughts too. He sighed and shook his head.

"You always think things are going to work out for the best," she said. "It's always some big surprise when something doesn't go perfectly."

"God," he stood up and put his hand on his hip. "Now you sound just like her."

"Well maybe she had some sense after all," she said, her hand touching her cheek again. "And maybe she whacked a little of it into me."

She gazed at him a while, still as winningly handsome as he'd always been. But she knew he felt the same as she did: that the moment should've been happier. They both stood there like shamed children, sent down here to the barn to think about what they'd done.

"Put the cover back on it," she said, looking down at the car. "I'll drive it tomorrow at the race."

"You need to take it for a drive." Charles stood and pointed at the engine. "To learn how to control it."

"I don't particularly feel like going for a drive just now." Prudence stood with her arms crossed. "And I would appreciate it if when I say 'no' to you, that you listen."

"This is different ..." he said. "It could be dangerous if you don't."

"No," she said, walking out of the barn. "It's no different at all."

PRUDENCE AWAKENED on the sofa in the front parlor of Charles's house, unwilling to sleep in one of Maria's beds. A clear blue sky was shining outside the large window. She shed her blanket sometime during the night and now the sunlight covered her body, her fingers nearly translucent as she lifted them to shield her eyes. She'd seen Charles stirring during the early hours, passing through for a glass of water or to use the toilet. And now she plugged in her hearing aid and heard him flipping open kitchen cupboards, his low, tuneless whistle echoing through the hallway.

She stood from the sofa and folded her blanket, fluffed the pillows, and when she finished, Charles was standing in the beams of light shining through the windows, looking out at the Ferrari, strapped to the Chevy's trailer.

"There's nothing to eat here," he said. He stood by the parlor window as he buttoned up his rumpled shirt. "She didn't even leave a crumb."

Prudence watched him a moment, thinking of last night, how she'd left him standing there in the barn. From now on, she would be making her own decisions. She turned from him again and pushed the front door open, felt the cool early morning breeze brush over her. The walkway stones were wet, and there in the circle driveway the cars were glistening with dew.

The three cars sat in the shade of the tree, the marble fountain in the driveway's center, a woman with her outstretched hands dripping streams of water. The scene struck her as odd, as she had never quite grown accustomed to the fact that this was indeed her own life that she was living. That this was something she was never supposed to see or feel, as if she had gotten off the train at the wrong stop. It made her wonder if her future was always out there, that each moment already existed and was waiting for her to arrive. And at times like this she felt as if she'd tricked fate, altered its course — not just this morning — but since she'd left home nearly a year ago.

She shivered and slid her feet into her canvas shoes. He came and stood in the doorway beside her, his eyelids puffy, his hair a tousled mess.

"Let's get going," she said, stepping out onto the walkway towards the Chevy, packed with their luggage and all her racing gear. She turned and saw him looking at her standing there in the driveway of his house. He had that lovably pitiful look to him again. She turned and went back to him, throwing her arms around him and pecking him on the lips.

"I'm tired, Steve," he said, holding her tightly and putting his head on her shoulder. "I'm just so damn tired."

"I know," she whispered, rubbing the back of his neck, breathing in the scent of his aftershave. "You'll be back home soon enough, and there will be no one holding you down."

"One more day with that woman and I don't think I would've made it." He put his hand to his head, his shoulders heaving as he breathed in and out. He combed back his hair with his fingers and tried his best to smile.

"Come on," she said, turning and taking his hand. "Why don't you drive, clear your head."

He smiled, following after her into the driveway, as if he'd forgotten that they had a race today. That he wasn't coming back here ever again, except to collect the Porsche to bring it back to the shop. That soon the ranch would be sold, and he'd be gone from this country. As she climbed in the wagon after him, he looked up at the house. She saw his eyes glistening, and he turned away from her and wiped his eyes with his sleeve.

"Let's get the hell out of here." He started the wagon and wrangled its big wheel, driving past her Porsche and up the driveway, leaving it behind in a cloud of dust.

ON THE way down to Palm Springs, she felt the contemplative mood of that morning traveling with them. Charles drove, humming along to the radio, while she lay in the Chevy's back seat with her race suit folded up as a pillow, furtively re-reading the end of a long letter she'd received from Vi just the day before:

> ... *sometimes I sit here in this old drafty house while John is away and think that this is just a body, this is just a life. I look out the window for hours. And it's like I'm staring out at someone else's eyes looking in at me.*
>
> *And being with a man, the way John is when we're together. Alien and natural at the same time. I must admit that I like it more than I ever did. Not just the sexy part, but having a man in my life. Especially one as caring as John.*
>
> *I'd forgotten too how nice the country is in the winter. How quiet. John had a new barn built while I was away. He wants some horses, and he has a new tractor that he cuts the grass with. It's amazing what occupies a person's time. If you aren't careful, the chores of life can*

Owen Duffy

consume you.

I like this new part of me. I don't want for anything. But sometimes I feel like I'm missing out on something that I'll never be able to get back. Like when it was just the two of us in that apartment, having breakfast together or reading the papers. But maybe that all wasn't such a great time either, because we didn't know where our lives would take us next.

Last week I went out into the shed, and there behind the watering cans was a black snake, coiled like a rubber hose. I saw the little tail of a field mouse sticking out of that coil, limp and still. The snake flicked its tongue at me and I just backed out and closed the door.

And now sometimes at night I lay awake in bed beside John and I feel like that mouse. Like my feelings for John are gripping me. A feeling of love that I've never had. A frightening sort of love that holds me there as tight as it can, and I hear a voice whisper, "You're mine now. I own you."

But in a way that feels good. Maybe you need to feel bad for a while, so you can feel good again. That's what I think happened to me. I just wish you were sitting here beside me now, rocking in one of these old chairs, talking to me.

I hope you'll come see me sometime, you and your little baby. Stay for as long as you want. Life doesn't have to follow everyone else's plan — you and I both know that by now.

I dream about her sometimes, your child. It's a girl, somehow I just know. I can picture her when I close my eyes. Brown hair and red lips. It sounds strange, but she looks like John in my mind. I see the girl running around here, circling the house. I hear her laughing. See her shadow, peeking over the edge of the porch to spy on me and John as we talk.

I think she's here, and she's looking, waiting to meet you ...

Love always,
Vi

Prudence tucked the letter in the pocket of her Levi jacket when she finished reading. She thought of the apartment; she could be gone from the place with all of her things, which might fit in a single carton, within hours of returning home after this race. Sell her furniture back to the store where she bought it, turn the keys over to Jeffie, and be headed north to visit Vi.

She fished the last cigarette from her pack and held it to her lips. She struck a match and held it before her, but then blew it out and tossed the cigarette away. She was still feeling the occasional nausea she had in earlier weeks, but she'd gotten good at holding it at bay. Most of the time, when she was pretending to be normal around Charles, she almost forgot she was pregnant at all. But then alone, she felt herself pressed to make a decision about which way she'd go: with Vi, or with Charles.

Prudence knew there was no way that she could have the baby, a career, and a relationship with Charles. As much as she respected him, being with Vi felt innately comfortable, nearly familial. Vi was the one person who understood her, like a sister she'd never had. Someone she would need in the coming months. Having an illegal procedure wasn't something she could live with. And having child out of wedlock was something she was not prepared to do alone, given that she was unwilling to entrap Charles as Maria had done.

"I talked to a contact in Mexico yesterday," Charles said, breaking the long silence, "who gave me an update on the boy's condition. It sounds like he's going to be just fine. Kids are very strong." He looked up at her in the rear-view mirror. "They don't get hurt like you would think."

"That's great," she said, sitting up. "Why didn't you tell me sooner? We need all the good news we can get."

He shrugged and looked back out the windshield. "Well, there were a lot of things to do yesterday. I just forgot to mention it."

She didn't reply, afraid of replaying yesterday's incident with Maria. But she'd been waiting for this news and now she leaned her head back on the seat, smiling. She'd been so concerned in the passing days, feeling a maternal sort of affection for the child, still wishing she could have gone to see him.

An hour later they stopped for an early lunch at a roadside hash house that promised hot loose-meat sandwiches and ice-cold soda pop. Charles stepped from the car, his hair disheveled, his shirt sleeves rolled up. At the thought of a sandwich and a Coca-Cola, she was suddenly starving. They went inside and sat at the counter, ignoring an open booth along the wall. But she was disappointed that her appetite vanished when she smelled hamburger meat frying, the greasy steam fizzling above the grill.

She ordered the first thing she saw on the menu, and when it was placed before her a few minutes later, a wet loose meat sandwich and a vanilla milkshake, she nudged them away. Thankfully, Charles talked about the race and nothing else, reminding her that Colonel Brown was making the long trip down to evaluate her driving.

Catsup and grease dripped down his fingers as he took a bite of his sandwich, wiping his mouth with a crumpled napkin. "I'm having one of the other mechanics meet us down there," he said. "That boy, Adam, from the shop. You tell me how you like working with him, because he'll be coming with us to Italy."

Prudence twirled the straw in her melting milkshake, hoping this wouldn't be a repeat of her relationship with Rudy. She knew Adam from the shop, but had never worked directly with him.

"Don't you know anyone over there?" she asked, hoping he somehow might delay their going to Italy for a while.

"Not that speaks good English. You want to be able to talk to them, right?" He took a long sip from his soda pop, set it down and wiped his hands clean. "Now, I've already made the flight arrangements. We leave for Italy in two weeks, Prudence. I've taken on a co-owner at the shop who will be running the business while I'm gone. I can make even better relationships with the car makers in Italy, build up my business even more." He leaned on his elbows. "But the rest of my time with be devoted just to you and your career."

Prudence nodded, knowing that his mind was made up on all of this, and there was no use trying to change it.

He looked at her untouched food. "Aren't you going to eat?"

Prudence looked down at her plate. She quickly lifted her sandwich and took a big bite, filling her mouth, the taste of the greasy meat turning her stomach. She forced it down, the soggy bread roll scraping on its descent, her eyes watering as it settled in her stomach. It wasn't so much the feeling of nausea that bothered her, it was the sudden realization, as she looked around the restaurant at all the customers, the traffic rushing by on the highway, that she was — now more than ever — in over her head.

As she looked up at Charles, she saw he expected her to do well today, as without the Colonel's investment, she would not be able to afford to continue. She would have to learn to drive the Ferrari by the seat of her pants. And as another slight wave of nausea passed, she realized that she was not just risking one life any more, but two.

Charles chewed the last of his hamburger, staring in the mirror behind the counter.

"Prudence?" Charles asked when he caught her pale reflection in the mirror. "Are you okay?"

"I'm fine," she said, looking away, pressing her napkin hard against her lips to stanch the nausea, the words, the truth from rising up in her. "Perfectly fine."

Seventeen

THAT AFTERNOON in Palm Springs, as Prudence came from the hotel in her race suit, there was a bitter scent to the air that signaled the start of winter. A cool sea wind was blowing the dead branches from the trees, and as they fell and snapped in the street, she strolled the half mile from their hotel to the track, where Charles was already prepping the Ferrari for the race. She heard the sound of the distant race engines echoing down the avenue as she walked along with spectators heading to the race. Christmas decorations hung in storefronts along the avenue, and Prudence paused before an appliance store window to stare in at a large console television, much like that one her father had given her mother years before. Prudence remembered how her mother's singing voice, warm and mellifluous over the piano strings, had been replaced by the constant Dippity-Do hair gel jingles and images of marching Lucky Strike cigarettes.

Prudence remembered her mother cleaning the rectangle of dust from the floor after the piano was hauled away. She could still see her mother on her knees in stockings, the notch of her spine imprinted through her dress as she passed the duster across the floor. Prudence remembered that night, sitting in the dark, listening to her mother laughing at *I Love Lucy*, relieved of her musical talents, the hope of re-starting her career. And yet, her mother was unaware that by turning her back on those talents, she would soon begin to wither.

Prudence turned from the storefront window and followed behind men and women with their arms around their children, protecting them from the blustery weather. Prudence felt ashamed at how easily she often remembered the bad in her mother. In just a few days, it would be a year since she died. And Prudence had yet to recall the really good things about her, the generosity and encouragement her mother had shown her in all her athletic pursuits.

As she walked, Prudence's hand touched her stomach and the pleasant thoughts faded. Her mother never would've pretended she didn't exist. Her mother never would've turned her back on motherhood, and this made Prudence wonder at the type of mother she would be. It was a rare instance that she'd wondered about the sex of the child, or what she'd name it, what the child would be like as it grew. Her step faltered midway through an intersection. She stood immobile under the pendulous weight of guilt, there beneath the swaying electrical stop lights that hung above the street.

A car stopped in front of her and honked. A man in a black Cadillac. It took a moment for her to collect herself, and then she moved to the sidewalk while the car accelerated by. As she passed a café window she caught her reflection. She noticed how perfectly she resembled her mother now: her long hair, her figure filled out some. It was frightening how close her mother seemed to her just then. Prudence moved closer to the glass to find the slightest difference that might set her apart from her mother, but besides her lighter coloring, there was none. There was that same arch to the eyebrows, the same large and bright eyes, the same shape and height to their bodies. And then for a moment, she felt as if she was looking in at her mother as a young woman. Standing right there in the middle of the café.

A bell tinkled and a man came out of the café. As if the open doorway had created a vacuum, she went inside and stood by the workingmen eating a late lunch, huddled together along the counter. Thick wristed, muscles bulging under their shirts. And the cook's fat belly pressing against the counter, his skin like pig flesh as he poured their coffee, the man beside her licking his fingertips and opening his newspaper.

"Can I help you, Miss?" the cook said, wiping his mouth with a dirty rag and tossing it over his shoulder. The workers at the counter looked over at her, chewing slowly.

"No, I don't think so," she said. She didn't move, and they all continued to stare at her. "I don't think so."

THE REDOLENT feeling in the air was gone when she arrived at the track. Their new mechanic was there, Adam, and she smiled when she saw him, his dimpled cheeks and freckled nose. She sat listening as Charles talked to him, offering advice while chomping on a piece of gum. Adam listened to him the same way as she often did, with interest, but knowing that it was too much advice to take in at once. Prudence turned and looked at the big Ferrari strapped to its trailer. And then beyond it was the racetrack, slowly revealing itself through a patch of fog.

The course was similar to the other homegrown road courses she'd raced in Stockton, Salinas, Santa Barbara, and Torrey Pines: racetracks that utilized old public roads or parts of abandoned military airstrips, sparsely outlined by hay bales. This course looked longer than the other courses she'd raced, and it reminded her of the photos she'd seen of the eastern NASCAR tracks in *Speed Age* magazine.

The pits bustled with mechanics prepping their cars for the race, the drivers smoking and sipping coffee from thick paper cups. They stared at the Ferrari as Adam and Charles rolled it off the trailer. Other cars in her class also began to appear near the paddocks, equally large and exotic. She recognized the well-known names painted on the cars, *Dan Gurney, Phil Hill*, and knew that she was certainly not of their ilk.

"Is the Colonel here?" she asked Charles, looking around for the colonel's broad shouldered, imposing presence. It had been months since she last saw him in the club, but the image of him sitting there in a booth, a big cigar stuck in his shiny bald head, had left a lasting impression in her mind.

"You won't be meeting him," Charles said, "but he'll be here, watching from somewhere in the crowd. That's just his way."

Prudence looked into the hundreds of spectators in the crowd but didn't see him among them, and wondered why he didn't want to come down and meet her. She had never officially been introduced to him. Even at The Scotch House, he had never so much as glanced at her. As she scanned the crowd, she knew he was there, somehow she felt his presence. And as she looked at Charles, unwrapping a piece of Blackjack licorice gum, she saw that he felt it too. He popped the gum in his mouth and chewed it slowly; a new habit he'd acquired to help him try and cut back on smoking.

As she was lacing up her shoes, Vi's letter fell from her race suit pocket and was taken by the breeze. She cursed and went running after it, the laces of one shoe still undone. As she chased it, watching it blow farther and farther away, she saw a few nearby mechanics watching her, shaking their heads.

The letter stopped by the feet of a young man who was passing by, wearing a tight white tee shirt, blue jeans, and cowboy boots. He knelt down and handily picked it up. She halted and looked at the letter, then at him. He was short but very handsome, with a sly grin and sandy blonde hair. He playfully held the letter out in front of him, just out of her reach.

"Can I have that please?" she asked.

"Looks important," he tittered, "for you to be running like that."

"It is," she said, looking in his eyes. "Give it please, I'm in a hurry."

He handed it over, ending his game just as easily as he'd started it. As she took it, he stared at her a while. "You're not driving your Porsche today?"

She narrowed her eyes at him, wondering if they'd met before.

"I seen you drive it in Torrey Pines. We were racing together. I was in the silver Speedster, and you blew by me in that Spyder of yours." He laughed and adjusted his tortoise shell glasses, a pair of sunglass lenses snapped over their frames. "I need to get me one of those Spyders one of these days." He offered his hand. "I'm Jimmy."

"Prudence." She shook his hand and then looked back for Charles, to see if he'd noticed her chasing after the letter.

"Well, good luck today," he said, lighting a Chesterfield King with a match. "I'll be seeing you out there."

She smiled as he turned and walked off.

"You know him?" Adam asked, suddenly standing beside her.

"No," Prudence said, tucking the letter in her race suit. "He seemed to know me though."

"That was James Dean," Adam said, watching as his figure receded into the crowd. "I've seen him around here before. He's a really good driver."

"Jimmy Dean? The country and western singer?" she asked.

"No," Adam laughed. "James Dean, the actor. Don't you read your celebrity magazines? He's supposed to be the next big thing."

"I don't have time for that stuff," she said, looking through the crowd after him, but he was already gone. She quickly turned and told Adam she'd meet him down at the paddocks, then she returned to the wagon, hid the letter in the pocket of her Levi jacket. She then buttoned the neck strap of her race suit, buckled on her helmet, and pulled her long pony tail out behind it.

"You ready?" Charles asked when she arrived at the pits. He snatched a large wad of cotton from his pocket, pulled off two tufts for himself, stuck them in his ears, and instructed her to do the same. She looked at him blankly and then at the cotton balls.

She brushed him aside, climbed into the Ferrari, put her feet on the narrow pedals, hands on the wood rimmed steering wheel. The seat cupped her body, the door jamb pressing against her left arm, the metal tonneau pressing on her right. She reached forward on the dash and adjusted the rear-view mirror, and saw that only her head and shoulders were exposed from the Ferrari's body.

She put the car in neutral and flipped on the fuel pumps, heard them whine. The engine churned as she then depressed the starter, the carburetors drawing air as the engine turned over. When it caught, a loud crack shot from the side pipes. The sound gave her a jolt, and as she fiddled with the vibrating rear-view mirror, she practiced working the gear lever and clutch.

She blipped the throttle as the car warmed up to keep the engine from dying. Adam climbed on the metal tonneau beside her as she let out the clutch and let the car lurch forward. She feathered the accelerator, trying to keep the car from stalling. His laughter rose above the ripping exhaust as they bounced along, his fingers holding the windshield braces.

She looked back at Charles, trotting alongside the car as they headed towards the track. His expression was only of earnestness, and perhaps a tinge of regret that it was not him, but she who was driving this machine.

As she neared the track, Adam slipped off and stood beside the idling car. He was smacking his hands together, bouncing up and down. The sun was hidden behind his head, his face a shadow, his hair aglow. He then gave her the thumbs up and a big smile, which she returned. She could see why Charles liked him, and she was growing to like him herself.

When she stopped the car at the edge of the track, Adam came around and strapped her in the Ferrari's safety belt. He did so loosely, smiling at her because Charles was standing behind him, instructing him not to try and get fresh. But after she was fastened in, Prudence felt too restrained and began undoing the belts.

"What are you doing?" Charles yelled.

"I don't like them!" Like a lot of other drivers, she'd decided she would prefer to be thrown from the car than trapped if it flipped over, which would mean certain decapitation.

"Put them on!" He yelled, but already she'd gotten the signal from the flagman to begin her qualifying laps.

She inched forward again, the crowd watching her from the grandstand as she slipped on her driving gloves. Charles ran on the pavement beside her, leaned in and kissed her quickly, his breath heavy with licorice.

"Don't push it too hard," he yelled, his hand resting on the door as he jogged. "Just make smooth, consistent laps. Remember, the Colonel's watching."

She affixed her goggles and stopped the rumbling car at the entrance to the course, looking out over the dash, the small windshield and the Ferrari's long hood. She was going to be only the second driver of the day out on the track. Already she felt hurried, nervous that she'd be allowed only three qualifying laps on cold tires and on a cold track. As she sat there, revving the engine, the flagman waved the flag, signaling that the current qualifier was safely off the track, and she pressed on the throttle and the engine spat out a loud, insistent rasp.

She felt the crews all turn their eyes to her and the Ferrari as she shot out of the pits. The fog had mostly lifted as she pulled out onto the course. The sky was clearing, although the sun still had yet to burn away the soft clouds that hung above the track. As she began her warm-up lap, she noticed too that portions of the track were still slick with the morning's rain and she drove the lap slowly until her tires were warm.

The engine shed a vociferous sound as she pressed the accelerator. Her stomach sank back in her body until it felt like a balloon pinned to her backbone. The speedometer needle flicked behind the glass dial, the car responding to every input she made, feeling tight and solid as she wound faster and faster along the track. Hay bales shot past, strands of it fluttering across the asphalt track, the cold wind in her face. The wind lifted and buffeted her goggles, and tears streamed along her temples and tickled her ears.

The Ferrari's power felt urgent. Taking the big car through a series of wide, sweeping blind turns, she was reminded of Mexico, of not knowing what came after each bend. But now she felt that she could intuit the mysteries of what lay ahead, and so she took each curve as fast as she could, as if she'd driven it a hundred times before.

She felt the rear end trying to slide out from under her as she took a turn wide and flew past the grandstands at over a hundred miles an hour. The spectators, nearly a thousand of them now, flashed by in a series of colors: reds, greens, yellow and white. They stood as she passed, the women with their bobbed blonde hair and dark sunglasses, and she felt the bitter rush of wind blowing her pony tail out behind her as she blasted down the long straightaway. The infield sparkled with the camera flashes, and in the pits crew members sat on the fence as she neared the end of the warm-up lap.

She saw the starting line, a hundred yards away now. She downshifted, pressed the accelerator to the firewall, sliding back in her seat as she blasted by the waving flag. She felt consumed by the rising engine noise, her bones and teeth rattling as the car skipped over the airstrip's rough pavement. The Ferrari wanted strong and decisive steering input, and she cut deliberate lines through each turn, her arm muscles straining as she fought to hold the large steering wheel steady. The red and white painted curbs trailed quickly in her rear-view mirror, and she knew, as she negotiated the course's toughest turn, that she was laying down a good lap time. As she came to the slight uphill grade, she looked over the Ferrari's flat, roofless body and planned how to attack the next turn.

It was a broad, shallow S-shaped chicane, and Prudence braked hard and felt her shoulders banging between the door and tonneau cover as she swung through the apex of each turn. She felt the car's rear end begin to lift again, warning her that she'd pushed into the turn too hard. She yanked back the wheel to compensate, hit the gas pedal and performed a hook slide. Breathing hard, she straightened the car out and hunched down behind the windshield, promising to take the chicane more smoothly on the next lap.

On the next turn, she cursed herself for coming in too fast yet again. The Ferrari was heavier than her Porsche and she realized she needed to give herself more time to brake. She overshot the turn and again the rear end lifted and swung out even further. Her leading outside tire hit the hard sand that lined the raceway. Instinctively, she let the steering wheel straighten itself, balancing it with her fingertips. She accelerated and heard the sound smack off the hay bales that surrounded the straightaway, felt their distance by the sound of her engine.

　　　　　　　　　　　　　　　　　Owen Duffy

Prudence felt her face get hot, her heart fluttering. She gripped the wheel and pulled back onto the course. The car was so lithe and powerful it was as if she'd strapped on a super human body, the car itself a part of her, as if they were connected by a bundle of nerves. The car urged her to go faster and faster yet, and as she rocketed up through the gears it began to feel as if the car had overtaken her senses, that she was forgetting everything Charles had ever taught her. The speedometer needle was indicating over one hundred and thirty miles per hour when she came to the last corner of the track, right in front of the grandstands. There was a low spot in the track there, completely covered in shadow, and the rain water from the infield had begun to leak across the pavement. In the corner, she saw a puddle glittering in the grey afternoon light. The car grunted as she downshifted, fighting her as she tried to steer around the puddle.

When she came to the turn she hit the slick and felt the car shudder. It twitched, tossing her off balance. When the rear wheels gave up their grip, they did so quickly, and she felt the car swap ends. She found herself staring back at where she'd just come from. She jabbed the brakes as the car slipped off the track into the hard packed sand that lined this section of the course.

The Ferrari skidded sideways across the sand as if it were ice, the brakes having no effect. It felt as if she was falling from a great height and for a moment she wished she could fall like this forever, the pleasant feeling of weightlessness. The car continued to slide until the edge of her tires caught, digging into the sand. The car lurched onto the outer edge of its left tires, and as the axles buckled, she was flung under the metal tonneau on the opposite side of the car. Her feet tangled in the pedals, she felt the Ferrari tilt on its side and then begin to flip over.

Eighteen

PRUDENCE OPENED her eyes inside the dark cockpit, her chest pressed hard against her knees, so each breath came only a mouthful at a time. She tried to move, but she was lodged beneath the metal tonneau cover, where she'd been thrown when the car flipped. Her wrist throbbed as she reached through the blackness and pushed against her door, but it was stuck shut. Then came the heady smell of raw fuel and she realized the engine was still running and the tires were rubbing the fenders so the car was shaking violently. As she lay curled inside the cockpit, she began yelling for help, but her voice was swallowed by the noise.

After a minute, the side door was pried open and she saw daylight. A pair of hands reached in and yanked her from the car and laid her out on the ground. She blinked and looked up at the silhouettes moving around her. Beyond them, the sun was fiery orange and the sky plain blue. Rays of light shot across it in distinct parallel lines. Several faces were peering down at her, circling around and around, their mouths moving but their voices mere whispers, the sand in her teeth and the ground hot to the touch as she tried to sit up.

Charles was kneeling beside her, talking and holding her as the world slowly came into focus. She blinked again and looked at the wind blowing through his hair, the rims of his blue eyes peering over his sunglasses. Her hearing aid had become dislodged, and yet she could hear her throbbing pulse inside her helmet. As she began to run her hands over her belly, checking on the baby, she felt a searing pain shoot up her arm and saw that her glove was soaked in blood.

"Just lie still." Charles grabbed her shoulder and pushed her back down. "Help is on the way."

Prudence winced and lay back, and when she looked over to her side she noticed a dozen men were crouched around the Ferrari. They lifted the one side and then slowly rolled the car over. It came down hard on its ruined wire wheels, the windshield and steering wheel smashed, the paint dented and scratched. A man then reached inside the car and killed the engine, as another man sprayed the car with a fire extinguisher, its jet of white froth covering the smoking engine.

Soon she saw an ambulance tearing across the track, trailing dust. Within seconds it was stopped just a few feet from where she lay. Two men climbed out with a gurney, set her on it, lifted her up and slid her inside. Charles climbed in after her, carefully resting her head in his hand, stroking her hair. As the ambulance began to move, she raised her head.

"I'm pregnant," she shouted, over the sound of the racing engine. "I'm pregnant, Charles."

He leaned closer and looked at her, a shadow coming over his face, as if he was putting together the clues that he'd seen over the last month. He then opened his eyes wide, as if dumbfounded that he hadn't figured it out sooner.

"I killed it," she said, and put her hand to her face and began to cry, ashamed that she'd waited so long to tell him, ashamed that she'd considered getting rid of the child, and now that she'd let it die.

Charles shouted to the driver over siren's grinding wail. "How much longer until we get there?"

"Just a few minutes," the driver shouted back.

He turned back to Prudence, crouching low, closer to her. "Everything's going to be all right."

When they arrived at the hospital and wheeled her in, and before the doctor even began to stitch up her wrist, she implored that he check if her baby was okay. The doctor was spindly looking, wiry gray hair and silver framed glasses. He looked at her a moment, as if he had misheard. Charles, who was standing beside him, nodded.

"How far along are you?" the doctor asked in a detached tone.

Prudence looked at the doctor, then at Charles. "About three months, as near as I can figure."

Charles looked away and cleared his throat. The doctor lifted his stethoscope to his ears, as if to humor them, and listened in her belly for a heartbeat. She watched his expression as he moved the cold diaphragm over her skin. He tilted his head and listened closely. After a moment he stood back, took off his glasses. As he rubbed his eyes, he assured her that pregnant women suffer accidents all the time, and that only time would tell if the baby or the pregnancy had suffered. That she'd just have to wait and see.

"Didn't you hear anything?" Prudence asked him, trying to sit up

"It might be too early for your baby's heart to have formed. Or else …" The doctor looked at Charles and then back at Prudence. "Well, every woman is different. When you get home you should see a doctor who specializes in these things. There's no one here right now, I'm afraid."

It was quiet in the room, and she knew the doctor was only trying to avoid an unpleasant conversation. She closed her eyes, leaned her head back and listened, hard. Her mind went into that dark space she often visited, one that existed below this room and this place. Like an earthen cave that she could stand next to, her hands resting on its wet rocky mouth, and listen. She felt the cool air it breathed, moist and anthracitic, bringing with it the sound from down within its deepest caverns. A sound so faint but so primal, that each patter of her child's heart sent an electric jolt through her ears.

"I can hear it," she said, opening her eyes, looking up at them. "I can hear the heartbeat."

The doctor exchanged glances with Charles, and then they stared at her. She knew she sounded like a crazy woman, but she was satisfied that she'd heard it. A nurse came in the room then, pushing a cart with silver utensils and bandages. Prudence lay back and let out a long sigh, watching as they mended her bloody arm, stitching it up and swathing it in bandages.

CHARLES WAS waiting by the wagon when a nurse walked Prudence out at dusk, her arm in a sling. She'd been given a sedative and it made everything feel warm and tingly, and when she looked up at the evening sky, the night wind blowing across the parking lot felt like rabbit fur brushing against her face.

Charles held her jacket out to her, and as she neared, she saw Vi's letter tucked in the outside pocket, where she'd put it after it had fallen out earlier that afternoon. As he draped the jacket over her shoulders, she looked down at the now crumpled letter and knew that he'd read it. That he now knew how long she'd been trying to keep her secret from him, along with her intimate friendship with Vi.

"So now you know everything," she said, her voice sounding hollow and tired. She turned and looked straight at him. Her hair had fallen in her eyes but she didn't brush it away.

"Why didn't you tell me?" he asked. "I don't need secrets in my life right now."

"Open your eyes, Charles," she said, glaring at him. "This wasn't all my doing. And I was going to tell you as soon as I was certain."

"Certain about what?"

Prudence looked down and shook her head, wobbling slightly

under the sedative.

Charles took her arm and helped her to the wagon. As he opened the door and helped her into the passenger seat, she looked back and noticed the trailer was no longer latched to the wagon. As she sat, she instinctively let her hand fall to her belly, the first time she'd done so in front of him. There was a dull pain in her arm, her body feeling slippery and warm from the drug. As she sat and stared out the window, she knew that her decision not to wear the safety belt had saved her and the baby's life.

Charles started the car and pulled out of the hospital parking lot. As they entered the bi-way a few minutes later, heading north towards home, she leaned her head against the cold window.

"You were lucky." He looked over at her now with that same bloodless, astonished expression he'd had when he was leaning over her at the track. "Very lucky. When I saw that car go over," he said, pressing his fingers to his eyes, "I thought I'd lost you. And I don't know what I would have done then."

Prudence ran her fingers along the shoulder sling, the strap circling her neck and connecting at her wrist. "I thought I was a goner too," she said. "I keep looking around and I can't help thinking that I shouldn't be seeing these things. That I should be dead."

"Well you're not," he said, putting his hand on the back of her neck and pulling him to her. "You're just lucky. Damn lucky."

"I'm sorry about the car," she said, looking up at him. "I hit that wet patch and there was nothing I could do. The car just went out from under me."

"Remember what I said?" Charles said, kissing her forehead. "I don't give a damn about cars, only racing." He reached for his breast pocket, where his cigarettes usually were, and then slapped his hand back on the wheel.

"Where's the Ferrari?" she asked.

"Adam drove the wagon to the hospital for us. He wanted to check on you." Charles unwrapped a stick of gum and popped it in his mouth. "He's friends with another team and they're towing the Ferrari home for us. We'll fix it back up soon enough."

"And what about the Colonel?" she asked, sitting up and moving back to her side of the car. "He's not going to be investing in me now." She looked at the street lamps overhead, like glowing orbs being hurled past them. "What bad timing, all of this."

"Don't worry. We'll be fine without him." He looked over at her. "We'll be free agents. Go wherever the wind takes us."

A long moment passed. He rubbed his jaw and she had her hearing aid dialed up so loud, she heard the sound of his fingernails against his whiskers. She looked down at her hands, fiddling with her bandage.

"I'm sorry I didn't tell you sooner," she said. "I was afraid you would think I was trapping you. That I did it on purpose. Or that you wouldn't let me race if I told you about it."

"I wish you had, just the same." He let out a long, thin breath. "We were careful. And it was just about a few times, and then down in Mexico." He looked over at her. "What luck."

"I wasn't with anyone else," she added quickly. "Nobody."

He looked at her and nodded. "And me neither."

A quiet moment passed, just the sound of the bi-way rushing under them. She knew he was deep in thought. Perhaps thinking how her pregnancy had derailed all their plans and again put him in a position where he had to do the right thing. When she knew he probably just wanted to run away from her now, and she wouldn't blame him if he did.

"You know," he said, his voice lowering, "a year ago I didn't see anything wrong with who I am. I thought I was happy with my life. But now I see that there was a lot I could've done differently."

Prudence brushed the hair out of her face and looked at him. "You weren't so happy when we met, I don't think."

"Maybe not." He glanced over at her and then back at the road. "Maybe I should've been more responsible about things. Not just some child playing with his toys while the house was burning down around him." His words drifted off, and Prudence leaned back in her seat. There was no way to say what they were truly feeling, and the time for reasoning had passed. They had walked too far past the wellsprings, where the water flowed cold and clear, and were now standing in the murky swamp.

She reached in her purse and pulled out a pack of her Pall Malls. She shook one out and offered it to him.

Charles took the cigarette and cleared his throat. "If you don't want to talk now, that's fine. We've got a long drive and you should try and rest."

She stared back out the windshield. Another long silence passed and Prudence rolled down the window, the breeze like soothing fingers through her hair. She lit the cigarette and then offered the lighter to him but he waved it away and tossed his unlit cigarette out the window.

Charles ran his fingers slowly through his hair. "I suppose we have a lot to think about now."

Prudence pulled hard on the cigarette. She thought of all that had happened in her life, and decided that the bad things could never be resolved, that they were a part of her, the way a tree grows through a barbed wire fence and eventually becomes part of the fence, the fence a part of the tree.

She thought of her father for the first time in a long while, and for once, she missed him. His simple, unclouded way of looking at the world; a viewpoint she herself was only now beginning to appreciate. She remembered the expression on his face the day she left home, as if he knew all too well what awaited her out there. He had been right about the world, that there wasn't some great meaning or understanding to be found out there. He'd get some satisfaction that she'd come to this understanding herself, and that she had likely, in his eyes, become the frivolous, impulsive woman he always expected she would be.

THEY ARRIVED outside her apartment at dawn, the yellow door and the large windows reflecting a lavender morning haze. He helped her from the car, although she tried to resist and do it alone. She had slept most of the way home, but now the drug had worn off. It had been a fitful sleep that made the pain in her arm sharper and cast into relief the general malaise she otherwise felt.

He led her up the stairs and into her apartment, where he immediately opened the windows to let in some air. Jeffie was still asleep in her room and she watched from her chair as he changed her bedsheets so they'd feel fresh against her skin, then helped her undress and get into her bed. He drew the windows closed, shut the curtains and crawled in beside her, assuring her that he'd be there when she awakened.

As she drifted off to sleep, she felt him there beside her. Although his eyes were closed and, flat on his back, his fingers laced across his chest, she felt that he was wide awake and deep in thought, his body nearly humming with a current of activity.

She awakened hours later and immediately recalled what had happened back in Palm Springs, the accident still fresh in her mind. Never before had she felt so consumed with regret, a feeling that was compounded by all the tasks and challenges that lay before her in the coming days.

Charles was still there in the apartment as promised, although she sensed he'd been out already, over to the dealership and making final preparations for them leaving for Italy in a few days.

She was stiff and sore as she lashed the sling around her neck, grimacing as she sat up in bed and tucked her bandaged arm in it. Out the window a soft rain fell, and she sat on the edge of the bed and watched Charles through her open bedroom door; he hadn't yet noticed that she'd awakened, and he was searching through the kitchen drawers. She watched him moving, consumed in his simple task, his fingers reaching through her empty cupboards, searching for something that wasn't there.

As she watched, Prudence felt a gushing warmth fill her entire body. He'd helped her career at such a great cost to himself. He'd tried to understand her even when it was impossible for her to articulate what she was feeling. He'd given her nearly everything she wanted, and yet she felt, rising from inside her, the notion that he was the one who needed her now. He needed her help in trying to understand himself. And she knew that he could never come to that understanding as long as she was in his life. That he would always be thinking of her first, and that he would be better off without her and this baby.

"How do you feel?" he asked, turning cheerfully when he noticed she was awake.

"I feel fine," she said, rubbing her eyes. "What time is it?"

"Almost noon." He walked over to the bedside, looking at his wristwatch. "Your roommate just left for work." He was still dressed the same as the day before, but he'd showered and shaved already. He sat on the bed beside her and she moved her legs aside to give him room.

Prudence looked around the apartment, where she'd spent so many nights alone and with Vi. She thought of herself the first day she moved in, how naïve and hopeful she'd been. And now she felt so much older than twenty. She wanted to reason with the girl she'd been back then, but she knew that girl wouldn't have listened. And Prudence knew that there was no going back, that the girl was gone.

She looked back to Charles, smiling at her. As if sensing her thoughts, he grasped her knee and shook it.

"Hey, everything's okay," he said. "You're fine. Your arm will heal soon and then when we get to Italy, you can rest until the baby comes. Then when you're well, you can race. You might miss the big races this year, but maybe that's a good thing. We'll get you some more practice in the larger cars."

She looked at him. She felt his nervous energy again, and knew that he was eager to be moving forward. That was always the way he'd been since she first met him. Rushing when he should be still and receptive to the present. Talking when he should've been listening.

He told her how he'd already made all the preparations for them to leave, and the great expense it had been. Plane tickets to New York, where he had business, before they flew to Rome. He rehashed how he'd made one of his top salesmen a partner at the dealership, and had left him to watch over the American side of the business. He'd entrusted his lawyers to settle the divorce and an agent to oversee the sale of his property in Palo Alto. He was willing to lose money on these things, cut his losses to see to her career, to invest in their future together.

"Look," he said, when her mood didn't brighten, "you aren't responsible for anything. Not my divorce, not anything. You only made me realize the bad things in my life. And I know this isn't the right way to ask, and I wasn't planning on mentioning it until we got to Italy, but I want us to get married. I've wanted it a long time."

Prudence felt her mouth fall open and hang there a moment. Charles was looking back at her, his elbows on his knees, his toe tapping on the floor. She snapped her jaw closed and turned, pressed her hand to her face. Her mind felt slushy, her palms instantly clammy. When she looked at him again, she saw that he didn't really mean it. His personal sense of duty was so strong, and she knew he was grappling with his responsibilities to her. And yet, he was offering her everything she ever wanted, but it didn't feel right, and it wasn't the way she'd imagined it happening at all.

She nodded anyway, smiling broadly, slapping her hand on his and squeezing it. Even after the shock of yet another accident, she was still excited about going overseas with him. The safety of marriage, of knowing their child would be cared for and protected, was an overwhelming relief.

Charles arched his eyebrows. "Well?"

Prudence opened her mouth, but her throat made no sound. She then leaned towards him, a sleepy smile on her face, and put her head on his shoulder. He put his arms around her and held her there in the bedroom of her soon to be evacuated apartment, and for a minute it seemed like everything was going to be okay.

PRUDENCE FELT the following days pass quickly. She sold off what little furniture she had; she bought a small luggage set with her sponsorship money and packed all her good clothes in them, discarding the ones she'd brought from Oregon, save the ugly mouton coat. She even planned to take her mother's old pasteboard suitcase, which now had a respectable amount of wear, and use it to store her racing suits.

She'd been thinking about her father since she dragged out the old suitcase, and after she had finished packing, she went into the den and picked up the phone. As she waited for the operator, she sat there on the arm of a chair, chewing a jagged fingernail.

A flat-toned woman's voice came on a moment later, a rush of noise behind it. "Operator. What number please?"

"Long distance," Prudence said, taking her finger from her mouth. "Twin Falls, Oregon."

"Please hold."

The line went quiet a moment, then another voice came on the line, one she recognized from years before.

"Twin Falls. What number please?"

"N-3476."

"One moment."

Prudence listened as the phone began to ring. She pictured her house, her father rising from his chair and slowly walking across the den. She could imagine his faded buffalo checkered shirt, his impeccably clean chinos, and the sound of the phone ringing throughout the house.

She listened, shredding her nail, as nine rings passed.

"I'm sorry, but there's no answer, Miss," the operator said. "Would you like to try again later?"

"Yes, thank you," Prudence said, leaning against the phone after she set the receiver down, breathing deeply through pursed lips.

She looked at the time, jumped up and headed out the door. She went and made a deposit at the bank, picked up some Dramamine for the flight, then went to see a doctor about the baby and to check on her healing arm. He assured her that everything looked fine for a woman in this stage of pregnancy. He was even able to make out the heartbeat under his stethoscope, said it sounded strong. Most of all, he said, as he removed her bandages and cleaned the wound, she needed to *rest*. That she shouldn't even think about traveling or doing anything strenuous right off.

Prudence sat there, winding her wristwatch, her toe tapping on the floor. There were so many things to get done before she left for Italy. Vi was a strong vision in her mind as she left the doctor's office and ran her errands, then packed up the last of her belongings. She pictured Vi on the porch of some old farmhouse, up in Washington. A misty, mossy place. It seemed to her then that Vi was the one person who could empathize with her now, because Vi too had chosen marriage rather than living alone.

As the day of their departure neared, Prudence felt her body cramping. Each muscle tight and rigid. She knew it was because Charles was only trying to do the right thing by her. Chivalry seemed like an antiquated courtesy in these circumstances, and it only entrapped them both. And although the fear of being alone in her condition was ferocious, she knew that Charles had been an unsettled man when she met him, and staying with him would only make him more so. That giving up his racing career had been the biggest loss in his life, and they both knew it. Marrying and having a child with her right now would kill what remained of his spirit, and all of hers.

THE MORNING of their departure, the city was quiet and still, as if it had pulled the sheet over its head and gone back to sleep. After the long taxi ride through traffic to the brand new San Francisco Airport, the airline attendant snatched their luggage from the trunk and set it on the curb. Already she could hear announcements for their flight over the loudspeakers, the sound of propellers blatting across the tarmac. Charles helped her out of the taxi and they stood there under the awning in the blowing wind. She watched him tender the money to the driver, and felt a string of words rising up her throat, like her body was trying to purge them.

"I'm not going with you," she said after he turned, her voice sounding more sure of itself than it ever had. She'd been thinking about it all morning, all week, but the sound of her own words surprised her. "I want you to go without me. You're the one who should be in those races this year, not me."

His brow furrowed, and he set his hat farther back on his head. People brushed past in heavy coats, carrying their luggage and clutching their tickets. He stared at her a while and then chuckled uneasily. "You are joking, right? Surely this is just a joke."

"No," she said, clamping her jaw and shaking her head. "You know I'm right. You have to race. That's what you need to do, and you know it." Prudence glared at him, knowing that she'd never be able to convince him that she wasn't crazy.

The attendant coughed, set their bags down and stepped away. More passengers brushed by, hurrying into the terminal. She and Charles looked at one another and she knew he understood her, but he didn't want to.

"What are you talking about, Steve? I can't leave you alone like this."

"I'm telling you that you can." She stepped closer. "You know I'm right. You don't need this put on you right now, and I'm not going to put it on you. I am going to go home, Charles. I'm going to rest and clear my head, and I'll write you every day." She looked at him. "So go and race again. You'll go crazy if you don't."

The plane was leaving in a few minutes, but he just stood there, staring at the ground. "I can't just leave you here. I want you with me."

"Look at me," Prudence said, wrapping her arms around him.

"I'll be fine. We'll both be fine."

"I can't," he took her good arm. "Let's go. We don't have time for this."

"You're not listening!" Prudence yelled, yanking her arm back from him. People nearby stopped and looked at her. "I'm not saying it's okay for you to leave me, goddammit, I'm saying that you *need* to leave me now. That if you don't get on that plane, I'm going to leave *you*." She shook her head. "It's not your decision to make. It's mine. So don't argue with me any more."

"No," he said, "it's not just your decision. We planned for this all along. This was the plan." He held up the plane tickets.

"*This* wasn't the plan," she said, placing her hand on her belly. "This has changed everything."

"And what do you plan to do, raise it alone?"

"I don't know. But I'll write you, and we'll figure it out."

Charles pressed his hat down on his head, tapped the tickets against his wrist.

"Don't think I'm not scared out of my mind right now," she said. "But this is the way it has to be."

"Okay," he said, stepping back. "But I don't like this one bit. Write me at that address I gave you, and I'll write you back every day."

"After the baby's born," she said, uncertain whether or not it was a lie, "we'll come to you. I promise."

"Promises never come true."

"This one did." She kissed him, then turned to the attendant and had him load her bags in a waiting taxicab.

"Are you sure?" he asked.

"Charles." She put her hands on his cheeks and looked up at him. "Thank you. Thank you for all you've done for me. I mean it.

Now get on that plane."

He looked at her as she got in the waiting cab and slammed the door, her heart racing and a tissue out and already blotting her eyes. *You're a fool Prudence Baylor*, she thought, looking straight ahead, *you're a damn fool.* As the cab jerked into traffic, she glanced back one last time and saw Charles pick up his luggage, limp into the terminal and disappear into the swirling crowd.

Nineteen

HER WRISTWATCH indicated half past seven in the morning as the taxicab arrived in front of Pieretti Motor Company. She stepped out and slipped the key in the front gate and went inside the lot. No one had arrived yet for work and she was the only one there. Her Porsche sat over in the corner and she went and lifted its canvas cover. She knelt and saw the faint markings of the dent were still there, the dimpled aluminum and flaked-off paint. She ran her hand over it again, feeling where the boy's body had hit. You can't unbend the accident, she thought, standing and wiping the grit from her knees. It can never be undone.

Prudence tossed a box of her trophies and two of her suitcases in the passenger seat. When the smallest one wouldn't fit in the front trunk — her mother's old pasteboard suitcase with her race suits inside — she left it in the shop. It was dark and empty in there, and she had the distinct feeling of being utterly alone, as if the world around her had vanished. She opened her old desk and found a stamp and an envelope, addressed it to the hospital in Juarez. She wrote a letter and then a check for a thousand dollars from her account, stuffed them inside the envelope, and licked it closed.

She then went across the lot and opened the front gates wide. It was still foggy and a breeze was blowing down the street. There was no traffic yet, and she leaned against the car a moment, reading a road map, tracing a line north through California, Oregon, and up to Washington. It would take her a few days get up to Raintree, driving mostly along the highways. The car was licensed and street legal, but it would draw unwanted attention on county roads, and she didn't

292   Owen Duffy

want to find herself in some hayseed town with a cop asking her a lot of questions.

Prudence then climbed in the car, running her hands over the wheel, her head leaned back on the headrest, looking skyward. She imagined pulling down some country lane at dusk a few nights later. Vi rising from where she sat on her porch chair to greet her. A field where she could park the car, a soft bed where she could rest. Where there in the dark she could whisper to Vi all the things that had happened to her, so far behind them that it would all feel like a dream.

The Porsche had no heater, so Prudence buttoned up her old mouton coat and slipped on her leather gloves. She started the car and headed to the Golden Gate Bridge, out of the city and towards the Marin Headlands. Before she reached the bridge, she stopped at a curbside mailbox. She slipped the letter with the check inside it into the slot. Although it may have been futile, the contents of the letter explained her remorse for what had happened. And she hoped the check would go to pay the child's bills, with enough left over to care for him a while.

She stood on the street corner a moment, gazing into the mailbox's black slot and felt as if she had dropped the letter into some dark void, where such foolish errands always came to rest. But she slipped back into the idling car and sped north. It was nearly nine hundred miles to Raintree, which would take several days of driving. It already felt like a weary kind of race, her eyes half-closed, the car's worn engine bellowing wisps of blue smoke. She drove hard anyway, passing slower traffic on the bi-ways, cruising until it was dark and she had to scan the map with her cigarette lighter.

She passed through Eugene, Oregon, at daybreak the next day, coasting down the long sloping stretches of road, across the freshly built highway. She passed a cop at dawn on the outskirts of town. As he gave chase, she furtively slipped into a vacant meadow and shut off her lights and watched him sail past, his red light cutting through the morning fog. She slept briefly in the car in the meadow, covered in her blankets, awakening to the sound of dairy cows being put out to graze after their milking.

She ate at a roadside diner and then pressed on. That afternoon she saw signs for Twin Falls and without knowing why, she detoured off the highway and found herself driving through the downtown. It looked just the same as she'd left it. Its old brick buildings, its wet streets, the tree lined square. She felt a faint affection for it now, the crumbling courthouse and even the greasy Twin Fall Café where she once worked.

Prudence jabbed the brakes when she came to the intersection of Sheridan and Main. A new storefront sat on the eastern corner, right across from Black's General Store. Above the brightly lit window, in red and white neon, was a sign that read: *Baylor Radio & TV Sales & Repair.*

Prudence feathered the gas pedal, staring at the sign with her mouth hanging open. The rows of televisions facing the streets, the customers inside, perusing the goods. A car honked behind her and she put it in gear and pulled away, smiling.

As she turned on Sheridan Street, it seemed that the town was indifferent to her passing by. The after-work crowd walking along the sidewalk didn't even notice the small Porsche or who was driving, as here it was always just an ordinary day, and no one expected anything unusual to happen.

Prudence drove past her old church, the old rubber boot factory. The ivy covered high school. She came to her street, Maple, and she turned and drove under its rain soaked pine trees and soggy looking houses, the sky dark grey above. She stopped down the street from her house, the engine rumbling loudly. The street was otherwise quiet and her house was dark. It still looked the same, albeit empty, and the shrubs and the lawn needed trimming as usual. Seeing the old house, memories flashed in her mind: the pleasant times, as well as the dark ones.

She parked and stepped from the Porsche, looking up at the house as she walked slowly towards it. It had sat there while almost a year had passed, while everything in her life was changing. She walked up the cinder driveway and saw that her father's work truck was missing but her mother's old Dodge was sitting beneath a tree, one flat tire, its roof algae-stained and leaves matted to its hood. She shook her head and clucked her tongue against the roof of her mouth. She went around the side of the house and stopped by a window, stood up on her toes and peered inside.

The same wood floors and old heavy Mission furniture. For a moment it was like she was looking at a still life painting. Forgotten memories returned, of when she was young and the house was alive during this time of year. Relatives laughing and her mother at the center of the festivities. She saw her father's favorite old chair, and remembered how she used to sit on his lap as a child when her mother sang. As her eyes focused in the corner of the den she saw an unlit Christmas tree. Already trimmed, a few gifts placed under it.

She continued scanning the room, and seeing no one, she went around and found the back door unlocked. The door creaked slowly on its hinges as she opened it and stared into the dark kitchen.

The house was cold inside and smelled faintly like the piney wood polish her mother used to use. And then heavier, the familiar burnt, dusty, electrical smell of her father's ham radio equipment. As she walked around the kitchen she saw that everything was just as she'd left it — even the calendar that hung from its peg, with the cartoon soap advertisement still displayed. She lifted the front page and saw how yellowed it was, her mother's handwriting on some of the dates, appointments and social events, some well past the day she died.

Prudence shook her head, wondering why her father hadn't taken it down, put it away. The hallway was dim as she walked along it, looking in each room until she came to stand in the den. She saw that the big console television was gone and in its place stood a piano. Not her mother's old upright, but a modern spinet.

She stood there beside the Christmas tree, running her hand over its keys. Then she sat slowly in her father's favorite chair and looked beside it at the liquor cabinet. Gone were the assortment of bottles that always stood on it, replaced with magazines and books. As she leaned and opened its doors, she saw that it was empty inside.

She stared out the rain-flecked windows until her eyes felt bleary and began to ache. It had been a long drive with the bitter wind blowing in her face. She looked around the den some more. She wondered if her father had remarried and these things belonged to his new wife. She wanted to snoop around and satisfy her curiosity, but she couldn't leave the comfort of that chair. But the longer she sat there, the more she felt like an intruder. That her welcome here had left along her mother.

As she stood to leave, she heard a noise outside. When she looked out the window, her father's red work truck was in the driveway. Her heart began to squeeze tightly in her chest. Her father stepped out with his mackinaw and his hat. His hair looking a bit grayer now, his figure a little thin. She figured he'd come home early from the shop, not something he usually did when he was making service calls. And not something she'd been counting on him doing today.

She looked at the front door. Ten steps away. She could dash to it and throw the bolt, run out of the house and never see him again. But she was suddenly so tired. Tired of running away from him and this house. And so she stood there in the hall with her shoulders arched as her father opened the back door and came into the kitchen. He flipped on the light and looked up and saw her standing there.

He slowly took off his hat and set it on the table, looking her up and down with a strange expression, as if he mistrusted his eyes; eyes that stared into television screens all day for anomalies, eyes that could not measure what they were seeing now. He walked slowly towards her, his boots heavy on the wood floor. He stopped a few feet from her, his breathing succulent and heavy, his face appearing much the same as it was when she'd seen it last, outside the bus depot almost a year ago.

"Well?" he asked, his voice gruff and thin, as if she should explain why she was standing there.

She looked at him, and after a moment she asked: "Do I look like her?"

He looked her up and down with a cold, detached expression. "Your mother is dead, Prudence. Don't be silly."

She nodded quickly, as if expecting he'd say this. As if he was incapable of seeing the resemblance that everyone else saw.

"I came back to see her grave," she said, although she hadn't considered the idea until that moment. "And I was passing by and I just thought I'd come in and see the house."

Her father moved closer to where she was standing.

"A lot has changed since I left," she said, looking up at the ceiling.

"I can see that," he said, coming even closer. "And you do look like her." He wagged his head slowly. "When I walked in the door, I didn't know what I was seeing."

An awkward silence passed, her father just staring at her. Prudence clasped her hands behind her back. He seemed different. Calm and less angry.

"That's not what I meant," she said, leveling her eyes at him. "What's changed is that I've forgiven you." As soon as the words left her mouth, she knew that she meant it. When she studied his face, she knew he wouldn't argue about what it was that she'd forgiven him for.

He nodded. She saw his stooped shoulders and grey whiskers and knew that she was very different from him, and a little bit the same too. A year away made him seem smaller, and granted her a perspective that now made him appear unassuming, harmless.

"You bought a piano." She set her hand on it, wiped away the dust.

"I didn't watch that television much." He shrugged. "I tried to get back the piano we sold, but the owner wouldn't do it. Their kids are learning to play on the thing."

Prudence nodded towards the liquor cabinet. "You stopped drinking?"

"Not long after you left," he said, looking down at the floor.

"And the presents, who are they for?"

"They're for me," he said, "from my customers. Same as every year."

She nodded, as if not completely satisfied that her suspicions about another woman had been allayed. "Is there someone else?" she asked. "Another woman?"

He glanced up at her, shaking his head quickly. "No."

"Well, I should go now," she said after a long silence. "I'm glad you finally opened that shop."

He stepped forward, then looked down at the floor. "I read all the papers," he stammered. He went over to the bookshelf and took out a folder and laid it out on a side table. It was a scrap book of newspaper clippings. "Some other people in town were helping me. We had to send away for some of the papers, and I clipped out the articles that mentioned you." He turned to her, his voice lowering. "That race in Mexico. Those were the hardest ones to get."

Prudence nodded as she stood looking at all the clippings. They were all there. All the ones that she remembered. From her first race, to her appearances at county fairs, the Artichoke Festival and all the way down to Mexico. As she looked at them, she was afraid she would turn and press her face against his chest and sob. Her arms wrapped around him, all the pain he'd dealt to her immediately forgiven. But the pain wasn't forgotten. It still felt very real.

Real enough, that as she stepped back and looked at him, she saw that he was the same as he'd always been. He may be sober now, but he still only cared about people privately, never showing his feelings, and instead collected them in a book. When he could've written her months ago, to tell her that he'd cared about her and her career.

"I have to go," she said, and turned quickly and left him there and walked out the front door. She felt his eyes on her as she went down the front steps and along her street towards the First Presbyterian Church graveyard, only a few blocks away. Her neighbors were home for lunch too and some of them looked at her as she passed, perhaps surprised to see her, or the way that she resembled her mother, who hadn't walked these streets in a long time.

Once she was past their gazes, she ducked into the woods, and cut along a trail of matted leaves, through the park and into the cemetery.

It had begun to drizzle, and through the pine trees daylight waned. Above, a crow chattered from a tree limb and Prudence stopped mid-trail amongst the wet trees. It was raining too hard to continue into the woods, and she looked over the shadowed ground and the gnarled tree roots jutting from it. She took another step forward and stopped when she heard the crow squawk. She looked up and saw it resting on a rocking branch high up in the tree. It squawked again and she turned, sensing something behind her.

There was a shadow coming up the trail. She stood there, only the sound of her breathing and rain falling on wet leaves. As a minute passed and the figured neared, she saw it was her father; he was moving fast, but then he stopped and leaned against the base of a tree, breathing heavily.

He looked at her a long moment, panting. He averted his eyes from her, held out an umbrella. She walked slowly back along the wet ground and looked at the umbrella in his outstretched hand, then up at him. She reached out her hand, and instead of taking the umbrella, she looped her arm around his.

"Come on," she said, and led him forward along the trail. She guided them both over the tree stumps and fallen logs, and though it was dark, and he hadn't opened the umbrella, she realized that he knew the trail well. He then took the lead, his feet knowing exactly where to step to avoid each hazard.

When the rain became heavier, he opened the umbrella and they huddled under it, continuing along the trail until they came to the cemetery. They walked along the pea gravel road until they were standing over her mother's grave, beneath a dark spruce.

It was a simple headstone, the size of a washboard, stuck in the ground. Prudence knelt and plucked the leaves from the headstone and read her mother's name. She then stared at the ground a long time, deep in her thoughts, unsure if there was a way to make sense of how her mother had died.

Often she'd asked herself what she could've done, what one small change she could've made that would've brought a different outcome. But there was nothing. No reasoning could align what had happened and what should've been. No speculation could avoid the inevitable conclusion: that what had happened was simply a tragedy.

Her father's voice cut through the stillness. "You may not believe this, but I did everything I could for your mother. There's a lot you don't know about her. About us."

Prudence didn't turn, but stayed hunched down below him, listening.

"Your mother was a sad woman. Always was," he said. "I tried to help her, but we both came to understand that nothing could be done. Because your mother didn't want to help herself. She just didn't know how."

He cleared his throat. "I don't mean to be talking like this, standing here. I just mean that I did my best. I was the one who sent away for that songwriting contest that she won. I bet you didn't know that. I thought it might lift her spirits, give her hope. And when she won, they invited her to Portland, but she didn't want to go. She *couldn't* go. It was just like all the other times in her life, when she was younger and someone wanted her to come sing. She was just afraid. Of what exactly, I don't know. Just afraid."

"And then here she had wanted to turn this new corner in her life. Bought a new dress and everything, so we could go to Portland. But in the end, she couldn't leave. And that broke my heart, and I think it broke something in your mother too."

Prudence remembered the dress. Navy blue with tiny white polka dots.

"So then she said she didn't want to look at the piano any more. So I got rid of it. And that settled something finally in your mother." He cleared his throat. "I never told you that then, because I didn't want you to look badly at her. And if your mother was here and I was down there, she could stand here and say all that I kept myself from doing with my life. I could've gone to college, been an engineer, and all I have are a handful of excuses why I didn't."

"And you're not like either of us. What you have inside you, I don't know where you got it from. You're different than the both of us. And while I always wished you were like everyone else, for your own good, who you are is a good thing. I was always worried you'd find disappointment like your mother and I always did. But I think what I see in you now is that those disappointments have only made you stronger.

"I'll leave you here." Her father leaned down beside her and handed her the umbrella. "I know you didn't come back to see me. So I want you to keep going, wherever that is. I have a feeling it's somewhere better than here. So I don't want to see you coming in for dinner or to say goodbye to me. I just want you to keep going like you have been because it makes me proud. And it would make your mother proud."

He moved closer beside her. "And I've been reading in those papers about what happened down there in Mexico. They say that child was starving. That he'd been abandoned by his parents. I don't know if I can even imagine a parent doing such a thing. What happened was an accident, pure and simple, and if you let it ruin you, then you've let those people hurt you too. Understand?"

She stood slowly and then she grabbed her father and held him, the warmth of him and the rough wool of his jacket against her cheek, her shoulders quivering as she sobbed. He held her a moment, patted

Owen Duffy

her arm. And then he turned and started down the path towards the road.

She watched him go, then looked back at the headstone and the rain falling on it, there beneath the spruce and the dark sky where at last she felt some relief for what had happened to her mother, some understanding, and finally, peace.

WHEN SHE returned from the cemetery to her street, a light was on in the study of her house. As she neared, she saw her father sitting in the far corner, facing the wall. She could envision the work table he sat at, chipped and worn. As she came to the edge of the driveway, Prudence watched the back of her father's head under his work lamp. The way his hair looked shiny as he bent over an intricate electrical part. The bright boxes of vacuum tubes on the shelf above him, the rack of tools, the sizzle of the iron against solder. The white wisp of smoke that rose up past the window, where outside a light had flipped on, illuminating the side of her house.

Her father looked up for the source of the light. From where she stood, Prudence could see the light had come from her neighbors, who were sitting down to supper across the way. Children that were all grown up now. She knew her father could see it too. When she'd come home from college, she often sat and watched them from her bedroom window, heard their laughter, then the flicker of the television screen against the walls, their figures huddled before *The Roy Rogers Show*, or *The Adventures of Superman*.

Prudence adjusted her hearing aid, touching the cord that twined down to the battery box on her hip, and turned up her volume. She walked closer and heard the rain dripping from the eaves, a squirrel chattering in a tree, and lower, that familiar fundamental sound, a trembling beneath the roots of the trees that bent over the driveway and shadowed her where she now stood. That rumbling sound filled her body, shaking the ground. It rose in intensity, and then came to a stop just behind her. Breathing noisily and finally ready to be seen.

But she didn't turn around. She could sense it there, hovering over her, as if it had expected to find her overripe and filled with rot. She just kept looking at her father in his study. He picked up a sandwich from a plate and she watched the mechanical action of his handling and chewing the food. Then after a moment, she turned and slowly crossed the street, got back in the car and drove away.

Twenty

W<small>HEN</small> P<small>RUDENCE</small> arrived in Raintree late in the afternoon on the third day, the Porsche was trailing blue smoke. She stopped at a Red Crowne service station where a young attendant stood hosing mud off a battered truck. As she pulled up beside him, he looked at her and then the Porsche, the hose spilling water on the ground. Her engine was clattering and he went to lift the front hood, but she revved it and he stepped back. She handed him Vi's address on the piece of paper, her gloved hand trembling. His eyes darted between her and the scrap of paper. When he pointed to where the Knowles farm was, she tore out of the service station and shot down a dirt road that sat beside a stream.

She wound deeper into the woods, speeding faster, feeling herself getting closer. The engine rod was knocking now, the sound of a hammer wailing against metal. She spotted the driveway, marked by a rusty mailbox with *KNOWLES* painted on it. As she turned, the exhaust boomed like a shotgun, the rear wheels locked, and the car skidded to a stop. The sound rolled deep into the woods. She sat there in the long driveway with the engine purging oil on the manifold, wafts of smoke bellowing over her.

While the smoke cleared she jumped from the car, and with the door flapping she began walking up the leaf-strewn driveway. Rain dripped in puddles and ran in rivulets along the side of it, rushing and gathering into an adjacent stream. She hurried faster along the muddy lane, then came to the edge of a broad clearing and saw a chipped, white farmhouse, a pond and a barn beyond it.

Prudence stopped at the edge of the woods, breathing hard and gazing across the clearing. The scenery filled her eyes. Lush and green, smelling of fresh fallen rain and the thick onion grass that grew in the open field. The big red barn, the tall, stoic farmhouse. The house was still nearly a hundred yards away, but she stood there a moment, to consider how far she'd come since she'd first met Vi.

As she did, the farmhouse's front door swung open. Prudence held her breath as a figure stepped out and looked over the field, as if coming to see what the noise had been. Tall and slender, a shock of blonde hair, she walked along on the porch, her arms folded across her chest. When Vi looked up to where Prudence stood, she shouted and waved her arms. She ran from the porch and across the long field, through its glistening blades of grass.

Prudence hurried along the lane and came into the clearing. She watched Vi running, dressed in a big wool sweater and paint-splattered chinos. She yelled out and then heard Vi's laugh echo back through the field. Vi was yelling and Prudence was holding out her arms and when they embraced, with the tall shadowy trees surrounding them, both of them laughing and crying and whimpering, Prudence felt like she was somewhere. Here with Vi, finally, after all that time apart, and all that had happened.

"C'mon," Vi said a moment later, clutching her hand and leading her towards the house. "I can't wait for you to meet John."

Vi led her down the rest of the driveway, up the wet steps and inside the warm farmhouse. Prudence looked around the dark, wood paneled room, its grey windows, flames licking inside the open doors of a pot belly stove.

"John!" Vi yelled to the figure sitting beside it in a rocking chair, holding a smoldering pipe. "*Prudence!*"

John smiled as he stood, wearing a Pendleton flannel and Levi's, his wild hair piled atop his head. He was tall and thin, his weathered face lined with thick, pleasant creases. He came and embraced Prudence like the ragged refuge she was, with her damp clothes and windblown hair. She felt her tears continue to flow as he held her, the wooliness of his whiskers against her cheek, the smell of wood and pipe smoke in his clothes.

Vi wrapped her arms around them both, and Prudence knew then that they were all refugees in their own way, and that she would be safe here with them. In an unspoken sense they seemed to be acknowledging her arrival as an inevitability; that here in this house, at last, was the natural order of things.

Prudence stood there when they let go, smiling. She basked in the blazing heat coming from the pot belly stove, smelled what was cooking in the kitchen. A trimmed, undecorated fir tree stood in the corner of the room, pine boughs fallen to the floor, a pair of scissors on the table. She looked out the nearest window, back into the cold, and up into the tumbling clouds that hung above the pines.

"My car died out in the driveway," she said, breaking the silence. "All my things are in it."

"I'll take care of that," John said, in a thin, academic tone of voice. "But for now, you must be starving."

Vi quickly went and set out hot bowls of stew and warm bread on the kitchen table. Prudence sat with them and ate ravenously, huge chunks of bread mopped in the thick stew. Hot coffee in large, steaming mugs. Thick slices of fresh bread, torn from the loaf and slathered with fresh butter. As Vi and John watched her eat, they laughed, because they must've known all she'd been through, and what it had taken for her to get there. That there'd been times in their own lives where they'd known hunger, and the joy in having it sated.

Afterwards they talked until the sun began to set, and Prudence told them everything that had happened since she'd last seen Vi; the race in Mexico and in Palm Springs. She didn't mention the accidents, and as she talked she seemed to forget about them herself. And for now she only talked about the good things that had happened: the places she'd seen, the people she'd met, and the competitors she'd bested.

She told about her reunion with her father, of visiting her mother's grave. They both nodded solemnly as she talked, with a deep appreciation and understanding for what she was saying. And through it all, she noticed a levity in her voice that she seldom heard, a new sense of perspective. As if she was finally where she was meant to be.

And then after dinner, the dishes dried and put away, John went out and brought in her luggage from the car, then went back out the door. Prudence watched him enter the barn, then come out with a big Farmall tractor and begin to tow her dead Porsche along the driveway towards the barn.

The image of her ravaged race car being dragged along that farm road, still painted up from the race in Mexico, struck her as both serene and sad. The Porsche had been partly responsible for her being the first woman to finish that race. And although it seemed sentimental, it felt like she was watching John take an old dog of hers into the woods to put it down. She shook her head at the thought of it, but she knew her feelings were true: a person could care deeply for a machine as if it were a living thing.

Vi came and stood by the window, watching as the car and tractor disappeared into the barn. She patted Prudence's back, took her arm and showed her the room where she had all her paintings, and then the room beside it where Prudence would be staying, one of the biggest rooms in the house. The room had a big bed and large windows, which overlooked the pond and the barn. Beyond the barn the faint shape of a distant mountain rose into the sky, so vague and shadowy that it looked like a picture from a slide show being cast on a bed sheet.

Vi helped Prudence unpack, and then they sat down together on the bed. They held hands and smiled at each other without saying a word. It seemed like such a long time since she'd seen her. Her blonde hair was longer now, gathered loosely behind her head, and she was wearing her diamond ring on her finger.

Prudence stared at Vi and then asked quietly: "Are you happy here?"

"Quite," Vi said, closing her eyes and nodding. "You inspired me to come up here. To start painting again. And John." She shook her head. "There are no unanswered questions between us. That's something I never got with anyone else." She laughed. "Hell, no one else even cared how I felt, or what I thought. But John does. And God, does he love me."

"I'm glad," Prudence said, relieved, as this definitively answered the question she'd been carrying around.

"I want you to know that you can do whatever you want," Vi said. "You can stay here as long as you like. John wants to make sure you're taken care of. He made this room up for you. It was filled with junk a month ago, but he cleared it all out in hopes that you'd come."

"Well I thank him for that." Prudence sank back on the downy bed pillows, looking at Vi, studying her face. How different she looked here, how much happier.

"Prudence," Vi added, taking her hand. "I don't want to get on you right away, but I wanted to know if you'd thought about what I said in my letters. About what you wanted to do. About the baby."

Prudence looked at Vi and took her other hand. "That's why I'm here." She wanted to tell her more, about what had happened in

Mexico that made her change her mind about an operation, but there would be time for that later. Right now she just wanted to rest. She was more tired lately than she'd ever been.

Vi nodded slowly, and as if reading Prudence's cue, stood and kissed her forehead. "I'm glad you're here." She then went to the windows and began to draw the curtains.

"No," Prudence said, "please leave them open. I want to wake up and look out at that beautiful mountain."

Vi smiled, drew the curtains open again, went to the door, and began to close it behind her.

"I thought about something else you said in those letters," Prudence said. "About you and John. Watching the baby if I need to go on to Europe."

"We can talk about that tomorrow." Vi opened the door wider. "You may feel differently later on. For now you should just rest."

Prudence watched as Vi shut the door behind her.

As she fell asleep that night in that large bed, she thought of Charles awakening the next morning in New York City. Blinking and looking around some strange room, just as she was doing now, filled perhaps with the same hope she felt when she raced. And then her thoughts turned inward, to the life coiled tight against her insides, and she knew that this child was finally safe.

Out the window, stars reflected in the farm pond. The barn shingles sparkled in the moonlight. A gathering of stars shone above the tree line, and between the water and her reflection on the window, it looked as if a hand had dipped down from the sky and stirred them together. She stood a moment and moved across the dark room, closer to the window. Her reflection came into focus more clearly; a face not much different than her mother's, and her mother's mother before her. But then in a moment the image of those faces was gone, and then it was just her own.

Prudence sat on the bed and looked up in the lamplight and noticed one of the walls was covered in newspaper. Each new layer pasted to the next, white then yellow, white then yellow. She smiled at the memory of that old woman in the paper house, but her smile softened as she recalled the newspapers that her father had put in his scrapbook, the only proof that she'd overcome her great fears. But just the same, she knew all those newspapers were already burnt in the incinerators, and that like smoke, all memory of her soon would fade.

As she lay back and drifted to sleep, she began to dream of the placard that hung in the civic building in Castroville. The one she'd stopped to look at that morning a month ago. Her name placed below Marilyn Monroe and the other Artichoke Queens. She dreamt of the man in his workshop, inscribing her name in a brass plate, then tacking it to the placard. And she pictured it hanging there beside the photo of the largest artichoke, becoming tarnished by time, the only proof that she had passed through there.

Soon she was dreaming of the subsequent queens inspecting the plaque, early on the morning of their own parade. They'd come and stare at the names as the sun rose outside, pausing on hers a moment because of the sound of it: *Prudence.* A strange name. A name from a another era, one they could only guess at. Or they might like the way her name felt on their tongue, worn by time until it was soft as thistledown. They would stand in the foyer of that old civic building, the sun rising higher out the windows, spilling on their faces in a neat line, until the room was filled with light. And they would know then, just as she did now, that it was a life full of magic, where dreams were made in an instant, and could vanish at a touch.

Owen Duffy's fiction has appeared in various journals such as *Passages North, New South, Storyglossia, New Delta Review, PANK, and Hawai'i Review.* He holds an MFA in writing from Rutgers-Newark and currently teaches and mentors young writers. He lives with his family in Charleston, South Carolina.